A Life Lived-
Ruth Ellis

First published in the UK 2025

For a complete listing of the author's other work, including the best selling Miriam and Morrow novels, please refer to the rear of the book.

www.a-romp-in-time.com

Introduction

In June 2005 I wrote a novel, best described as counterfactual, about Edith Thompson who was executed in Holloway prison on the 9th of January 1923. In it we stepped into Edith's life and hypothesised events which could have been. An authentic life, emotionally moving and even humorous. It focused on her one child, her new husband, family and profession. We journeyed with her as the twentieth century unfolded, as she experienced the Second World War, and after into her old age. She begins new relationships, watches her grandchild and her other adopted children grow. Finally, she remarries, moves abroad, and finds refuge from the publicity she has generated all her life. The publicity of the woman who was almost hung.

Although not as successful as some of my other novels it nevertheless did well and I followed it with a sequel called, The Following Years, a semi fictional story about Edith Thompson's family and how they dealt with the horror, guilt and shame of having a family member executed. It followed the life of Edith's family concentrating on her sister, Avis.

I have no idea how many, if anybody, picked up on the fact that Ruth Ellis was mentioned in the first book, albeit briefly. In my biography it mentions, "he is noted for including 'easter eggs' in his work and incorporating coincidences and parallels from our real world" and that is exactly what I did there. For those of you who have the first book, think Westminster Bridge!

However, 2005 was a long time ago and in 2025 in July it will be seventy years since Ruth was, in my opinion, unjustly executed and for some considerable time I have wondered how her life may have been if circumstances had been different. This then is my counterfactual account of how her life may have played out had she been allowed to live. And to commemorate her passing, this book will be released at one minute past nine o'clock in the morning on the 13th of July 2025.

Chapter 1

The cells on B wing were unusually quiet on the 13th of July 1955. This was traditionally out of respect for what was going to happen that morning. Such an event had not happened for seven months when Styllou Christofi had been put to death, the fourth woman to be executed in Holloway since it had been constructed in 1852 although many had been reprieved.

However, outside the public was milling. Opinion was divided that hanging was monstrous, barbaric and evil. There was singing, chanting and mounted police did their best to keep public order. The famous millionairess and abolitionist, Violet Van der Elst was there of course making her presence known and the authorities knew very well who she was as she was more than capable of causing disorder.

It was not possible to say with any certainty why these ghouls felt the need to be present. Perhaps they felt it was the nearest they could get to death without dying themselves. Or perhaps they wanted to offer respect for the woman who was about to undergo the ultimate punishment.

But there they were outside the fortified prison waiting for nine o'clock when they would read the notice officially notifying the world that Ruth Ellis had undergone the sentence the law allowed.

At 8:30 that morning, Ruth had been awake for more than three hours and with the assistance of two experienced female warders she had come to know well, she had washed, dressed and had drunk half a cup of tea while refusing breakfast. Now, so close to the time, all she wanted to do was sit, smoke and stare into the distance. She did her very best not to think about what was going to happen to her after nine o'clock, that is, where she will be and what she would be doing.

Instead, by looking at an indistinct spot on the floor she brought into her mind various images of her past, some happy and some sad and those sustained her. The wardens saw her wipe her eyes as she held her teacup but were loathed to say anything. Outside the cell it was unnaturally quiet. Ruth took a deeper breath, broke her focus and spoke.

'I've never asked you this, but where is it going to happen?'

The older of the two wardresses stood and took two steps towards her. Her name was Grainger and she joined the service in 1936. Now a grey haired senior prison wardress, she was chosen for the position that day as she was a childless widow and the governor of Holloway Prison, May Doris Charity Taylor, knew she was a strong woman who would been able to deal with any difficult situation that might arise. As she very well did concerning Styllou Christofi.

Taking care of prisoners who were due to be executed was not an order. As soon as a prisoner was condemned a notice was put up for volunteers and a rotor was chosen which was to last for three weeks. Only the most experienced staff would be allowed to guard the prisoner during her final days and especially on her final twenty-four hours. The prisoner was always guarded twenty-four hours a day by two wardresses.

'Ruth…I'm sorry…I'm not permitted…'

Somehow, Ruth smirked. 'It's behind that cupboard isn't it? I've noticed the markings on the floor. It doesn't matter. How long have I got?'

'Not long. A little while.'

'Why is it all so quiet out there?'

'Being respectful, that's all.'

Ruth glanced across at, Hobson, the other wardress who was sitting at the wardress' table. She was younger, about the same age as Ruth and had been friendly but now sat still not looking at her at all, her face frozen, her lips almost a straight line. Grainger turned.

'Hobson? Buck up.'

She stood. 'Yes, mam.'

Grainger turned back and offered no explanation for her colleague's odd behaviour because there was no need to and Ruth understood. She nodded slowly and a tear formed and ran down her cheek as her lips trembled. Grainger took another cigarette and lit it for her. As Ruth took it, Grainger placed her hand on Ruth's and there was an unspoken communication between them before Grainger spoke.

'You are the bravest woman I have ever met. I will tell everybody about you.'

Ruth was about to nod again when they heard the low clatter of boots on the iron stairways. Grainger turned and Hobson moved closer. With the unlocking of it and a loud clang, the iron door opened and the governor, the chief medical officer and the senior chief officer entered as well as two more wardresses. Grainger, noticing immediately that Albert Pierrepoint was not among them, turned on the spot and took hold of Ruth's arm and offered her a glimmer of a smile. But Ruth was too confused to acknowledge what that meant. She still sat. The governor, May Doris Charity Taylor approached her holding a piece of paper.

'Ruth Ellis, by order of the Home secretary, William Lloyd George, your sentence has been commuted to life imprisonment.'

When Ruth thought about that moment later on she expected some form of joyous expression but what she got was a stunned silence as if they were waiting for her to say thank you. But she didn't have time to say anything because she simply dropped her cigarette, her eyes rolled upwards and she collapsed into unconsciousness.

The hospital wing. Ruth has only vague memories of being carried from the cell and along the corridor of B wing. Vague memories of light that bedazzled her and sounds of screaming and cheering but nothing more. She thinks there was a short period of darkness and quietness before she fully came around to find an unknown stout nurse taking her blood pressure and shining a torch into her eyes before retreating.

Still horizontal she saw Doctor Brightman hovering over her. A man she instantly recognised. A man whom she knew was not at all fond of her.

'So, you've got your way then, Ellis.'

Ruth never answered.

'A lifer then? You seem all right. BP's high. Bit of a fright, that's all. To be expected. Nurse? In here for twenty-four hours then put her in general. Liaise with the PPO.'

'Yes, doctor. Any special requirements?'

'No, none at all.'

He left abruptly without uttering another word. He was a thin man, around fifty and as Ruth was to write later, as he had been in the job for twenty-five years, he had probably witnessed too much tragedy and had had his heart broken too many times. All the same, she did not like the man because he had treated her sharply since she had entered the prison on remand. For whatever reason, it remained unknown to Ruth.

'I don't suppose you ate breakfast, did you?' asked the nurse.

'No, just a cup of tea.'

'Do you want anything?'

'Perhaps a slice of toast?'

'All right. I'll get it sent in with a cuppa. You compose yourself. You are one lucky bitch.'

Ruth closed her eyes and listened but all she could hear was the sound of pigeons cooing and for some unknown reason that upset her for it was a sound she never expected to hear again and once again her eyes began to sting. But in the silence of the room she could hear her breathing and if she concentrated she could hear her heartbeat and that too frightened her to the point of disbelieving her senses.

For three weeks she believed she was going to die and she was settled in her mind that that was the only course her life was going to take. That her heart would stop beating at 9.00 am that morning. But now it was still beating, that her soul would be free from all guilt and her spirit would be united with David so nothing made any sense. What had changed the Home Secretary's mind? Yes, as she lay in the prison bed in a separate room at 9:20 am nothing made any sense at that moment.

A wardress unlocked the door and a small woman in her thirties with a pronounced limp wearing prison garb advanced with a metal tray which she placed to one side on a small wooden cupboard. On it rested a mug of tea and a plate containing two thin slices of toast. Their eyes met and the prisoner ruefully smiled as Ruth lifted herself into a sitting position.

'Thank you.'

'Sugar's already in it. Always is whether you want it or not.'

'That's enough, Baxter. Away with you.'

Baxter limped out and the door slammed shut. The tea was hot and very sweet but she welcomed it because she was used to it by now. She knew she would have to accept many things that she would have previously complained about because, being close to death changes a person's perception in more ways than one.

As soon as she drank the tea and finished the toast Ruth felt instantly tired and snuggling under the bed clothes she fell asleep. She was awoken by the clatter of the door being unlocked and a wardress and another woman in prison garb entered, this time with a bucket and mop. This one did not look at her but immediately began to mop the floor in silence while the wardress wrote on a clipboard. Ruth, with no particular purpose, watched the middle aged prisoner as she energetically worked her mop moving rhythmically and silently. Then she looked at the wardress.

'Excuse me, could you tell me the time please?'

'There's no reason for you to know the time. You're in prison now. Same as you don't need to know what day it is.

Or what week it is. When your time is up to leave you'll be told. Come on, Nicholls, get a move on!'

'Sorry, mam.'

Ruth was left alone again with only the noisome smell of strong disinfectant to keep her company and soon her eyes closed again. This time she slept for far longer, for when she was woken it was time for another examination by Doctor Brightman and then lunch. As usual he was his normal arrogant self and treated Ruth as if she were little more than a piece of meat.

'Yes, everything's pretty much back to normal I would say. You've had a fortunate escape, Ellis. Not the first one I've dealt with I might add. But one that was near to the limit I will say. Three minutes was cutting it close.'

'Is that what it was? Jesus!'

'And I'll have no *profanity* here is that understood? The governor will not stand for it and neither will I.'

'I'm sorry.'

'As well you ought to be as it was Him who saved you.'

Ruth noticed a gold ring on his finger upon which there was engraved a cross and she was intelligent enough to remain silent. Yet despite her recent close encounter with eternity her old personality stood gaining ground because she was still alive. She had dealt with this type of arrogant weasel before of course. The type of man who had become so indifferent to women that he had lost whatever humanity with which he had been born. He had become a technician only, a futile man. Stone cold in his habits and in his belief of God. A hater of her sex. As he put away his stethoscope Ruth eyed him without passion and wondered, not for the first time, if there were any women doctors in Holloway.

One other thing Ruth noticed was that the only other person in the room was the wardress who silently stood by the door and the expression on her face was telling. Ruth had been on remand in Holloway for two months before she was condemned so she had already become accustomed to the system and she had recognised the young wardress. She did not know her by name but any woman can recognise a scowl given against a man. Then, in his usual manner, Doctor Brightman left and she stepped forward. Did Ruth see a hint of chagrin?

'You have to stay in here until tomorrow. Lunch will be brought to you.'

'Yes I understand. Is there anything to read?'

'There's a Bible in the cupboard. But I'll see if I can get you a magazine. How do you feel?'

'A bit strange to be alive. I don't know how I feel. Part of me feels as if I don't have the right to be alive while part of me is glad that I am alive, if that makes any sense.'

'I can't imagine. I've only been working here two years and I'm not experienced enough to look after prisoners who are due to be…you know so…I shouldn't even be talking to you like this.'

'I won't say anything. What made you become a prison officer?'

'My mum was one and she thought it was a good life. She was twenty-five years in the job.'

'How are you finding it?'

'It's better now but it was tough in the beginning. It was a lot to learn. And being here it's a quick way to grow up.'

'Do you have a fella?'

'I can't answer that. That's too personal. I don't mind chatting but we are told not to talk about personal things.'

'Of course. I'm sorry. I understand. Well, I'll be grateful for that magazine if you can find one.'

'I'll do my best but I will have to get permission from my SPO first. It'll be after lunch if I can.'

Lunch was delivered by the same limping prisoner called Baxter and was supervised by the same wardress who remained silent this time but Ruth smiled at her because accompanied by the meal were three dog-eared copies of Readers Digest. Upon removing the metal cloche, Ruth was surprised to see a handsome meal of two sausages, mash and peas with gravy and all of it hot. She looked up in surprise at the wardress.

'Am I getting special treatment?'

'I'm not too sure. Let's say, someone in the kitchen is pleased you're still alive!'

'Do you think the governor knows about this?'

'I'm sure the governor knows about everything that goes on in Holloway. Now eat that before it gets cold.'

One other thing that brightened Ruth's day that lunchtime was the grey sky that had dominated the morning had dissipated and the sun began to shine casting its light into the room. Accompanying the meal was jam pudding and custard and after finishing it Ruth chose one of the magazines and was about to read it when a sense of reality overcame her. The reality of being locked in Holloway for life.

In the excitement of still being alive, in the fragility of still being herself, the idea of continuance had not occurred to her. Now her belly was full and she was contemplating the reality, the full reality of her situation which was one of long term imprisonment fell against her and it felt like an iron door slamming in her face. Instantly memories of her time in the clubs, reckless times, drinking times, cocaine times, dancing times, sexual times, flooded over her and these were times that were now lost to her and they were times that would never again be repeated. Memories only. Now she was going to live with five hundred women for the next sixteen or so years to reappear, if she survived, to somebody completely different, an entirely new person.

Ruth let the magazine fall and stared at the wall opposite her breathing slowing as if the walls were closing in on her, the weight of her situation becoming unbearable. Why had she killed David?

'How the shit am I going to survive this?'

Chapter 2

Ruth was moved immediately after Doctor Brightman had made one more cursory examination the next morning and declared her fit enough to join the general population. The vetting was done in silence and after breakfast the same wardress took her to the governor's office where she was made to wait outside for five minutes. This suite of offices was set apart from the main prison where it was light and airy and was part of an area where solicitors and barristers met their clients. Where she sat, a number of prisoners were at work scrubbing, cleaning and polishing and Ruth imagined they all knew who she was by the way they surreptitiously stared at her. Because they were on official business the previously friendly wardress showed no sign of being amiable so they sat in stony silence until they were called.

She was instructed to enter by a far older woman whose uniform was immaculate and was told to stand on a chalk line and face the governor who sat behind her desk. The governor's office lay behind a thick institutional door along a hushed corridor, its distance from the cell blocks lending it an eerie calm. The room was functional yet unmistakably personal, a space shaped by the woman governor who ruled it: May Doris Charity Taylor.

Sunlight slanted through the sash windows with wire reinforced glass, casting a patterned glow over the dark wood floor. A modest coal fire burned behind a brass fender, its scent barely masking the must of old paper and disinfectant. The walls were an uninspired shade of pale sage, the paint curling above the radiator. A framed photograph of Queen Elizabeth II hung above a map of the prison grounds, beside a softly faded reproduction of, The Light of the World.

Governor Taylor's desk was a broad oak slab with claw feet and scuffed edges. It bore the hallmarks of someone both orderly and overburdened: neatly stacked paperwork, an inkwell, a blotter smudged with old corrections. A black rotary telephone sat ready beside a typed list of the day's appointments. Most items were lined up with near military precision, except the well thumbed copy of, The Prison Rules 1949, which rested askew, open at a page concerning reprieves and transfers.

Ruth Ellis stood awkwardly in the centre of the room. Governor Taylor remained seated as Ruth entered, then rose with quiet formality. She was tall, upright, mid fifties, with greying hair fastened into a stern chignon. Her eyes, magnified by thick glasses, were unreadable.

'Ellis,' she said, her tone neither warm nor cold. 'Please sit down.'

There was no ceremony. No sympathy, either. Simply a directness that Ruth, in her shock, found oddly comforting. On a small table nearby stood a tray with two cups, a teapot, and a tin of condensed milk, though the governor made no move toward it. Behind her, on a shelf of reports and orderlies' logs, stood a vase of lilies, artificial, and dusty, but placed with care.

In that small, tightly composed office, the course of Ruth's life had shifted from death to an unknown span of years. The only certainty was this woman, May Taylor, and the formidable institution she represented.

'Ellis. You are looking more composed.'

'Yes, mam.'

'Doctor Brightman has signed you off as being fit for return to the general population.'

'Yes, mam.'

'And how do you feel about that?'

'I'm unable to answer that, mam.'

'Oh? How so?'

'I am alive, mam when I should be dead and so I am…'

'Yes, I believe I understand. You have had three weeks to prepare yourself for the ordeal of the unknown. And then a reprieve. Yours is not the first case that I have had to deal with in this manner you understand.'

'Yes, mam.'

'So you mustn't think me unsympathetic. Although I cannot possibly conceive of how you must be feeling I have a reputation for progressiveness, education and rehabilitation and so for that reason I will not be putting you on general duties at the moment.'

'Yes, mam.'

'In the next couple of days I want you to see welfare and the chaplain and we will take it from there.'

'Yes, mam.'

'Do you have any questions?'

'I probably do, mam but I'm too confused at the moment to remember any of them begging your pardon.'

'I understand. Well, when you do, speak to the warder on your floor in the morning. Now, Ellis, I want to give you a piece of advice.'

'Yes, mam?'

The governor leaned forward and intertwined her fingers and made direct eye contact.

'Now you may take this in any way you prefer but I'm saying it for your own good because you're going to be here for a very long time. And my advice is, lose the phoney accent. It will do you no favours in a place such as this. I trust you take my meaning.'

'Thank you, mam. I will try.'

'All right then. You're going to be placed into B wing and my advice is, obey the rules and keep your nose clean. Dismissed.'

After visiting the stores and collecting clean bedding, a towel, soap, a new toothbrush and other essential items such as a mug, plate and a spoon, Ruth was escorted back to the wing which was as noisy as she remembered it to be.

However, this time she was taken to the third floor where an empty cell awaited her.

'You'll find life far more regulated than when you were on parole but you'll get used to it.'

'I suppose I'll be given some form of work to do?'

'Of course, but not yet as the governor said. Tea and recreation is at five and I'll lock you in until then. Use the time to sort yourself out.'

'When will I be able to write and receive letters?'

'I'll have to check. Normally it would be three months but I don't think that will apply to you. But normally, twenty-eight days.'

'Thank you.'

'Settle down now. You have your magazines?'

'Thank you, yes.'

The wardress nodded and closed the heavy door and locked it. Ruth close her eyes at the ugly sound as she held the items the stores had given her. But then she was finally forced to open them and saw her single bed made of iron with its thin and discoloured mattress and its equally thin discoloured pillow. Outside the cell she could hear constant screaming and yelling and because Holloway was so huge the sounds echoed and echoed and echoed. She instantly wondered if she would ever manage to sleep. Then a greater fear came upon her, that she would go mad within such a small space. The window directly in front of her with its grotesquely thick iron bars showed only the sky and it would be an effort to climb up to grasp the bars had she felt a need to. In a desperate panic, she fell to her knees and placed the bundle on the floor and placed her head on it and that is where she stayed and wept until she fell asleep.

The same wardress was concerned to find her on the floor but as she was dealing with all the inmates on that landing she did not have time to give her any special treatment.

'Ellis? Tea and rec. Look lively. Line up outside. Get your mug.'

Tea and recreation meant exactly that. A trolley pushed by two trustees delivered tea in a stainless steel urn along with a thick slice of bread and butter. The tea already had milk and sugar added. The recreation part meant that the door was left open so the prisoners were free to visit each other. It did not take long before a woman rapped her knuckles on Ruth's door and smiled.

'Hello! Any one in! You're Ruth Ellis, aren't you? We've been expecting you. Mind if I come in?'

Ruth offered her a fatigued smile. 'There's nowhere for you to sit.'

'Oh, I'll just plonk myself down on the bed, darling. My name is, Wilson but my first name is Sally. Can I call you, Ruth?'

'Of course.'

Sally was a blur of peroxide blonde hair and nervous energy, a thin figure leaning around the cell door like a curious bird peering into a cage. She gave a lopsided grin, her bright eyes darting around the drab cell before settling on Ruth with an expectant flicker, as if they'd already met in another life.

Sally looked younger than her years, all sharp cheekbones and wide, eager eyes, the kind that seemed to drink in every detail of her surroundings. She had the sort of face that could melt into a dozen expressions in as many seconds–a flicker of mischief, a trace of worry, the hint of a laugh always lurking at the corners of her mouth. She wore her prison issue dress with the casual disregard of someone who had never mastered the art of taking life seriously.

'I'm not much for being quiet,' she admitted, plonking herself down on the iron framed bed. I thought I'd pop in, see if you fancied a natter. Better than staring at these bloody walls all day by yourself, ah?'

She gestured vaguely at the peeling paint, the grimy bars, the stale, motionless air–the entire grim reality they found themselves in–before flashing Ruth a conspiratorial smile. 'Reckon we'll get along, you and me.'

'Where do you…which is…?'

'Where's my cell? Next door, darling. Well, you're a lucky girl! Rumour has it that you only had minutes to go and then you got reprieved. Was that true?'

'Yes, they said it was about three.'

'Bloody hell! Excuse my French! You've been all over the papers. Not that we're allowed to read the papers but the news gets through anyway.'

'You don't get to read newspapers?'

'Not allowed, my old darling. Not allowed at all. Maybe if you have to go outside for a hospital visit you might get to see a newspaper but while you're in here, no chance! So I suppose you've been given life then?'

'That's the deal yes, although I don't know what that means. When things get clearer in my mind I will have to talk to my solicitor.'

'What it means, darling is about sixteen years if you're a good girl and you play by their rules. Then it means you'll be released on license. I can see by your face that you haven't given it much thought.'

'*Sixteen* years? I can't imagine that. I went through a period in that death cell wanting to be hung. I wish they had done it now.'

'You can't talk like that. I've been here a year and it gets better and you get used to it, trust me.'

'Can I ask how long have you got to go?'

'Me? I am an old timer. I've got another nine years before they let me loose.'

'So you've got… *ten years*? That's… I dare not ask you why.'

'Because I was a bad lady, Ruth. I killed my children. My three beautiful little Christian children.'

Sally looked to be no older than Ruth but because of her circumstances and her middle class upbringing she looked younger. She wore her blonde hair long in a single ponytail and wore spectacles. She had intelligent eyes, a small nose and a small round mouth. She was of average height and now she had mentioned it, Ruth could see she was the kind of woman she could see going into church on Sunday accompanied by her children, mild mannered and dutiful.

Ruth had no immediate answer to her statement and it hung in the cell unquestioned. until Sally provided the answer.

'My husband, Benny, short for Benedict is an Anglican vicar and one evening he was chairing a meeting when he telephoned me and said he had forgotten the minutes of their last meeting and would I bring it over. So I did but as it was a five mile drive and I couldn't leave the children for that long I had to take them with me. The journey there was fine and I left the children in the car. When after I delivered the ledger to my husband one of his friends gave me a glass of port which I accepted as it was a cold night. It was only a small glass of port and I quickly drank it and left. On the way home I began to fill dizzy and I lost control and I crashed the car leading to the deaths of my three children. A subsequent police investigation proved not only had I taken alcohol but that I had taken cocaine as well and I was convicted for the manslaughter of my three children and given ten years. Despite all the efforts of my legal team the identity of the man who gave me that drink was never established and so here I am. How's that for a story? My children were Mary, eighteen months old, Daphne two and a half years old and Roger, five years old and my husband is in the process of divorcing me and I have another nine years to go. The only people that visit me is my mother and father so Ruth, that's my story… Ruth? why are you crying?'

Ruth quickly wiped her face in embarrassment.

'I'm sorry. I've got two children and I haven't treated them well at all. Your story has made me feel ashamed.'

'Holloway is full of shame, my darling as you will come to know. Did this fellow of yours treat you as badly as the rumours say he did?'

Ruth nodded. 'Very badly and looking back I was a fool.'

'I hope we can be friends, Ruth seeing as we are next door neighbours! Now we know the worst of each other.'

'Of course. I need a friend. Someone who can steer me through this maze. But I never in a thousand years imagined that I'd ever get friendly with a sky pilot's wife.'

'You are not a Christian, Ruth?'

'I was raised as one in Wales but somehow, well you know how it is.'

'Did you pray to God when you were… in that cell?'

'Never once. Do you think that's strange?'

'For me, yes. If I had been in your position I would've been on my knees day and night.'

'But you see, Sally at the time and during those weeks I wished to die because I wanted to be reunited with David. My solicitor couldn't understand that.'

'You must have loved him very much.'

'Let's say I was stupid and confused which amounts to the same thing. You said that only your parents visit you. What about your husband?'

'The last time I saw him was at the old Bailey when I was sentenced. He stared at me, I remember that. He simply stared at me and then I was pulled away. I called out his name but I don't think he replied and he's never visited or written. But three months into my sentence my solicitor received a notification that divorce proceedings have been put in place so there is my answer. My parents, try as they might, can get nothing out of him and they have stopped trying now. I killed our children. I was high on alcohol and cocaine and this is my punishment.'

'But Sally, did you have any previous convictions for drugs?'

'Of course not. I've been a model citizen. Not even a parking ticket.'

'Then this whole thing sounds like a fit up. It's disgusting.'

'Whatever you call it, my sweet, I'm in here and here I'm staying. Now let me tell you about the routine while there is time. There are about seventy cells on each level and I can tell you the daily routine is endless. Let's start at nine o'clock, exercise, one hour then ten o'clock we go to work. Those on governor's adjudication see the doctor or welfare. There are special visits to solicitors and at the same time, legal remand for collection on appointment times by allowed visits.'

'Does this go on all the time?'

'Every day except Sunday. Anyway, at nine-thirty, the Governor and chief officer tour the prison and inspect all wings and mostly dealt with applications for the governor who then carry them out at eleven o'clock. At eleven-forty-five, the workshop workers are returned to their wings and are always searched before leaving the workshops. The tools are accounted for and the girls counted in and out. Lunched is served at twelve o'clock and there is a lunch patrol. At twelve-thirty we are locked in our cells. After, another roll check the staff go to lunch leaving a skeleton staff patrolling the wings and checking on prisoners. At one-thirty, the staff came back and the wings are unlocked. At one-forty-five, we are returned to work. At two o'clock, the domestic visits start and end at three-thirty. At four-forty-five, all work stops and we are returned to our wings after our tools are accounted for and we are counted in and out once again. At five o'clock we get tea and then at five-thirty, we are returned to our cells where we are locked up again. There's another roll check and after, the evening staff take tea. At five o'clock the main day staff began to go off duty and then at six o'clock we get an association period which is one hour which includes lessons and lectures. But by seven we are returned to our cells. Reception staff dealt with new receptions and returns from court throughout the evening. During the evening staff and reception count any monies from prisoners and complete their paperwork. The night staff come on duty. At nine o'clock prisoners are locked away for the night and there is always a roll check before handing over to the night staff who count us all before accepting. And then after, the evening staff go off duty. Throughout the night, staff patrol wings and there are constant checks on prisoners. On Saturday there are no courts appearances, but some can receive some prisoners association between the times of ten and eleven. On Sunday, there are no comings or goings of anybody. There is a church service between nine and ten o'clock. Exercise is normally between ten and eleven and association is between two and four. Think you can remember all that?' Sally smiled.

'I knew it was regimented because I was on remand but you have surprised me.'

'You'll get used to it.'

'What sort of work do they give us to do?'

'The work is almost all labour intensive such as sewing mailbags, wing cleaning, painting and gardening. There are a few plum jobs if you can get them but they're preserved for those who've been here years and earned the privilege, such as working in the library. Do you have any special skills?'

'Such as?'

'Cooking?'

'I can fry an egg!'

'That won't get you in the kitchens then. Anything else?'

'I can run a nightclub!'

'Oh I think you're fit right in here! Actually, it's not such a bad time to be in Holloway because the governor is a soft touch and she's one of those that's all for rehabilitation and all that so I think there is going to be opportunities for learning.'

'What do you do?'

'I work in the greenhouse. During the war I looked after pigs and grew veg and as we have a small holding here that's what I do. The gardens.'

'In here?'

'Sure. We have an area at the end of the greenhouse. The governor at the time started it during the war and it's continued. It might be a bit of a stretch but I can always ask if you fancy it. It gets you out and into fresh air every day and that's something.'

'Thanks I'd like that. I'm not afraid of hard work.'

'Then I'll ask. Hello, that's our time over. We get coco at nine so I'll see you in the morning. Slop out is at seven. Just follow what everybody else is doing. And don't use the toilet with the big red X on the door!'

'Why?'

'Because that's only meant for those if you've got VD. Didn't anybody tell you that? Well, don't worry. It get's easier!'

A different wardress locked her in and that characteristic sound hurt Ruth's ears because it was so ugly. Not having anything else to do she arranged her bed clothes and pillow and then did the same with her cup, plate, spoon and toothbrush. The prison undergarments were uncomfortable but practical as was her prison dress. Her fall from exotic nightclub hostess to this rag woman was complete and she was glad that she did not have a mirror.

She imagined her cell had to be the quietest on B wing as she heard a great deal of shouting and screaming. She wondered if there were any others on the wing that contained a person like her, a first timer. Ruth was a woman of imagination but she was unable to imagine settling in such a place. She touched the walls and they were cold. Escape was impossible. When she was on remand she had heard it mention that during all the years it had been in use not one person, man woman or child had ever escaped from Holloway prison. For in the olden days it was a man's prison and they used to keep juveniles there as well.

Once that door closed Ruth didn't know what to do. She felt the only thing to do was sleep but she knew coco was coming at nine o'clock and she also knew that if she slept then would she be able to sleep during the night? No, she would try and keep awake. She had magazines and she would try to occupy herself.

But such was the noise of the prison she was unable to concentrate on anything but her circumstances and when nine o'clock came around and the door opened the wardress found her not ready and willing to receive her Coco but found her on the floor her pillow over her head.

'Ellis, come on, get up. This won't do. Pull yourself together. Now listen to me. You have a choice. Deal with your circumstances or I'll make an order for you to go down where they will put you to sleep and that won't be good for you do you understand?'

'The walls keep coming in on me.'

'I understand. Look, take this. It's allowed.'

From her pocket she took a jar and from it shook out a small white pill which she gave to Ruth.

'It'll give you a good nights sleep. Take it now.'

Ruth did as she was told and the coco tasted as sweet as the tea.

'Good. Now you prepare yourself for bed. Lights will be out shortly.'

The door was locked.

Ruth remembers changing into her pyjamas and remembering how cold the bed was and remembering only drinking half of the cocoa because she didn't like the sweetness of it but that was all. She only faintly imagined she heard the soft roar of London traffic but that was all. She thinks she heard her son, André calling her name but that was all.

Chapter 3

The next morning, the first full morning as a regular prisoner of Holloway began early at seven o'clock when her door was unlocked and she was expected to slop out. This meant taking her bucket along to the communal toilet and emptying it and washing it and then returning to her cell. It was a confusing, messy and smelly procedure and Sally was not on hand to guide her so she simply followed the other women by example. Sensibly only eighteen cells were opened at one time. If Ruth had thought the previous evening had been a low point she was mistaken. After that she was locked in again.

Ruth quickly discovered the routine in Holloway was a bath once a week while at the same time a change of clothes was issued. This was when inmates washed their hair with the coarse yellow bar of soap with which they had been issued, or if they had brought some at Holloway's shop on the ground floor, a penny packet's worth of shampoo. It was also the time when the women were probably at their liveliest, with much of the conversation taken up with crudities and even some singing. She was not surprised at all to discover that each inmate was weighed once a month and any deviation from a supposed norm, resulted in a change of diet.

She remembered what Sally had told her from the night before. That when personal items went missing from the kitchens and workrooms, the entire prison was locked down, and a thorough search was initiated. This was not popular at all and caused much resentment. Prisoners who had to get rid of things quickly tossed them out of their windows. Ruth had been warned early on that nothing of a personal nature was to be kept in the cell when they left it, as, because the door was not locked, anyone could enter and take whatever they wished. She learnt early on that there was no honour among thieves. Therefore, Sally had obtained a small bag from a workshop for her, and Ruth now carried it wherever she went. In it was everything she owned. Letters, and everything else of a personal nature. Even her soap and toothbrush.

Breakfast came soon after but this time she took it by herself as Sally was still not available. Clearly, she thought, dealing with plants was an early part of the day.

After a great deal of shouting of orders and after the wing had cleared because the inmates had left for work her door was unlocked once again and another wardress entered.

'Ellis? You are booked in to see welfare this morning.'

'Yes, mam. Now, mam?'

'Yes.'

'Follow me, don't dawdle.'

The welfare office was part of the same spacious landing where the governor's office was and was run by two women, Chief Officer Parker, and her middle aged civilian secretary. The wardress, Brown stayed outside in the outer office with the secretary while Ruth was ordered into the senior officer's room. A sunshine lit south facing room which illuminated how cluttered it was.

'You may sit, Ellis. I am Chief Officer Parker and your visit here today is part of a mandatory program set by the government and implemented by the governor. Briefly the intention is to providing emotional support. To help prisoners cope with the challenges of incarceration, offering guidance. I can also help provide access to various services. That is I can connect inmates with healthcare, education, and rehabilitation programs. I understand you have family, Ellis?'

'Yes mam.'

'Very good. I can assist you with maintaining relationships with them, which can be vital for emotional stability and reintegration. And finally, I may advocate on behalf of prisoners to ensure their needs are met within the system. Is any of that unclear? Do you have any questions?'

'I am grateful to meet you, mam. There is one thing that has been troubling me over the last month but I've not mentioned it to anybody because as I saw it, because I was going to die there was not much point. But now I am going to live it seems I must speak.'

'Is it a problem concerning this prison?'

'I think it will concern the prison, mam.'

'Then I would advise you to speak plainly. You may do so in this room.'

'Sometime during my remand, my… please excuse me this is difficult for me, my… discharge began to be different. I said nothing as there was no point. I had enough on my mind to deal with. And then when sentence of death was upon me it didn't matter. But now everything has changed once again except that… so now I know, how only a woman does, that something is very wrong and I would ask that I be properly examined preferably by woman doctor if that could be possible, mam.'

'You have been examined by Doctor Brightman is that so?'

'Briefly yes, just my heartbeat and blood pressure, that was all.'

'I see. And you suspect your condition is serious?'

'I am in pain, mam and what comes out of me is not normal. I don't wish to go into details.'

'I see you have had several miscarriages.'

'Yes, mam.'

'I have read of the details of your trial of course. It was he?'

'Yes, mam. He was violent.'

'All right, first things first. When you leave here you'll go down to the nurses office and she will take a blood and a urine sample and we will send them away to get them analysed and then we will take it from there.'

'Thank you, mam.'

Officer Parker leaned her head forward a little and squinted.

'I remember you coming in on remand. You've lost weight. When was the last time you were weighed?'

'In the death cell, mam. They weighed me every day for some reason.'

'Well, yes… no, you were also booked in for the chaplain this morning. If you don't feel up to it I can book you in for another day. How do you feel about that?'

'Perhaps another day might be better when I can… Perhaps another day might be better, mam.'

'All right then.'

Chief Officer Parker pushed an intercom button on her desk.

'Officer Brown can come in now.'

The nurses station was on the ground floor at the grand intersection known as, The Centre. This was a vast space from where it was possible to see the long arms of A, B, C and D Wing at the same time as seeing all four tiers of landings on each wing which included Ruth's own cell. Clearly visible of course was the tight wire netting slung between each floor and the iron staircases that connected all the landings. When James Buntstone Bunning developed the radial design in January 1848 so that one officer could see everything from one central position he knew exactly what he was doing.

Told to wait on a bench, Ruth was able to see the fabled vase of flowers which stood on a round table. These flowers which were delivered every day had become part of Holloway's daily life and she had been told about them when she was in the death cell. Ruth imagined that prison would be noisy but even she was surprised at the level of noise several hundred women could make as they went about their duties. From wardresses with their huge chains attached to their belts shouting their orders to the prisoners themselves scrubbing, cleaning, dusting, singing, chatting and whistling it was cacophonous. And within the bounds of the church like structure made of metal and stone, everything reverberated.

Nurse Hatfield, a mature civilian, treated her pleasantly even though she knew who she was and by the way she chatted it was clear she believed Ruth ought not to have had the death sentence. This was made doubly clear before Ruth left her small office because she offered her a genuine smile and mentioned she had signed her petition. For which Ruth thanked her.

'How long will it be before the result comes in?'

'About a week. But can I say? You have done the right thing because simply looking at your sample, from experience I can tell something is not right with you.'

'I knew it.'

'You are in pain?'

'Yes, a little. Here…'

'Then you must rest as much as possible. I will inform Chief Officer Parker and Doctor Brightman. In my opinion it might be sensible to put you in the hospital wing for the time being. Better food and more peace and quiet.'

'That sounds ominous.'

'Better to be safe than sorry. Leave it to me.'

The rest of the day was spent in her cell, sleeping and reading and the door was only opened for lunch and afternoon tea and recreation. It was only during tea that Sally visited her.

'Hello, cell mate! Been to welfare and chaplain today?'

'Hi Sally, Just welfare. You look…messy!'

'Boy! What a day it's been. Old Carpy's had us running around in circles all bloody day.'

'Who is, Old Carpy?'

'Oh, she's in charge of the allotment. Wardress, Carpenter. Been here since the place was built I think, or close to anyway!'

'What happened?'

'It's because it's been pissing down all day.'

'It's been raining? I had no idea.'

'That's the thing about prison. The weather never affects us. Here's a queer story. I heard about some old lag, she was in here for twenty years. I never knew her of course but so the story goes, on the day she was released it was pissing down and she walked out the main gate and instead of walking away she stood where the cars are parked now and just danced in the rain for ages. Sounds crazy doesn't it?'

'Sounds like she must've been mad, poor thing.'

'Well, we certainly got soaked today.'

'So that's why you look knackered.'

'And I smell like you know what as well. We've been spreading it about all day. We got a delivery from a farm. All four of us do. And that's not the end of it either. Not many people know that the allotment sometimes produces enough food to supply about ten percent of the food for Holloway so if things go wrong the governor will not be happy because she likes to spend the prison allowance on other things like rehabilitation.'

'How often are we allowed baths? I heard a week?'

'That's right. But I'm going down after rec as they know that I stink like a farm yard! How did you get on today?'

'Sort of interesting. I saw welfare and then a nurse who took blood. She thinks, well, I don't know…'

'You didn't get to see, Chaplin? If you want to get a way into getting out of your cell and doing things then he's the man to see. It doesn't matter whether you believe in God and all that sort of thing. He's a decent bloke and he will help you one way or another. But the only thing with him is you have to play it straight. Because he will see through any bullshit. Because he's been here a long time and he's seen it and heard everything. Every line, every bullshit you can imagine so when you see him just tell the truth and he will help you. Why didn't you see him today?'

'Not sure really. The nurse told me to come back here and rest. Perhaps he was busy.'

'She used those words? Why did she take your blood? Have you got VD?'

'I don't think so. I'm sure I haven't.'

'I wonder why welfare sent you to the nurse?'

'Don't know. The way I feel Sally, which is overwhelmed, I'm just obeying orders.'

'I can remember feeling like that, but you'll soon find yourself. Right, I'm going to get myself cleaned up. Ta ta for now.'

Ruth was locked in for another two hours expecting the next time to be coco but the door was unlocked unexpectedly when no other cell doors were. Chief officer Parker the welfare officer and a wardress entered.

'Ellis? Gather your personal items together.'

'Mam? Where am I going?'

'To the hospital wing. The governor believes that will be the best place for you at the moment given your circumstances. Hurry up now, I should have gone off duty an hour ago.'

Although it was late in the afternoon, Holloway was still a very busy prison and as Ruth was escorted through innumerable passageways and multiple massive iron gates which had to be unlocked and locked behind them, she gained the impression that the place never fully slept. In order to get to the hospital it involved walking to the Centre and then walking along the entire length of C Wing and then for a brief moment into the outside world under a metal structure onto which rain still fell. Ruth took in a few deep breaths of the cold fresh air, the first she had since being arrested and stood still for a moment looking at the rain. But she was quickly urged to move forward. Then they entered the hospital wing itself.

She had no idea why she was placed a private room but it was a pleasant room not at all like a cell. It was painted in pastel colours and there were bars on the window and flowers in a vase by the bed. A staff nurse welcomed Ruth and Chief Officer Parker and the wardress. Chief Officer Parker spoke first.

'Staff? This is Ellis, first name, Ruth. I trust her papers have been sent to you?'

'I have received them thank you, chief officer.'

'Well, Ellis, I'll leave you in staff nurse's good hands and I wish you well.'

'Thank you, mam.'

Chief Officer Parker nodded only once and she and the wardress left leaving Ruth and the staff nurse looking at each other.

'I'm thinking this must be somewhat confusing for you, Ruth. Am I correct?'

'A little, mam.'

'You may call me, staff. And as I am a humanist I will call you, Ruth if that is okay with you.'

'Thank you mam…Staff.'

'Very good. Now, I see you have a very few things with you so let's get you sorted.'

'Staff? May I ask you a question please?'

'Of course you may.'

'Apart from being put into a hospital wing almost straight away I am surprised to be placed in a room separate from other women and I wondered if there was a reason for that.'

'My full title is, Staff Nurse Chambers. Come sit on the bed here for a moment. Now, I have been a nurse for many a year. I trained in Oxford before the war and then I became a member of Queen Alexandra's Imperial Military Nursing Service doing frontline medical care. We nurses worked in field hospitals, treating injuries from combat and that included burns, amputations, and infections. We assisted in operating rooms, helping surgeons perform lifesaving procedures and provided emotional care to soldiers suffering from trauma and shock. You might be wondering why I am telling you this. Well, the reason is because I have seen it all. Nothing shocks me anymore. I know why you are here and what you have done but none of that matters while you are in this room. The fact of the matter Ruth is that I can be honest with you and I have seen the sample you gave this morning and spoken to Nurse Hatfield and I don't think things look good for you in my considered opinion. So let us speak plainly and openly. How long have you had this unusual vaginal discharge and pain?'

'Honestly? I think when I was on remand. There was a problem with getting pads. The wardresses were unsympathetic.'

'I see.'

'You think there is something seriously wrong with me?'

'Again, my honesty comes to the fore. Yes, I believe there is something wrong with you and that's why you are here. The tests will either confirm or deny my suspicions but until then your best option is rest and you need looking after and the best place for that is here.'

'What do you think it could be?'

'I'm afraid I'm not going to be that honest. We will have to wait and see. Now in the meantime let's get you settled.'

'And the reason for being placed in a private room?'

'One word will be sufficient for the answer, Ruth and that would be gossip. Your case generated a great deal of controversy and if they had executed you, you would have been only the fifth person to have been executed in Holloway prison in its long history. I made the decision to keep you separate because placing you with a lot of sick women who have nothing else to do but gossip would not be in your best interests. Does that satisfy you?'

'Yes, I take your meaning, thank you. But this doesn't feel right you know.'

'What doesn't?'

'My life outside the prison was hard. I tried so very hard and got nowhere. And now I'm in prison and perhaps for the first time in my adult life strangers are treating me with kindness and it's upsetting me and it feels odd and… wrong.'

'So, you had better get used to it, Ruth.'

Ruth turned away towards the window and the iron bars and Staff Nurse Chambers knew why. She stood.

'In that cupboard over there you'll find everything you need and so I'll leave you to settle in. In half an hour there will be dinner. I'm afraid the regulations of locking doors still applies here but that's Holloway rules. I'll speak to you soon, Ruth.'

At least the sound of the door locking was a normal door and not one of those huge iron ones that was in the main prison and Ruth heard it as a soft click. Wiping her eyes, she opened the cupboard and indeed found everything that she needed. The room had a separate toilet and bathroom and was centrally heated. The bed was even soft and the view from the window because it was on the ground floor was pleasant with a range of plants and trees.

'Well, it could be worse,' she sighed.

Chapter 4

The results of the blood and urine tests arrived quicker than Ruth expected. They had mentioned a week but during the afternoon of the fourth day, her door was unlocked at an unusual time, between lunch and afternoon tea. Even without any means of knowing the time or what day it was, Ruth was already beginning to recognise patterns of behaviour from beyond her room and therefore she looked up sharply from the book she was reading.

Nevertheless, as much as she was in solitary, those four days seemed to her to be some of the longest days she had ever experienced as there was very little else to do but sleep and read the few books that Staff Nurse Chambers had offered her from the limited prison library. It most definitely reminded her of the time when she was seven years old and had mumps and her mother made her stay in bed for over a week in the blazing summer of 1933.

She remembers watching her friends from her bedroom window playing in their gardens and often calling at the front door asking her mother if she could come out to play yet. But what was worse was when her friends were not in their gardens for she knew exactly where they were. Because they would be at the seafront enjoying manically splashing about in the sea and perhaps even eating a twopenny ice cream. And surprisingly about this time she also remembers missing school and being concerned about missing lessons because Ruth was an intelligent and creative girl who enjoyed her lessons.

During those four days she had become the subject of intense scrutiny by two other nurses who regularly took her temperature and blood pressure several times a day. When she asked why, Ruth was given the non committal answer that, 'it's a function and responsibility of my job.'

However Ruth's slight paranoia told her differently. They thought she was going to do away with herself. And the truth was, that that notion had not been absent from Ruth's mind during the long nights when she concentrated on how long sixteen years was. And that was if she behaved herself. Because by now she had calculated that, even with good behaviour, when she might be released on license, the year would be 1971 and she would be forty-four years old, middle aged, most probably fat and a frump and the truth was that scared her more than anything else in the world. That scared her more than the results of any test. But then she looked up from her book and felt a chill as not only Staff Nurse Chambers entered but a clergy man as well as a wardress. As she was only lying on top of the bed she swung her legs over and stood.

'Ruth, please sit,' Staff Nurse Chambers sat beside her. 'Let me introduce you. This is, Reverend Woodswalker.'

'Well, this doesn't look good if you have to bring along a vicar.'

'Not at all. Now, I have the results of your tests and I'm afraid it isn't entirely good news. You do have a very serious illness for which you need to go into hospital and be treated immediately.'

'What's wrong with me?'

'I'm afraid you have cervical cancer. At this stage I cannot say with any certainty how developed it is and we won't know until you are examined properly.'

'Am I going to die? Oh, this is a joke isn't it? Sentenced to death and then reprieved and now this!'

'Ruth? Having this type of cancer nowadays does not mean a death sentence. I want you to understand that. That is, if it is caught early, which I believe it is at the moment. It is important that we get you to hospital immediately do you understand that?'

Ruth nodded. 'In chains I suppose?'

'The situation has been approved by the governor and you will be under supervision all the time of course and while you are in hospital you will have a private room and that private room will function as an extension of Holloway. That is how it must be.'

'When is this going to take place?'

'You will be going to the London and an ambulance will be collecting you at five. This is Wardress Martin who will be accompanying you. Ruth? Why are you smiling?'

'Sorry, I sensed irony. The state did their utmost to kill me and now they're doing their upmost to save my life! It's just so stupid it made me smile. I'm sorry.'

'That's alright, Ruth you must be in shock. Let me assure you once again that your condition does not mean you are going to die. Cancer is very treatable nowadays.'

'But do I want to die or do I want to live? Because I've been thinking about it as well. Sixteen years here. It'll be 1971 when I'm released if I'm lucky. I'll be old and fat.'

'You must not think like that, Ruth. All you have to do is think about the next couple of days. Will you do that for me?'

Ruth nodded.

'Then I'll be back at five and I'll leave you with the reverend.'

The Reverend Woodswalker stepped forward. He was a tall bald and skeletal man who Ruth thought could do with a good meal. He was hesitant in the way he said her name which gave Ruth the impression that he had been advised not to use her surname as he normally would have but to use her Christian name.

'Er…Ruth, I see you are C of E?'

'Yes, sir…reverend, but it's been a long time since I've been to church.'

'God is patient, my child. He welcomes sinners.'

'Well, I am one of those. I'm not a believer, reverend. I'm an honest woman and I won't tell you an untruth.'

'And I am much obliged for that. For it's a good starting point.'

'Do you expect to convert me, reverend? To see the light? You must know of my history, let alone of the reason why I am here. Drugs and prostitution.'

'I do not have the power to convert anybody, Ruth. If I had, my job would be so much easier! I am simply here as an agent of God to listen that's all. And through me you will come to your own conclusions as to how you wish the rest of your life to be.'

'That's not how our old vicar used to put it when I was a child back in Wales. He was a fire and brimstone sort of man and that me and my sister would burn in hell for our sins. Frightened the shit out of…oh, sorry reverend, frighten the Dickens out of us kids he did.'

'I'm afraid that's the way some believers work but it is not my belief.'

'Do you mind if I ask you a question, reverend?'

'Go ahead.'

'How long have you been working in Holloway?'

'I came here in, let me see…1938. Yes, that would be right, in the summer. That was a baptism of fire for me!'

'Was it very different then?'

'It was pre war so yes, very different indeed. Holloway in those days was a strict and entirely unforgiving place.'

'It doesn't seem very forgiving now.'

'It *is* a prison you know!'

'Do you expect me to confess all my sins, reverend?'

'Unless you convert to Catholicism then I would be useless to you. I expect nothing of you, Ruth. But I do expect you to get better and I do expect you to come and visit me when your health fully returns. Will you promise me that?'

'You have that much faith I will survive?'

'I do. I do have faith you are going to survive. God saved you from the gallows and I believe God will save you from whatever evil is growing inside you. That is my belief. God *will* save you. And I will pray for you and I will ask others to pray for you.'

'I don't think anybody has ever prayed for me. That's an odd thought that anybody should ever want to pray for me.'

'Well I shall and now I will leave you and you can prepare yourself for the journey ahead.'

'Thank you, reverend. When will I see you again?'

'I'll be close by. Goodbye for now, Ruth and good luck.'

After Reverend Woodswalker left, Ruth asked the wardress the time and she was told she had an hour to go. The door was locked and apart from changing her underclothes, Ruth did nothing else but lay on the bed listening to the birds and trying to take in the life changing news that that had been delivered to her.

Once again irony came upon her and she felt how messed up everything was. What could have caused the cancer? Was it the multiple abortions? *Where* was the cancer? Was it the amount of alcohol she had consumed? Or had it been the drugs? Had it been her lifestyle or was it partly all or some of the above? Certainly she had not lived the life of a choirgirl but neither had her friends but they had not come down with cancer. But they had not killed the love of their life and been sentenced to death either so was that a factor?For Ruth had heard that stress could do strange things to the body. Desmond had mentioned that more once. And he ought to know he had insisted. And she reasoned that during the last three months she had been under extreme duress.

Ruth was not allowed to walk to the ambulance as a wheelchair was provided and the procedure for leaving the prison was complicated with forms to sign and gates to be unlocked and locked. She was told she was going to be accompanied by three wardresses all the time who were going to work on a rolling eight hour shift so somebody would be outside her private room day and night as where she was going there would be no lock on the door.

The ambulance driver, a young man, did not seem surprised at his passenger. Ruth pondered as he watched her being loaded aboard if he knew about her notoriety. If he did it did not show on his face and after signing more forms, the ambulance was soon moving away from the towering grey fortification that Ruth thought she would never see again from the outside.

Now partly freed from their authoritative duty the three wardresses relaxed somewhat and smoked and offered Ruth one as well which she gladly accepted.

'Sorry to put you all out, ladies. I don't know how long this is going to take.'

'Don't mind us, Ellis. We're getting a special rate for being away from our families.'

'And I tell you,' said the eldest, 'it's a bloody holiday for me!' she smiled.'

The inside of the ambulance descended into informality and that was strange for Ruth to see the women in an entirely new light for these were ordinary women doing a job. They were stripped of make up, their hair was tied back in tight buns and their uniform disguised any femininity but watching them smoking, chatting and smiling for some unknown reason caused Ruth to feel sad. For these were the same type of women that accompanied her for three weeks in the death cell while she waited and waited to be executed. How were these ordinary women able to do that? How were these ordinary working women able to watch a woman day by day disintegrate almost to the point of living insanity and then go home to their husband and children and pretend as if nothing had happened? What sort of system indoctrinates a woman to do such an occupation and remain so detached? Or did they choose particular women that were unique? The question occupied her for most of the journey and another cigarette.

Preparations for her entrance into the London hospital in Whitechapel had been clearly made in advance for the ambulance did not take her into the usual bay but entered the hospital by the back away from the eyes of the public. Placed once again in the wheelchair the entourage was met by a ward sister and a nurse. But the sister was a woman who clearly was not at all happy being surrounded by dustbins and other assorted rubbish.

'Good afternoon, Mrs Ellis, I am, Sister Stockinger and welcome to the London. We are going straight to your room and I have all your details and I will be supervising your treatment. This is, Nurse Canham who will be looking after you personally. I aim to make your stay with us as pleasant as possible.'

'Thank you, Sister.'

'I hope you'll forgive the cloak and dagger operations. This is not the way I would normally administer a patient into hospital but my feelings over the matter were overruled. I simply wish you to know that. Admitting a patient under these conditions is abhorrent to me no matter the circumstances.'

She briefly glared at the three wardresses knowing full well they had nothing to do with the arrangements but Ruth gained the impression it made her feel better.

'So, come along then and we'll get you settled in.'

Nurse Canham wheeled Ruth up a ramp, along a short corridor and the wardresses followed. It soon became clear she was not going to stay in any part of the hospital where any normal patient would stay and all too quickly she found herself in a ground floor room that smelt strongly of bleach and which was completely empty except for a bed and looked as if it had been removed of rubbish and cleaned especially for an occupant.

'I'm only going to apologise the once, Mrs Ellis. The management in their infinite wisdom would not allow you even to have a private room in women's surgery so I'm afraid this room and its separate WC was the only alternative. And on behalf of myself I can only apologise profusely.'

'That's really all right, Sister. I'm here to be cured of cancer and I really don't care where you do it. I'm grateful however it is done. You obviously know who and what I am. You probably know that it's only by God's Grace that I am here anyway. I ought not to be alive so existing in this small room is a miracle to me so please do not give it any more thought.'

'That is very gracious of you. Thank you, Mrs Ellis. But this room is warm and the bed is soft. Everything is clean and fresh, I have made sure of that. Now, nothing is going to happen today so you may rest but you will be taken tomorrow morning for an examination and an X-ray and then tomorrow afternoon you will be seen by a consultant, Mr Delauney.'

'And then I will have the operation?'

'I am not in position to second guess the consultant I'm afraid. We will have to wait for his diagnosis. Now you see that button beside the bed there? I have had that installed to connect to the nursing station above so if you need anything please press that and Nurse Canham or another will see to your needs. I understand one of these wardresses will be outside during your stay so with that in mind I shall leave you for now and I'll see you tomorrow morning. Do you have any questions?'

'None, thank you, sister. Thank you, nurse.'

'I understand how concerned you might be but try not to be. We have hundreds of cases like yours a year and we have a high success rate so bear that in mind. Oh, one more thing. No more *smoking*!'

Glaring at the wardresses, the sister and the nurse left leaving Ruth alone with the three wardresses.

'Where are you all going to sleep?'

'We've been booked into a hotel over the road.'

'Ellis? Don't even think about climbing out through that window.'

'Why would I do that? I'm here to be cured of cancer. If I climbed out of the window I'd still have the cancer!'

One of the wardresses spoke deliberately to the other. 'Marshall didn't say anything about a ground floor room with a window without bars. We have to phone this in. We have to cover ourselves. I'll speak to that sister. Perhaps we can get somebody to put a lock on it.'

'I'll do it. You're on first watch anyway. Right, well, we'll leave you in peace then, Ellis.'

Ruth nodded and the door closed. The view from the window was uninspiring and consisted of a pile of broken bricks, a short alleyway and dustbins.

'Lovely…'

Out of interest she tried lifting the lower half of the sash window up but someone had painted over them a long time ago and it wouldn't budge. Returning into her bed she laid on it and closed her eyes and smelt the bleach.

Chapter 5

Ruth will remember her first night in the London for the rest of her life because when she awoke she found herself on her back on the floor with one of the wardresses on top of her struggling to hold her down by her wrists.

'Ellis! Ellis! Wake up, Ellis. ELLIS!'

Ruth's eyes opened and stared at the young woman's frightened face and they stopped struggling…frozen.

'Ellis? What the bloody hell? Get up.'

Wardress Smith helped Ruth stand and pushed her back on the bed before she closed the door. Ruth wore the white hospital nightdress that had been worn by so many previous patients and now she sat, her head sunk, her hair dishevelled, her hands touching her throat, the single electric light bulb throwing harsh shadows as it was four am.

'Ellis? What was that all about?'

'It was a nightmare. I'm sorry.'

'What was you doing on the floor?'

'I must have fallen out of bed.'

'Has that happened before? I'll have to make a report. I said…'

'I was being hung…'

'*What?*'

'In my dream. God, I was so frightened.'

Wardress Smith sat on the bed next to her. Although young, having a husband and a daughter and having strong opinions opposing capital punishment and because of the job, she had become somewhat more quick to anger than she used to be before beginning it.

'What happened?'

Ruth looked at her with an expression that would have broken any heart. It was in her eyes.

'I was in the cell…that cell and on the wall was this giant clock that was ticking away the seconds. You know we're not allowed clocks in cells. Especially in the death cell. So that was strange and I could not stop looking at it. Then it was all chaos. Men came in and grabbed and pulled me and then there was a rope around my neck and a vicar was speaking a passage from the Bible and then I was falling and chocking and then I was staring at you.'

'Bloody hell, Ruth! How often do you have nightmares?'

'Never. Not since I was a kid.'

'I'm surprised the whole hospital hasn't woken up. It's ten past four in the morning.'

'I'm sorry.'

'When I heard you screaming I thought you were being bloody murdered! Then seeing you on the floor I thought you were having some sort of fit. Have you ever fallen out of bed before?'

Ruth shook her head. 'It was the dream. I'm sorry.'

'You feel better now?'

'Not really, mam. I can still see him putting the rope over my head.'

'But it was only a dream, Ruth. You were spared the reality. Try and put it out of your mind and get some sleep. I'll make a report to Chief Officer Parker. Just for the record.'

Ruth did managed to sleep for three more hours and was awoken by Nurse Canham who had been told of the events of the night. As she checked Ruth over she sounded breezy and efficient.

'So, you had an eventful night then? The warder mentioned it. Are you a woman who suffers from disturbed sleep patterns?'

'No, nurse. I normally sleep like a baby. But I'm sure that given my previous circumstances I think the dream was inevitable don't you think?'

'I think it must have been terrifying and dreadful if it was powerful enough to pitch you on to the floor!'

'When I came around, the wardress was on top of me holding me down. God, I was so frightened.'

Mrs Ellis? I understand that you are troubled this morning but I'm afraid I have to inform you that today's examination must still go ahead. You understand that? There are rotas…'

'Oh yes, I wasn't… No, of course not. I want this thing over and done with as quickly as possible.'

'Very well then. Now, your temperature is fine and I can see no reason for your examination not to proceed so I will be back at nine o'clock. In the meantime take your breakfast and do try and relax.'

'Thank you, nurse.'

Much to her surprise, because she wasn't expecting it to be tasty, breakfast actually was and she enjoyed toast and scrambled eggs and coffee. Wardress Smith had now been replaced by Wardress Floyd, an older woman in her mid fifties and one she now recognised as one of the chosen few that had guarded her in the first week of her death cell experience. Surprisingly, Wardress Floyd decided to eat her breakfast with Ruth.

'I heard all about last night's ruckus.'

'A nightmare. I've apologised. I recognise you now, mam. I didn't before.'

'I was wondering about that. You looked at me in the yard and your face didn't show any recollection.'

'You only were there for the first week wasn't you.'

'That's right.'

'Can I ask why?'

'You can ask.'

'I see. I understand. Have you been a prison officer long?'

'Let me see…coming up to seventeen years. Joined in the summer of thirty-eight. Straight out of college. Failed at everything!'

'Failed?'

'My parents were both mathematicians and that's what I was supposed to be. However I didn't have the brains and I didn't get the grades so here I am! And that's all the personal details you'll get out of me.'

'I'm sorry, I didn't mean to pry. You're just somebody to talk to.'

Wardress Floyd finished her food and lit a cigarette blowing a cloud of blue smoke away from Ruth.

'Sorry, I know you're not allowed to have one. All right, yes the reason I wasn't present at the second or the third week was because I opted out. That's the reason. That sort of work is all volunteer anyway. I was present when they hung, Christofi. Remember her?'

'Christofi? That was last year, wasn't it? Didn't she do some woman in with a frying pan?'

'She did. Her daughter in law. And then tried to burn her body. But I can tell you now I spent a great deal of time with her and in reality she was just a tired old confused grandmother who ought not to have been in this country at all and in my opinion was suffering from a severe mental health problem. And I said so at the time to the chief medical officer but would she listen to me? Of course not. And it would not of made any difference anyway.'

'What happened?'

'I was present that day at nine o'clock in the morning and she really didn't know what was going on. Pierrepoint was his normal efficient self and it was over very quickly but it took me weeks to recover and I swore I would never go through that again and the experience haunted me.'

'Why did I see you then in my first week?'

'I put my name down because I wanted to see if I had got rid of my ghosts. And after a week it was clear I had not. And I would not have been able to go through seeing you hang. In my mind it was clear the establishment wanted you dead.'

'And now I've got cancer.'

'And a life sentence.'

'If I survive. Can I ask you what the time is please?'

'It's eight-fifteen. I'll let you alone for a while so you can get yourself together and collect your thoughts. I'll be outside.'

'Thank you for chatting, mam.'

Wardress Floyd offered her a sight wink. 'Just between you and I…did he really punch you in the stomach when you was pregnant causing you to lose your baby?'

'Yes, mam, he did.'

Wardress Floyd hesitated for a moment before sighing and silently turning away.

Nurse Canham collected and wheeled her herself and accompanied by Wardress Floyd, they made their way through numerous corridors and a lift until they were in the heart of the hospital. Ruth was only too aware of how many people were staring at her because of the wardress and she could not have felt more conspicuous if she had been in handcuffs

The X-Ray department was first and that was a particularly uncomfortable experience because it was cold as she still only wearing the thin nightdress and dressing gown and Ruth thought the technician was as frigid as the room. It was the way he had uncomfortably and silently glared at her, as if she had shot *his* son.

Then it was on to a room where they were forced to wait for over an hour for the X-Ray to be developed. Which Ruth didn't mind at first except that it was a social room which meant it was being used by members of the public which meant she came under further scrutiny as people came and went. Recognising her uncomfortableness, Wardress Floyd gave her a magazine and she therefore spent the time with her head buried in it. Then finally Nurse Canham entered and surreptitiously nodded to Wardress Floyd.

Doctor Jackman did not look up from whatever he was writing when Nurse Canham wheeled Ruth into his office and the three women remained silent until Wardress Floyd gave a deliberately loud cough as she stared at the top of his bald head.

'Doctor?' said Nurse Canham, 'your next patient, Ruth Ellis.'

'Yes, yes. Blasted paperwork…get her on the table nurse behind the screen. And I suppose *you* have to remain in the room?'

'I do, doctor, *yes*.'

'What do you think she's going to do? Jump out of the first floor window?'

Wardress Floyd never answered.

When Ruth was settled, Nurse Canham retired and silence ensued while Ruth was examined. Doctor Jackman then washed his hands and returned to his desk and Nurse Canham helped Ruth back to her wheelchair. She immediately recognised how distressed she was.

'Mrs Ellis. Come forward please. Now, I have the results of your blood and urine and I have examined your X-ray and from what I have seen I am afraid I have some uncomfortable news for you. I am sorry to tell you that it is my belief you have cervical cancer. Normally, under other circumstances this would be confirmed by a biopsy but from experience I can see an abnormal growth on the X-ray itself.'

'I see…'

'When did you feel there was something wrong?'

'A few months ago.'

'I see. And how do you feel in yourself?'

'Given my circumstances… Not too bad I suppose. Some pain.'

'Yes I understand. Now your age is twenty-eight?'

'Yes, I'll be twenty-nine in October. I never thought I'd say that.

'And you already have two children?'

'Yes, a boy and a girl.'

'Mrs Ellis, let me be forthright with you. The options for treating you at this stage is limited but I do believe your condition is at an early stage. There are two options one of which is radiotherapy or megavoltage therapy but in your case I think surgery would be best considering your age.'

'Surgery, doctor? What sort of surgery?'

'What is known as radical hysterectomy. It's often used for early stage cervical cancer but considering you already have been blessed with children the operation will involve removing the uterus, cervix, and surrounding tissues, including the lymph nodes. Obviously, this will mean you will never be able to conceive again.'

'But it means I will be cancer free?'

'It means you will be cancer free, yes.'

'I see. Then yes, I would like that done…please. I want to live.'

'Very well. Nurse? I will mark this as urgent and I will speak to Mr Delauney's secretary at lunchtime.'

'Yes, doctor.'

'Will you be doing the operation, doctor?'

'No, Mrs Ellis. I am not a surgeon. The surgeon who will be performing your operation will be, Mr Delauney, a highly experienced gynaecologist attached to the London. You will be in safe hands.'

'Thank you.'

'Doctor? I have to send constant reports back to Holloway. Have you any idea when the operation will take place and how long the recovery will take? I ask because there are three of us wardens and we have to make further arrangements if Mrs Ellis is to stay here any longer.'

'Yes, I see. I will find out this lunchtime and let nurse know. At the moment that's the best I can do. As to recovery time? Mrs Ellis appears to be a healthy young woman so I would expect her to receive post operative care for several days, possibly seven in the London and then full recovery could take up to eight weeks thereafter.'

'Thank you, doctor. That's enough information to give my superior.'

'It's Nurse Canham, isn't it?'

'Yes, doctor.'

'A little bird tells me that Mrs Ellis has been dragooned into the basement.'

'Oh, I only did what Sister Stockinger told me to do, doctor. To prepare that room.'

'I see. I shall speak to her then. But after Mrs Ellis' operation I will make it my business to make sure she has a bed in women's surgical.'

'Yes doctor.'

'And *your* name is?'

'Floyd. Mary Floyd.'

'Very good. You might inform *your* supervisor that premium recovery depends upon good nursing and I cannot have nurses scurrying up and down stairs to the basement checking on one patient. Besides, recovering in a favourable atmosphere amongst other women will do her a power of good psychologically.'

'Yes, doctor. I will mention that. But she is to remain in the London for at least seven days?'

'At least.' Doctor Jackman stood. 'Now, put all other thoughts out of your mind, Mrs Ellis. Your consultant, Mr Delauney is the best we have and I'm sure the next time we meet will be under far conducive circumstances. Goodbye for now.'

Although Ruth had no money, Wardress Floyd took Ruth to the small hospital shop where she purchased a paperback and a choc ice for her.

'For goodness sake, don't tell anybody! But I saw your face after he had done with you and I was upset. What did he do?'

'It was the examination. He didn't hurt me. It was just uncomfortable. I just want this day to end. Thank you so much for this. I can't remember anybody being so kind to me. I don't deserve it after what I've done.'

'Ruth, you are being punished. You have been sentenced to life in prison. You have not been let off scot free'

'I know. That's something I've still yet to come to terms with. The evil I have done in the cold light of day is beyond my imagination. Mam? Do you think you'll be able to stay for the duration while I'm in here?'

'It looks likely. Me and the others were chosen for the job so it looks like we'll be staying.'

'What's your hotel like?'

'An utter dump. Hard beds, dodgy food and full of foreigners. We've already made the decision to eat out every evening.'

The hospital shop near the main foyer was a busy place and a microcosm of the city and for a few minutes Ruth sat and enjoyed her ice cream watching the sick, the lame and the lazy pass her while they in turn stared back at Wardress Floyd wondering who she was as it was evident she was not a police officer. For nobody in Whitechapel had ever seen a uniformed woman officer enjoying an ice cream in public.

Chapter 6

Nurse Canham gave Ruth good news that evening when she brought her, her evening meal.

'Best enjoy this, Mrs Ellis because it's your last meal if you'll forgive the wording. Your operation will take place at nine-thirty tomorrow morning which means only water from nine o'clock this evening.'

'Am I being moved?'

'Not this evening. But you will be recovering in a private room on woman's surgery before being transferred onto the main ward for the remainder of your stay. It seems you have made an impression on Mr Delauney and that's a feat in itself.'

'I wonder why? I'm a convicted murderer. Why should he show me any leniency?'

'Ask him!'

'Maybe I will! After!'

'You sound as if you are better now. More chirpier.'

'You got that right, nurse. I don't know. Talk about a ride on the Waltzer. Sentenced to death then reprieved then found to have cancer now it's being taken away. It's all... I don't know. It almost makes me believe...'

'In God?'

'Do you believe in God, nurse?'

'What a foolish question! Of course I do. I could not do this job otherwise. You do not?'

'I believe we must have had very different upbringings, nurse.'

'I see. Yes, my faith keeps me true. The devil chose Whitechapel for some reason and it is easy to spot him lurking and practising his evil in every corner.'

'And I suppose you see him in this hospital all the time?'

'Are you making fun of me?'

'I don't mean to. It's just that I don't believe in the devil and God. I suppose I believe in tragic circumstances that happened to bad people and good people and we get caught up in things sometimes for no reason. That's how I feel about my own life.'

'Well, it's far too late in the day to debate philosophy with you, Mrs Ellis and I have work to finish and a home to get to. But I will be on duty tomorrow morning and I will be collecting you first thing. I will be giving you an injection to make you drowsy and remember, only sips of water this evening. Would you like a pill to help you sleep?'

'No thank you.'

'Then I shall leave you with your capable guard outside and I shall see you in the morning.'

Ruth's third wardress, Wardress Malone was older and far less talkative. Ruth imagined she was close to retirement age and all she was interested in was doing the job by the numbers. Therefore, Ruth turned off her light early and tried to sleep with a great deal on her mind knowing the next day might be her last if things did not go as planned.

But as she had been in that situation previously, oddly she did not feel agitated. Indeed, she felt a sense of calm. As if she were wading out to sea. Moving beyond heavy violent waves that were crashing against her body repeatedly while she could see the calmness of the ocean spread out before her. And with that image held closely in her mind, she fell asleep.

Eleven hours later the next day, Ruth opened her eyes to a dark room and heard whispering and felt someone's fingers curl around her hand before a familiar face loomed over her and smiled.

'Ruthy! My darling! It's me, Muriel.'

Ruth's eyes closed again.

'It'll take a little time, Miss Jakubait,' said the current nurse. 'May I suggest you find yourself a cup of tea and come back in perhaps half an hour?'

'I've been drinking tea all bloody day. No, I'll wait.'

After some encouragement from the nurse, Ruth regained her senses a little more and this time she was able to focus on her sister.

'Ruth? How do you feel?'

'In pain. Oh God! In pain.'

'Nurse? Is she getting anything for the pain?'

'Of course she is. I'll fetch a doctor now she's woken up. He won't be pleased to see that she's got a visitor here.'

'You think I care? When bloody Holloway didn't even tell me that she was in here with cancer and I had to find out myself from the bloody Daily Mirror?'

'That's not our concern. Our concern is that the patient is kept calm.'

She hurried from the room.

'Ruthy? Did you hear that? Bloody Holloway didn't even tell me that you were in here with cancer. The Daily Mirror actually phoned me and told me you were in here and I almost had a fight with the old devil on the door there to get in here to see you.'

'Muriel? Can you speak softer please? My head is splitting.'

'Oh, I'm sorry. I've been waiting hours for you to wake up. It was such a shock to find you in here.'

'I did ask if I could let family know but everything moved too fast. Did the nurse say anything about the operation?'

'Not to me and I haven't seen any doctor.'

'What is the time?'

'It's just past ten o'clock at night.'

'So I've missed an entire day.'

Ruth closed her eyes and remembered when they came for her at nine o'clock. It was all very efficient and professional and she was taken to the theatre in a wheelchair. A nurse had at eight o'clock already given her a sedative and so by the time she had arrived there she was already drowsy. She vaguely remembers standing and being placed on a flat surface first near a window and then a wall but after that things became very unsteady. The final thing she remembers was Mr Delauney wishing her good morning and hoping she had had a good night sleep and then oblivion.

A doctor returned with the nurse and stared at Muriel.

'Excuse me, who are you?'

'I'm her sister. And she tells me she is in pain. What are you going to do about it.'

The doctor turned and stared at the wardress who stood in the doorway.

'Is this *person* allowed? Sister Stockinger has spoken to me.'

'My duty, doctor is to make sure the prisoner does not escape. I am doing my duty.'

Doctor Harris, a youngish man in tweeds who was doing his best to grow a moustache, snorted in embarrassment then approached Ruth's bed and began his examination in an awkward silence and then wrote his notes. By the furious way he wrote it was obvious, he was most put out.

'I'm in a lot of pain, doctor…here.'

'Nurse? Morphine 5mg every four hours to begin with. I'll call in again after my evening round.'

He never got the chance to slam the door because the wardress closed it for him but Muriel was sure he would have done had he the chance.

'God! What a pig!'

'I've no doubt the doctor's going to report you being here.'

'Then let him! See if I care. Bloody Holloway's kept me away from my sister for months.'

'Yes, but...'

'But what? Because she is prisoner? Because she shot a man? Why don't you say it? That's right. It's none of your bloody business. Your job is to help her get well and look after her.'

'Mrs Ellis? I will return shortly with the doctor's recommendation. Is there anything else that you need?'

Ruth shook her head slowly and closed her eyes. 'Get rid of this pain please and if I'm allowed, a cup of tea?'

The nurse grimaced, nodded and left leaving Muriel to take her sister's hand again.

'Ruthy? God! It pains me to see you like this. Mum sends her love. I haven't had time to see anybody else. You poor darling, but you're going to pull through this. When we heard about the reprieve it was unbelievable that our dreams had come true because we didn't think it was going to happen even though we had prayed and prayed.'

'I wanted to die, Muriel. Almost up to the end I thought I had to die, I thought I deserved to die, I really did. I suppose God had other ideas.'

'God? That's the first time I've heard you speak religiously since you ran around in a little frock! Are you going all religious on us?'

Ruth managed an odd smile through the pain and Muriel saw how her sister's eyes were glistening but she could not tell whether that was from pain or from some other emotion.

'I did speak to somebody about your operation and it's a big thing, Ruth. It'll take ages for you to recover so I suppose you'll be in here sometime. Good thing you've got two kids already.'

'They think about a week here and then a couple of months recovery until I'm better. Hopefully that will be in the hospital wing in Holloway so that will be good.'

'What's it like there, you know in the ordinary part of the prison?'

'Too early to say but it's noisy and busy.'

'How are you going to deal with it?'

'I'll just have to. You'll visit won't you?'

'Of course I will. Mum will and André of course although I don't know about dad.'

'I don't want him visiting me. Make sure of that please.'

'I'll make sure that he doesn't then, don't worry. Oh, Ruth!'

'Muriel? One favour please?'

'Go on.'

'Look up Desmond and tell him I don't want him visiting either. Can you do that for me? It's important he doesn't visit. Ever, do you understand?'

'I understand. I also understand that he should be in bloody prison as well.'

'That's beside the point and that's between you and me.'

'Oh, Ruth!'

'His time will come eventually.'

'But you know the truth could make a difference to your time here.'

'I don't know any such thing, Muriel. I deliberately put four bullets into a human being and I'm going to serve out my time in prison, case closed.'

'You were always such a free spirit, Ruth. Always so gay and happy. I can't imagine how this free bird is going to manage being caged for so long and how it's going to change you.'

'I expect it will in ways I cannot imagine but perhaps I will be released one day if I behave myself and then we will see.'

The door opened again and the nurse returned with a tray. Professionally she administered the morphine by way of an injection in Ruth's arm and within moments the tension that Ruth had been holding was palpably released and she genuinely smiled.

'Oh, God! That's better! That feels warm.'

The nurse stared at Muriel.

'I have spoken to Sister Stockinger and now she is aware of your presence she is currently speaking to the Consultant, Mr Delauney. He will deal with you. But being here on the first day of her recovery is most irregular. Mrs Ellis? Tea will be brought to you shortly.'

'Thank you, nurse.'

Muriel felt some relish at having a confrontation with the consultant but never got the chance because she left before he arrived. She did not have any grievance with that particular man of course and later felt gratitude that he had done such a splendid job in saving her sister's life. But the fact was, minutes after being given the morphine, Ruth fell asleep and so there was no reason for her to remain. When a nurse arrived with a cup of tea and found her asleep she left it to one side, informed the wardress and then went about her business. Ruth slept through the night until she was woken by Nurse Canham with a cup of tea.

'Good morning, Mrs Ellis. No more nightmares I trust? You must be thirsty. Here we are.'

'Oh, it's morning. How long have I been asleep?'

'According to your notes, all night. The night nurse has been making notes on you every hour. That morphine put you right out which is unusual. How is your pain level this morning?'

'Much less than last night but it's more of a pressure if that makes sense. I had a feeling that I ought not to move.'

'And that makes very good sense indeed because I do not want you to move. You have had a lateral incision in your abdomen and that will take time to heal. Now, you are going to be put on a regime of antibiotics and painkillers and a rather strict diet I'm afraid but that's all for your benefit. I see no rise in temperature which is good and if this continues I will move you up into women's surgical ward tomorrow morning. So you will be pleased to get out of this dull old room I'm sure.'

'What about my security out there?'

'That is a matter to be discussed between them and the hospital management. It should not be a matter which concerns you.'

'Nurse? The cancer? Has it gone?'

'I have been reliably informed by the consultant, by which I mean I have not spoken to him directly as I am only a humble nurse not worthy enough to wipe his nose, but I have seen the notes and I can say that the tissues that were cancerous have now been removed.'

'You can't take away my sixteen year sentence so easily can you?'

Nurse Canham smiled. 'I'll be bringing around your breakfast and your first round of tablets very shortly. Enjoy your tea, Mrs Ellis.'

By the end of her second day in that room, Ruth's pain had eased a great deal. Late in the afternoon she had a lady visitor from the London Patience's Society, a charitable body organised in the late nineteenth century to ease the suffering of patients and their families. The arrangement provided light counselling and friendship for those who had no visitors, helped people find family members and even on occasions provided fiscal help for those in dire need.

The lady who visited her was very old, walked with the assistance of two canes and wore clothes more appropriate to the Edwardian age. Nevertheless, she had a most pleasant way about her and she chatted with Ruth for over an hour about her operation and about herself, offering any help she could. Ruth thought she was a dear old soul, but she was shrewd enough not to release too much information about herself even though she surmised the woman knew a great deal about her. All the same it was a pleasant way to spend an afternoon with somebody that was not paid to either look after or imprison her.

Chapter 7

The next morning Ruth awoke with a headache and was disappointed when the nurse refused to give her anything for it telling her that simple aspirin which is what she asked for, would not be allowed given her condition.

'Mrs Ellis, you'll have to mention it to the doctor on his rounds. I'm sorry.'

'But aren't I going upstairs today?'

'I couldn't say. Doctor will advise you.'

Unfortunately, the doctor that arrived was Doctor Harris, and as soon as he and a nurse breezed into the room and picked up the clipboard, Ruth put aside her cheap novel with a sigh of disappointment which he noticed. All the same he remained professional.

'Good morning, Mrs Ellis. I understand you are a little under the weather this morning?'

'Just a headache, doctor. Probably from yesterday which by the way I apologise for my sister. She's a hot head. Always has been and as my older sister she's always been protective of me. She found out where I was from the Daily Mirror. The prison told her nothing and she was very angry.'

'Well, she had no right to talk to me as she did of course but thank you for apologising on her behalf. I see your temperature has remained steady which is excellent. Now I should like to examine you. Nurse if you please…'

That was the first time Ruth had seen the incision they had made and it shocked her. She only caught a glance because Doctor Harris' arm was mostly in the way but it was at that shocking moment she realised her complete recovery would take months. With a sense of rising panic she asked the same question.

'Is it all gone, doctor?'

'I'm assuming you mean the cancer?'

'Yes.'

'I am no oncologist, Mrs Ellis but Mr Delauney is a surgeon of high standing. Have you talked to him?'

'Yes, he says it's gone I just felt I needed to ask again.'

'I understand. You are healing very well, Mrs Ellis. It is time for you to leave this room. I will speak to Sister Stockinger this morning and we should have you settled by after lunch. What is going to happen to your friend out there?'

'Her? I don't know. I suppose the prison will make some arrangement. I have no idea. I hope they don't provide a chair for them to sit by the bed!'

'Highly unlikely. Sister would not allow that. There's a possibility she might be posted at the entrance to the ward. The ward is on the first floor so you would be unlikely to escape out of the window! Especially given your condition!'

'You smile, doctor but I don't think I'm even capable of walking at the moment.'

'Indeed, I should hope not. No walking whatsoever. If you need to go anywhere you will be taken by wheelchair. That's understood nurse?'

'Yes, Doctor Harris.'

'All right then. I am lowering your morphine and putting you on tablets which will be easier for you and that should ease your headache as well. Nurse? Make sure she drinks at least two pints of water a day.'

'Yes doctor.'

'Alright. Nurse, go into Ward Eleven please and wait for me. I wish to have a few words with Mrs Ellis privately for a moment.'

'Yes, doctor.'

Doctor Harris waited for the door to close and Ruth could see the dark uniform of the wardress through the frosted glass. She wearily looked back at the doctor. But he looked almost apologetic.

'Mrs Ellis? I don't really know how to ask you this or even if I should but given the circumstances of you being here, I am going to take the bull by the horns as it were and I am going to ask you a personal question if I may.'

Ruth never answered so he continued.

'You see, working in a hospital I naturally see a lot of life and sadly a great deal of death. I see it all and although I am far from being an experienced doctor, yes, I know, death is still an issue about which I still have to come to terms with when I see a patient dies.'

'You want to know how I felt when it came for me to die?'

'That's perceptive of you, Mrs Ellis. You have been in that position. You faced the blackness and you returned. My patients never come back. They never get to tell me how they felt. So how did it feel?'

'You wish for the truth, doctor?'

Doctor Harris grimaced. 'I don't think I do really, but yes.'

'On the day, on that morning as it approach nine o'clock I was never so terrified in all my life. I think my bowels were about to turn to water. What is that phrase? Shit scared! It is not something you would put your worst enemy through. I've been told I looked calm enough but that was me putting on a show because I knew that reports would go out about my final few minutes but inside, in my head I don't think I was there at all. There was some part of me left there but most of my personality was floating with the stars, floating with memories… floating with anywhere but what was going to happen when the clock struck nine. And then they said you're reprieved. And I did the only sensible thing a person could do. I fainted. But of course, I am talking about being executed not dying peacefully in a bed with a head full of morphine.'

'Quite so. I apologise for invading your thoughts but you are very special woman, Mrs Ellis and I could not…I hope you can forgive my impertinence in asking you the question.'

'I forgive you of course. I forgive you because I understand. My position is privileged. The woman who lived. The woman who also died. That's so odd. I can live with that! In a way that makes the next sixteen years rather easier to bear.'

'It does?'

'Yes, for some reason that does make a difference. Thank you, doctor. I know you probably won't but should you ever have a day off and you find yourself at a loose end then this old prisoner would welcome a visit!'

'There's a thought, Mrs Ellis! All right then. More patients to see. I shall see you in women's surgery this evening.'

Ruth was moved with the minimum amount of fuss that afternoon and found herself in a long ward occupied by thirty women. When the green screens were finally removed she found she only had one neighbour and she proved to be chatty.

'Hello, me ducks! You've got the wall space! Premium spot that is. I'm, Dot. Dot Bell. You just come in, have you?'

'Now, now, Dot,' said Nurse Canham, 'enough of your chatter, this patient has had a serious operation and needs a great deal of rest so don't you go tiring her out with your silly questions.'

'Alright, nurse.'

Nurse Canham brought her face close to Ruth and spoke quietly.

'A little tip, Mrs Ellis, don't give away who you are. She's a talker if you get my meaning and she's simple. Best stay clear if you can.'

'Thanks. I don't suppose I'm allowed to smoke?'

'If you can get out of bed you can smoke! Do you have any cigarettes?'

'No…'

'There's your answer then! And I don't approve of smoking.'

'Is there a smoking room?'

'In that room over there.'

'That wardress that came up with us is called, Floyd. Can I have a word with her?'

'I have got other patients to deal with you know. All right.'

Mary Floyd smiled at Ruth as she approached her bed causing a ripple of surprise among many of the patients that saw her uniform who imagined she was a woman police officer. But out of the corner of her eye she saw Dot make a sudden move and pulled a sheet over her head while muttering, *'oh gawd!'* and that made her smile. Turning back to Mary she said.

'I think you've made an impression there!'

'Who's she?'

'I'm not too sure yet,' Ruth whispered, 'could be she thinks you are the law!'

'How are you feeling and settling in?'

'A bit too early to say although it's a step up from that room. The doc thinks I'll be here for about a week.'

'Yes, We've been told that. We've booked the hotel for seven days.'

'And they found you a place outside?'

'Yes a nice hard chair and we have to pay for our own tea and coffee.'

'There was some talk about me escaping from the first floor window.'

'Yes, I'd like to see you do that with what I understand has been done to you.'

'That's what I said. So, seven days? You must miss your husband and family.'

'That's very sneaky of you, Mrs Ellis. Because I bought you an ice cream doesn't mean I'm going to share personal information about myself with you. First rule of the job, never share personal information. And you having been on remand must have been given the same advice as well? Don't go gabbing to other prisoners because they will use that information against you.'

'I'm sorry. Actually, whether you believe me or not I was not fishing for information. You have been the only person that's been kind to me and I was just simply making conversation when you talked about the hotel for seven days what came out of me was natural. I just thought of who might miss you. I'm sorry.'

'You're a deep one, Mrs Ellis. The newspapers paint you as an uncertain woman. A woman of a particular type but I'm beginning to believe…'

'That I am somebody different?'

'You did shoot that man stone dead.'

'I did shoot him dead. I wanted him dead. It was my intention to kill him dead.'

'But what drove you to it, Mrs Ellis? Now it's my time to apologise because this is not the sort of conversation I should be having with you. It is a conversation you should be having with the chaplain not somebody as low in rank as me.'

'Perhaps you are the perfect person to talk about this with.'

'I doubt that very much indeed. You mustn't look at me like that!'

'I suppose you heard about the hospital run in with my sister?'

'Yes I did. Runs in the family I suppose.'

'She always looked after me, my big sister.'

'That's lovely. I'll let you know that I had a big brother that did the same for me.'

'Careful! …had?'

Mary's eyes momentarily lost their sparkle. 'He fell in northern France in '44.'

'I'm so sorry. How old was he?'

'Thirty-four. He'd only been married two years and his wife had just delivered a son.'

'What a tragic word we live in. I'm so sorry, mam. I won't say anything to anybody I promise.'

'No, I believe you won't either. I believe you're a good person, Mrs Ellis. A good woman who found herself in extraordinary circumstances and if you don't mind me saying so, I feel sorry for you but at the same time glad that you escaped the noose.'

'When I get back to Holloway will I go back to B Wing?'

'Not immediately of course. From what I understand you will spend as long as two months in hospital and then it will be up to the governor. And if that sounds cushy then I can assure you it will not be because lying in bed for two months with no work to do will drive any sane woman mad! After two months you will probably be screaming to get back into some sort of normal prison life. Trust me, I have seen it all before.'

'Then I will do my best to get well as soon as possible.'

Wardress Floyd glanced at her wrist watch.

'I'm going for a smoke now as I'm soon to be relieved. You behave yourself!'

'Thanks for chatting, mam.'

'Remember what I said. Keep your lips closed.'

Ruth had no sooner made herself comfortable and settled, opening her novel, when Wardress Malone appeared. Silently, she pushed something under Ruth's pillow and gave her a direct but benign look.

'Not from me.'

Taking a brief glance around the ward, she left leaving Ruth to bear the stares of the other patients until she felt her cheeks redden which surprised her. Burying her head in her book she surreptitiously felt underneath the pillow and retrieved a packet of Player's cigarettes and she smiled.

Ruth was offered a pill that would help her sleep that first night in the ward but she refused. However, she regretted that decision around 3am as the amount of coughing and unusual feminine noises as well as general hospital sounds were disturbing and the nurse on duty told her that she did not have permission to issue her with any drugs. Therefore, her first night was long and, she hoped not inauspicious for the months ahead when she would be spending the nights with ill women.

By the time she had eaten a decent breakfast, she told the doctor she was hardly in any pain at all so he reduced her tablets once again and surprisingly told sister she could be given wheelchair access from the next day once an examination took place that afternoon. And then like all doctors on his rounds, off he went leaving a multitude of questions unanswered.

It took Nurse Canham to answer them. She returned after the doctor and sister had left the ward because she remembered the confusion on Ruth's face.

'Mrs Ellis? Glad to see you are looking so much better.'

'Thank you. I'm getting used to all this. I won't want to leave soon! What was the doctor talking about? Wheelchair access?'

'Yes, it's a common practice here on this ward. Helping a woman, restoring her to health after illness. In your case because of your stitches, we do not encourage walking but at the end of the ward there through those doors there is a day room with a south facing veranda where patients are encouraged to sit and enjoy the sun. Now you would have to walk there which we cannot allow but if we put you in a wheelchair you will be free to wheel yourself hence the wheelchair. And you will be able to smoke those cigarettes as well!'

'Oh you noticed.'

'Yes, Mrs Ellis. There's not many things goes on here that we do not know about.'

'The wardress won't get into trouble, will she?'

'Not by my hand she won't.'

'Where's Dot gone? Something happened to her as the sun was coming up I think and then they took her away.'

'Don't worry about her, Mrs Ellis. Dot is a mental defective and that's all I can say about her. She'll be back tomorrow. Right, must get on. I'll find out the time of your examination and let you know.'

Her examination was performed by no less than the consultant, Mr Delauney himself and behind the green screens he took his time examining her and her notes before asking some general questions about her health. Then he smiled.

'Well done, Mrs Ellis. It's a wheelchair for you from now on! But I will still urge you to be careful getting in and out of bed. And you must be accompanied to the WC I'm afraid. At least for the next three days. I have no wish to return and have to adjust my senior nurse's fine needlework!'

'Thank you, Mr Delauney. Thank you for all you've done.'

There was a momentary silence between the consultant and Ruth as if he wanted to ask her a question and Nurse Canham saw him wet his lips but the moment passed. He nodded and moved away out from the green screens.

That night Ruth took advantage of a sedative and enjoyed her first full nights sleep and awoke refreshed to find Dot back in her bed. However, when breakfast was being served it was clear this was not the same chatty person that Ruth had spoken to before. Dot was sitting up in bed and was eating her cereal and drinking her tea but she was silent, staring apparently into space.

Because Ruth had been a night club hostess she had always taken an interest in people especially men of course and she prided herself on gaining a knowledge or an awareness of a specified kind about people because that was a skill she had honed over the years. Nevertheless, when she looked at Dot her theories fell apart.

In age, Dot could have been anywhere between 20 and 40. Her hair was unkempt and a greater percent of it was grey. Her eyes were sunken, she had a hooked nose and a mouth that looked as if she had few front teeth. Her frame was small. The woman meant nothing to Ruth except, where was the chatty woman that spoke to her before? She briefly recalled Nurse Canham's words, 'Dot is a mental defective.' Where had they taken her? What had they done to her? But then, a larger question rose in Ruth's mind. One that shocked her. Why was she asking these questions? This woman meant nothing to her!'

Ruth felt cold despite the broad and bright sunshine that was streaming in through the tall and wide windows. The ward was bustling and warm yet the cold she felt was not physical. The cold she felt was an oddity she did not understand. She found herself looking at Dot and asking herself why was she bothering herself with this woman's silent and odd behaviour?

Ruth was 28 years old and had spent a majority of her adult life in the company of dubious men and women many of whom were egoists, narcissists and sex and drug addicts. She had done things that would have shocked a majority of middle England. And finally she had killed a man, a man she loved. And now she was paying the price of that hedonistic lifestyle. She knew she had at least sixteen years of prison to endure and how might that change a woman?

Ruth *felt* queer. She felt distinctly different. She remembered when André fell over as a child and injured his knee she felt concern and pity of course as a mother should and that was natural. But as she glanced once again at Dot, this woman who meant nothing to her, the same feelings of pity rose up and she felt it in her eyes and felt her cheeks swell. What had they done to her? Where had her spark gone? If she had been drugged, Ruth reasoned, surely she would be asleep and lying down not sitting bolt upright staring into space like a zombie while mechanically eating cornflakes?

But as the canteen assistants began to fill their trolleys, the cleaners began their daily grind and the nurses continued their administration, Ruth's attention wavered and she returned to her novel after seeing a nurse cover Dot with a blanket and tuck her in.

After mid morning tea, finally and with a great deal of effort, Ruth was placed in a wheelchair and she was able to wheel herself to the day room while nodding to the various women who were eyeing her. She was more than aware of her appearance. No makeup at all, her hair hadn't been brushed for days and the hospital dressing gown looked as if it had been sewn back in the 1920s. What would some of her former clients have thought of her now?

Chapter 8

The day room was painted in standard government green and was as bland a place as Ruth could have ever imagined. But it did not take much imagination as it reminded her of some rooms in Holloway and it crossed her mind that the same paint was used all over government buildings. But this one smelt of something she could not immediately identify. Then it came to her. A powerful odour of sweaty pants, which she remembered from school, and strong disinfectant mixed with tobacco. It was an oblong room devoid of any imagination or beauty and currently only three patients were using it, only one of which used a wheelchair. As that woman appeared to be the same age as Ruth and was already smoking, she wheeled herself over.

'Hello, can I trouble you for a light please?'

The woman swivelled her head slowly and gazed unemotionally at Ruth for some seconds before she answered. Only when Ruth looked at her face directly did she notice she was older. Her cold grey eyes and flattened nose was an indication and around her mouth were those perioral lines so often prevalent in older women. Her long black hair was greasy and unkempt and she wore glasses of an old fashioned wire framed type.

'I know who you are. Me and my old man had some rare old words to say about you.'

Ruth hesitated, unsure of how to respond but she needed a light. At that moment she did not recognise the woman's accent.

'Can I trouble you for a light please?'

Although the woman had a box of matches on her lap instead of handing them over she passed her own cigarette across and Ruth lit her own from it then handed it back.

'Thanks.'

Almost a full minute passed in silence while Ruth enjoyed the sunshine and silence.

'So you recognised me then.'

'Nope. I was trying to sleep and I heard two cleaners talking. They said, "I hear that murdering bitch, Ruth Ellis is coming in here for some operation" and then you arrived.'

'You're not English are you?'

'I'm Texan born and bred. A proper daughter of the Lone Star State.'

'How long have you been in England?'

'Came over in '25 when I was fifteen with my ma and pa.'

'So, can I ask you? What were these rare old words you and your husband had about me?'

'You wanna know? We Texans are straight talking people. The English hasn't beaten that out of me as much as it's beaten everything else out of me.'

'You sound bitter.'

'Bitter? I guess I do. Dang! bless your heart, honey. Maybe you and I are more similar than I first thought given what I think I know about you.'

'You probably don't know anything truthful about me. The newspapers… You can't believe a word anybody writes about me. Tell me something about you.'

'Pa found me a nice boy to marry when I was twenty but he turned out to be not so nice. Oh, he was okay when Ma and Pa were there but as soon as they were gone it was a different matter. And then ma and pa died in an accident in '22 and that's when it started. That's when I became a punchbag and I put up with that for years until he got called up. And so it was in the army for him. The best day of my life. No, I tell a lie, the second best day of *our* life because the first day of my life was when he got blown to bits in 1943 in North Africa.

'So you must've remarried.'

'Dadgum, you're quick! Yup! Got myself a Harry in 1950 and a better man I couldn't find. But a man more soft in the head I couldn't find.'

'How do you mean?'

'Because and this is going back to you. He was pleased you weren't hanged whereas I thought you should've been strung up and that was our difference of opinion.'

'Let me get this straight. Your first husband beat you, is that right? The same as the man I killed. So you don't have any sympathy for me?'

'None at all. Why should I have? You put six bullets into him…'

'Four bullets.'

'Six bullets, four bullets, who cares? You killed him. In Texas that's a slam dunk.'

'All right. How long did your first husband abuse you?'

The woman paused. 'about nine years… yeah about that. Ended up in hospital a few times after Ma and Pa died.'

'For *fuck's* sake! What's your name?'

'Louise. Louise Howard.'

'Well, for a proud Texan you put up with a lot of shit! Did it ever cross your mind to do the same thing as what I did?'

'Never! I wasn't brought up like that and you don't have guns in England.'

'So if you had had a gun? And you had been living in America?'

Louise turned once again towards Ruth and this time she bore the hint of a smile but only a hint.

'I think you ought to retract your statement about me.'

'I will not.'

'I know. You're a proud Texan. Changing the subject ,what are you in here for?'

'Gallstones. The worst pain I've ever had and that includes spending nine years with Theodore. I had my op three days ago but I've been told I'll be here for another eight days I think recovering.'

'Do you spend much of your time out here?'

'Nothing else to do. Harry visits me every day and that's about it. So I sits out here and smoke.'

'Do you have kids?'

'No, Theo never wanted any and with hindsight I can see that was a good thing because what a son of a biscuit he would've been. You have though haven't you?'

'Yes, a son and a daughter although I'll probably never see my daughter again.'

'You shouldn't think like that. You'll be in prison a long time but you should keep in touch with her.'

'It's not up to her. She's far too young. It's my first husband that's the problem. Listen, speaking about a different subject entirely, I'm at the bed right near the entrance and there's a woman right next to me…'

'You mean, Clementine.'

'I don't know her name. Is that her name? That's a pretty name. Do you know anything about her? I mean, when I first arrived she was very chatty and then they took her away and now she's like a bloody zombie.'

'Yeah, she's had the knock.'

'The what?'

'The knock. You know. She comes from the funny farm and they've given her the knock.'

'I know what a funny farm is but what's the knock?'

'Well there's a proper name for it I guess but it's known as the knock. It's where they put a chisel in your eye and they kind of knock some sense into you.'

'Oh, wait a minute. Do you mean a lobotomy?'

'Yeah, I guess. So that could be it. I overheard a nurse say she was brought in because of she got herself pregnant somehow so I suppose they've taken steps to prevent it happening again.'

'For God's sake! I was warned off talking to her on the first day I was here.'

'Probably for a good reason.'

'Do you work?'

'No, I'm just a housewife. Harry's on the buses and that suits me.'

'What do you do with yourself then?'

'Not much. Shopping. Go to the flicks. Go up West when I can and see a few friends. I fill up my day.'

'If ever you wanna break you can always visit me.'

'In Holloway?'

'Yeah why not? See how the other half live?'

'I don't think so, sweetheart. I don't think my Harry would like me going to such places.'

'Suit yourself but the offers open to you. Write to me and I'll give you permission.'

'Oh it's like that is it?'

'Yeah. You can't just turn up at the gate and say, let me in, I wanna see so and so. It doesn't work like that.'

'That's not for me. Sorry. I hear there's things like good behaviour and things like that. When do you expect to get out?'

'You might be surprised but I haven't given it much thought. It's so long in the future because we're talking 15 to 16 years. I haven't given it much thought but I suppose I could be thinking about…1971. God! Just saying that gives me the willies. It seems impossible. I'll be 44 years old. A bloody old middle age woman.'

'You'll be one year older than what I am now.'

'Really! Oh sorry, you really look a lot younger.'

'Thanks.'

'You're 43? That's astonishing. I thought you were about thirty,' Ruth lied.

'Must be the cream I put on my face every night. Another cigarette?'

'Thanks.'

They continued chatting in a more or less friendly manner and so a nurse having noticed they were enjoying each other's company, placed a table between them and they continued their banter during lunch, during which Ruth found out a great deal more about her American and how much she suffered at the hand of her first husband.

At first Ruth was perturbed as to why she had become so concerned why Dot had been so poorly medically treated for Ruth was not one of life's natural carers. Yet over lunch with the American and listening to how much she had suffered and reconciling with her own wretchedness concerning David, she gave some thought as to what had happened to Dot to change her into what she was. Was she born a chatterbox and childlike? Was she born simple? And was knocking her brains out the best solution? For Ruth had read about the devastating consequences of lobotomy in a scientific journal in George's surgery and was angry when she returned to her bed mid afternoon to see Dot laying on her bed, her eyes open, staring at the ceiling and Ruth bit her lip. Yes, now she remembered from the journal the countless operations performed on females because they didn't conform. Just like perhaps herself.

Ruth sat by the side of her bed and waited for help to get her into it. She didn't have to wait long and was relieved when Nurse Canham noticed her.

'Mrs Ellis! Have you had a pleasant day? I saw you made an American friend. You are ready to get back into bed now?'

'Thank you, nurse.'

'One moment then.'

With the assistance of one other nurse she was soon gently moved and arranged.

'So, settling in then, I hope. Doctor will be round later. He'll answer any questions you have.'

'Will he?'

'Whatever you do you mean? Of course he will.'

'Will he explain what happened to her?' Ruth nodded towards Dot who lay looking little better than a corpse.

'I shouldn't be concerned about her, Mrs Ellis.'

'My first husband was a dentist. Anybody who has been following my case they would know that and I read some of his professional journals so I know what a lobotomy is and I know how prevalent it was twenty years ago and why they mostly did to females and and also how it's fallen out of fashion. When I came in here the woman was chatty and normal. Look at her now. She's not no more is she? And I have to say, I'm angry about that.'

'Mrs Ellis? It would be wise if you kept your opinion about other patients to yourself. Really, it would be to your advantage if you kept your opinions silent, do you understand my meaning?'

Nurse Canham glared at her but in the friendliest way possible. There was a great deal of emotion in her expression.

'Yes I understand. You want me to keep my mouth shut because there's nothing I can do for the poor thing but it's not right is it and I think you know it's not right because you're a good nurse.'

'Mrs Ellis, be that as it may, the decision was made and the die has been cast by those on high well above my station. I am just a simple paid nurse and I have no control here.'

'But you do have an opinion.'

'Perhaps. But we already know the procedure's long term effects and ethical concerns eventually led to its decline.'

'Then why is it still being used?'

'Because under special cases it's used when all other alternatives have been exhausted. I'm sorry, Mrs Ellis but you can't just come in here and tell us our job. The doctors, physicians and consultants know exactly what they're doing and we have known Dot for a very long time and she was an unhappy neurotic and hysterical woman with no hope of recovery or leading an ordinary life so her next of kin gained gave us their permission. She is under sedation at the moment but when she comes out of it she will be, kinder, gentler and more pleasant and that is all you need to know. Now is there anything else I can get you?'

'Not me but you might at least put a sheet over her because she looks like a corpse lying there!'

Nurse Canham drew up a chair after checking the time on her small watch.

'Mrs Ellis? Ruth? You seem more than usually upset. What's upset you really?'

'Honestly, nurse? Just now when I had mentioned George my first husband, that part of my life came strongly back to me including giving birth to Georgina of course and I wondered if I truly would ever see her again. I suppose it's a possibility that she might seek me out when she's old enough but it's highly unlikely that George will bring her to see me. If I did see her what could I say to her? How would I explain myself? I'm your mother, the infamous murderer. No, why would she want to meet me?

'I didn't just feel a sudden sense of strangeness in this ward, nurse. I think it was there from the beginning. I only just become aware of it. That I was not a free woman in amongst this bunch of women who were all free to leave any time they wished. And that was a very strange feeling. To know and to understand that at all times there's a guard on the door of the ward that would prevent me from leaving. And in less than one week I'll be taken from here back to prison where I will spend the next sixteen years locked away in a small cell. Last night I found myself repeating this under my breath as if it were entirely new knowledge, as if someone had just told me, as if the last three months had not existed at all and it was most definitely a sudden sense of strangeness which was accompanied by a sense of disbelief.

'I am one of those unfortunate women who are never satisfied. When I am here I want to be there and when I'm there I want to be here. Do you understand what I'm talking about?'

'Perhaps. I think my sister would more though.'

'I'd like to speak to her. As an example I was brought up in Wales by the sea and by the time I was a teenager I longed for city life, some high life. And then I got it and more. And then it all went wrong. And so then I wanted the country again. And there I was bored. So I am a woman who can never be satisfied. But I have to be satisfied now. Satisfied with a small cell. Constricted to a cell. My punishment for killing a man I loved. My David. They ought to have hung me. Being hung would be better than this. This uncertainty and yet certainty is now all I've got, so it's madness do you understand?'

'I think this is a serious situation that you ought to talk about with somebody who's qualified in the prison, probably the chaplain. I think you're talking about deep mental issues here, Ruth that I can't help you with. I wish I could but I can't. But I do know how prison works and I'm not going to tell you why but will you put me on your list and I will come and visit you. Will you do that?'

'Of course I will, thank you. You can bring cigarettes!'

'I will bring you cigarettes. Now close your eyes and then it will be teatime.'

'Thank you. I keep saying thank you to everybody here and I do mean it. I don't think I've said thank you so much to anybody. It's a strange feeling.'

Chapter 9

There were no great number of goodbyes on the day the prison van arrived to collect Ruth although Nurse Canham did inform her an hour beforehand that it was coming so she was able to give her best wishes to Louise and two other women with whom she had become acquainted. Because these women knew who she was and what she had done Ruth did not expect much but all the same they seemed genuinely sad to see her leave and their expressions affected her more than she was prepared.

At the time, Ruth felt she had to draw on that hard bitten, iron clad personality that she had fabricated but she felt the falseness of it as she shook their hands. Later that evening, alone in her bed trying to sleep, not having had a chance to speak to the other patients in Holloway's hospital ward, she would think of them and come to realise that those ill women in the London were probably the first genuine and honest women that she had been friendly with for a very long time. And that caused her to think profoundly about her entire previous existence since leaving home.

Naturally, she had little in the way of personal belongings and when she left the ward accompanied by two wardresses, that was uncomfortable being transferred to the waiting van. Equally as embarrassing as being wheeled through the hospital and what was worse, through the main front entrance where she became an object of intense curiosity by onlookers. But as much as Ruth wanted to look down and avoid their stares, at the same time she wanted to take advantage of the last time that she would view the open free world for a very long time and the reality of that gripped her.

Whether or not wardress Mary Floyd had negotiated her way into escorting her back to Holloway Ruth didn't care but she was glad to see her when finally her wheelchair was loaded and made fast and Ruth was transferred to a seat on the prison bus. With the two wardresses in front, they left the London and headed west along the busy Whitechapel Road. Mary Floyd spoke quietly so the other officers didn't hear.

'Morning, Ruth. You look so much better.'

'Thanks. I missed you. I thought you'd been given the sack or something for speaking to me.'

'No, I was transferred to another duty for a few days that's all. How are you feeling? How went the op?'

'I'm still on morphine tablets but only just. I was doing fine until two days ago and then my temperature went up so they shot loads of antibiotics in me but now I'm okay again. They did wonder whether I was okay to be moved but… here I am ready to be thrown back into prison.'

'But you are going into the hospital wing which will be similar to where you've been in the last week. You won't be going into the main prison for at least a couple of months.'

'Hooray for that!'

'Ruth? You must try not to be difficult and try and settle. I'm going to try and do what I can for you. I'm going to get the chaplain to visit you because you are going to need some form of help. You understand that don't you?'

'Yes, I'm beginning to understand how dreadful it's all going to be and that I have two choices. Put up with it or to kill myself. And I haven't decided which one I'm going to choose yet. I'm sorry to be so frank.'

'It's just an idea but it might help you if you were to speak to another lifer. It could help if you understood how she managed to put things into perspective.'

'You think so. Well it couldn't hurt I suppose.'

'You are not the first person that I've had this conversation with.'

'They should have just killed me. I killed, David. I deserve to die and that's it.'

'I shall send the chaplain to see you.'

'Oh yes, the good old chaplain. The God squad. I wonder what his job will be? I wonder how he will deal with somebody like me?'

'The same as he deals with other murderers I suppose.'

Ruth appeared thoroughly shocked.

'That's the first time you've used that word against me but it's true of course. Because that's what I am. A murderer! A cold blooded murderer. I don't deserve to go into heaven do I? I don't deserve to go anywhere except in the ground and stay there with David. Look at all those men. Walking this way and that way. Walking home back to their loving wives and then probably going to beat the shit out of them. Maybe they have little children that they won't see anymore. What is it all for, Mary? What's it all about?'

'Ruth? Do you know what prison is for?'

The unusual question caused her to look away from the chaotic scenes outside and she looked puzzled.

'That's a strange question.'

'Not as strange as you think because the true answer is not what you are thinking of. The truth is, Ruth is that, yes it's a place of incarceration, a place of keeping a person away from the general population so they can no longer hurt people. A place of punishment that's true but that's only part of the reason. Holloway is a woman's prison and our esteemed governor has taken it upon herself to provide funds because she is enlightened and she wants to help battered and injured women like yourself. And she means to understand why you became battered and to help lift and raise yourself above your previous circumstances so you may never return to them.'

'I never felt battered when I was running my clubs. I was on top of everything. I was in charge of everything. In control. I dressed well, I looked good so forgive me but I don't understand what you mean by any of that. I was no ugly housewife surrounded by kids and being thrashed with a stick because I didn't have his dinner on the table in time when he came home from work.'

'No, you were surrounded by ugly, fat, jeering drunken men who took advantage of your body for money. You allowed them to do that.'

'They weren't all fat.'

'You want to make a joke of this? I think you know exactly what I mean and I think you are intelligent enough to know that men used you in exactly the way I'm portraying. And I'm saying that Holloway is there as a space and a time for you to change yourself. It's a time for you to look at yourself and make alterations to your personality so that when you are released you will be a different person. You're only twenty-eight years old, Ruth and I can only imagine that my words must ring hollow to you but I have seen women transform for the best in Holloway and I feel that can happen to you because you are intelligent and now, you have the time to change. I like you, Ruth and I think you have potential. I would ask you to give it a little time that's all. One day at a time.'

It was while the van was at the bank interchange waiting at the traffic lights that Ruth happened to see a newspaper vendor and read his leaderboard which exclaimed to the world that Ruth Ellis had left hospital that she turned to Mary.

'Can you see that? It says I've left the hospital. How do they know that?'

Mary shook her head.

'Informants everywhere. Someone knew and got paid for it.'

'How can anybody be interested in that?'

Mary shrugged her shoulders. 'I wouldn't be surprised in the next couple of days if there is a first rate account of your week's visit there by some anonymous person.'

'You mean somebody will be paid for information about my stay there?'

'I think you can be sure of it.'

The van moved away along Princes Street and Ruth took a last look at the interchange and the bank of England. She would not see it again for many years. She was glad of the cigarette that Mary offered her but depression overcame her as the van trundled on towards Holloway and such was its darkness that it reminded her of the day she signed her divorce papers from George.

She had been sitting in her parents parlour at the time by herself and she had consumed half a bottle of whiskey and she had been staring at the form on and off for over a day. But it was a signature that was necessary and she signed it eventually with a sad but determined angry flourish. Now, from her new perspective, as she watched central London slip away, free from the governing rules of marriage, she saw how easily it had been for her to slip back into prostitution.

'I did a sum in my head and if I'm a good girl I might be free by 1971.'

'I think that's a normal reaction. But it's not a good thought, Ruth.'

'I think it's something to hang onto.'

'You'll find other things better than that I can assure you.'

'Better than my freedom?'

'You've only one thing to do now, Ruth and that is to accept what's happened to you. once you've done that everything will be easier.'

Ruth turned back again to the passing world. A vibrant moving world she knew she would not inhabit for decades and she found she could not speak so the rest of the journey was made in silence.

Over the next twenty-four hours, apart from acknowledging a few yes and no's to the staff and Doctor Brightman, she remained taciturn becoming withdrawn and unresponsive even to a visit from the chaplain who was unable to elicit any real reaction from her whatsoever. She overheard Doctor Brightman tell one of the nurses that it was nothing serious, in that she did not need any specialised treatment but merely thought she was undergoing some slight neurotic disorder which will eventually pass.

'How nice for me,' Ruth thought.

Nevertheless, her stoic condition eventually warranted a visit from Chief Officer Parker, the Welfare officer who did manage to gain eye contact.

'Ellis? Prison regulations state that no prisoner may receive or send a letter or have a visitor until three months of her sentence has passed. I am aware that a letter or a visitor might bring you out of your ennui but I cannot break the rules. I wish you to know that so this is one thing you will have to endure.'

'What choice have I got?'

'Exactly, you have no choice. The same as the other five hundred women in here. You are all being punished because you've broken the law. I cannot pretend to understand how you feel, Ellis but I am glad your cancer has been dealt with. But now is the time to lift yourself up and reorganise yourself because only you can do that.'

Ruth slept well in the hospital wing because of the tablets they gave her and because the other fifteen women were also given the same tablets. Therefore it was a quiet wing. During the day it was not so quiet and the other prisoners did make an attempt to be friendly but they soon got the measure of her and by the third day they mostly avoided her. As in the London, she was allowed to be placed in a wheelchair and there was a very small room where the prisoners were allowed to smoke and that is where she got on talking terms with a prisoner called, Barbara Bulley but who preferred to be called, Babs.

When they first spoke it was a day of persistent rain and it was hammering on the windows and they were the only two in the room. Naturally as Ruth did not have any cigarettes she asked the unknown woman if she could have one.

'So, come out of your shell now have ya? Sure, if you can roll one.'

'Oh, I don't…'

'Okay, just this time then but you'll have to learn. There are few ready rolled in here.'

'Thanks… I'm Ruth,'

'Oh, we know who you are! I'm Babs. And before you ask I'm doing six years for killing me kids. One down and five to go with good behaviour. Yep! I killed 'em. Drunk in charge of my car on the A20 on the Sidcup Bypass when a tyre blew. That's all it took. I walked away with bruises but my kids…' Babs stopped babbling for a moment and Ruth had the sensitivity not to speak but she was instantly reminded of Sally in B Wing.

'So, we all know about you. Got out all the cancer, did they?'

'They said they did. I hope so.'

'And now you're all quiet. I know what you're going through 'cause I went through it. One minute I had a husband and kids and a job and a home and next, no kids, no home and my husband of five years is divorcing me. None of my former friends are speaking to me and only me mum is writing to me.'

'Why were you drinking?'

'I'd had lunch with a friend in Eltham and I'd had four glasses of wine. Then I picked up the kids and was taking them down to me mum's. I felt perfectly fine but I was over the limit. If it hadn't of been for that tyre everything would've been alright.'

'Why are you in the hospital wing?'

'Ah, that's my good news. I'm dying!'

'I beg your pardon?'

'Yes, isn't it strange how things work out? Recently I had a blackout for no reason and fell down some steps. So they X-rayed me and found something nasty in me noggin. Something I can't pronounce. But it turned out to be serious and they can't operate but they told me I ought to go into a hospital but the authorities have said no, so here I am to stay until it's good night sweetheart.'

'You mean…?'

'That's exactly what I mean. That's exactly what *they* mean. Brightman says it could be a month perhaps two at best so I can give two fingers up to the rest of the sentence.'

'I'm sorry. And nobody is visiting you?'

'My mum is going to visit shortly so I've been told but I'm not looking forward to that.'

'And your dad?'

'He won't come. A miserable little turd he is. A man born without a spine.'

'And is there no operation that can be done at all?'

'No. They said it was about the size of a golf ball according to the X-ray. There's nothing they can do. They were surprised it got that big without me showing any symptoms except looking back I think there were symptoms but I just ignored them.'

'What like?'

'Strange lights in my eyes, tingling in my legs, numbness in parts of my body. My diet changed, weight loss, stuff like that. You just put down to tiredness.'

'I'm sorry, Babs. And here I am feeling sorry for myself because I'm living.'

'Yeah, and you survived being hung and having cancer. God must want you to live. He must have a purpose for you.'

'You believe in God?'

'I do. I was raised as Methodist and that is my faith and it is unwavering. I drank those four glasses of wine. Did he cause the tyre to burst? I don't know. Did he cause the cancer? I don't know. But I have found some peace within myself and I'm ready for the next step. But your silence since you came in here, Ruth tells me you're not ready at all for your next step just as I wasn't ready for my next step when I came in here. Is that not true?'

'Can I have another rollup please?'

Babs was a thin woman, younger than Ruth but luckily she was talkative. And that was exactly what Ruth needed at that particular time. Someone from the inside who could explain how the system inside the main prison worked. It did not take her long to reason that her length of stay in the hospital wing was about the same time as Babs had to live and that thought she found anguishing. She found herself asking in her head what was going to happen to Bab's body. Would her mother take it? Would anybody attend her funeral? Would anybody send flowers? The entire situation was upsetting and what was discomposing her more than anything else was there was nothing she could do about it.

This was a familiar feeling she was to feel often about being in Holloway. The fact she felt powerless. She was a cog in a living machine from which she would not be released for at least fifteen years and that is what she had to come to terms with. From once being a living breathing laughing drunken mannequin pleasing men at her whim to being locked in a cell every night of every day of every week of every year until they decided her term of imprisonment was over.

'Babs? How did you get used to this when you first came in?'

'I cried a lot. I cried for my children. I still cry for my children. When I think of what I did to them, their poor tiny twisted burnt bodies and how they suffered in that fire… So

I think I suppose being in here was my penitence and I suppose that made it easier.'

'*Penitence*? Yes, that's why I'm here because I shot David. Penitence? Yes? I can understand that now. I am here because of penitence. Okay, I accept that then. Thank you Babs. That helps. I needed something to hold onto. To get me through and you've given me something, so thank you.'

'All right. Glad to have helped.'

'Can I ask? How old were your children?'

'Julie was almost three and Bobby was eighteen months.'

'And the car caught fire?'

'After it rolled over a few times. I was flung clear and when I came round, it was burning and there were people trying to put it out but they couldn't. It was terrible that I could feel the heat and I was screaming but it was no good.'

'Were they in the back?'

'Yes, poor things. I've had some terrible dreams.'

Ruth took the unusual social step of touching Bab's hand and it felt cold.

'I wish I could say something to offer you more comfort, Babs.'

'Thank's, Ruth. My comfort is hoping that my children will accept me when I meet them again. That's all I have.'

Ruth smiled.

Chapter 10

Ruth spent a total of five weeks in the hospital wing during which she became convinced Doctor Brightman had a problem with drink. This first occurred to her on the third week when her temperature rose again over the course of a few hours one evening and he was called in as an emergency to administer more antibiotics and his breath was found wanting. The night nurse noticed it too and Ruth and she both exchanged glances. The nurse's expression made it clear to Ruth that it wasn't the first time either.

Sadly during that time she also watched the disintegration of Babs who was eventually confined to her bed becoming more heavily sedated. This was because she had begun to wander and twice attempted to leave the ward wondering why she was being kept in there. Soon her confusion was dreadful to witness and sedation became the only answer.

The only thing that soothe her was when Ruth sat by her bed and held her hand. A token that did not go unnoticed by the matron although she was ridiculed by a couple of the older and more hardened prisoners when the wardresses were not around. One evening Ruth found an occasion to have a word with the matron. Babs was on constant oxygen by this time and had lapsed into permanent unconsciousness two days before.

'Mam? I know you aren't allowed to tell me anything personal but is her mother ever going to visit before…you know?'

'Ellis, I suppose it makes no difference for you to know. Her mother will not be visiting because permission has not been given. An application was made to the Home Office but it was denied.'

'That's awful! How long has she got?'

'Not long. As you can see, her breathing is slow and is slowing. I would say no more than two or three days at most. Maybe four.'

'Will her mother get her body?'

'If she wants it.'

'Her hand is very cold now.'

'Her heart is slowing, Ruth. I must say, you are a different woman to how your reputation proceeds you. Five weeks ago you had no idea this woman existed, now you hold a vigil for her. Why is that?'

'I'm not sure of it myself, matron. Oh, maybe I do. When I was in the death cell, I was alone. As alone as anybody could ever be. And I knew what they were going to do with me afterwards because when they thought I was sleeping, I heard the two wardresses talking quietly. Buried in the ground with no priest or ceremony along with the other women that have been executed. No headstone or anywhere or anything to say where we are buried. That's all part of the punishment. How wicked is that? That's like something out of the 17th century. That's punishing the families that is. And now because of her punishment they won't let her mother in to hold her hand before she dies and I believe that's cruel. A mother has a right to say goodbye to her child. *She* hasn't done anything wrong. It's a wicked system.'

'Don't get yourself worked up, Ellis. I know you mean well but there's a time and a place for your thoughts. What you are doing is enough for now and is all you can do. I can see you've been a good friend to her in the short time you've known each other.'

'I was hoping to do her five years with her.'

'I understand. But there will be others.'

'Matron. Please don't let them move me while she still lives because nobody is going to tell me what happens to her and I'd like to be here to say goodbye.'

'You know I can't guarantee that. If Doctor Brightman recommends your transfer then it's out of my hands.'

'Then I might fall over…accidentally!'

Matron looked at her watch. 'Right, time to do things. I didn't hear that.'

However the situation with Babs ended undramatically. For Ruth awoke the next morning to the normal sounds of the hospital wing to see babs' bed was empty. Asking the nurse, an explanation was given. Babs had died during the night and was now in the morgue. The reason the prisoners had not woken was because of the powerful sleeping tablets which they were given each evening.

By this time Ruth no longer needed the wheelchair and that morning she treated Doctor Brightman as if he himself had denied Babs mother's entry to the unit. But her lack of communication suited him as he studied her chart.

'Very good. You've healed well, Ellis. It is time I believe. No more soft option for you. Transfer this afternoon, Matron.'

'Doctor? Is there to be any follow up examinations for her?'

'Oh, I don't think so but we'll monitor the situation. I'll see her in a month.'

Ruth and the nurse caught each other's eye but neither said anything before she moved away and followed the doctor to the next bed.

Ruth was escorted back to B Wing by a young wardress she had not met before and from when she collected her it was obvious to Ruth that she intended to do her job as efficiently and as correctly as possible for she hardly spoke. Ruth had heard about the way new wardresses were supposed to treat prisoners. That is unemotionally and this one was being professional. Although the worst part of being transferred was the chaotic and noisy atmosphere of the Centre. After her name was entered into the book by the Chief Wardress she was taken to the stores where she once again was given the same items she collected previously: clean bedding, a towel, soap, a toothbrush and the other essential items such as a mug, plate and a spoon before being escorted up the iron stairs and along the tiers of the third floor where to her surprise, her old cell awaited her.

'I'm locking you in for now. Tea is in two hours.'

The metal door slammed and that was that. Ruth was able to feel the hot August sun on her face when she placed herself against the bars and she felt numb. As if she was in a place that did not matter. Nothing mattered at all. She felt as if it was all some hideous dream from which she was never going to wake. She was only just able to see the rooftops of the local houses and idly wondered about the families that occupied them and wondered what they were doing and who they were but was unable to imagine how different their lives were compared to hers. Her only option was to make her bed and then to lie on it and cry.

Afternoon tea and recreation happened eventually and during it, Sally tapped on her door.

'Hello, cell mate! Remember me? So, you're back. You've been in the wars?'

'Hello, Sally. Yeah, they've reserved my room.'

'You better now?'

'All better. How's your allotment?'

'The same! They say you had a big operation.'

'Yeah, no more kids for me.'

'What was it? We heard it was cancer.'

'That's right. Lucky to be here. Twice.'

'Someone's looking after you. So now you've got to get into the swing of things here.'

'I suppose so. Next stop, Welfare and Chaplin I suppose.'

'Yeah, you need to start work because you can't sit in here all day long because it will drive you crazy. Do you like plants?'

'They're all right. Why?'

'It's an idea I have. There's four of us girls on the allotment and Mary, she's due to go out in about a month and there might be a vacancy…'

'Are you saying that you could get me a job there?'

'I can't promise anything. A job on the allotment is a privilege position but I could have a word with Old Carpy who could have a word with the Welfare officer. It wouldn't hurt. It's out in the fresh air all day.'

'But it's hard work isn't it? But I'm fresh out of hospital and I'm supposed to take it easy.'

'But it wouldn't be for at least another month so you'd be stronger by then.'

'I like the idea of working outside and with a friend so, sure.'

'Of course if you are chosen, every lag in the place is gonna hate you!'

'Why?'

'Because it's a privilege position. Same as working in the library or in the storeroom. That's a sweet job if you can get it. Most lags who come in here start off by cleaning or working in the kitchen or the laundry or even working the boilers.'

'The boilers?'

'Yeah, well the place has to be heated doesn't it and I'll tell you, you won't wanna mess with those dykes.'

'Oh?'

'Yeah, I seen 'em on their early shift and they're a tough bunch of buggers. No, I reckon you'll probably be put on mopping to start but I'll try and put in a good word.'

'Thanks. Sally? How long did it take you before you settled in?'

'I know why you're asking that question, my old darling. Let me see. About three months but that was me. It might take you longer it might take you quicker. Everybody's different. You're in here for life aren't you? So that's about sixteen years with good behaviour. That's tough but it will go quicker the longer you're in here so they say. After I settled in, the months flew by really. So it's been a year and it's flown by. Only another nine to go.'

'When I was in the prison hospital I met a woman called Babs who had done something similar to what you did. She got six years.'

'Oh yeah?'

'Yes, she died last night from a brain tumour.'

'Lucky her then. Oh, that sounded callous didn't it? I didn't mean that but I suppose I meant that she didn't have to… well you know what I mean.'

'I know what you meant, Sally. Shit! I'm beginning to get the measure of this place.

There was no work for Ruth the next morning when Wardress Brown unlocked her door. After breakfast she was taken once again to the same welfare office as before on the same spacious landing where the governor's office was and she was soon standing in front of Chief Officer Parker. Her office was as cluttered as it was previously.

'You may sit, Ellis. Are you recovered?'

'I am, mam, thank you.'

'So, it was cancer?'

'Yes, mam. Caught in time for which I am grateful.'

'Very good. Well, my word. You have had a great deal to put up with. Now work is the thing I believe and something not too strenuous to begin with so I'm going to place you in the library and that will not involve you in delivering books because as you may have noticed there are no lifts in Holloway and taking the books to the upper parts of the prison entails a great deal of endurance not to say strength.'

'Thank you, mam.'

'I have already received letters from your family for visitations and this will be allowed after another two months. I'm afraid home office rules are sacrosanct for new prisoners. Three months is regulatory to allow prisoners to settle in.'

'Yes, mam.'

'And in time I can facilitate your education with work programs, vocational training and educational opportunities to prepare you for life after release. I have initiated several programs here which may be of interest to you. I hope you will take advantage of them. It will be in your best interests to do so.'

'Thank you, mam. I don't know what I could do but I'm willing to give anything a try.'

'That's the spirit. That's what I like to hear. All right then, Ellis. Good luck and keep out of trouble.'

'Thank you, mam.'

After lunch, Wardress Brown escorted Ruth to the Chaplin's small office which was a small room off the Centre and as with when waiting to see the doctor, she was told to sit on a bench and wait her turn. As usual the Centre was busy with dozens of prisoners mopping, polishing, fetching and carrying, an order of discipline very evident. An equal number of wardresses shouted orders their keys jangling from chains hanging from their waists. Ruth wondered if she would ever become used to it. Then her name was called.

Reverend Woodswalker looked as thin as he did the last time she saw him but this time he smiled and did not hesitate.

'Hello, Ruth. Please sit. May I first say how pleased I am that you survived your ordeal. I trust you are healing well?'

'I am, vicar thank you.'

'Although our last conversation was a short one I have given it a great deal of thought. Do you remember you thought you was not going to survive?'

'I do remember that you said you were going to pray for me.'

'And I did most fervently.'

'Your prayers appear to have been answered.'

'I detect a note of cynicism!'

'I'm sorry vicar. I truly am. The honest truth is that I am confused. At the risk of repeating myself, I thought I was going to hang and then I'm alive then I was told I had cancer and then I'm cured and my head is spinning and spinning and now all I have to look forward to is sixteen years of this hell and the nights are long and lonely and I've been having some very queer dreams. Not exactly horrifying dreams but unusual dreams.'

'Would you care to describe them?'

'Describe them? They take the form of me going on a long journey I think. An endless journey. Yes, a journey without end. Travelling through clouds, through rooms, through fire, through water, along passages, endless journeys until I wake up having gone nowhere. I don't know what it means.'

'How often do you have this dream?'

'Every night. I think I've been having them ever since I had the operation.'

'Have you spoken to anybody about them?'

'What for? It's just a dream. A stupid dream.'

'You are different now to what you were when you were reprieved. Are you aware of this?'

'In what way?'

'There was a particular kind of brashness to your personality when I spoke to you before. You have softened. Do you not recognise that?'

'I don't know. Maybe. Well, maybe having your guts ripped out of you does something for a woman.'

'An operation that saved your life.'

'A life that now seems endless.'

'Ruth? In my seventeen years here I have been witness to a great deal of suffering and much on a scale greater than yours. But in all cases, if I may put it like this, there is one solid antidote and that is, work. Decent hard work will lift your spirits and settle your mind and that is what I advise.'

'It's been mentioned to me by Chief Officer Parker that I will be going to work in the library.'

'Indeed, that is a fine recommendation.'

'Although I'd rather work at the allotment.'

'The allotment?'

Ruth then spoke about Sally's mentioning of working with her and Reverend Woodswalker made a note.

'Very good. I shall look into that. Now, for the present, remember that should you wish to see me at any time then you need only ask for a reception letter at breakfast. I think that's all we need to talk about at the moment.'

'Actually, vicar can I speak about one more thing?'

'Of course. What is that?'

'I know this is nothing to do with me whatsoever but it concerns the body of, Barbara Bulley? The woman I knew as, Babs?'

Chapter 11

Ruth never began her library work for another three months. Instead, supposedly only for a week, she was ordered to spend her working days with a mop and a pail of hot disinfected water along with three other prisoners. On each level there were three wooden toilet doors, and each had a large space between them and the floor, affording no privacy whatsoever. One had a large red cross painted on it, and, drawn by the safety that the sign represented, only certain women used that one. Of course, with foresight, she knew what that X meant.

By October her routine had became so familiar that she no longer had to think about it. Before she was unlocked she had washed her second pair of underclothes, made her bed and washed her face and wore her grey skirt ready for work before most prisoners and only then given an early breakfast. All too quickly afterward, a wardress would assemble her and three others on the ground floor at the Centre where they would be given instructions on where to work that day. When they stopped for lunch they were returned to their cells where they were locked in for an hour and then continued working until afternoon tea and recreation. Then it was another two hours work before, 'Exercise' was shouted.

This was another daily ritual which became ingrained into every prisoner's routine and consisted of walking outside in a well worn circle round and round for an unknown period of time because nobody had the ability to tell for how long. Many prisoners by that time were hungry and although they enjoyed the fresh air, most were keen to return inside for their evening meal but it was a chance to speak to friends and gossip and Ruth often found Sally when she was available and they would chat. When she was not she made other friends.

Hot scolding water would always be available throughout the day and the four women's job was simply to mop the floors, the staircases and the toilets of B Wing. When gathering at the Centre, Ruth had the chance to witness the other groups of cleaners that lived on the other wings and the groups of women there looked as gaunt and as miserable as her group did. Although most women sensibly looked at the ground, for only the foolhardy made direct eye contact with a wardress, Ruth could not but help notice one strikingly, tall woman in C Wing who who did nothing but stare at her which caused her to feel uncomfortable. Almost every time when standing in the Centre, there this woman was, staring directly at her, pretending to polish or clean. But then it was time to begin that days work and she was told to move.

But one day, by chance, Wardress Mary Floyd happened to be issuing the orders for that day and Ruth decided to ask an impertinent question after the wardress had finished and dismissed them.

'Mam? May I have a quick word please?'

Wardress Mary Floyd took a brief look at the Chief Officer who was at her desk supervising. A woman known for her efficiency. She took two steps to one side and lowered her voice, more than aware she could be overheard.

'What is it, Ellis?'

'I'm sorry, mam but that woman? Her over there? Who is she? Every time I'm here in the Centre, all she does is stare at me.'

'Yes, I know who she is. Keep away from her. Now, get on with your work.'

It was an unsatisfactory answer but there was nothing Ruth could do but continue the days work of mopping the landings. However that day was to prove why Ruth spent an extended time on cleaning duties instead of being placed into the library. For after lunch, the four woman continued their duties and Ruth continued working on the ground floor close to the Centre when someone violently pushed her to the ground.

Ruth was a small and slight woman and this level of unexpected violence took her by surprise and more so when she saw it was the tall woman who had done it. Ruth was no stranger to physical violence having taken it on many occasions and she had learned to fight when she had been at school and her first and only instinct was to get to her feet and attack which she did much to her attacker's surprise. But all she managed to do was slap the attacker's face before she was grabbed by two wardresses and pulled away.

An immediate inquiry by Governor, May Doris Charity Taylor was held and while she was sympathetic she made it clear that violence was never acceptable and therefore her punishment was an extended time in cleaning. As Ruth was not there when the other prisoner was sentenced for starting the fight she had no idea what her punishment was but for months afterwards she never saw her at the Centre so she figured she must have been rehoused at probably ether E or F Wing.

Ruth, although an egotist herself, after several months and with that word, penitence still uppermost in her mind and sensibly regarding the position she was in, notwithstanding the huge overall effect that Holloway prison was designed to have on those incarcerated in it, became silently compliant. This was an issue that pleased the Chaplin and the day she arrived for Sunday service because she felt she attended for herself other than it was somewhere else to go, as almost all other prisoners felt, was a fine relief for him and as her cleaning duties ended, he called for her. When she entered his small room, she was offered a chair immediately.

'Your enthusiastic singing did not go unnoticed on Sunday, Ruth. I saw the governor's head turn twice towards you. That's some voice you have.'

'Yes, that's me. A bit of a loudmouth.'

'Yes, that's you. Always putting yourself down.'

'What can I say, vicar.'

'Did you enjoy the service?'

'Yeah, I did. It was nice. Different from the old service that we took back when I was a kid in Wales, but nice. You'll think I'm soft but I found it comforting.'

'I'm not going to rise to that. But I am going to make an observation that I think you are adapting to life here and that is good.'

'That's because I never think about the future. If I do then I'll collapse and die. So I don't. In my low periods I keep reminding myself that I'm here because I did shoot a man dead and I'm here to be punished and that's it.'

'So you are telling me that your day to day existence is one of wickedness?'

'Yes. I am a wicked woman. And I am being punished. There is no other reason for me to be here.'

'But what about the forgiveness that God can offer?'

'Yes, maybe he can but I think I will have to complete my punishment first.'

'I see. So in fact you have placed a timetable on God's forgiveness. Do you think you have the right to do that?'

'You're trying to catch me out, vicar. That won't work. I'm a tough nut to crack and more so because I can't escape. I am in here for the duration and all I have is my penitence, my anger and sometimes, when I can remember to do it, my praying and that's enough for me right now.'

'You remember that woman who attacked you?'

'Of course I do. Who was she? Do you know? Are you allowed to tell me?'

'I cannot tell you her name but I can tell you she was a friend of David Blakely.'

'A *friend*? I've never set eyes on her before. But he had many friends. How did she end up here?'

'I am not in a position to tell you that but it is clear she knew who you were and decided to get a little even.'

'Well, thank you. That clears up the mystery somewhat.'

'I thought it might.'

'I'm sorry, vicar. I know I might seem like a hopeless case to you but I suppose I am.'

'Not at all and in all my years here I have seen women a hundred times more damaged than you, believe me.'

'That's a hard word to hear. *Damaged*. You believe I'm damaged?'

Reverend Woodswalker nodded.

'It's a word deliberately chosen, Ruth and I think it perfectly encapsulates the way a majority of women have been treated and how Holloway becomes their final destination. Because you see, most people think of prison and they think bank robberies and that sort of thing but the truth is, in a woman's prison many women are in here because of problems pertaining to men such as yourself.'

'Such as?'

'Soliciting, abortion and infanticide. Of course yours is on a different scale entirely. But there is also drunkenness, vagrancy and simple immorality. All these I would classify as being done by people whose upbringing has been damaged in some way.'

'My childhood was perfectly normal, vicar.'

'But may I ask you a question then, Ruth?'

'Of course, ask me anything.'

'Why have I not received a single letter from your father asking to visit?'

The Reverend Woodswalker had his answer before Ruth managed to speak as he saw her fingers tighten against each other as her lips compressed and her eyes narrowed.

'You see, you are soon to have your first visitor session from your mother and sister and your father's name is not on that list.'

'What is this, vicar? You want to open up my head and get all the answers? My dad's probably working that's all. He's a busy man.'

'Too busy to visit his daughter who has been repealed from a death sentence?'

'You make it sound bad when it isn't. There's probably a perfectly simple explanation.'

'Yes, Ruth. I think there is an explanation but I have a suspicion it's not all that simple.'

'I have no idea what you mean.'

'I won't press you. It is beyond my purview to do so.'

'What does that mean?'

'It means it is beyond the scope of my influence or concern… Unfortunately. I am not a psychotherapist.'

'Are you saying I need to see a shrink?'

'I believe things have happened to you, Ruth. Awful things and that taken together and that without resolution these events culminated in the events of what happened on the night of the tenth of April.'

'I shot him because…'

'Yes?'

'Because I was pissed off!'

'Of course you were, Ruth. Everybody gets pissed off sometimes. Except we don't go around shooting people. So there must've been something else happening in your head. Can't you see that?'

'I loved him. I still love him. He was my world and I couldn't go on without him.'

Ruth began crying.

'I shouldn't have done it. Why did I do it? Why did I do it? Why did I do it?'

Ruth sobbed silently for several minutes until she wiped her eyes and composed herself.

'Sorry.'

'Ruth? Let's kneel and say the Lord's Prayer together.'

Although Ruth had not uttered the prayer from the Gospel of Matthew since she had been a child, it came easily to her. And the vicar was able to tell that doing that had been the correct thing to do as he had by experience used it before.

'Your visit is at 3:30 tomorrow afternoon.'

'Yes, and I must say I am nervous.'

'And how do you feel about your father not being there?'

'More about my father, vicar? But if you want to know the truth, I'm glad he's not going to be there, *all right*?'

'Then I won't talk about him anymore, *all right*.'

'Thank you.'

'But don't expect such generosity in the future. Yes, you are like a lock, Ruth. A lock with a secret. One day you will be released from this place and I believe the secret of living a long and happy life is to release that secret and it would be beneficial if that secret was told to one other person because that's the way it works. Very intelligent people discovered that a long time ago.'

'I didn't understand much of what you said there but maybe we can talk about it sometime.'

'I'm glad to hear you say that. Now best be off. It'll be exercise shortly.'

At exercise Ruth fell in with a young woman of Indian heritage who had been sentenced to three years for aggravated assault which took the form of hitting her mother in law over the head with a hot frying pan. Laila was a petite woman, easy to talk to unless her family was mentioned and this Ruth learnt early on. Laila was currently eight months into her sentence and therefore had sixteen months to go with good behaviour. Only two things really concerned her. The first was that she was forced to wear the standard prison uniform, the dull grey dress which exposed her legs, and what was going to happen to her upon discharge as her husband's entire family had disowned her.

Brought over from Alappuzha as part of an arranged marriage in 1949 it had now been made clear she was no longer needed or wanted in any circumstances.

'I've just had a mad conversation with the chaplain.'

'Oh? What about?'

'I don't really know. He made me cry though. What's going on with you? Did you get your letter through?'

'He's trying to seek a religious annulment saying we were weren't legally binding.'

'But you went through a perfectly normal marriage didn't you?'

'He's struggling with the shame of having an imprisoned wife. It's all about dishonour and social stigma. His fucking mother! I should've hit her harder!'

'Laila! It's not like you to swear!'

'It's this place, isn't it! You know, even if he gets a civil divorce, in our religious community, he might still be seen as married. That's the worst thing.'

'So, what's going to happen to you? You know, when you get out?'

'I don't know. I can't live here and I don't have the money to go back to India. And if I do go back to India, I can't go back to my family so I might as well kill myself because I'm a wronged woman.'

'Isn't there anybody here that you can talk to? Can't you talk to the chaplain?'

Ruth noticed Laila had tucked something into the sleeve of her prison dress. It wasn't contraband — too small, too worn. Simply a folded square of yellowed paper. They were circling the yard slowly, their boots scuffing on the wet gravel.

'What's that?' Ruth asked, nodding to it.

Laila glanced down. 'Just a picture,' she said, almost shyly. 'Of a God.'

She didn't elaborate, and Ruth didn't push.

After a few steps, Laila added, 'My beloved mother gave it to me when I left Alappuzha. She said I'd need it one day.'

Ruth gave a small, lopsided smile. 'Do you? Need it?'

Laila shrugged. 'I don't know. But I talk to him sometimes. It helps. When they let us sit in silence, I talk to him in my head. Better than talking to myself, anyway.'

Ruth kicked a stone aside. 'As I said, you could ask to see the chaplain. He's always floating about looking for souls to rescue.'

Laila gave her a curious look then spoke softly.

'He's not mine. And I don't need rescuing. Only a bit of remembering. My God doesn't need to speak English.'

Ruth didn't reply. A crow landed on a tree nearby, black against the steel grey sky.

Laila went on, mostly to herself. 'I think Gods understand when you're far from home. Even if you forget the words. But a Chaplin's no good to me. No, I've already asked if he could bring in a Hindu priest for me.'

'You asked the Chaplin that?'

'Yes. And he said he could see what he could do.'

'I hope it works out for you, Laila. What's it like working in stores?'

'Smelly!' she smiled.

Chapter 12

The next morning Ruth awoke with an immediate sense of anticipation and horror because the the last time she saw her mother and sister was twenty-four hours before she was due to be executed and the drama of that day she had never been able to remove from her memory. The memory of her family being dragged away pleading and crying was an event no person should ever have to undergo. Ruth could only have imagined what had happened to them after, and furthermore, the next day and the day after that and the day after that and she continued to feel the shame and pain she had brought upon them.

Her working day was unspectacular and followed its normal routine but she was approached mid afternoon by a wardress and told to follow her. Excited but disappointed because Ruth knew what was happening, but upset for she had no time to prepare her hair or wash her face, she silently followed.

Ruth expected to go to where she had previously spoken to the senior wardress, but knew immediately this was not going to happen. All too quickly she found herself at the Centre where the wardress spoke to the senior wardress on duty and her name was ticked off a list. Then Ruth was escorted past several massive doors, each of which had to be unlocked and locked until they came to a wide room which was divided into compartments. She was shown to one and told to sit at a small, bare wooden table, which, besides the chairs, was the only item of furniture.

Light streamed in through some high windows and while she waited she found herself holding her breath and feeling her fingers trembling. Then another door opened and she stood as she saw her mother and her sister walk towards her in silence and they too were overcome with emotion. All flung their arms around each other and tears sprang forth naturally.

'Sit down. You have thirty minutes. No passing of anything is allowed. If I suspect anything has, I will order a search immediately, and the visitors are to obey those rules.'

The wardress pointed to a cream coloured poster on the wall and for her efforts all she got was a hard look from Muriel.

Comfortably, they sat around the table touching each other's hands.

'My God child, what have they done to you?'

'I know, mum. I can't do anything with my hair. It's not by choice.'

'Are you going back to being natural then?'

'I might have to. In someways I might not have a choice.'

'Forget your locks. How are you coping, sis?'

'Well it's been a couple of months and I'm getting used to the routine. I'm not thinking about the future just taking it day by day. What else can I do? It's so wonderful to see you both. I've thought about nothing else. No André?'

'I know you put him on the list, darling but he's only eleven and we thought he was too young to see his own mother in prison. It's simply too early.'

'I understand. But you'll give my love won't you and you'll tell him that I'm thinking of him all the time?'

'Of course we will, my darling. Have no worries on that. He was so relieved you weren't…you know.'

'And Georgina?'

'She's well, little scamp! What we hear of her anyway.'

'Mum, I can't tell you how sorry I am. I could write a million words and it wouldn't be enough. I'm sorry, I'm sorry, I'm so sorry. I let you all down.'

Bertha looked hard at Muriel, unsure of this new fragment of her daughter's personality. A temperament that was before always so brash and hard and outgoing. She was unable to tell whether she was playing yet another theatrical part or not.

'Ruth, darling? We ought to be upfront and tell you that dad's never gonna visit.'

'That's a relief anyway. I didn't expect he would and I don't want him here. And you know why. I don't want him here, mum and Muriel knows why as well. No, don't look shocked, mum. Being in prison you get to hear a lot of things of what men do and few are acceptable and he's the one who should be in prison. The same as that bastard, Cussen.'

Her mother squeezed her hand tighter.

'Then you are going to do something about that?'

'No I'm not gonna do anything about that despite what happened before my reprieve.'

'But why?'

'Because what would be the point? I can't be put on trial again and although I'd like to see him go to prison for a long time the fact is he may be complicit to an act of murder and he could be executed and I wouldn't put anybody through that.'

'But if he assisted you with the gun he deserves to die.'

'That's not how I see it, mum. You don't know what it's like in here. It gives you time to think and reflect. I'm not the same woman now. I've changed. I've spoken to some decent people and I'm becoming somebody I thought I would never be. It's hard to tell you about it. You look at me and see the old nightclub queen and she's gone. I don't know who I am at the moment but I'm not she. The one that you knew. The old brash, cocaine taking, cocktail drinking, gay, prostitute... yes that's what I was, mother. I was the host of the party. Let's face facts. In here I've learned to be honest and that's what I was. A bloody prostitute.'

'Don't upset her please, mum. Ruth? What do you do with yourself? Do you have a job?'

'Yes, everyone has a job and we get paid a very small amount of cash which we can buy things from a little shop. Things like soap and other things. Very small things that we need. My job at the moment is mopping floors but apparently I'm soon to go into the library which is a better job.'

'And you've recovered from the operation?'

'Yes I had a secondary check about a week ago. I suppose it's difficult to tell because we're not allowed clocks but I'm fine. No trace of cancer.'

'Thank heavens for that.'

'And are you both okay?'

'I'm fine. Mum's not been well, have you mum?'

'It's nothing serious. Just rheumatism. Old age creeping on. I'm fifty-five so it's to be expected.'

'Is André doing well in school?'

'No darling, he's not. He's dealing with the shame of having his mother's face plastered all over the news as a woman almost hung for murder so no he's not doing very well at all if the truth be told.'

'And I'm stuck in here and I can't help.'

'But I'm speaking to his headmaster often, Ruth.'

'Thanks, mum.'

'Ruth, I don't know whether I should tell you this or not but I did see, Cussen.'

'Oh? When was that?'

'I deliberately went to his flat but he wasn't there so I went to your old club and made a fool of myself and shouted at him and then I got asked to leave.'

'Why did you do that, Muriel?'

'Because I was angry. Because I was frustrated. Because it was him that caused you to be in here. Because I know the truth that my sister is rotting away in this place that's why.'

'And nothing will come of anything you do so leave it alone. I know your intentions are coming from your heart but there's nothing you can do, Muriel. I'm in here and you're out there and you have to live your life now and make the best of things. You can't concentrate on me. You have to continue at your job and go out and find a young man and get married and have children and live your life.'

'Darling, I'm thirty-five so who will have me now? And I'm far too old to have children!'

'Mum? Please talk some sense into your daughter.'

'She's strong willed like you. I've lost control over both of you. I lost control a long time ago.'

'Mum? You lost control of me? Well you know when you lost control of me.'

'Can we please not talk about that today, Muriel?'

'Yes, let's not talk about *that*. Let's not talk about the thing that I protected, Ruth from.'

The abrupt drop in silence caused the wardress to turn her head and stare at them.

'Anything wrong here?'

Ruth offered her a weak smile. 'No mam, nothing wrong.'

'Do you have anything to give to the prisoner?'

This hard question by the wardress was abrupt and to the point and it broke the spell. Muriel noticed her mother's expression harden when she heard the officer refer to her daughter as a prisoner.

'What are we allowed to give her?' asked her mother.

'Prisoners are allowed hair grips, curlers and hairnets. And you may send in flowers if you wish. The option to do so will be offered to you when you leave.'

'Are we allowed to send in things because we haven't brought anything today?'

'You may.'

'We'll send in things, Ruth then. We didn't know what to bring.'

'That's all right, mum. It's hardly the sort of thing you would know.'

'How often can we visit?'

'I'm not sure. About every three months perhaps? I'll have to check.'

'So the next time will be after Christmas. What is going to happen in here at Christmas?'

'Your guess is as good as mine. Do they celebrate Christmas in here? I don't know. Mum, as I said I've come to take it all one day at a time. I've made a couple of friends and soon I'm going to be working in the library which is easy work and I think I'm changing into a better person. My old life, the brash kind of gay woman you knew and who stood up in court and said I killed him deliberately, well, she's gone or at least she's disappearing and honestly good riddance.'

'Ruthy? With all my heart as your sister I wish I could take your hand and just lead you out of this place right now and take you home. It's the most dreadful feeling in the world that I'm feeling right now.'

'Well you can't, Muriel. Like me you have to be practical. I'm in here for the next fifteen years. Fifteen long years so that's my life. If I live that long what will I do afterwards? Who knows. I'll be a different woman I know that. What sort of woman I have no idea. I know how old I'll be but I have no idea what sort of world I will step into or what I will do in it. But I know one thing.'

'And what's that, my child?'

'You haven't called me that, mother for a long time.'

'But you are my child. What do you know?'

'I know that by the time those fifteen years have passed I would've paid the penitence of killing David. I would be free by then in my head I mean and I look forward to that. If you like, if I can put it that way, that's what sustains me. Do you understand?'

'Not really, darling. As a family we were never all that religious.'

'I do, Ruth. I think I understand you.'

'Then I'm glad somebody does, Muriel. The chaplain here, he's a nice fella and I think he understands me.'

'So are you going all religious?'

'It's not a question of going religious, mum. It's a question of finding a way through to deal with being here. That's the best way I can think of it or explain it. And if it's through religion then it's through religion.'

'Oh, Ruth!'

'Don't feel sorry for me, mum. I don't feel in the least like that. When I speak to the chaplain it's almost as if I'm speaking to the first decent man I've ever met in my life. Can you imagine that? Here is a man that doesn't want to fuck me or take advantage of me in any other way.'

Bertha looked away too shocked to reply and even Muriel closed her eyes because it was said loud enough that the wardress must have heard.

'I'm sorry, mum but that's the cold hard fact of prison life. Things are very real in prison. You see, we speak the truth without hindrance. It's difficult to hide away in prison. It's only when things are spoken about that things get resolved. This is the sort of thing that I'm learning. It may not be to everybody's liking but that's why they call it therapy here and it's good for the soul.'

'Well, it's certainly not good for the ears. Your father would have a fit to hear you say such a word.'

'I would prefer you to never speak of him, mother and you know why. And so does Muriel.'

Her mother took a deep breath unable to think of what to say next.

'Two minutes left.'

Muriel glanced at her wrist watch. 'Really? Already? Ruth, please write and if there's anything you need that we are allowed to post to you just say and we will do our best okay?'

'Thanks, sis. It's great to have that lifeline at last. A lifeline to the outside world, to family. That will make all the difference to my time here. Any letters will be a godsend. So Mum? I guess I'd better wish you, a Merry Christmas right now and hopefully see you in 1956.'

'Oh darling, what nonsense you speak!'

They stood and hugged and then sobbed until the wardress told them it was time. With almost unbearable reluctance they parted and Ruth watched them disappear through a door once again to leave her alone. She abruptly sat dejected looking at the floor until the wardress returned.

'Up you get, Ellis. That's your first visit isn't it?'

'Yes mam.'

'It will get easier. Come along, they'll be calling exercise shortly.'

Chapter 13

Ruth was entirely wrong about Christmas in Holloway because even the staff made an effort. On Christmas day the food was nicer and in the afternoon on each wing two Christmas films were shown courtesy of the Salvation Army who set up a projector on the ground floor and this event was enjoyed by all prisoners except those in hospital and in solitary.

There were two places of worship in Holloway, for Protestants and Catholics and each were packed each Sunday. Even those who never before attended church went simply as somewhere different to go to break the monotony. Ruth enjoyed sitting next to Sally and together they enjoyed singing the hymns as Sally had a fine voice as well.

It was at Sally's insistence or recommendation that Ruth made a decision that even surprised her. But once she did she felt so much better about herself. It happened in February as they were walking around the exercise yard one windy afternoon when Ruth's hair would not behave itself and she had lost several of her clips. By this time the blonde rinse that she had been allowed back in July in the week before her execution was growing out and was making her look extremely obvious. Even by Holloway standards with women and their tattoos and she admitted it was getting to her.

'Let me do your hair, Ruth.'

'What can you do? I don't have the money to dye it one way or the other.'

'Cut it!'

'What! And look like a bloody dyke!'

'No, you won't. Look, I did hairdressing when I left school. I can make a pretty good fist of it if we can get some scissors.'

'And where are you going to get them?'

'We'll get it done in the salon.'

'Oh, right. Of course. We'll just take a cab over to Knightsbridge shall we? What are you talking about?'

'Didn't you know? Holloway has a salon. It's not much but we use it. Where do you think women get their hair cut?'

'I hadn't thought about it but I suppose you're right. Somebody's in here for years, I suppose, yeah, they need to have a haircut otherwise it would be growing down to their knees wouldn't it? Okay, how do we go about that then?'

'Usual thing. Ask for a reception letter at breakfast. Then tell them you want me to do it.'

'Where is it? This salon?'

'Do you remember coming in and going to reception?'

'Yes.'

'It's just behind there. It's cosy. There's only three chairs but it's nice. A warder will supervisor us of course to make sure we don't stab ourselves to death!'

'How short is short?'

'Your natural colour is growing quickly so you won't look like a boy!'

'I bloody hope not.'

'Not with your figure, darling!'

Therefore by the beginning of March 1956, Ruth finally, and for the first time for as long as she could remember, appeared in public as a brunette, her hair styled in the manner of a pixie cut. It certainly surprised her mother and sister when they visited. And more than that for they noticed a definite change in her personality as well because she was softer and less challenging. After the usual hugs her mother took a step back and glared at her before she sat.

'What have they done to you, my darling?'

'Leave her alone, mum. She looks great. She looks… younger.'

'Thanks, Muriel. How are you both keeping?'

The exchange of information would be the same that would continue for years and would consist of very little else but family and light substantial conversation. As the years progressed her mother due to illness visited less often but Muriel never missed a visit and she always made sure she supplied her sister with everything she needed. It would not be an untruth to say the two sisters became closer than ever during that time when they were physically apart.

The therapy of which she mentioned to her mother and sister was part of a new and grand rehabilitation program she had been allowed to join under the guidance of the Reverend Woodswalker who, with the permission of the governor, May Doris Charity Taylor, brought in a qualified psychologist to run group sessions for those prisoners whom she thought might benefit and Ruth was chosen to attend as one of those. Because the group was intended for recidivists it was felt that they could benefit from the perspective of a long term prisoner and that is why Ruth was chosen.

What, May Doris Charity Taylor did not realise was that that having a famous name attending the psychologist's session did not do her professional work any harm at all at the London School of Economics where she was based.

The psychologist's other five guinea pigs were an eclectic range of prisoners selected from the four wings and it was clear that the single wardress who was there to maintain order did not approve of governor's modern methods of rehabilitation as anybody could tell from her flat expression and the way she crossed her arms after everybody settled.

The psychologist, she introduced herself as, Professor Rushingham, appeared nervous as she shuffled her notes but first gave thanks to the governor for her insight in allowing this new form of interaction/rehabilitation program to begin.

'Anything that gets us out of our cells for an hour, prof is all right by me,' chuckled a heavily tattooed elderly thin woman. This prompted some general sniggering and caused the wardress to speak loudly.

'Be quiet, Gilbert.'

'No, that's all right,' smiled Professor Rushingham. 'I hope in time to foster a safe place where each woman will feel comfortable enough to give rise to their feelings, whatever those feelings may be. This may come as a surprise to you but this is new territory. This is 1956 not 1856 and we are here at the forefront of testing new methods of understanding why women are in prison and more importantly why women keep returning to prison. Now, that is my short introduction over and done with does anybody have any questions?'

'What if I don't want to talk about my feelings?'

Professor Rushingham looked at her list.

'What is your name?'

'Lucy Stone.'

'Ah, here we are. Mrs Stone. You see, the first thing I'm going to offer you is respect because I believe you deserve that. As a woman and as a mother. To me you are not a number, you are a person. And people have feelings and in my long experience it's people's emotions that often get them into trouble. So, may I ask, would that be the case for yourself?'

Ruth saw immediately the woman was placed in the spotlight. A place she did not expect to be and her eyes flashed from one person to another. Ruth had spoken to this woman a little on exercise and although she did not know her story she knew she was in there for a two year sentence.

'It might be. I was brought up not to blab and show my emotions.'

'By your family?'

'That's right.'

'Why was that?'

'I don't know. That's the way it was.'

'And can I ask, why are you here?'

Lucy Stone's head dropped.

'At this point let me inform everybody in this room that whatever is said here is private and may never be revealed to anybody else. I am making myself absolutely clear. Think of this as a courtroom. And this applies to everybody. Please continue if you wish, Mrs Stone.'

'You know why I am here.'

'Yes, and I should imagine many of the women in here know as well but for the purpose of the reason we are here today the words need to be spoken. You will understand this later. So why don't you try?'

'I…I had sexual intercourse with a minor.'

'And how old was he?'

'Fifteen.'

'And how old were you at the time?'

'Twenty-two.'

'And what was your relationship with him?'

'I was his English teacher.'

'You were his English teacher. Thank you, Mrs Stone. And besides being given a three year sentence how else has this changed your life?'

'My husband is divorcing me and my family will have nothing more to do with me.'

'Indeed, it is a tragedy.'

Lucy Stone raised her hands to her eyes and began to silently sob which caused anger in another woman.

'What was the fucking point of dragging all that up? We all know what she's done. It's not as if she's molested a fucking kid. I mean the fucking boy fucking probably enjoyed it. He was fifteen for fuck's sake. And look at her. She's not fucking ugly is she?'

Professor Rushingham lifted her hand to the wardress who had risen from her chair.

'That's fine. Would you like me to tell me your name please?'

'Yeah, Sharon Nicholls, Miss. In here for fifteen months for assaulting my pimp who fucking deserved it.'

'Thank you. So I gather from what you say you are a prostitute?'

'Part time, yeah.'

'And your age?'

'Thirty-one.'

'May I ask, when did you decide to become a prostitute?'

'No one decides to become a prostitute. It just happens, doesn't it.'

'I do apologise, Miss Nichols. So, somebody forced you into it. May I ask who that was? Miss Nichols? Miss Nichols, are you uncomfortable with that question?'

'What do you think?'

I think that is an uncomfortable question for you. Then perhaps I can ask another? How old were you when you first earned money from prostitution?'

'I was sixteen.'

'Quite legal then. Yet there is a note here…'

'I was raped alright? The fucker raped me.'

'And how old was your rapist?'

'You know how fucking old he was so why don't you just tell everybody?'

'I'd like to hear how old he was from your own lips.'

'He was fourteen. Very mature for his age.'

'And was he prosecuted?'

'Was he fuck! His dad was a copper so was he fuck!'

'And his family secretly paid for an abortion according to these notes. That is correct?'

'You've got all the answers haven't you?'

'No, Miss Nichols I do not. I do not know why your family, your mother and father do not visit you. Have not ever visited you on your many occasions that you have been arrested, tried and committed.'

Miss Nichols jerked her head at the wardress. 'Do I have to be here?'

'You put your name down for it, Nichols, as did seventy others. You got the short straw like the other five here.'

'Miss Nichols? Ladies? If I may speak plainly for a moment? Rehabilitation is a term much used of late, but not always understood. It is not a soft alternative to punishment, nor is it a promise. It is, rather, an opportunity, a chance to rebuild, carefully and deliberately, the person one wishes to be. And this is a program of rehabilitation. Let me explain. It does not demand perfection. What it does require is effort. A willingness to reflect, to face truths that may be uncomfortable, and to take personal responsibility for the life that lies ahead. These things cannot be imposed from above. They must come from within.

'In my work, I have seen women leave institutions like this one prepared to live quietly, honestly, and with purpose. I have also seen others return, unchanged and embittered. The difference is seldom in their circumstances. It is nearly always in their resolve. You are not beyond hope. Nor are you invisible to the world. The law may have judged your actions, but it has not fixed your future. Let this time be more than mere waiting. Let it be the beginning of something better. Rehabilitation is not about forgetting the past. It's about finding a new way forward. At its core, rehabilitation means restoring someone, anyone, to a place where they can live safely, responsibly, and with dignity in society. It's a process, not a single event, and it starts with the individual.

'As a concept in criminal justice, rehabilitation recognises that people can change, not through punishment alone, but through education, reflection, support, and the development of better choices. Through this kind of therapy we can explore the reasons behind behaviour, the circumstances that led to it, and the tools needed to avoid repeating it.

'This isn't about being fixed by someone else. It's about learning to take responsibility of your actions, your future, and your role in the world. That might involve building practical skills, addressing addiction, understanding trauma, or simply relearning how to trust yourself.

'This is not achieved overnight, nor by coercion. It is a gradual process, requiring your own willingness to reflect, to learn, and to confront past choices with honesty. Education, discipline, and the cultivation of habits, both of mind and conduct are the pillars upon which this effort rests.

'Society expects not only punishment, but progress. And while the past cannot be undone, the future remains unwritten. Each of you has, within reason, the opportunity to leave this place not as the person who entered, but as someone prepared to contribute in whatever quiet or modest way to the world beyond these walls.

'It is, perhaps, the hardest work of all. But it is work worth doing. The aim isn't perfection. It's progress. If rehabilitation works, the outcome isn't just a release date, it's the capacity to live meaningfully, with purpose and without causing harm. You're not here to be forgotten. You're here, perhaps, to begin again and that is not weakness. That is strength, Miss Nichols.'

The room fell silent and Ruth even noticed the wardress was moved. A young woman sitting next to Ruth, whom she didn't know, began sobbing and the original woman who spoke jeeringly at the professor, Gilbert, an elderly toothless lag and one whose arms were covered with tattoos from her armpits to her nails sank back into her chair. Ruth had heard about this woman. Her nickname was Laggy on account of the decades she had spent in prison and Ruth had been forewarned that given the chance, Laggy would waste a person's time telling tall tales of what prison life was like in the 1930s. She even told people she had been on remand in 1921 in the week when Edith Thomson had been hung and she had a story or two to tell about that day.

Ruth raised her hand.

'Yes? Your name please?'

'Ruth Ellis.'

'Yes, Mrs Ellis? You have something to say?'

'I've come to realise that in the few months I've been here that I have to suffer penitence for what I've done.'

'And what is it that you have done?'

'I killed a man.'

'And how did you do that?'

'I shot him four times.'

'Why?'

'Because I loved him.'

'Did he love you?'

'I don't believe he did. I thought he did but I don't think so. I was mad at the time.'

'That is an interesting word you use. Penitence. Would you care to explain that?'

'It came from another prisoner who I befriended. I won't say her name but she told me her story and it resounded in me and it felt right. It's regret for having done wrong. I admit it and I am paying the price with my freedom.'

'But this is important, Mrs Ellis. How did you feel once you accepted what you did?'

'I am assuming you want honesty? Like shit! Depressed and miserable but truly that passes. Afterwards comes clarity and hope but it takes awhile to get there. But there is the anger and there is a lot of anger.'

'You have been in Holloway how long?'

'I don't even know what month it is.'

'It's March.'

'Then I've been here…eight months but it feels like eight years.'

'Then I would suggest you have a way to go yet, Mrs Ellis and despite your calm demeanour I would like to see you in our next weekly session. Now, who else would like to speak? We have forty-five minutes left.'

Her eyes turned to the sobbing woman who looked up and wiped her face with her sleeve. She was young and frightened and because they were in a circle, her neighbour, Ruth, placed a comforting hand on her shoulder. Professor Rushingham waited.

'I'm Dorothy Davies.'

'How old are you, Dorothy?'

'Eighteen.'

'And what brings you to be here?'

'I killed my father.'

'And what did your father do?'

'Do?'

'What was his profession?'

'He installed telephones.'

'And how did you kill him, Dorothy?'

'With a knife. I loved my daddy!'

'Why did you kill him, Dorothy?'

'You know why. Everybody knows why.'

'But I want you to tell me. It's important for you to tell me.'

'Because I couldn't bear to think of him being hung.'

'How did you kill him, Dorothy?'

'I slit his throat in the garden, it was quick.'

'And therefore deprived his victims families justice.'

'I couldn't think of them.'

'What was your sentence?'

'Five years.'

'I see your mother is serving ten years for conspiracy.'

'Yes.'

Professor Rushingham looked at the wardress. 'Do you know in what wing she is being held, officer?'

'No, mam, I'm sorry.'

'No matter. This is a place to be truthful, Dorothy. The bodies of nine women were found in your father's garden. Did you have any inkling at all of his murderous activities?'

'No, as I told the police, I found that necklace and I put two and two together with that description in the newspaper. And then when I found that set of teeth in his shed and found that bone under that hydrangea I got really suspicious. And then when I read his diaries and all the dates matched up with when the women disappeared what else could I do? I loved him. I couldn't see him hang like a pig. I only wish he knew why I did it.'

'Many people would have wished to have known why he raped, tortured and killed so many women. He was an evil man and you helped him evade justice.'

All Dorothy did was lower her head and wring her hands.

Although Ruth had made a verbal promise not to speak about what was said in that room she broke it when she was visited by Muriel a month later who came by herself. Ruth showed surprise as she had signed for two tickets.

'Is mum alright?'

'No, she's under the weather today. She wanted to come but her belly is giving her some jip. She sends her love. I say! I love the hair do! It's growing out nicely. I haven't seen you looking that natural since we were kids. So, how are you getting on?'

'So, so. At last my job's been sorted out. First I was mopping for ages and ages when I was supposed to be in the library and then I was in the library but then they put me in the garden but then they took me out of the garden and now I'm back in the library. Honestly, one hand doesn't know what the other hand's doing in this place.'

'So what do you do in the library?'

'Nothing much, just sorting books as they come in and out. Because of my operation, there is no heavy lifting so I don't deliver books to the cells, I just sort them in and out. But listen, I have to tell you about this therapy gig that I've been allowed to be on and I tell you some of the things that I'm hearing would blow your mind let me tell you. And then you can tell me what's going on in the real world.'

They were allowed to chat for the regulation thirty minutes and before Muriel left she handed one of the wardresses a bag containing the things Ruth had asked for along with letters from her mother and André. It was one of hundreds of visits that her sister made over her time in Holloway and Ruth was forever grateful to her.

Chapter 14

In the quiet counting of 3,497 nights, a life was remade.
9 November 1965

Ruth opened her eyes and heard the clanking of the hot water pipe. The noise immediately reminded her of the boiler house and the loud and constantly swearing girls that attended the boilers. When working they seemed to live in a world of their own, almost completely separate from the prison.

Without moving Ruth looked around her cell, at the few pictures on her wall, the calendar with its days crossed off, her books, her writing pad and her little blue clock and felt….nothing.

Which concerned her because she knew that soon her door would be unlocked for the last time. Her eyes now became frozen on the door, her hearing acute as she remembered the events of two days previously when she had been told to attend the governor's office mid afternoon.

As usual, Joanna Kelley's modest but tidy office was spare but orderly. Files were stacked neatly on her desk. A clock ticked quietly and sunshine filtered through the barred window. The governor, in uniform, compassionate but dignified, stood by the desk holding a letter. Ruth, now forty, was escorted in. She was composed, her posture dignified, her expression unreadable. She nodded politely as she entered, her face was calm, but her eyes carried decades. The governor gestured to the chair opposite.

'Come in, Ruth. Sit down, please.'

'Thank you, Governor.'

They sat and there was a moment of silence. Joanna Kelley regarded her gently as she opened a folder and referred briefly to a document before fully meeting Ruth's eyes and after clearing her throat spoke gently.

'I have called you here today to inform you of a significant development in your case. As you may be aware, the Abolition of Death Penalty Act received Royal Assent on the eighth of November, this year. The Act formally abolishes capital punishment for murder in England, Wales, and Scotland. As a result of this legislation, and given that your sentence of death was previously commuted and held in abeyance, it has now been reviewed. I have been instructed to inform you that you are to be released from Her Majesty's Prison Holloway. The formal arrangements for your discharge will commence immediately.'

A long pause. Ruth blinked once, twice. She didn't react with joy — just an audible exhale, as if something impossibly heavy is finally lifting.

'I never thought I'd hear those words. Not really.'

'I know. And I'm sorry it's taken so long.'

Ruth took this in with a slow and steady breath.

'May I ask when this is to take place?'

'The process will begin today. There's paperwork, naturally. Provided all administrative processes proceed without delay, you will be released within forty-eight hours. There are people who can help you with housing, work... whatever you choose. You won't be alone, Ruth.'

'No, just a woman stepping into a world that's forgot her.'

'The world's changed, yes. But you haven't been forgotten. And you're not the same woman who walked in here ten years ago. You've survived. That counts for something. Your conduct during your time here has been noted with consistency and restraint, Ruth. I trust that will serve you well in your return to the community. There are arrangements that can be made—accommodation, supervision, employment and guidance. You will not be left without support.'

A silence settled between them. Not uncomfortable, but full of the weight of time.

'Thank you, Governor. That is appreciated. For not treating me like a ghost.'

'You've always been very much alive, Ruth. It's time the world remembered that it may take some time to adjust, Ruth. But I hope you will find peace beyond these walls. You have borne the weight of many years with dignity.'

'Your kindness is not forgotten, Governor. I thank you, and your predecessor...for your fairness.'

'Then I shall simply wish you well. And a quieter chapter ahead. However there is one more thing that must be discussed if you will now follow the warder.'

Ruth stood and soon she found herself in another office where she was received by a tall woman. She was in her mid forties, clipped and precise. A file was open before her. The atmosphere was quieter and more procedural. Ruth was invited to sit.

'Mrs Ellis? I'm, Miss Hazel Ford and I'm your probation officer. Now that your release has been approved, there are formalities we must observe. I am here to explain the terms under which you will be released. Which are, you are being released from custody under what is known as a life licence. This means that although you will no longer be confined within these walls, you remain, in the eyes of the law, under sentence.'

'So I'm not… free?'

'You are at liberty, yes — but not beyond the reach of the Crown. The licence conditions are not intended to restrict your life unduly, but you are expected to abide by them fully.'

She took out a typed document and slide it toward Ruth.

'You must report to a designated probation officer — initially once a week. You are to reside at the address provided, and any change in your circumstances must be reported immediately. You may not leave the country without written permission. Employment is encouraged but must be approved in advance. And, of course, any further criminal offence could result in your recall to prison.'

'And how long will I be on this licence?'

'Indefinitely. The licence remains in force for the rest of your life. Only the Home Secretary may revoke it.'

There occurred a silence. Ruth looked at the paper, her fingers lightly touching its edge.

'It's strange… They said I'm not to be hanged, and now they say I'm not to be entirely free. It's as though I've stepped from one prison into another.'

'A different kind of prison, perhaps. But you'll find, Mrs Ellis, that the world outside has a different rhythm. And people do forget…eventually. If you comply with the terms, we will do all we can to support your reintegration. There are charities and services that assist women in your position. You will not be without guidance.'

Ruth gave a faint nod. She picked up the pen and signed the licence.

'Very well. If this is the price of the years I have left, I shall pay it.'

The dreaded sound of the key in the door dragged her away from her comfortable memory and the familiar smiling face of Warder Hopkins peered at her.

'Come on, slow coach! Up and atom! Anybody would think you lived here!'

Half heartedly Ruth pulled herself from her bed and then spent the next ten minutes attending to her toilet taking as many congratulations as she could from other prisoners on the landing who knew exactly what was going to happen to her that day. Then it was breakfast which she took with her friend, Chinmayi Sharma, an Indian woman who lived in the cell once occupied by Sally.

'Her problem is she's too bloody happy! She would not have lasted five minutes years ago. The old lags would have eaten her for breakfast.'

'I think, Hopkins is a nice woman.'

'Yes, you're right and that's the problem.'

'You are unhappy. Why is that, Ruth? You're getting out today!'

'I'm getting out to what? The truth is I'm frightened. The truth is I like it here.'

'But everything is arranged for you. You're starting a new life with Sally. You have a business. You have this wonderful new skill, making things.'

'And I have this cloud of my past hanging over my head. Maybe a cloud that people will not let me forget what I did.'

'Ruth? You don't look anything like you did ten years ago. People will not recognise you and you can always change your name if you want to.'

'I'm not too sure about that. This licence conditions I'm on it's fairly strict but we'll see.'

'I'm going to really miss you, Ruth. I've got a whole year to go yet and I don't know how I'm going to manage without you.'

'You'll manage in the same way I managed without Sally when she left.'

'You two are going to have such a lot of fun working together.'

'It's a dream come true I admit. Who would have thought this of me? Selling silly pots for a living!'

'But they're not only pots are they? They're works of art.'

'So they keep telling me! I'm going to miss you too, Chinmayi. You have to come down and stay. You know he won't take you back, don't you.'

'He might.'

'But you stabbed him!'

'Only a little bit!'

'He lost his kidney!'

Chinmayi sighed deeply. 'He might forgive me.'

'He's a lost cause, darling. Let him go.'

Warder Hopkins reappeared on the landing encouraging everybody to finish their breakfast and prepare for work. Chinmayi looked sadly at Ruth before they hugged.

'Please write to me.'

'I will, don't worry.'

'Say hello to the outside world for me.'

Ruth nodded and Chinmayi stepped away. After gathering a few things she waited to be escorted to the storeroom and afterwards to reception where she was glad she had taken the advice of the Principal Officer years before and put by a small amount of money from her earnings in order to purchase a relatively modern suit, blouse and shoes because as it was explained to her at the time she couldn't possibly wear the same outfit she was wearing when she entered Holloway.

After changing and collecting what cash she had earned which amounted to £40 and saying goodbye and shaking the hands of many people, the Chief Officer escorted her to the main gate where she shook her hand and offered her her own advice.

'Keep out of trouble, Mrs Ellis. I don't want to see you in here again!'

The small Holloway prison gate opened with a heavy mechanical clunk. Its sound was absorbed by a damp fog. Ruth, in a simple grey coat provided by the prison charity, stepped out. Her hair was tidily set. She carried a cardboard suitcase, scuffed but serviceable. An unfamiliar world awaited her.

Parkhurst Road was quieter than she expected as she walked towards it. A dog barked, an unusual sound. A car hissed past. A young man watched her from across the road as he waited for a bus. Ruth stood still, beyond the threshold, her breath visible in the November air.

'It doesn't smell like I remember. It smells newer. Louder. Faster. But people still walk the same way. Hands in pockets. Late for something.'

A woman in a smart coat and a kindly manner, approached her with a gloved hand extended.

Mrs Ellis? I'm Mrs King, from the Aftercare Society. I'll take you to the house. You must be freezing!'

'Hello. No colder than I was yesterday.'

After shaking hands they began to walk away. Ruth glanced back at Holloway saying nothing. The policeman on guard looked at her but then looked away.

That first night Ruth found herself in a halfway house and she had a bedroom to herself. It was a modest upstairs room in a Victorian terrace run by a pleasant but taciturn woman who introduced herself as Mrs Green. She was immediately taken to her room where she noticed the wallpaper was curling at the edges. She had a kettle, a single chair and a lamp. It was clean but impersonal. Ruth sat on the edge of the bed and folded her hands, her suitcase remained unopened. A clock ticked. From outside she heard faint laughter and a car horn. Eventually she took off her shoes, reverently, as though unsure if she is allowed. Then she laid back, fully clothed, and stared at the ceiling.

'The bed is too soft. I didn't expect that. I thought it might be the softness that broke me. But it's the silence. It's too large.' She turned on her side, eyes open.

Next to her, a laminated welcome note rested on the side table. It read: "You are safe. You are free. You are not alone."

Ruth read it once, then turned the card face down.

'I am free, they say. But free to be what? Not Ruth Ellis. Not the woman who stood in court. Not the girl in the club. So who am I?'

A tear slipped down the side of her nose, unnoticed. She blinked slowly. The clock ticked on. Outside, London breathed. A train clattered in the distance. Ruth closed her eyes, but only halfway. Today was going to be an important day in more ways than one.

She thinks she has an awful dream during the night but by the morning she has forgotten it but whatever it was it terrified her. As she had forgotten to pull the curtains the sun woke her up by shining full on her face, something she had not experienced for ten years and she did not know what was happening.

It was then she felt foolish being scared of the sun. Dressing in the same clothes she made her way down to the communal dining room where muted sunlight filtered through net curtains illuminating plain tables and mismatched chairs. Ruth heard the clink of crockery. A radio murmurs in the background: the weather forecast, then the Beatles faintly singing, "In My Life."

Ruth, freshly washed, entered leaning heavily on her cane. She carried herself with composure, but there's hesitance in her eyes—like someone trying to learn another language. Three other women, also ex offenders, are already seated. They look up briefly, then return to their toast and eggs.

A woman, Evelyn, a grey hair lady in her early fifties, nods politely. She's been here a while and has the air of a settled inmate turned guide.

'Tea's hot. Milk's on the side. We eat 'til eight. After that it's your business.'

'Thank you.'

Ruth poured herself a cup. She doesn't sit right away. She looks at the chair as if it might be the wrong one. Then she slowly lowers herself, folding her hands before her plate. She lifts a piece of toast. It crunches loudly in the quiet room. She chews carefully, eyes lowered. Evelyn watches her , then softens.

'They let you out late, didn't they?'

'Ten years.'

Evelyn blinked several times. 'Christ! I did five and thought the world had started speaking in tongues. You must feel like you've landed on the moon.'

'No one tells you how loud the silence is when it isn't locked in with you.'

Evelyn considered that, then gave her a half smile and pushed the jam across the table.

'Here. Helps with the taste of the bread. Everything here tastes like cardboard until about week three.'

Ruth accepts it. For the first time, her lips twitched in the direction of a smile.

'That's something to look forward to, then. But I won't be staying. I'm only here until after I speak to the probation officer which I'm hoping will be tomorrow morning.'

'Oh, you've got a job lined up already?'

'Yes I hope so.'

'Then good for you. Honestly there's a lot of rigmarole to be honest so if you can sort yourself out you'd be better off.'

A silence. The women eat. Not exactly friends — but not strangers anymore, either.

The probation office was a plain municipal building in Islington and with the help of the landlady she was able to find it easily. By ten o'clock she found herself in a small sparse interviewing room consisting of two chairs one desk and a window which overlooked nothing in particular. Ruth faced Mr Riley, a short man who wore only a shirt and waistcoat with no tie. He acted professionally, but not unkindly. He was a man who kept his emotions behind his paperwork.

'Mrs Ellis. Thank you for arriving promptly. My name is, Mr Riley.'

Ruth offered him a faint smile that didn't reach her eyes.

'I've reviewed your file. You've been assigned to me for the duration of your licence period. We'll be meeting weekly, at least to begin with.'

He pauses, studying her. 'I understand you've been provided accommodation through the Aftercare Society?'

'Yes. Just up the road. It's…clean.'

'Good. That's a start. Employment—we'll need to look at that. Given your circumstances, it may be a gradual process. We'll start by exploring voluntary work. Some women find the Red Cross or hospital kitchens a useful stepping stone.'

'Excuse me, Mr Riley may I interrupt you for a second?'

'Er, if you must. What is it?'

'If you look at the back section of my file you will find a letter from the superintendent of Holloway addressed to the probation office stating that I already have a place to live and an occupation and both are to start on the 12th of November. That is tomorrow.'

'I see. One moment… Ah…yes… Well, congratulations, Mrs Ellis. In which case our interview is at an end. However, I shall write to you at this address and foreword you the address of the nearest police station where you will report to them for the time being on a weekly basis. I hope that is understood.'

'It is.'

'Now, Mrs Ellis, a word of advice. I won't pretend this will be simple. There are people who will remember your name. Some will remember your photograph. You may encounter curiosity or hostility. Even misguided sympathy. You're not obliged to answer to any of it—but I advise caution.'

'It's nothing I didn't face on the front page.'

'Yes. But the difference is: now you have to live with it, not simply endure it.'

She meets his eyes for the first time—level and unreadable.

'Mr Riley, I've lived through worse than gossip.'

'I don't doubt it.'

He closed the file gently.

'The probation office is not here to judge you, Mrs Ellis. It's here to keep you out of prison. That means structure, consistency, and a willingness to engage. If you find yourself struggling—financially, emotionally—speak to us. Don't drift. Drifting is how people end up back inside.'

'I understand.'

'You've done a long time. You now have some say in what the next chapter looks like.'

Ruth nodded and he stood. The meeting was formally over.

'Thank you, Mr Riley.'

As she left the room leaning heavily on her stick, Mr Riley watched her leave, his expression was unreadable.

Ruth left the probation office with a slight headache forming behind her eyes. The interview had been polite enough—a checklist of questions and some scribbled notes from the officer with no tie. But her temples throbbed and her thoughts were elsewhere.

Outside, the afternoon was flat and grey, the kind of London sky that could never make up its mind between dull and sunshine. She turned up the collar of her coat and stepped into the murmur of Highbury Corner. The florist's stall by the station was still open. She bought daffodils—a small, sun coloured bundle wrapped in damp newspaper. Barbara had once said they were her favourite, so many years ago now back in the hospital ward. Now was the time to pay her respects for she had the information. She had waited ten years...

She boarded the Number 30 bus to King's Cross, then caught the tube to Cannon Street. The train to Eltham was nearly empty—an old Southern Region service, its seats worn smooth, windows etched with condensation. She sat alone, the flowers on her lap. The rhythm of the train blurred her thoughts as the soot blackened terraces of southeast London flicked past.

She arrived at Eltham Well Hall Station as the clock read four o'clock. The wind had picked up and carried with it the sharp smell of wet leaves and cold earth. She walked briskly along Westmount Road, the daffodils pressed against her chest. The cemetery came into view behind wrought iron gates—quiet, green, and oddly familiar, as though she'd visited it before in a dream.

She found the grave with surprising ease and the headstone was modest:

Barbara Ellen Bulley
1930 – 1955
Kindness is never wasted

Ruth knelt. Her knees sank into the damp grass. She didn't cry, not exactly, but her throat tightened in that helpless way throats sometimes do. She placed the daffodils neatly against the base of the stone, brushed away a few windblown leaves, and rested her hand briefly on the cold marble.

Ten years. And yet it hadn't faded. That short time in the prison hospital together — the word tumour said so matter of factly to be fully believed, the quiet confidences, Barbara reading aloud from a magazine while Ruth dozed, the extraordinary meaning of the word penitence which changed Ruth's life around so much. Then the sudden silence when she'd been taken away overnight. The nurse's face, not meeting her eyes.

'Goodbye, my darling. Rest in peace. And thank you for being there when I needed you.'

After a while Ruth stood. The wind had picked up. She pulled her coat tight and walked back the way she came, her hands empty now, but her steps a little steadier.

She retraced her steps slowly, letting her boots find their rhythm along the cracked pavement of Westmount Road. A passing car stirred the daffodil scent still lingering faintly on her hands. Behind her, the cemetery gate creaked shut.

The walk back to Eltham Well Hall Station was only fifteen minutes, but Ruth's mind was already loosening its grip on the present.

The corridor of the prison hospital came flooding back — sterile and humming with distant clatter, but softened in her memory. Barbara had arrived on a gurney back from getting an X-ray and within days had somehow won over the entire ward. She was all quick smiles, pale shoulders, and a voice like warm tea.

And then — as quickly as she had arrived — she'd gone with the whisper of a tumour. Then nothing. Simply silence and the dim echo of her voice.

A gust of wind tugged Ruth gently back into the present. She glanced up — the station was ahead, squat and grey under a sky the colour of steel wool. A train was due in five minutes. She stepped inside, her chest hollow and oddly light, like a memory had been left behind on that grave — not the flowers, but the ache.

Chapter 15

Mrs Green, the landlady attempted to be friendly at breakfast but the truth was, Ruth wanted to be left on her own. She was used to being on her own. When she worked in the library she was on her own and the only time she talked to people was on recreation and that's how it had been for years. Even in classes she had done her best to keep herself to herself and the classes had been good for her for that is where her talent for creating art had come forth…in silence.

But ten years was a long time and as Holloway consisted of so many diverse women, eventually Ruth found a few that did resonate with her and one of those was Sally. Although she had been given a ten year sentence for killing her children she and Ruth enjoyed a friendship until 1960 when Sally was unexpectedly released under extraordinary circumstances after only serving six years. The case was shocking enough to reach the national newspapers.

For although her ex husband Benedict had divorced her, he had in the interim, continued to investigate what had happened that awful day and through a great amount of effort and money, eventually caught and successfully prosecuted a man who had spiked his former wife with cocaine. A man who had attended school with Sally and had been enamoured with her for a long time. He now was serving a fourteen year sentence and the High court judge had issued Sally with a pardon.

However, Sally's immediately and sudden release was both a blessing and a curse for their friendship. A blessing for obvious reasons but a curse for the same and Ruth easily remembers the conversation they had while walking during exercise.

'I know I'm pleased for you, Sally but what are you going to do?'

'Well, that's the other thing. Benedict, bless him, he feels as guilty as sin. I didn't see him at the interview but his solicitor has told me that he's set aside a place for me to live.'

'He's done *what*?

'It's true. He's given me some sort of small holding I think he called it. A place where I can live. Part of his family's. Not short of a bob or two are they, his side of the family. He must be feeling very guilty.'

'He doesn't want you back?'

'No, he's already married some other bird so I think this is his way of doing the best he can to erase his guilt if that makes any sense.'

'I am going to miss you so much.'

'But Ruth, I want to say, when you get out, please come and visit me and come and live there with me. Will you do that? You can sell all your work, your lovely pots. You can make a new start there. We could even set up a business.'

'Sally? I won't be let out until about 1970 and who knows what's gonna happen? We might all be destroyed by nuclear war by then! It's a lovely thought but you will have probably remarried and will have kids and you certainly won't want an old woman hanging around. Of course I'd love to visit but as I say, I'll be some old bag and you won't want me hanging around.'

'Just come and visit anyway, please say yes.'

'Yes, I'll come and visit.'

Evelyn arrived and this time after pleasantries had been exchanged, Ruth had a chance to observe her as she began to chat. At first glance she looked like a perfectly ordinary woman born sometime in the 1920s. Thin, upright, honest, straight talking, clear voice, chisel features, blue eyes. Yet it didn't take long to recognise the multiple tattoos on her hands, her false teeth, her obvious wig, and her distressed clothes. She gave the impression of an upright honest woman who had fallen on hard times and moreover one who was afraid of the world.

'Miss Evelyn? Are you familiar with this house?'

'You mean am I a recidivist, dear?'

'I suppose so. I don't like that word.'

'Yes, I'm one of those. Of course I know who you are. I remember who you were. The one who almost got her neck stretched.'

'Yeah, that was me.'

'That was big news.'

'At the time I suppose. But the world moves on, I hope.'

'So what you gonna do now?'

'I'm gonna stay with a friend… in Scotland.'

'Far away from it all eh? Good for you.'

'What are you going to do, Miss Evelyn?'

'I have a little hole in the wall in Greek Street and that's where I'm going for the time being. I'll see my ex husband and we'll see what happens.'

'What did you do there?'

Miss Evelyn smiled as she poured tea. 'Same as you did, ducks, but for a lot less dough.'

Ruth stopped smiling. 'You're right about this bread! It's terrible!'

The next morning, bright and early, Ruth stood on platform fourteen in Victoria station close to steam which curled along the platform. The station was a cacophony of sound. Porters calling, whistles blowing, suitcases thudding against tiles. Ruth stood near the edge of the platform, clutching her small leather handbag. Her coat was smart, if dated and she felt out of place, like a black and white photograph dropped into a colour film. She felt as if hundreds of eyes were on her, judging her. Yes, we know who you are. You are that woman, the murderer.

The train idled. It hummed like a metal creature about to wake. An overhead announcement garbled its way through the tannoy: 'The train now standing at Platform fourteen is the ten twenty-seven service to Bognor Regis…'

Ruth mumbled to herself. 'Victoria Station. I stood here once with Desmond. I remember… I bought a sandwich in a brown paper triangle. I thought it was a marvel. That was…before. Before it all became a blur of courtroom steps and iron doors.'

She boarded the train and chose a window seat. The interior smelt faintly of coal dust, soot, leather and upholstery cleaner. An older couple entered the carriage and nodded politely. Ruth gave a tight smile to them and turned to the window.

To the accompaniment of a whistle the train jolted forward and all London began to slip away, chimneys, rooftops and people not noticing her at all.

'So many faces, all rushing toward something. Or away from it. I'm not sure which I am.'

For a while because it seemed so dream like that she should be travelling so fast, Ruth stared at the passing scenery feeling the occasional lurch as the train gathered speed. Because her life had consisted of a small brick room and a hard iron door, now to be able to see the far horizon and to see the changing clouds and overall scenery did seem dream like and unreal. It was beautiful, mesmerising and emotional and the experience lasted for the entire journey.

At midday the train pulled into Bognor Regis station with a screech and a sigh. Ruth stepped onto the platform, blinking into the unexpected light. The air was softer here, tinged with salt and gulls cried constantly overhead. The station was smaller, quieter, almost sleepy and for a few moments she stood still taking it in. But then she walked through the ticket hall and into the open where the first thing she saw was a palm tree swaying uncertainly in the breeze and somewhere nearby, a carousel tune drifted faintly on the wind.

'It smells of the sea. Even through the fumes and the steam…there it is. Salt and sand and…oranges? No, fish and vinegar. That's it.'

For a moment she became aware that in London there was this place called Holloway, a cold and hard grey place where hundreds of women were suffering and she was not able to understand how two such places were able to exist in the same world. But then she forced herself to throw off that memory.

Ruth began to walk slowly down the main street, her shoes clicking on the pavement. People passed her—late holidaymakers, locals in cardigans—even a group of schoolboys in short trousers, jostling past holding writing pads. Nobody noticed her.

A sudden gust of wind lifted her hair. She stopped and faced the seafront. The sea stretched out before her, vast and glimmering and she caught her breath.

'I thought it would be louder. But it just… rolls. As if it's always been here, waiting. As if it knew I was coming.'

As there a was a bench close by overlooking the water, she sat, hands in her lap, staring at the gentle waves as the sun played on her face. A small smile flickered at the corner of her mouth, fragile but real. For a moment, she simply sat. Alive. Outside. Unnoticed.

After having lunch in a little cafe called, Hunger Cure, Ruth approached a taxi rank where a line of black cabs stood. She approached the front one where a driver in his sixties stood next to his car, smoking.

'Excuse me. Could you take me to, Haven Farm? It's… north west of here?'

'Haven? Aye, I know it. Bit of a winding run. You alright with bumpy roads and the odd sheep?'

Ruth smiled. 'I've had worse.'

The cab smelt faintly of tobacco and lavender air freshener. She sat in the back, watching the streets melt into fields. The car passed shops, pubs, hedgerows, old stone cottages and a wooden sign for, pick your own apples before she saw sheep begin to dot the landscape.

Again Ruth mumbled to herself. 'Every mile feels as if it's being given back to me. Inch by inch. A country road instead of a corridor. A gate instead of a door that locks.'

As the cab rounded a corner, a hand written sign came into view: HAVEN FARM.

Pulling into it, a short gravel drive lead to a cluster of converted outbuildings and a whitewashed farmhouse where chickens strutted about freely. To one side a collie lay half asleep by a fence unconcerned the place had visitors.

After the cab stopped, at the same time Ruth stepped out helped by her stick, the farmhouse door opened and out walked Sally, sun reddened, hair in a bandana, hands on her hips. She wore boots and an old jumper. She broke into a wide grin the moment she saw Ruth and she rushed into her arms.

'Bloody hell! You really came.'

Ruth stared at her, then let out a short breath that sounded like a laugh. Or like a relief.

'You said the kettle would be on.'

'It's never off. Come on then. You've come at a great time. It's such a warm autumn we're having. Let's see if you remember how to shell peas!'

After Ruth paid the taxi and took her bags, she followed Sally up the path. As they walked, the collie, now awake, trotted alongside them, tail wagging.

'This is Benny, ie: potato head! And he's as daft as a brush and he's lovely.'

'You look so different.'

'Sunlight'll do that. And not being shouted at every five minutes. Suits me, I think.'

They reached the main door and Sally held it open. Ruth hesitated for half a breath, then stepped inside.

'Maybe freedom isn't all fireworks and parades. Maybe it's tea and mud and someone waiting at the gate.'

'Come in, darling. Of course I got your letter and I knew you would be arriving sometime but look at you! When did you get out?'

'The day before yesterday. I spent two nights in a hostel dealing with stuff.'

'But you found me okay?'

'Yes the taxi man knew of your place. So this is what your ex gave you?'

'He did, yes lock stock and barrel. All in my name forever and ever. I've never seen Benedict so guilty as when he signed it over to me.'

'Well, you spent six years in jail for nothing so you deserve this. Not to mention you lost your three beautiful children.'

'And he knows that but let's get that tea and I've got buns! And then I want to know why you're walking with a bloody stick! You've never mentioned that in your letters!'

'Okay yes, there's a story which I will tell you as I drink my tea.'

After admiring the 19th century kitchen stove from which the buns were retrieved they buttered them, poured the tea and ate them in the cosy low ceilinged living room.

'Do you live here on your own, Sally?'

'Not now you're here.'

'Is that offer still open? Truly?'

'I meant every word. We get on well don't we? Come and live here. You can continue your work and if you like you can help me with mine, which is basically chickens.'

'Chickens? I saw a few outside. How many have you got?'

'I've got about a thousand.'

'A *thousand*!'

'Well, about two hundred came with the farm but I think I've done rather well!'

'You manage all those by yourself?'

'Oh God no! I'm an employer! I got three girls and one fella that come in every day and without them the place would go to hell! There's feeding, egg collection, cleaning, and in general looking after the little bitches! And that goes on multiple times a day to prevent breakage and ensure freshness. Every egg has to be cleaned, graded by size and packed. We need to look out for broody hens and predators as well. There's a lot to do.'

How many eggs do you get?'

'What, a day? Off the top of my head that's difficult but I can say that one laying hen produces an average of…250 to 280 eggs every year. Now I got about a thousand hens so that's roughly… 250,000 to 280,000 eggs annually.'

'Christ! that's a lot of eggs!'

'Sure is. It's a busy business!'

'I can't see it, Sally. As much as I think I'd like to live here, I can't see what use I'm gonna be to you.'

'But didn't we talk about this? We are friends. We are jailbirds! This is a place where we can well, this is the opposite of Holloway. This is our freedom. Nobody to shout at us. Nobody slams doors. Here is a place where we can walk about in freedom, eat good food and do whatever we like. It's comfortable and you can stay as long as you like and when you think you need to move on, you can. It's what we talked about, Ruth. You have no need to work here but there is a little place out the back where you can continue your work with pottery and I know there is a place where you can actually sell them in St Jude, the village. I mean they were a success in Holloway weren't they? People love them. Your designs I mean so you should carry them on here.'

'That whole pottery thing was a bit of a fluke. Whoever thought I could design pottery and ceramics must've been a bit potty themselves!'

'But it worked out didn't it? You're a potter and a bloody good one.'

'Yes okay, I'm a potter. Alright, I'll stay, thank you.'

'So come on, at last what the hell are you doing walking with a stick? You're drinking my tea, you're eating my buns, now give me the story.'

'This is a lovely little sitting room it's really cosy and nice.'

'Forget the bloody sitting room. Get on with the story!'

'Alright then, now it was March I think and I had been in there for about seven years and I was helping out mopping the floors, the staircases and the toilets of B wing because of an outbreak of something of other. You know, all hands to the pump in a crises. So I just happen to catch the eye of this tall woman who was standing in C wing and all she did was stare at me. It was in the Centre and I remembered her from years ago when I first arrived. I thought she'd been sent away to another prison but it looked as if she was back. She made me feel really uncomfortable. Every time when I was standing in the Centre there was this woman pretended to clean something. So years before, there was this wardress and I asked her who this prisoner was and she said, just keep away from her and told me to get on with my work which I did. But that afternoon I was mopping and suddenly I was pushed to the floor and this tall woman stood over me. She didn't say anything. I got up and managed to slap her but then the warders came and broke up the fight. I learnt later that she was a friend of David but I never recognised her. Do you remember all that? Anyway, that was that and I never saw her again. I assumed she'd been transferred to another prison. Anyway, all these years later, out of the blue, on a Sunday, she jumps me when I was walking along a staircase. She flew out of this open cell and took hold of me and threw me down the stairs. I mean she was really strong and I passed out and that was it. I came around in hospital. I mean proper hospital outside the prison and I was told that I had two broken legs and hip and concussion and that was it. I was proper bashed up. I was in hospital for a long time. And then when they took the casts off, my legs were bent and my hips were off and they gave me a stick and this is the stick so that's the story.'

'Why did you never write and tell me this?'

'I didn't want to worry you about it.'

'You silly mare! Do you know what happened to this bitch?'

'Her name was, Marissa Gordon-smith and she got eight years added to her sentence. I went to court to give evidence. But how she actually knew David I still have no idea. She never returned to Holloway. I'm guessing she was in love with him!'

Chapter 16

Ruth stepped into the small bedroom at the back of the farmhouse and paused, her fingers curled lightly around the doorframe. The room was quiet, thick with stillness, as though it too were holding its breath. A wash of late afternoon light spilled through the lace curtains, dust motes suspended like pollen in the golden beam. Everything smelt faintly of lavender, old books, and polish. These were strange, intimate smells after years of institutional soap and boiled cabbage and carrots.

The bed was narrow but looked soft and stood against the far wall, a handsome handmade quilt was folded neatly at the foot. Its patches were faded and mismatched—florals, stripes, a square of red gingham—but it had been stitched with care. A single pillow rested against the headboard, fluffed and waiting, like an invitation. Ruth stared at it momentarily, almost suspiciously. She had grown used to coarse blankets and thin mattresses, to sleep without softness…without choice.

A wooden chest of drawers stood beneath the window, the varnish worn at the handles from years of use. A photograph, a black and white image of hens in a field, leaned against the mirror, alongside a small vase holding a sprig of dried lavender. Sally's touch, no doubt. She had always had a knack for small, thoughtful gestures. Her cell had always been cluttered with such touches.

Ruth lowered her handbag, the same battered one she had carried when she'd first arrived at Holloway, ten years and a lifetime ago, onto the stool near the dresser. She stood in the centre of the room for a long moment, her arms hanging loosely by her sides, unsure of what to do next. There were no keys turning behind her, no shouted names, no metal bed frames bolted to the floor. Just the slow ticking of a clock in the hallway, and the distant cluck of hens beyond the window.

She crossed to the bed, sank down slowly, and ran her palm across the quilt. The fabric felt almost impossibly soft under her fingers. She had forgotten the feeling of pure cotton. She looked at her shoes, sensible lace-ups, scuffed but clean and felt so aware of herself. She slipped them off and let her feet press into the cool wooden floor.

Outside, a breeze stirred the branches, and somewhere on the farm, Benny barked. Ruth leaned back on her hands, breathing in the scent of the room again. It smelt like a life. Not hers yet, perhaps. But it might be. It might become hers, if she could let it. She closed her eyes and listened to the hush, and for the first time in years, no one told her to open them again.

That evening she and Sally talked about the old days and there were plenty of memories to get through. They talked about friends they had lost who had been released and those who had died prematurely. They talked about wicked women and those that were never ever going to be released. They spoke of long forgotten family who were never going to forgive them and the tragedy that had encompassed them but they also laughed a great deal while drinking two bottles of wine. Sally promised to show her everything the next day including introducing her to her staff and also to her new pottery shed.

'Do your staff know about you?'

'Oh yes, they know I'm an ex con!'

'And what do they think I am?'

'That's up to you. I'm going to introduce you as my friend. But they are a sharp little bunch. They'll probably work you out! But they're young and they don't care.'

'Sally? How old are you?'

'Thirty-six. Why you ask?'

'Haven't you got anybody? You know…interested in you?'

'Can't say that I have. Don't really have the time. But having said that, there is a guy in the village that does like me. He's made advances but, I don't have the time! What about you. Have you got an itch that needs to be scratched?'

'Oh, God, no! Never again and who'd have me any way? A murderess? I can't see many men lining up to date me, can you! No, It's a clean life for me now. Which reminds me, Sally. Where's the nearest police station?'

Ruth woke slowly, as though her body couldn't trust that sleep had been allowed to linger. For one long moment, she lay entirely still, the faint creak of the farmhouse settling into her bones, her mind reaching for the familiar weight of cold stone walls, the sound of the hot water running through the pipe and the metallic taste of prison mornings let alone the discordant and familiar sounds of female screeching. But the air around her felt softer, warmer, carrying the scent of earth and something sweet, like damp grass and sun warmed wood.

Her eyes opened to pale light filtering through gauzy curtains, the room painted in soft gold and muted shadows. No iron bars broke the view, no chipped paint or bolted frames. Just a simple window, glass glinting with the first hints of daylight, the sky beyond it streaked with peach and lavender. Unlike former times her toes and legs felt warm and she arched her feet in delight.

For more than a few minutes, she stared at that open stretch of sky, her breath caught somewhere between disbelief and something far more fragile. Ten years of waking to steel and slate had taught her not to expect anything beyond what she could see and touch and yet here she was, blinking into a world that stretched wide and unbroken. Oh my word! Those chickens were noisy!

Ruth shifted under the quilt, its warmth comforting against her legs, enjoying its weight. She had slept.

Properly slept, without the distant clank of keys or the heavy scrape of boots down corridors. No one had banged on her door. No one had shouted her number, 5486.

She breathed in, deep and steady, and the air tasted like wood polish and lavender again, mingled with something faintly metallic, the scent of dew creeping in through the window frame. A loud clucking noise drifted from outside, the hens were alive! Somewhere farther off, she heard the low murmur of young female voices. Sally's employees, probably already tending to their early duties.

Eventually, Ruth pushed herself upright slowly, her body stiff but lighter than she remembered and felt a slight pain in her head and remembered the wine. Her gaze moved back to the window, lingering on the world beyond the glass. There was a tall tree outside, she hadn't noticed it the night before, its bare branches etched against the sky like ink strokes on paper. Beyond that, open fields rolled into the horizon, dotted with outbuildings and hedgerows. No walls. No watchful eyes.

A small, disbelieving laugh slipped from her lips, barely a sound at all. She pressed her palms against the quilt, grounding herself in the softness beneath her. For the first time in ten years, there was nothing between her and the morning but glass and air.

She swung her legs over the side of the bed, toes meeting the cool wood of the floor. Her shoes waited beside her, just where she had left them, and the simple normality of that moved her. She didn't have to ask for them. She didn't have to wait for permission to move. From her case she found a skirt and blouse and quickly dressed and after brushing her hair she looked at herself in the mirror. She would do. Outside, a rooster crowed, sharp and defiant against the quiet. Ruth smiled, slow and uncertain, and let the sound settle into her chest.

'No bars today.'

Taking her stick, Ruth crossed the hallway, one hand grazing the wall as though needing its reassurance. The farmhouse was still quiet, the wooden floor cool beneath her soles. She reached the front door, hesitated, then lifted the latch. It gave with a soft click, and the door swung inward on a soft morning breeze and Benny greeted her.

'Hello, Benny! Good Boy!'

Ruth found it so strange to touch and stroke an animal not having done anything like that for so long. It was a queer sensation to look into his eyes and she spent a little while talking to him. But then it was time to move on.

She stepped onto the flagstone path. For a moment, she simply stood there, blinking against the brightness, her body caught in that strange twilight between memory and present. The air smelt alive, soil, chicken feed, grass, and the faint tang of woodsmoke from the nearby stove house. It wrapped around her, thick and vivid and overwhelming.

The sky stretched wide above her, far too big and too open. She felt the weight of it pressing down in a way that was both frightening and yet beautiful. The fields ran out like open arms, brown and green and gold, hedgerows still damp with dew. A cluster of hens scratched at the dirt near the coop, feathers flashing in the sun, their soft clucking drifting on the wind. One, white and sleek, paused to stare at her as if assessing the newcomer.

Ruth took a step forward. The crunch of gravel underfoot was sharp and startling. There was no echo, no hard surfaces to throw it back. Only the sound of her own footsteps, unaccompanied.

A swallow dipped in the air above her, swooping low over the yard. She watched it, her breath caught somewhere between awe and sorrow. In Holloway, the only birds were pigeons and the occasional crow. This felt so different.

She eventually looked toward the barn, where its door stood ajar. A radio played faintly inside alongside the soft hum of voices, crackly and distant. Another type of life that she had not witnessed for years was taking place in there.

The farmhouse's kitchen was warm and heavy with the smell of toasted bread and fried eggs and bacon. Sally stood at the stove in a blue cardigan and worn corduroys, her hair pulled back in a loose plait. She glanced up as Ruth stepped in, and gave her a quick, easy smile, the sort that didn't need words.

'Morning, darling! How did you sleep?'

Ruth nodded. 'Strangely, very well. But the wine hasn't sat right with me. Out of practice I think.'

'Aspirins are in that drawer there. Help yourself. Yeah, I had the same problem. I stick to shandy when I go out.'

'Thanks.'

'Glad you slept well. Some people find it a bit too quiet.'

Sally turned back to the pan and flipped it with a practiced hand.

'Tea's made. Bit strong, maybe, but it'll do the job. Eggs and bacon all right?'

The table was set simply. Two plates, two mugs, a chipped sugar bowl and pats of butter resting in a saucer. A pot of tea steamed gently in the centre. Ruth sat slowly, her hands brushing over the worn wood of the tabletop. It had knife marks and burn rings, a history written in scratches and stains.

Sally slid a plate in front of her. Eggs, bacon and toast, with the yolks still soft. Ruth stared at it for a moment, not moving.

'It's alright,' Sally said, pulling out a chair. 'Tuck in. No one's going to take it off you.'

That struck her. Some thin, brittle layer inside her and Ruth looked away quickly. She picked up her fork. The first bite was hot, buttery, and perfect. It was just an egg. But it tasted like a feast. Sally poured the tea and slid the sugar bowl closer.

'You can take your time, you know. There's no schedule. No whistle. You don't have to ask for anything. I know I'm being stupid saying those things but I know how you feel and it's important for me to say those things. You know it is, don't you.'

Ruth nodded.

'Yes, you're right. It is important you say those things, and it is stupid. We are so ingrained to do those things, to say those things, it's terrible.'

'But you'll soon get used to it. To the freedom I mean. It will take a few weeks but you will get used to your freedom, Ruth. Everybody does. Go on, tuck into that bacon. You enjoy it.

Ruth gave a small nod, her eyes fixed on her plate. It was almost too much, the kindness, the ease, the lack of ceremony.

She swallowed, 'this is going to take some getting used to.'

'I know, we all come back with a little Holloway stuck to our skin. But it gets easier, Ruth. Little by little.'

They ate in companionable silence for a while as Benny lay beside them occasionally flicking his eyes up at them. The clock ticked above the door. Hens clucked outside the open window. And for the first time in years, breakfast didn't feel like a transaction or a countdown. It felt like a beginning.

Chapter 16

After several more cups of tea Sally took Ruth on a quick whistle stop tour of the farm and introduced her to her four young employees as they happened to be scraping shovels.

'Good morning, gang! I'd like to introduce you to Ruth who you know is going to stay with me. Ruth? This is, my hard working team, Ava, Amelia, Daisy and David and I wouldn't advise shaking hands with them at the moment unless you want to smell like chicken shit!'

Ruth smiled. 'Hello. I've heard so much about how hard you all work.'

'Does that mean you're giving us a pay rise, Sally?' asked David with a friendly smirk.

'Well, we must get on,' smiled Sally. 'Ruth…come on!'

'See you all later.'

Ruth and Sally moved off but Ruth had become quiet enough for Sally to look sideways at her friend.

'Something wrong?'

'No it's nothing.'

'But I think there is.'

Sally touched Ruth's arm and they and Benny stopped by a barn.

'What is it?'

Ruth stared back in the direction of the young workers.

'I don't know. That one with the pigtail.'

'Daisy? The small girl?'

'Yeah.'

'You *know* her? You can't know her. I know her mother. She's a village girl.'

'No, I don't know her. How old is she?'

'Oh, I see. You're thinking…'

'Yes, I am. Sixteen years ago. She looks like I did at that age, Sally. She could be me. She could be my baby if I hadn't…'

'Ruth, nature is cruel sometimes. You can't blame yourself.'

'But the thing is, Sally, I still do. My bloody lifestyle I had back then. Two months to go and then I lost her.'

'But you still have two kids. Two more than I have.'

'Oh, I'm sorry, Sally, I wasn't thinking. Forgive me. I don't know how you cope with what happened.'

'I tell you how I cope, shall I? I cope knowing that it was not my fault. The one that caused it is still doing time. Although I wish they'd have hung him, excuse me.'

'No, that's all right. I'm over that now. A distant memory, thank Christ.'

'You are amazing, Ruth, you know that?'

'I don't know about that. Ex nightclub owner, murderer and jailbird. What's so amazing about that?'

'Oh, I don't know, let's see, award winning ceramic artist and survivor? Won't that do for a start?'

'Please show me your lovely farm.'

It had to be a quick tour as everybody was busy and when they came to the main sheds Ruth was astonished for she had never seen so many chickens in one place before.

'This is madness!'

'Yes, it seems like that but everything is in good order I can assure you. I have two sheds and there's about five hundred hens in each so that's my business. Now, I have something special to show you, follow me.'

The gravel crunched beneath their shoes as Sally led Ruth across the wide yard, past various outbuildings to a low, stone outhouse tucked against a grove of ash trees. Sally stopped in front of the door, grinning like a child about to reveal a secret.

'Go on, open it,' she said, handing Ruth an old iron key.

The door creaked open and Ruth stepped inside. Sunlight slanted through a wide, south facing window, catching motes of dust in the air. A sturdy worktable dominated the centre of the room, and in one corner stood a gleaming potter's wheel, its wood and metal freshly oiled. Shelves lined the walls, already stacked with new blocks of clay, glazes, brushes and tools, all laid with loving care. Opposite the work table were two huge sinks and a supply of fresh water and drying racks while opposite was an electric kiln.

For a long moment Ruth stood, unable to move. No guards. No shouted orders. No keys rattling on belts. Just space and peace. Her throat tightened painfully and she had to blink several times before she trusted herself to speak.

But then as Ruth crossed the threshold, the scent of raw clay rose up to meet her, sharp and familiar. For a fleeting second, she was back in Holloway's workshop, the low hum of the wheels, the coarse bark of the wardress' voice, the bars cutting the light into slanted stripes.

The workshop smelt of damp clay and something sharper, almost metallic, that Ruth could never place. Rows of women hunched over their stations, the grey light from the high, barred windows washing their faces into pallor. She sat awkwardly at a wheel for the first time, her hands uncertain as the wardress, a stout woman with ink black hair, barked instructions.

The clay was cold and stubborn under her touch. Ruth pressed harder, trying to will it into shape, but it buckled and spun out of control. She caught it instinctively, and the wardress, passing behind her, grunted approvingly.

'You've got a feel for it,' she muttered gruffly.

Ruth blinked, unsure whether she was being mocked, but when she looked at the collapsed efforts of her neighbours, she realised she had somehow, almost accidentally, drawn a tall, slim cylinder out of the mass.

From that moment, the afternoons in the workshop became an escape. She lost herself in the rhythm of the wheel, the wet, gritty texture under her palms, the slow, coaxing patience it demanded. Sometimes she would look at a finished pot and feel a faint, fierce pride stir in her chest, an emotion she had not felt in a very long time and she was so glad that the prison governor had decided that this type of rehabilitation was good for the prisoners.

But here, the air was warm with sunlight and birdsong, and the only bars were the wooden beams across the ceiling. The memory of Holloway slid away like a shadow, leaving only the steady, thrilling realness of this new place, this new life.

'Sally…it's perfect.'

Sally shrugged, pretending casualness, but her eyes were shining.

'I figured you'd want somewhere of your own. Somewhere to make things. Somewhere to continue your work.'

Ruth crossed the room slowly, running her fingers over the surface of the wheel. It was smooth and cool to the touch. Solid. Real. For the first time since stepping out of Holloway's gates, she felt a glimmer of something she had almost forgotten how to name: hope.

Later that evening, on her own, Ruth pulled out the battered wooden stool and sat, her hands resting lightly on her knees. For a long while she simply listened: the ticking of the cooling sun warmed stones, the distant cluck and chatter of the hens, the breath of the breeze against the windowpane. Then she reached, reverently, and touched the wheel's handle.

It turned under her fingers with a soft, reassuring weight, steady and sure. She closed her eyes, feeling the memory of muscle and movement stir awake inside her, the slow spin, the yielding clay, the shaping of something whole out of a lump of formless earth.

Not a prisoner now. Not a number. Just Ruth Ellis, sitting in a sunlit room, with the world waiting in her hands.

The faint, earthy scent of wet clay filled the small studio, mingled with the sharper tang of the cold December air which swept under the door. Ruth sat at her wheel, her apron dusted with fine white powder, her hands steady as they coaxed a shallow bowl into shape. Outside, the bare ash trees rattled in the wind, and the low winter sun spilled a golden light across her workbench, catching the delicate forms already drying on the shelves. Ruth looked down at Benny and smiled.

'Benny Bens!'

A week before Christmas, and orders had been steady. Ruth worked with a quiet, contained joy, shaping bowls, vases, and slender jugs destined for homes she would never see. People had heard of her, not through scandal, as once they might have, but through admiration. An article in a small arts magazine had called her, "a talent born from hardship," praising her fine, clean lines and the unmistakable emotional depth of her pieces. Another writer, more daring, had noted she was a, "survivor of Holloway prison who had turned silence into strength."

It had led to more commissions than she had dared to hope for. Each new order was a quiet validation, a reminder that she was building something with her own hands, not out of desperation, but out of grace. Today she was finishing a set of porcelain plates commissioned by a gallery in Cornwall. Plates so thin they rang softly when she tapped them. She turned the wheel slowly, trimming the foot of the latest piece, her mind pleasantly empty except for the feeling of the clay responding to her touch.

The door creaked open behind her, letting in a rush of cold air and the scent of woodsmoke. Ruth turned her head and smiled to see Sally standing there, still wearing her heavy coat, a square white envelope in her hand.

'Post came early,' Sally said in her normal warm voice.

Ruth wiped her hands on her apron and took it, smiling when she saw the handwriting was André's. She knew it instantly, bold, boyish, a little untidy. The last time she had heard from him had been months ago, a short note full of guarded words but unmistakable affection.

Sally hesitated a moment, reading Ruth's expression. 'I'll leave you to it,' she said softly, and pulled the door closed behind her.

For a moment, Ruth stood, the letter heavy in her hands. The wheel spun on slowly behind her, forgotten. She sat on the wooden stool by the window and slit the envelope open with a clay knife, her fingers trembling.

Inside, the words tumbled out: news of his work, plans for Christmas, a shy, hopeful suggestion he might visit if she was willing. Ruth read it twice, blinking hard against the sting of unexpected tears. She pressed the paper lightly to her chest, feeling the fragile, stubborn pulse of life continuing, clay shaped into bowls, broken bonds mended one careful word at a time. Outside, a crow wheeled over the fields, its cry sharp and free in the cold air.

The morning light broke clean and golden over Haven Farm, spreading warmth over the fields and hedgerows which were beginning to blush green again. Ruth stood by the kitchen window, her hands cradling a cup of tea, watching the dust rise behind the narrow country lane that wound up to the house. A car approached, small and sensible, bouncing over the ruts. Her heart lifted. It was André.

She moved to the door, wiping her hands absently on a dishcloth. The car pulled up, and there he was: tall, confident, with the same tousled hair and quick smile he had worn as a boy. Beside him, a young woman with a honey blonde cut climbed out, smoothing her skirt. Ruth had seen her once before, briefly, but this was different. This was real.

André spotted her and grinned. 'Mum!' he called, as if he were still fifteen and running home from school.

Ruth laughed, a low, surprised sound, and stepped onto the gravel. He hugged her tightly, lifting her off her feet for a second, before setting her down again with a boyish chuckle.

'Mum? This is Heather,' he said, stepping back and taking the young woman's hand with pride. 'My fiancée.'

Heather offered a warm smile. Her handshake was firm, her eyes steady. Her hair was fashionably cut and she was dressed conservatively. 'It's so lovely to meet you properly, Mrs Ellis.'

'Please, just Ruth,' Ruth corrected, her voice thick with emotion. 'Please come in.'

She ushered them inside, the kettle already humming. Over tea and warm scones Sally had left out earlier, they spoke of small things, the drive down, the blossom coming early this year, the plans for the wedding in July.

'I work in telecommunications now,' André said, sipping his tea. 'Mostly installations and maintenance for private businesses. It's decent work and it keeps me on the move.'

Heather touched his arm lightly. 'And he's very good at it.'

Ruth smiled, feeling a quiet pride she scarcely dared express. Her son, growing a life steady and true, beyond the shadows of the past.

Later, as the clock chimed half past ten, André glanced at his watch. 'We should get going,' he said. 'Matins starts at eleven.'

Ruth appeared startled. 'Church?'

'Yes,' he said, smiling. 'Heather and I, well, we're both fairly religious. It's important to us. Would you come? St Jude has a lovely church. We looked it up.'

There was a hesitation, just a breath of it, but Ruth caught it. She saw the kindness in Heather's eyes, the way André held his breath a little, hoping. They wanted her there. They wanted her to be part of their lives.

'Of course,' Ruth said, smoothing her hands down her skirt.

The walk to the church was short: the lane curved down past the paddocks and into the village of St Jude proper. Spring was fully in charge now: birds singing themselves hoarse in the hedges, the scent of fresh earth in the air, daffodils nodding along the stone walls and bluebells were everywhere.

St Jude's Church sat at the heart of the village, its square Norman tower was solid and was weathered by centuries of faith and storms. As they approached, its bells tolled softly, and small groups of villagers trickled inside, families in their Sunday best, older couples arm in arm and children with scuffed knees and polished shoes.

Ruth felt the shift the moment they reached the porch for heads turned. She caught the glances, some curious, some cautious but a few were warm. They all knew who she was. Everyone did, by now. The woman from Holloway. The woman with the son. The one who made those beautiful ceramics sold in the magazines.

She lifted her chin, not in defiance but in quiet dignity, and accompanied André and Heather inside.

The church was cool and dim and the air smelt faintly of stone and candle wax. Sunlight streamed through the high, narrow windows, painting coloured patches on the flagstones. They slipped into a pew near the back, Ruth again smoothing her skirt and folding her gloved hands.

The service began with the familiar cadences Ruth had not heard for many years. The opening prayers, the ancient responses, the gentle rhythm of scripture. She found herself mouthing the words almost without thinking, the phrases buried deep from a Welsh childhood long ago.

As the congregation rose to sing, Ruth hesitated a fraction, then joined them. Her voice was low, a little rough from disuse, but it found its way through the simple hymn. "All things bright and beautiful…" she sang, the notes rising to the rafters. Heather's voice beside her was clear and bright, and Ruth felt a small, unexpected welling of emotion in her chest.

During the sermon, Ruth's mind wandered a little. She studied the faces around her, Mrs Pembroke from the post office, Mr and Mrs Howard from the dairy, young Alice Brewer clutching her prayer book with earnest concentration. Most pretended not to look at her, but Ruth caught the quick, darting glances all the same.

There was no hostility, she realised. Only surprise. Perhaps even something softer, acceptance, curiosity, a hesitant welcome.

After the blessing, as they spilled into the sunshine, several villagers approached. Mr Howard offered a brisk nod and a 'morning to you, Ruth.' Mrs Pembroke stopped to admire Heather's engagement ring. Alice Brewer shyly pressed a daffodil into Ruth's hand before scampering off after her mother.

While standing on the grass outside St Jude's, its bells clanging joyfully overhead, Ruth felt something loosen inside her. A tether undone. A permission granted not by proclamation, but by simple human kindness.

'Are you all right, mum?' André asked, slipping his arm through hers.

She smiled at him, a real, radiant smile. 'Yes, I'm all right, love.'

They walked back to the farm together, as the village returned into its quiet Sunday rhythm behind them.

For the first time in many years, Ruth Ellis did not feel like a ghost. She felt like someone beginning again.

Back at Haven Farm, the kettle was soon singing, and the table was laid with simple care: cold ham, pickled onions, fresh bread and a jug of primrose wine picked the previous year. Ruth moved about the kitchen with quiet ease, feeling the deep, steady comfort of her home.

They sat together, the spring sunlight slanting across the scrubbed wooden table, their plates filling, the conversation moving easily from wedding plans to work and then back again to laughter and small stories.

Heather spoke about her family in Sussex: André told a funny story about an installation job gone wrong when a goat had eaten the engineer's paperwork. Ruth listened, joining in, feeling the warmth between them growing like a slow, steady fire.

At one point, she looked up and caught André watching her, a soft pride in his eyes. She smiled and reached across to squeeze his hand. No words were needed. The loneliness of old wounds, the slow ache of separation, the dark memories, all of it was being folded away into something smaller, quieter and more manageable.

The past was still there. It always would be. But here, at this simple Sunday table, it no longer ruled her. She was part of life again, and this was life, messy, beautiful, ordinary, and entirely, gloriously hers. That evening, after André and Heather had left for London, and the farm had fallen into its usual hush, Ruth sat alone in the small sitting room with only Benny for company as Sally was still away that weekend.

The fire crackled softly in the grate, throwing long shadows across the stone hearth and the worn armchairs.

On the low table before her, a pot of tea steamed gently, untouched for now. She cradled a cup between her hands, letting the warmth seep into her fingers. Outside, the spring night stirred, a fox barked somewhere in the distance and the wind brushed the hedges with a whispering touch.

Ruth gazed into the flames, her thoughts loose and slow. Today had been a day she once never would have imagined. A day when forgiveness, from others, from herself, no longer seemed an impossible dream. She thought of André's face, full of simple joy. Of Heather's clear, open smile. Of the daffodil Alice Brewer had placed in her hand, now tucked safely into a glass on the windowsill.

Ruth breathed deeply, the old ache still there but softened now, like a scar weathered smooth by time. She wasn't only surviving anymore. She was living. And the life that stretched ahead of her was no longer just a thread of duty and regret. It was a tapestry, waiting to be woven, rich with promise. The clock on the mantelpiece struck ten. Ruth smiled to herself, finished her tea, and stoked down the fire for the night. Tomorrow was waiting, and she would meet it with open hands.

Chapter 17

Benny was in his usual position next to Ruth as she worked in her studio. It was a glorious morning. The Conservative Party had won the 1970 general election and for the moment all seemed right with the world as Sally had predicted them winning would be good for business.

Currently Ruth was working on a twenty-one piece dinner set, a private order for a friend's daughter which she wouldn't normally do but as it was for her wedding she had relented. Mainly because the daughter reminded her so much of herself when she was nineteen.

And most likely that was the reason she felt so distracted that morning. Indeed why she had felt so distracted over the past two weeks while creating the set. It was certainly something Sally noticed when she took her a coffee.

'Benny's noticed as well you know.'

Ruth knew immediately what she was talking about.

'No he hasn't. Little potato head hasn't got the brain to notice emotions!'

'Oh really? Chickens know what I'm thinking you know.'

'No they don't.'

'Yes they do. My Rhode Island Reds definitely know when they're in for the chop!'

'Oh don't talk like that! Anyway, alright I've had things on my mind recently.'

'Do you want to talk about it?'

'I've been thinking of London recently and I suppose just once I think I'd like to see it all again. Not as the woman I was you understand, but as the woman I've become. If that makes any sense?'

'Perfect sense, my darling. I had the same thing happened to me. I think it's natural to go back and see where you've come from and to see how you've changed. A comparison if you like. There's nothing wrong with that. But are you going to do it or are you going to brood about it?'

'It frightens me if I were to be honest.'

'Don't you think enough time has passed? It's been what? Over five years? And where would you go? And what would you see?'

'It's true. I have been brooding And yes, there are a few things. I'd like to see the club where I met David although I'd think it's probably closed but it would be interesting to look at it from the outside and feel the memories. Then there's Goodwood Court and Desmond although I don't want to see him.'

'That's where you lived with him, isn't it?'

'Yes, I had some good times there with André.'

'What do you feel about him now?'

'Contempt. Some anger, that's about it. I wish I could forget him entirely.'

'What about the pub?'

'The *Magdala*? Oh God no, I couldn't go there. No, that would freak me right out, as the young people say. Freak me right out. I think I'd pass out if I stood outside there. No, no, no! I couldn't do that. I could never go back there.'

'How about if I came with you? Kind of like held your hand?'

Ruth looked away from her mucky hands and smiled at her friend.

'Could you take the time off? An entire day just for me?'

'You are a silly poppet! What do you think? Choose a day and we can take the train from Bognor and make a day of it. What do you say? Afternoon tea at Harrods? My treat!'

'I fancy that!'

So, four days later, the morning sun filtered through a gauze of soft clouds as Ruth and Sally stepped onto the station platform at Bognor Regis, Ruth's handbag clutched tightly against her coat. Sally, beside her, carried a thermos and a small shoulder bag with sandwiches and a paperback she was reading at the time tucked in the side pocket. They had dressed neatly, not ostentatiously: Ruth in a pale blue wool coat and a scarf tied at her throat, her dark hair pinned up as neatly as she could. The platform was busy with chatter and the rhythmic shuffle of weekday travellers. The train, when it arrived, eased effortlessly into the station, its carriages opening to swallow the next group bound for London.

They found a seat by the window, facing one another as the train began its slow roll through the outskirts of the town. Trees flashed before them, then open fields, and finally suburban rows of houses, all in perfect formation.

Ruth barely spoke for some while. She held her silence with the same deliberate care she held clay, cradling something soft and difficult that might crack if mishandled. Her eyes were transfixed on the world outside, and Sally understood she wasn't watching the scenery.

Finally Ruth spoke. 'I used to take this journey in reverse, you know. Years ago. From Victoria to Brighton or Worthing for a weekend with…well, with someone.' She didn't say his name.

Sally gave her a gentle smile. 'You don't have to go through with this if you're not ready.'

'I am sure,' Ruth replied quickly. 'It's just…it feels like walking back into a dream you've long since awoken from. And wondering whether you dreamed it at all.'

A small child a few seats away dropped his comic book and wailed. A businessman read a copy of The Times. A teenager chewed gum and looked miserable. Ruth closed her eyes for a moment, leaning her head against the window. The glass was cool and she could feel the train's vibrations humming through her skull.

She thought of the last time she had worn makeup in London, applied expertly in the club's mirror while the pianist played, "These Foolish Things". She thought of Desmond's cologne, of cigarette smoke curling into the air. She thought of the corridor in Holloway, of the footsteps echoing on concrete, and the sudden finality of steel doors and in particular what lie behind that cupboard door in her death cell that was never opened...

'I'm not going back to that version of myself,' she said softly, more to herself than to Sally. 'I want to see what's left.'

Sally reached across and gently squeezed her hand. 'And when you're ready, we'll come straight home.'

Ruth smiled, grateful. The train surged forward, drawing them toward London, a city she had once loved, once feared, and now faced again, not as a penitent, but as a witness.

Arriving at Victoria they made their way through the barrier and found themselves outside in strong sunlight where Sally linked Ruth's arm and pulled her towards a taxi rank. Everywhere was so busy they had to queue.

'Darling? Do you want to go there straight away or shall we get a cup of tea first?'

'Let's go straight away shall we? I think that's best.'

'Alright then.'

They waited in silence shuffling along every so often and then at last they were in a cab. The taxi eased through the congested streets of West London, its engine idling at every red light, almost as if reluctant to deliver Ruth to her destination. From the back seat, Ruth watched the city shift and shimmer behind the glass, more vertical now, more frantic, with horns blaring, scaffolding crawling up once familiar façades. Knightsbridge still carried its name like a crown, but it had changed in those fifteen years. She could feel it in the pace of the passers by, in the designer shop windows that hadn't existed when she knew this world.

'This was always my favourite part of the city,' Ruth murmured, as they turned into Brompton Road which was packed with traffic and fumes.

'There was a time when I thought I'd never leave.'

Sally leaned forward, glancing at the buildings. 'Where exactly was the club?'

Ruth hesitated, then pointed. 'There. That pale stone building. Number twenty-seven. The door was painted black then, not grey. And there was always a man with a red carnation waiting by it. You had to be someone to be let in.'

The taxi pulled up and stopped. The driver glanced back. 'This you?'

'Yes,' Ruth said, her voice smaller than she intended. She reached for the door handle but didn't open it. She stared at the building, now clearly a private office space, with a discreet brass plaque reading McDonnell & Partners.

No red carnation. No doorman. No laughter spilling onto the pavement with smoke and perfume.

Sally paid the fare and they stepped out. The sun, filtered by high cloud, laid a dusty sheen over the street as people of all classes streamed by. Ruth stood still, the past unspooling in front of her with a quiet cruelty. The Little Club had once been velvet and warmth and gin in a highball glass. She had danced here. Laughed here. Hidden here. And now it was nothing more than a smart doorway with a buzzer and no memory of her at all.

'I remember the wallpaper,' she said softly. 'Red and gold, tacky, but glorious. I thought it was the centre of the world. And I was part of it.'

They stood on the pavement a moment longer, two middle aged women in sensible shoes, looking at a building that had once held Ruth's heart in its throat. No one passing by gave them a second glance. Ruth tilted her head, half expecting to hear the muffled sound of a piano through the door. Instead, there was only the distant honk of a lorry and the rhythmic hiss of a bus' brakes.

Sally touched her friend's elbow's gently. 'You don't have to say anything.'

'I don't know what I thought I'd find,' Ruth replied. I think I wanted it to be frozen in time. So I could step back in and prove it happened.'

They began walking slowly over towards Harrods.

'It happened,' Sally said. 'It happened. You survived it.'

Ruth nodded. But as she glanced back one last time at the lifeless grey door, she felt a strange kind of mourning, not for the club, but for the woman she'd once been within it.

The crossing from the former site of The Little Club to Harrods took less than a few minutes, but for Ruth it felt as if she had stepped through a mysterious portal. One moment she was mourning a past life, the next, she stood before the grand green awnings of London's most famous department store. The gold lettered sign gleamed above the entrance as if time had politely chosen not to touch it.

Sally smiled. 'Come on. We're going to lunch like ladies.'

Inside, the atmosphere was opulent and almost theatrical, a far cry from the sterile scent of institutional corridors. The air held faint traces of perfume, roasting coffee and expensive perfume. They passed displays of fine china and cut crystal, all carefully lit as though each item were performing under its own spotlight.

Both women felt underdressed but not unwelcome. Harrods always had that curious ability to make a woman feel that if she were there, that she belonged. Ruth had only been inside it a handful of times, decades ago, and never for anything more than a few quick purchases. Lunch had always been something other women did: kept wives, debutantes, elegant widows in wide hats. Not girls from,

The Little Club. Certainly not ex prisoners, Not even one with a national art award resting on her mantelpiece.

But Sally was insistent, and soon they were seated at a table in the elegant ground floor tea room. Crisp white linen, silver cutlery, and waiters in black waistcoats. Ruth couldn't stop glancing around, as though someone might recognise her, but of course, no one did.

A waiter arrived and offered them menus. Ruth was about to decline wine, but Sally raised a hand.

'Two glasses of white,' she said, without consulting Ruth. 'You've earned it.'

Ruth raised an eyebrow. 'Are we celebrating?'

Sally leaned across the table, voice low but warm. 'You came. You faced it. And you're still standing. That deserves a toast.'

Ruth breathed in the perfume air as she closed her eyes and sampled the ambient sweet atmosphere. Yes, this was nicer than Holloway and she smiled.

'What are you smiling at?'

'I was remembering when you first put your head in my cell and introduce yourself and look at us now!'

'Silly cow! But I know what you mean.'

Their glasses clinked gently. Ruth sipped, letting the cold crispness of the wine fill her mouth before swallowing. It was better than she remembered. Or perhaps her memory of wine had grown stale in the long silence of abstinence.

'I thought it would be worse,' Ruth admitted. 'London. I thought it would swallow me.'

Sally nodded. 'You're not the same woman who left it.'

'I didn't leave it,' Ruth said softly. 'It left me.'

Their food arrived, delicate smoked salmon sandwiches for Sally, a warm goat's cheese tart for Ruth. She ate slowly, savouring every bite, as if she could taste not just the ingredients but the meaning behind them: freedom, normalcy and grace.

'People stare at me less than I feared,' Ruth said, glancing at the tables around them.

Sally smiled. 'That's because you're just another woman having lunch in Harrods. Nothing more, nothing less.'

And, for the first time in what felt like a lifetime, Ruth believed it might actually be true. The hum of conversation around them grew as lunchtime reached its peak, but their corner of the Harrods tearoom remained cocooned in calm. Ruth placed down her cutlery and looked at Sally. The tart had been perfect: buttery, sharp, warm, yet somehow it sat like a stone in her stomach.

'There's one more place,' Ruth said quietly.

Sally nodded. 'Devonshire Street.'

Ruth glanced into her wineglass. 'Goodwood Court. I should have gone there first, but I couldn't face it on an empty stomach.'

'You don't have to, you know.'

Ruth gave a faint smile. 'I do, though. It's not a sightseeing tour. It's...unfinished business.'

Sally said nothing. She simply waited, the way she always did when Ruth needed time to speak but couldn't get the words out.

'I think he was the one I expected.' Ruth said, barely above a whisper. 'More than anyone. Desmond. I didn't expect much. I know I didn't want him to visit but a letter? A single letter? *Something*?'

'He should have written.'

'Not a bloody word. After all that talk, you'll never be alone, Ruthie. I'll be there for you, Ruthie. But when it came to it...nothing.'

She picked up her napkin and dabbed her lips, although they were already dry. 'In the end it was strangers who stood by me. Not him.'

'He wasn't worth your loyalty.'

'That's the bitter part. He was, once. Or I thought he was.'

There was a long pause. Around them, plates clinked, chairs scraped and the outside world continued. Ruth stared past her friend, seeing not the mirrored walls or polished floor but a hallway in Devonshire Street, its pale wood panelling in the morning light.

Within half an hour another taxi turned into Devonshire Street after two o'clock and by that time clouds had begun to drift, casting patches of warm sunlight across the pale façades. The buildings were as Ruth remembered, tall, elegant, with a gentle Georgian uniformity. But the soul of the place had shifted. It was quieter now, far more clinical. Almost sterile.

'Do you want me to come up with you?' Sally asked, as the cab slowed outside Goodwood Court.

Ruth shook her head. 'No need. I won't go inside. I just want to see it or to stand outside the flat.'

The driver waited while Ruth stepped out, the breeze tugging at her coat. She walked toward the steps of the apartment block, as if each tread held a decade's worth of memory. She stood for a long time on the pavement, her eyes fixed on the entrance, the familiar glass doors and the brass nameplate now duller with age.

This was where she had once climbed the stairs with a key in her hand and hope in her chest. This was where Desmond had poured drinks and whispered promises. And this was where her silence had begun.

She closed her eyes. No one was watching, and even if they were, she no longer cared. The past didn't need witnesses to be real.

Behind her, Sally left the cab and stood back, giving her space. Ruth turned and looked up toward the second floor. That window, yes, that had been his. His study. His little fortress of secrets. The curtains were drawn now. No face behind the glass. No echo of her name.

'I used to think love was enough,' Ruth said quietly to herself. 'how stupid could I be?'

Sally stepped forward. 'You gave him the best of yourself. He gave you nothing back.'

Ruth's jaw tightened, then relaxed. 'Let's go. I don't want to be here when someone comes out and asks what I'm doing loitering on the pavement.'

As they returned to the taxi, and before she entered it, Ruth looked back one final time.

'You know what's odd?' she said. 'I don't feel angry anymore. Just…done.'

As the cab pulled away from Devonshire Street, a chapter of her life closed quietly behind her, not with drama, not with tears, but with a long exhale of understanding.

'Are you ready for our final visit, Ruth?'

'Are *you* ready, Sally?'

'I am, let's do it! Driver? Holloway prison please!'

The driver yanked his neck around and spoke for the first time in a surprisingly clipped middle class accent. 'You do know that place is closed down don't you know?'

'We know!' They chorused as they sat back and grinned while making faces at each other.

Due to heavy roadworks and diversions it took over an hour to reach there and so it was almost four o'clock when the taxi coasted up Parkhurst Road and stopped outside the prison. The streets around Holloway were quieter than

Ruth remembered, or perhaps she was simply seeing them with different eyes. Time and silence had rubbed the edges off everything.

'There,' Sally said gently, nodding out of the window.

Ruth looked hard. Holloway Prison loomed up behind a high metal fence, the outer walls softened by creeping ivy and disuse. The gates were shut, bolted tight. The great iron doors, once so final, were rusting into memory.

It was no longer a prison, not officially. The place had been shut for years now, plans in place for redevelopment that never seemed to reach completion. Only the shell remained. Cold, hollow and still, only the four bodies of the executed women so recently exhumed had been reburied at Brookwood Cemetery.

The taxi idled at the curb.

Ruth leaned forward, one gloved hand resting on the glass. She didn't feel the need to get out.

'I don't feel anything,' she said, her voice neutral, almost curious. 'I thought I might.'

Sally glanced at her, uncertain whether to speak.

Ruth continued, almost to herself. 'Ten years inside. I'd have thought the place would haunt me. But it just looks like a building now. Bricks. Windows. Bars. Empty.'

The wind stirred dust across the cracked pavement. A fox darted through a gap in the fencing. Beyond the outer wall, an old security light blinked erratically.

'I used to stare out of those windows,' Ruth murmured. 'Second floor. I remember the sound of the gates clanging shut at night. The smell of soap and bleach. The way time never moved…'

She wasn't crying. She wasn't even especially sad. It was as though the woman who had once walked those halls had packed herself up and left, just as surely as the wardresses and other inmates had done.

'They've boarded the windows,' she noted. 'Doesn't suit it, does it? Looks more like an abandoned castle now.'

Sally reached over and took her hand. Ruth let her. It was comfort, not pity. And she could bear that.

'I wonder if my name's still carved into the desk in the ceramics room,' she said, and gave a faint, dry laugh. 'Miss Davies used to pretend not to notice. I liked her. She had patience.'

The cab's engine hummed softly.

'I thought it would be harder than this,' Ruth said, blinking slowly. 'But I suppose I said goodbye to that place long ago. The walls just haven't caught up.'

Sally nodded. 'I get that. I feel the same, even after all these years. Six bloody years!'

Ruth glared at the prison once more, this time not as a former inmate, but as someone fully outside it.

Sally noticed the driver was tapping his steering wheel quickly and looking at his watch. She nudged Ruth and nodded at him. And unaccountably this changed Sally's attitude and she felt annoyed.

'Hello? Your meter's running Mr…' she spotted his registration card on his dashboard. '*Weis*, is it? Have you got somewhere else to go?'

'Well, I've got more important things to do than hang around outside here.'

'Oh lardy da! What is your problem? You're being paid. Your meter's running.'

The driver turned back and faced the road muttering, 'fucking jailbirds…'

'What did you say? I heard that.'

'Nothing. How long are you two going to be? I live in West London you know and it's getting late.'

Sally became more annoyed. 'I tell you how long we're going to be. We're going to be…this long. Come on, Ruth.'

Violently, Sally pulled Ruth from the taxi and slammed the door. 'How much?'

The taxi driver became instantly spitting mad. 'Hey! I'm expecting to return you to central London.'

'Tough titties! How much you arrogant German bastard.'

'Fifteen shillings and ninepence, without a tip.'

'Well you can go and fuck yourself for that.'

And with that, Sally flung a note and a handful of coins at him, grabbed Ruth's arm and began to walk northwards along Camden towards Holloway Road.

'Come on Ruth, we'll get a train.'

It took them fifteen minutes to walk to Holloway Road underground station but during that time neither said anything and they didn't speak again until they arrived at Victoria station when they entered a Wimpy bar and Sally bought two coffees. Only then did Ruth ask a question.

'*Sally*? What was *that* all about?' she smiled. 'Do you particularly hate Germans?'

'No, I particularly hate arrogant bastards. He reminded me of somebody that's all. It was the way he spoke to me, arrogant prick. Still he's gone now, it's over. He's a nobody. Can you imagine being married to that?'

Ruth wanted to push the conversation further but felt it was not the time. At least not that day anyway and she returned to perusing about their long day. All too quickly they brought tickets and had found their train.

Which pulled away on time, its wheels squeaking over the rails as the city receded. Ruth sat back, the seat cradling her spine with unfamiliar softness as the sun shone on her face. Sally didn't speak at first. She understood that silence was necessary now, that words might crowd out the quiet echoes rising within them both.

Through the window, the jagged skyline blurred and smudged with motion. For Ruth, once, this city had been her stage, her trap, her prison—each in turn. Today it had become a ghost. The faces of strangers passed by in flashes, the shouts and horns and scaffolding forming a dissonant chorus that had somehow failed to reach her.

Ruth breathed out slowly. 'It's like I've been walking through someone else's dream,' she said at last.

Sally smiled. 'Or a memory you've outgrown. That's how it's felt to me.'

They passed through tall buildings giving way to more trees and wider roads. As the city loosened its grip, Ruth felt her shoulders settle. The distance brought clarity. London, with its clamour and coldness, had not waited for her. It had moved on, become louder, faster, and somehow smaller. She had changed more than she had ever realised.

'I used to think I might want to come back someday,' Ruth said. 'I thought I needed to…to see it all again. But I don't. I don't belong to it anymore.'

'Perhaps you never did, darling,' Sally replied. 'Maybe not really. You simply didn't know there was another kind of life.'

They travelled onwards, the sunlight beginning to slant gold across the hedgerows. The rhythm of the journey soothed her now, the ticking of time between passing villages as steady as a heartbeat. In her lap, Ruth's fingers traced the edge of her handbag absentmindedly. It had been a gift from Sally when she first moved into Haven—a soft, practical, handmade handbag. It felt like part of her new life.

The thought of the farm made her chest swell — its quiet paths, the chickens, the clay drying on her fingertips in the studio. It was more than a place. It was home. And in that moment she understood something deeper. That survival had not meant enduring Holloway. It had meant choosing life again afterward. And she had.

By the time their taxi turned down the narrow lane leading to Haven, the last of the sun was brushing the tops of the trees. Sally leaned forward and tapped the driver on the shoulder. 'Thanks, Frank. I hope June's hip get's better. Pop over in the week and I'll have two dozen ready for you.'

The farm came into view, bathed in gold, and Ruth felt joy rise up in her throat. Not loud, not sharp, but warm and steady. As the car rolled to a stop, she smiled, not just with her mouth, but with her whole being as Benny came running to greet them.

'I think,' she said, 'I've never been so glad to be anywhere in my life.'

Sally reached for her hand. 'Welcome home, Ruth.'

For the first time that day, Ruth felt it fully. She was no longer looking back.

The next morning dawned soft and grey, the kind of light that made the garden seem blurred at the edges. A mist clung to the fields like a shawl and the sky carried the hush of a world not yet fully awake. Ruth stood at the window of her studio, a mug of tea cooling in her hands, her breath lightly fogging the glass.

Her body ached: not from age or illness, but from the deep fatigue of having carried too much memory in one day. Yet her mind was clear. Not buzzing, not brimming. Just still.

She set down her tea and crossed to the workbench. Everything here was as she had left it. The coils of clay wrapped in damp cloths, the half finished vase waiting patiently and the gentle hum of silence broken only by a robin trilling somewhere outside. This room had never asked anything of her except her presence.

Ruth slipped on her apron. The fabric was stained with ochres, reds, slip, and dust: a history in marks. She ran her fingers over the rim of the vase. The clay was firm now, ready to be shaped further. She took her seat and began to work, not with urgency, but with assurance. Her hands moved instinctively, smoothing the curve, centering the form. The rhythm was slow and meditative. Each breath fell in time with the turn of the wheel.

The experience of the previous day hovered at the edges of her mind—not sharp, not dominant, but present. Knightsbridge. The Little Club. Desmond's empty flat. And Holloway's cold façade. They had left her tired, yes. But not undone. Something had settled inside her. Some tension released.

As the shape grew under her hands, she began to realise what it was she'd been forming—something tall, graceful and restrained. It would be hollow, but strong. Not unlike herself. She paused, tilted her head, and smiled faintly. She wasn't sculpting the city. She was sculpting what had emerged from it.

Footsteps crunched outside on the gravel path and then came the gentle creak of the studio door. Sally stepped in with a fresh mug of tea. She placed it on the bench without saying anything. For a while, she watched Ruth work.

'She's looking beautiful,' Sally said softly, nodding at the piece.

'She'll hold,' Ruth replied. 'She's meant to.'

'Do you think you'll ever go back?' Sally asked.

Ruth didn't answer immediately. She sat back, wiped her hands, and looked out the window where the mist was beginning to lift over the hills.

'I already have,' she said. 'And I came home.'

Sally smiled. 'Then let's keep it that way.'

And Ruth, now truly at peace, returned to her work. The wheel began to spin again, her fingers pressing into the clay with quiet certainty. Outside, the robin sang on.

Chapter 18
July 1973

The summer sun fell in lazy dapples through the canopy of oak and ash, scattering soft light across the patch of meadow by the stream. The hum of bees and the occasional plop of a water vole were the only intrusions into an otherwise perfect silence. Ruth stood for a moment before stepping onto the grass, taking in the unspoiled scene. It had rained the night before, leaving the air sharp with the scent of wild mint and damp earth, but now the world was dry and warm again.

Frank, the local taxi driver had been hired to collect Ruth's family from the station and here they were at last. Ruth and Sally heard them before they saw them: Muriel's brisk voice rising above the others, issuing cheerful instructions, and André's low laugh, softened by adulthood but still recognisable. Then came Heather, gently coaxing her three year old boy, her words shaped with love. Ruth moved closer, a little slowly, she'd never learned to rush without purpose, and the sight before her brought an unexpected rush of something too complex to name.

She embraced all three then picked up Graham and held him high.

'Oh my! Heather! What have you been feeding him?'

'He eats like a horse. It's so good to see you, Ruth. You both look so healthy!'

'It's all the eggs and chickens we eat! Come on in. Coffee's on and we've got the most perfect picnic for us down by the stream. Thank goodness it's going to be a perfect day.'

They had laid a tartan blanket on a flattish patch of ground, its corners anchored with stones and picnic baskets and it didn't take long for Muriel to fuss over a folding chair that refused to behave. While Heather knelt barefoot in the grass, balancing Graham on her hip deftly spreading butter on a slice of bread, André stood ankle deep in the stream, trousers rolled up, skimming stones with the easy skill of boyhood.

'There he is!' Muriel pointed at André, 'always playing, that lad.'

Ruth smiled. 'I think he's makes a good father,' she said, smiling. 'Is he, Heather?'

'He's very attentive and he works very hard. I've no complaints.'

Muriel leaned across and kissed her sister's cheek, briskly, as ever, and then stood back to examine her. 'You've lost weight again,' she said with a mix of concern and accusation. 'You look healthy but I don't think you're eating enough.'

'I eat plenty,' Ruth replied. 'When I'm hungry. I'll be fifty in a couple of years and old people don't eat so much anyway do they? So anyway, come on, tuck in everybody. ANDRÉ! Come out of the water and eat!'

And André did and then was surprisingly hugging her, properly, warmly, and Ruth melted into him. The last time she'd seen him, Graham hadn't been born. Now the little boy clutched a strip of cucumber with determined teeth, bright eyed and curious, wholly unaware of the many lives that had quietly turned in order to deliver him safely to this gentle clearing by the stream.

They settled together on the blanket, Ruth declining the chair Muriel had finally conquered. She preferred the ground. Heather passed her a sandwich without asking what she wanted, tuna and cress, as it turned out, one of Ruth's favourites. 'Thank you,' Ruth said, and she meant it.

Sally talked a great deal about the farm and about the multiple flowers which grew everywhere and about the insects that flew around them, the dragonflies, the beetles the butterflies the different types of trees and her conversation about nature easily fused somehow with the conversation about London life and Andrea's work.

The conversation meandered like the water beside them as the day grew hotter. Muriel, ever the matriarch, recounted minor family dramas, most inconsequential but oddly comforting in their smallness: a cousin's divorce, an aunt's bunion operation, Their mother's constant nagging, the retirement of a neighbour's Labrador. Heather asked polite questions and offered soft replies, her voice easy on the ears. André listened more than he spoke, occasionally interjecting with a wry observation that made them all laugh.

It wasn't until Graham had fallen asleep, curled against Heather's chest like a warm pebble, that the talk deepened. Ruth was the one who shifted its course as the shadows turned.

'Do you remember when André got his head stuck between the bannisters?' she asked, her eyes fixed on the stream.

Muriel barked a laugh. 'God, yes. Poor thing. Screamed as if he was being murdered.'

'You were the one who calmed him down,' Ruth said, glancing at her sister. 'I was useless. Panicking.'

'You'd had barely any sleep in three nights,' Muriel replied, gently. 'That was the week of the measles, wasn't it?'

Ruth nodded. 'Yes. He looked like a little red balloon.'

André smiled. 'I don't remember any of that. I remember the photo of me looking furious.'

Heather chuckled. 'It's still on your mum's mantle. Next to the horse with the missing ear.'

They laughed. And the silence that followed was full of something more than peace. It was understanding, mutual and unstated.

'I wish it had all been so different,' Ruth said then, very quietly. 'I wish I hadn't been so bloody selfish.'

The air seemed to shift. Muriel opened her mouth, but said nothing. André reached over and touched his mother's hand.

'Mum? It's alright, It's all turned out okay,' he said.

Ruth didn't elaborate. She wanted to but she didn't have to. The missing years, the pain, the trial, the shame: none of it needed to be spoken about. They all carried some piece of it, but not here, not today. In this green corner of the world, there was no place for ghosts. Just sunlight, buttered bread, cool lemonade, and the sound of a child's contented breathing.

It was not too long after that there was some contented dozing in the sunshine accompanied by some gentle rippling of the stream and bird song. Then it was Graham who demanded some attention.

As they packed up the remains of their picnic, Ruth handed Muriel a jar of homemade chutney and a small tin of biscuits. 'You'll never make it yourself,' she said. 'And don't pretend you don't want them!'

Muriel smiled and accepted both. 'You know me too well. but you haven't asked about mum have you?'

'You know how I feel about her. She made her feelings plain to me in Holloway when she stopped visiting. That time she walked out of visiting I find it so hard to forgive her. She knows where I am and she hasn't written one single word since. Despite all I've done. Despite all I've achieved. Not one single word. And you and I both know…

well we both know what she didn't do concerning you so we're not gonna talk about that. But the simple fact is, Muriel our family is a mess. I think the way it is unless something big happens I'm never gonna see her again and I'm sorry but that's the way it is.'

'We've all had to adjust,' Muriel replied, her tone softer than usual. 'You made it hard not to.'

'Yes, I played my part and that's the way it is but I can't run my life on her expectations, you can see that can't you?'

'I can, Ruth. It's a mess isn't it?'

'Sure is, sister! But I do love you!'

'That's a great little family we have there.'

'I know, but what about you, my older sister? When are you going to get yourself a fella?'

'Me? I don't think so. Spinsterhood for me. I've got my little quiet life and I'm contented.'

After an evening meal of roast chicken with all the trimmings the taxi arrived to return them to the station and as they stepped outside under a twilight sky beginning to shine with stars, André hung back with his mother.

'I'd like to come again, mum. And not leave it so long this time if that's alright?'

'Darling, you and Heather will be welcome any time you like.'

'I love you, mum.'

'I love you too, my son. I'm so proud of you. You get home safely, all four of you.'

She felt the last warmth of the day on her skin and something similar to gratitude take root in her chest—not dramatic or overwhelming, just steady and quiet. For today, at least, she wasn't Ruth Ellis the infamous murderer, or Ruth the recluse or even Ruth Ellis the celebrated artisan. She was a mum, and a sister, and a grandmother. And that, she thought, might only be enough.

Easter Sunday, 10 April 1975

Ruth rose early with the help of her small alarm clock. The farm was quiet except for the chickens who never seemed to sleep. The sky was only beginning to lighten, the faint suggestion of birdsong was rising in the hedgerows. She hadn't slept much, yet she didn't feel tired. There was an odd steadiness to her, as if her body had understood before her mind what sort of day this was going to be.

Twenty years ago David had walked out of, The Magdala public house and into her path. And then it was all over: the sound of her own voice calling his name, the noise, the blood, the flash of the weapon in her hand. And afterwards came the cell, the sentence, the silence. Ten years. A life of shame in itself.

She dressed with care. Not in black, she had long since stopped performing grief, but in a dove grey coat and a plain wool skirt. Sensible shoes, her dark hair pinned up. She looked, to anyone else, like a late middle aged woman on her way to a church service, or perhaps to visit an elderly relative. She moved slowly though as she had been thinking of this day for over a year. The 20th anniversary.

By half past eight, she was on the road. She didn't take the train, too many people, too many eyes. She had hired a car for the day, a modest grey Vauxhall, and driven herself. She wasn't frightened. Not of London. Not of memory. What could the past do to her now that it hadn't already done?

The city greeted her with indifference. Roads she used to know like the lines of her own palm now felt unfamiliar, as if someone had shaken the map and moved things about. She approached the Magdala pub from South Hill Park noting the changes and the new housing and stopped outside turning the engine off.

The Magdala stood there, almost unchanged. A little smarter, perhaps. The paint on the façade fresher. But the doorway was the same. The window still bore the curve of etched glass. Even the pavement had the same slight dip where water pooled after rain. She sat for a long time as her imagination remembered what she had done that day twenty years previously.

Ruth felt a desperate need to step outside the car but she felt unable to move and her hands clung to the steering wheel as she fixed her eyes on the pub. How much courage would it take for her to leave the car and walk towards the pub? No, she could not risk it. Would not risk it. Once again in her imagination the dreadful scene played out again and she closed her eyes and released her hands and breathed deeply. The pub was quiet—Easter Sunday wasn't much of a drinking day.

Ruth didn't cry. She hadn't cried in years. But there was a feeling, not sadness, exactly, and not guilt. Something stranger. As if she were remembering a version of herself she could no longer reach. A young woman with her nerves frayed to threads, trapped in something she had once believed was love.

She stayed for twenty minutes and nobody bothered her. Then she started the engine and drove west.

The journey to Buckinghamshire took longer than she remembered and she lost her way more than a few times despite previously purchasing an up to date map. There were more roundabouts now, more signs warning of congestion and more signs depicting many things with which she was not familiar. But eventually she reached the village of Penn and its church with its flint walls and the little gate that opened onto the churchyard.

Holy Trinity stood quiet under the spring sun, its roof warmed by a wash of gold. Ruth found David's grave only by searching eagerly. His headstone was simple: His name, the dates and a simple inscription. His mother had arranged it, Ruth assumed. She had never met the woman. She wondered now whether it had been cowardice or kindness on her part to stay away.

There were fresh lilies on the grave. So somebody still visited and that caused Ruth's eyes to smart. She knelt and touched the edge of the stone, her fingers brushing the cool lichen.

'I'm not sure if this was a good idea,' she said aloud, but quietly. 'But I thought I should come. Twenty years is a long time. Just to make sure you're okay.'

The wind stirred the grass. Far off, a blackbird twittered.

'I've changed,' she said. 'You probably wouldn't recognise me now. I don't think I'd recognise you, either. And maybe that's for the best. We were both rather stupid back then, weren't we?'

She didn't say, sorry. She had said it before, in courtrooms and in interviews, to strangers and to ghosts. It didn't make anything better. The truth was more complicated than a single word. She had loved him. He had destroyed her. She had destroyed him.

Eventually with the help of her cane, she stood. Her knees ached. She brushed the moss from her skirt and looked around the churchyard one last time wishing she had brought some flowers but it was too late now. A young couple was walking hand in hand along the gravel path, pausing occasionally to read the names of the dead. Life carried on, as it always did.

On the way back to the car, she passed the parish noticeboard. The Easter service had begun at eleven, followed by tea and hot cross buns. It was a shame she had missed it but she would never have gone in anyway. She had always liked hymns. But this wasn't a day for ceremony.

She drove home in silence. No radio. No music. Just the hum of the tyres and the ticking of the traficator as she turned off the main roads and back onto the familiar country roads.

Back at the farm, Sally had left a note on the kitchen table: Roast chicken in the oven. Hope today was what you needed. Love you XX.

Ruth poured herself a glass of water and stood by the sink, looking at the fields. The daffodils were still in bloom. Lambs in the next field scrambled after their mothers, unsteady and eager. She didn't feel lighter, not exactly. But something had shifted. The day had passed, and she had walked through it. Twenty years behind her. Perhaps, at last, she could stop walking in circles.

The roast chicken had been cooked to perfection—golden skinned and fragrant, but Ruth only managed a few mouthfuls. Sally, wisely, didn't press her. They ate in a comfortable silence, with the radio off and only the ticking of the kitchen clock between them.

Later, with the plates cleared, Ruth poured them both a small glass of brandy, and they sat in the front room in front of a log fire. Outside, the evening had deepened into a pale mauve dusk. The trees at the edge of the field stood in silhouette, unmoving.

'Well?' Sally asked, at last, gently.

Ruth didn't answer straight away. She stared into her glass, the way people in stories always did when searching for words.

'I didn't go in,' she said. 'To the pub, I mean.'

Sally nodded. 'Didn't think you would.'

'I thought about it. But I sat in the car and looked at it. And it looked the same. Same doorway. Same step. Same windows. It's odd how nothing changes and everything does.'

'Do you think that was enough?'

'Maybe.'

There was a long pause. Ruth reached down and ran her fingers along the edge of the hearthrug.

'I don't know what I was expecting. Some kind of feeling. Closure. That's what people call it, isn't it?'

Sally shrugged. 'It's just a word. Sometimes you don't get an ending. You just stop looking for one.'

'That's very insightful.'

Sally smiled. 'That's what I'm here for!'

'I found his grave,' Ruth added after a moment, 'someone had left lilies. I didn't stay long. Just said a few words. Not an apology. Just…what I needed to say.'

Sally took a sip of her drink. 'Do you feel different?'

'No. But I'm glad I went. It's not something I want to repeat, but…it felt necessary. Like oh, I don't know. I cried a little.'

There was a quiet crackle from the fire. A log shifted and grustled, sending up a burst of embers.

'You've carried it for so long, Ruth. Longer than anyone should.'

Ruth gave a soft laugh. 'It's lighter than it used to be. But it's never gone. I don't think it ever will be. He's part of my story now, the worst part, maybe, but still part of it.'

'Is that why you went today?'

Ruth looked at her. 'Partly. I suppose I wanted to see if the past still had power over me. Whether I'd flinch. Whether I'd run.'

'And did you?'

'No. I didn't run and I didn't flinch.'

To this, Sally raised her glass in a quiet salute and Ruth did the same, and they drank.

After a while, Sally stood and poked the fire, coaxing a fresh flame from the coals. Ruth watched her, grateful, as always, for her presence. No probing, no judgement, just warmth and solid ground.

'I think I'll sleep well tonight.'

Sally glanced at her with a smile. 'You deserve to, my darling.'

Ruth nodded. Then, as if speaking more to herself than anyone else, she added, 'that chapter's over. The rest is mine to write.'

Chapter 19
January 1977

The frost had been hard that morning, silvering the hedgerows and stiffening the ground beneath the boots of the six young women that were currently employed at the farm. Ruth had been in the lower field, walking for inspiration, her face turned towards the low and rising sun, when she heard the crash: a sharp and unnatural sound that cut through the still air. Instantly breaking her revelry, she hobbled as fast as she could back to the courtyard where she faced a most horrific scene.

The farm's long wooden ladder lay broken in the yard, one rung splintered clean through and Sally was crumpled beside it, two of her legs were at an angle that made Ruth momentarily gasp. Sally's eyes were open wide with shock, and her breath came in short, shallow gasps. Ruth reached her at the same time as Anne and Valerie who had torn over from one of the sheds. Ruth screamed at them to phone for an ambulance and cradled Sally's head.

'Jesus, Sally. Help's coming.'

'I can't feel my legs,' she whispered.

Ruth pressed her fingers to Sally's wrist, feeling the rapid thrum of her pulse. 'Don't move,' she said, her voice steadier than she felt. 'Help's coming. Someone get a blanket please?'

The ambulance took far too long in Ruth's opinion but later on she supposed it arrived in about the normal amount of time, its siren wailing through the quiet countryside. Waiting with Sally so distressed and cold was agonising. But the ambulance men worked with practiced efficiency, stabilising Sally's spine and securing her to a stretcher. Ruth rode with her to St Richard's Hospital in Chichester, leaving the farm to the employees. It was the beginning of three very long days.

At the hospital, the sterile smell of antiseptic and the bright, unforgiving lights made everything feel surreal. Doctors and nurses moved around them, speaking in hushed tones, their faces grave. And after what felt like hours, a doctor approached Ruth. He was middle aged, with kind eyes and a clipboard clutched to his chest. He guided her to a waiting room and they sat.

'Mrs Ellis? She's sustained a fracture to her lower thoracic vertebrae,' he said, we're preparing her for surgery to stabilise the spine, but I must be honest with you, the damage is severe and it's unlikely she'll regain movement below the waist.'

'Oh God!'

'She told me she fell off a ladder?'

'Yes, nobody saw it though.'

'So you have no idea how far she fell?'

'No, no idea at all. No chance of ever walking again?'

'I'm sorry. I've seen cases like this before and the spine is severed.'

Ruth nodded, his words washing over her like cold water. 'Can I see her?'

'For a very short time only. Please remember she is sedated.'

Sally was pale against the hospital sheets, an oxygen mask attached to her face. She turned her head as Ruth entered a private room, not even managing a weak smile. Ruth brought her face close to hers and kissed her on her cheek and Sally managed to focus on her face.

'Looks like I've gone and done something daft,' she murmured.

Ruth took her hand gently. 'You're going to get through this, Sally,' she said, the conviction in her voice surprising even herself.

'Someone will have to feed the chickens.'

'I'll make sure the chickens are fed. You make sure you get better, alright?'

'I put you down as next of kin in case anything happens.'

'Don't talk nonsense. I won't hear of it.'

'They said they are going to operate, Ruth. What are they going to do?'

'They are going to make you all better, darling. Please don't worry about it.'

'I'm going to dream of huge dancing chickens!' Her eyes closed.

Ruth looked over her shoulder towards a nurse who was standing by the door and gave her a questionable look which was instantly understood and she stepped forward.

'Don't be concerned. It's the sedation.'

Ruth turned back. 'Sally? It's me, Ruth. I'll see you soon, my darling.'

But there was no response and Ruth stepped away and unnecessarily said, 'look after her please. She's all I've got.'

The weeks that followed were a blur of hospital visits, consultations, and the slow, painful process of acceptance. Sally faced her new reality with a quiet resilience, her humour intact even as she grappled with the loss of her mobility.

At the farm, Ruth made the necessary adjustments. She arranged for a ramp to be installed at the front door, widened doorways, and converted the downstairs study into a bedroom. She learned to navigate the intricacies of wheelchair accessibility, liaising with occupational therapists and builders, ensuring that Sally could return home with dignity.

Dealing with the company itself was an entirely different matter and it was decided to employ a manager to oversee the day to day running of the business, a position that previously had been Sally's. The man Sally chose was a graduate from the London School of Economics called

Harry who had a degree in animal husbandry and he settled in to the position quickly.

When Sally returned to the farm after eight weeks in rehabilitation, the winter sun was still low in the sky, casting long shadows across the yard. Ruth helped her from the car, guiding the wheelchair up the new ramp and into the warmth of the kitchen.

'I never thought I'd be so happy to see the old place,' Sally said, her eyes misting over.

Ruth smiled, placing a hand on her shoulder. 'It's not the same without you.'

They settled into a new routine, their roles subtly shifting. Ruth helped out more around the place despite the extra effort from the employees, while Sally still managed the accounts and correspondence, her sharp mind undiminished and Harry took care of the actual physical business of running the place. A single man, he proved himself to be an intelligent, decent and affable manager and found accommodation in St Jude from which he travelled in every day on his motorbike.

In the quiet evenings, the two women sat by the fire, sipping tea and talking about everything and nothing. The bond between them, forged over years of shared experiences, grew stronger, tempered by adversity.

One December night, as the wind howled outside and the fire crackled in the hearth, Sally put aside her book and spoke plainly to Ruth.

'You know,' she said, 'I've been thinking. When the time comes, I want you to have the farm.'

Ruth looked at her, startled. 'Sally, I...what are you *talking* about?'

'No arguments,' Sally interrupted, her tone firm. 'You've put your heart into this place. It's as much yours as it ever was mine.'

Ruth stared at her, emotion tightening her throat. 'what nonsense you do talk', she whispered. 'What's bought this on?'

'Ruth, I know we have a nice life here but let's face facts, my accident has not exactly extended my life has it? Indeed it's done the opposite if the truth be told. I'm unlikely to live until I'm a very very old lady. The amount of drugs I take is bad for my liver and kidneys et cetera, et cetera. You know how it is. I'm probably going to pop off before you so I'm going to make a will and I'm going to leave you the farm. That's it. You deserve the farm. If I still had my children of course I would leave it to them but they're in heaven cursing me probably. I don't know and you're my best friend and I want you to have it so please take it. It's a gift for being my best and closest friend. Will you do that?'

Ruth nodded.

Outside, snow began to fall, blanketing the fields in white. Inside, the two women sat together, the warmth of the fire and their shared history wrapping around them like a comforter. They drank home made wine and neither talked.

Three uneventful years passed until October 1980 when two days before the ninth, Sally, before their evening meal, asked Ruth if she could make herself available on the eleventh.

'But that's a Saturday. Is this anything to do with my birthday!'

'Of course it is. I'm going to treat you.'

'You little vixen! What are you up to?'

'Wait and see! Come on we didn't celebrate your fiftieth did we? Because of one thing or another so we are definitely going to celebrate your fifty-fifth.'

'And what have you got in mind?'

'That would be telling wouldn't it? Just be ready by six o'clock and wear your best frock. Don't worry about me. Hazel's going to stay behind and sort me out is all I'll say. Apart from saying I've hired a special car for me and we are going to meet up in London. So suck it up and don't ask any more questions!'

'Yes, mam!'

In actuality it had been on Ruth's mind that celebrating her 55th year of life was one thing she had not been looking forward to. It was true that her life in general was contented now for she had made peace with her past except for two sections, one of which was her father to whom she still did not speak and the other was her mother to whom she had fallen out with many years ago and who had died the previous year.

These were wounds but they were superficial, not deep, more like gentle scars that could be covered with light clothing. In the front of her mind increasingly as she aged she never forgot and was frankly amazed she was there at all considering she was once destined to be executed. Therefore, as far as she was concerned any day added to her lifespan was a day to celebrate.

Her relationship with Sally had deepened to a remarkable extent after Sally's tragic accident and it had most definitely had an effect on the running of the business for Harry, the new manager, had proved to be so efficient with his new ways of thinking, that with Sally's approval, he had managed to improve productivity a great deal which brought in more investors which had changed the dynamics of the farm itself.

Ruth, although she now took no part in the economic running of the farm and almost never discussed that part of the farm with Sally, nevertheless could tell that Haven was changing from being a cosy and small, business into a commerce now known throughout southern England servicing supermarkets and worth twelve times more than when Ruth arrived.

Ruth, who knew nothing about raising chickens, also understood nothing about buying extra acres, extra sheds and now employing forty people. That was the difference but Ruth remembered the original five helpers and especially that girl that looked so much like the child that could have been hers in another life.

It was a crisp, copper toned evening in London, with the Strand slick from recent rain and the leaves underfoot turning shades of rust and gold. Ruth stood outside Simpsons, pulling her coat a little tighter against the chill, the autumn wind threading through her grey streaked hair. Behind her, the familiar red and gold awning of the restaurant fluttered in the breeze. The smell of roasted chestnuts from a nearby vendor mingled with the city's diesel tang and the scent of damp stone.

She had chosen a charcoal wool dress for the occasion, simple but elegant, with a burgundy scarf looped carefully around her neck. It had been years since she'd worn lipstick, but tonight, she had applied a muted rose shade, not out of vanity, exactly, but because her birthday felt like something worth marking.

Sally arrived in the adapted car shortly after, reversing expertly into the disabled bay. The lift mechanism hummed smoothly as she manoeuvred her wheelchair onto the pavement, wearing a heavy green overcoat and one of her trademark knitted berets—this one russet, to match the season.

'You're looking very Soho 1953,' Sally said with a grin, eyeing Ruth up and down.

'And you're looking like you should be offering me a toffee apple and a wartime coupon book,' Ruth shot back, smiling.

'Happy birthday, my darling.'

They embraced carefully. It had been a time of adjustments since Sally's accident, the broken back, the surgery, the long weeks of rehabilitation in Chichester. But tonight, they were reclaiming something. Not just a milestone, but a sense of possibility.

'I can't believe you kept this secret,' Ruth said as she leaned down to help straighten Sally's lap blanket.

'Well, it's not every day you turn fifty five,' Sally replied with a grin. 'I thought we'd mark the occasion in style.'

Inside, the restaurant it was as grand as the photographs Ruth had seen: dark wood panelling, tall windows letting in pale evening light, and silver service performed with quiet ceremony. The clink of cutlery and the murmur of suited diners reminded her faintly of, The Little Club, though this crowd leaned more towards old money than old mischief.

Their table, discreetly placed near a window, had a fine view of the room and the head waiter, on recognising Ruth's name, had arranged a small bouquet of late season roses at their place. Sally ordered champagne, a half bottle, 'because we're not completely decadent' and they toasted to Ruth's milestone.

'To the woman whose artistic merit knows no bounds and who still makes her own jam.'

'To the woman who made sure I didn't drink myself into a ditch in 1968,' Ruth replied.

They laughed. The food was excellent, roast beef carved at the table from a gleaming silver trolley, horseradish so sharp it brought tears to Ruth's eyes, and Yorkshire puddings the size of teacups. But more satisfying than the meal was the conversation: full of shared glances, sly digs, and memories neither needed to explain.

Between bites, Sally leaned in, conspiratorial. 'You realise we're running a business now? Not just a farm.'

Ruth raised an eyebrow.

'Your work is selling better than ever. The last batch to that gallery in Chichester? Gone in three days. And your commissions? You're having to turn people away.'

'I work because I need to,' Ruth said, half smiling. 'It's not meant to be an industry.'

Sally shrugged. 'Doesn't matter what it's meant to be. It is. And if I'm not mistaken, you're enjoying it more than you let on.'

'I suppose I am,' Ruth admitted. 'Especially since you now do my accounts. You've turned into a right boss.'

'Someone has to be. You're hopeless at saying no.'

They were finishing dessert, a treacle tart and a light lemon sorbet, when a shadow fell across their table. A tall man in an expensive suit stood nearby, holding a brandy glass, his expression tentative but unmistakably interested.

'Excuse me,' he said in a deep, polished voice. 'I don't mean to intrude, but, I believe I know you. You're, Ruth Ellis, aren't you?'

There was a moment of silence and instant suspicion. Sally's fork froze midway to her mouth. Ruth, though startled, kept her gaze level.

'Yes,' she said. 'And you are?'

'If you would permit me? I am, Mark van de Watering,' he said, offering a slight bow of his head as he offered his card which Ruth took.

'I do apologise. I didn't mean to bring up the past. But I've followed your work for some time. Your pieces, they're extraordinary.'

Ruth's surprise deepened. 'You know of my work?'

'I own three pieces,' he said smiling. 'I have a small gallery in Marylebone, well, not so small these days. Would you ever consider visiting? I'd love to show you the space. And if you're open to it…perhaps we could discuss exhibiting?'

Ruth never answered immediately. She was aware of Sally watching her, eyebrows arched in approval.

'I might be interested,' she said carefully. 'Although I'm not keen on being in the spotlight.'

Mark nodded, unfazed. 'That's perfectly understandable. But my offer stands. I'll send a note with details. No pressure, just an invitation. And now my profound apologies for interrupting your meal. Goodbye.'

He gave them both a gracious nod and retreated, melting into the crowd like smoke.

As the waiter brought coffee, Sally leaned in again, voice low but gleeful.

'Well, well. Looks like fifty-five's going to be more interesting than fifty.'

'I don't know, Sally,' Ruth said, sipping carefully. 'He could be trouble.'

'All the best ones are!'

'That's prison talk!'

They stayed late, letting the evening unwind around them. When they finally emerged, the Strand was lit with amber street lamps and the rumble of late traffic. Ruth pushed Sally's chair carefully over the curb and helped her back into the car.

As Sally drove through the glowing city to their hotel, Ruth looked at the world she'd once feared would forget her and knew definitely that it hadn't.

London–One Week Later

The train pulled into London Victoria just after ten on a blue skied Wednesday. Ruth stepped from the carriage with a careful steadiness, coat buttoned high, wearing gloves and a familiar knot of nerves quietly churning beneath her composed exterior. It had been a long time since she'd travelled to London alone to meet a specific man. Decades, in fact, and the city felt like anything other than a memory best left alone. But now, here she was again, standing at the edge of something she couldn't define. What the Dickens was she doing here?

She took a black cab to Knightsbridge, letting the city drift past in autumn tones, commuters hunched in their coats, leaves skimming the gutters, noticing the glint of golden light illuminating the London trees. The cab turned down a quiet side street near Harrods, and she saw the gallery nestled between a florists and an antique bookshop.

'Van de Watering & Cole,' read the subtle, etched glass.

Ruth paid the driver and took a breath before pushing the heavy glass door.

The gallery was warm, surprisingly so, not in temperature, but in atmosphere. Soft, natural light poured in through high windows, spilling across polished oak floors. The space greeted her with quiet confidence, open plan, white walls, and lighting that warmed the clean architectural lines. But what truly struck her was the care in presentation. Sculptures, vessels, and art objects were arranged with deliberate simplicity.

Some were placed on plinths, others inside glass cases, and a few nestled along long oak shelves. The scent of wood polish and kiln fired glaze lingered faintly in the air. Walls were a clean white, each one showcasing a small but thoughtfully curated set of paintings, ceramics and drawings. There was space around each piece, room to breathe and a sense that nothing here had been chosen by accident.

'Ruth!' She heard a rich and familiar voice.

Mark appeared from a back room, wearing a dark turtleneck and slate coloured jacket, his manner professional but warm.

'You found us easily, I hope?'

'I did. Though I was half tempted to turn around at Victoria.'

He smiled. 'But you didn't.'

'No. I thought that might be cowardly.'

'I doubt you're capable of cowardice.'

She gave a short covering laugh. 'You don't know me well enough to say that.'

'Then perhaps I'll earn the right.'

He gestured around the gallery. 'Would you like the tour?'

She nodded, and they moved slowly from room to room. He spoke with an art dealer's rhythm, enthusiastic but measured, informed without arrogance. Ruth listened more than she spoke, her eyes scanning each work, noting the soft palettes, the figurative pieces next to the more experimental ones. There was an intelligence to the curation, but also a warmth, not one of the pieces felt deliberately obscure or self indulgent. This wasn't a space filled with canvases, it was one devoted to form, tactility, and craft. The collection ranged from contemporary ceramics and small scale sculpture to minimalist installations that blurred the line between art and function. It was, in Ruth's eyes, an honest gallery. Nothing gimmicky. Nothing desperate for attention.

'And here,' Mark said, pausing in the final room, 'is where I picture your work.'

Displayed here were pieces in muted earth tones burnished terracotta, deep oxide glazes, stoneware bowls with iron speckles and pale slip decoration. There was a hush to the room, as if it invited contemplation rather than reaction.

'I first saw your ceramics in Brighton, three years ago,' Mark continued. 'At a coastal exhibition on hand built forms. Your pieces were different. They had a kind of restraint, but also…one of feeling. There was one, a tall, lopsided vessel, cracked at the lip, I couldn't stop thinking about it.'

'I remember. He was called, 'Vigil,' Ruth said softly. 'I wasn't going to include him. He felt too personal.'

He nodded. 'That's exactly why it mattered.'

Ruth approached one of the plinths, running her gloved fingers above the rim of a celadon glazed bowl. Her own work was so often quiet, textural, intended to be touched and lived with. And yet here it would be placed on display, lit, examined, perhaps even judged.

'I'm not used to being treated like an artist,' she said. 'I still think of myself as a maker.'

'Mark smiled. 'That's exactly what this space honours. The art of making.'

He let the silence settle, then added, 'We're planning a winter exhibition, functional forms as art objects. Pieces that live in the domestic world but carry deeper meaning. I'd love for your ceramics to be a centrepiece.'

Ruth glanced at the empty plinths and clean display cases. She imagined her stoneware, the ash glazes, the rough textures from local Sussex clays, sitting among them. It was intimidating. And it was tempting.

'I'll need time to think,' she said. 'And I'll need to fire some new work.'

'There's time,' Mark replied. 'The opening is in March '81. You'd be the only ceramicist among sculptors and mixed media artists. I think that contrast would say something important.'

Ruth gave a slow nod. 'Perhaps.'

He led her to a small office at the back, where he poured coffee from a French press and offered her a slice of homemade walnut cake from a tin.

'My sister bakes,' he explained. 'I'm merely the grateful recipient.'

Over coffee, the conversation turned warmer. She asked about the other artists he represented, and he gently asked about her studio, her kilns and the way she worked. And in return he was genuinely interested in her creative process, in the quiet, solitary rhythm of her days.

'I still do everything by hand,' Ruth enthused. 'No electric wheel, no assistants. It keeps me honest.'

'I expected nothing less.'

They sat opposite each other in armchairs, steam curling from their mugs. Ruth relaxed, grateful for the quiet civility of the space.

'What made you recognise me the other night?' she asked, looking up. 'It can't have been an article.'

Mark hesitated. 'No. It wasn't.'

He met her gaze directly.

'My parents lived in Hampstead in the fifties. I was a boy, but I remember, the news, the headlines. Your photograph. The silence in our house when it came on the television. Years later, I read about your reprieve. And then I saw your work, in a small show in Brighton, I think. There was something…I don't know. It stayed with me. And then, when I saw you at Simpson's…it clicked and something moved me and I felt I had to speak with you.'

Ruth didn't respond at first. The past felt oddly distant, like a reflection in a moving train window, still visible, still hers, but moving away.

'Well,' she said after a long pause. 'I'm not that woman anymore.'

'No,' Mark agreed, 'but everything she endured is what makes you, you. And that's what people respond to.'

The October sky had now grown darker, promising rain. The afternoon had slipped by and Ruth rose and thanked him for his time, coffee and reassurance.

'I'll most definitely think about it,' she said again, this time more firmly.

Mark saw her to the door and hailed a taxi. 'Take all the time you need. And please keep in touch. You have my number. Goodbye.'

In the taxi she pulled her coat around her. London felt a little different than it had that morning. Not less complicated. But more open. A place with more possibilities. And with that, the taxi returned her to Victoria Station, her coat wrapped tight, her thoughts shifting with each moment toward the possibility of something entirely new.

Chapter 20
March 1981

Ruth's taxi stopped outside the gallery as the sky gave way to a fine spring dusk, soft as ash. Streetlights blinked into life along the pavement, drawing halos in the puddles left from an earlier shower. She paused before opening the door, her gloved fingers resting lightly on the handle. She exhaled slowly, watching the mist of her breath disappear into the evening. Then, with a steadying nod to herself, she stepped onto the pavement and into the next chapter of her life.

The gallery stood in quiet elegance, a narrow fronted Georgian building discreetly tucked along a side street in Knightsbridge. Its windows glowed gold in the fading light, and inside, she could make out the glimmer of porcelain under low, warm spotlights. Her name, painted modestly in a serif hand on the glass, still startled her: Ruth Ellis–Ceramics. It was the first time she'd seen it written like that, as if she belonged here, among the artists, the sculptors and the makers.

'Oh Sally! I wish you were here!'

She drew her coat tighter and walked to the entrance. A member of staff greeted her with a kind smile and murmured her name, then led her in. Her footsteps felt loud on the wooden floor. The room was already half full: strangers sipping wine, bending over the displays, nodding appreciatively. She had been warned it might feel surreal, like watching one's own life from behind a pane of glass. And indeed, it did.

Each piece of hers had been arranged with care: Mark had insisted on simplicity: low plinths, clean linen cloths, one or two items per stand. A white glazed vase with hairline cobalt etchings. A wide bowl, speckled like an eggshell. And in the far corner, her favourite: a tall, tapered vessel inspired by the Norfolk cliffs she'd visited years ago, the ochre tones running like veins through the clay.

Isabell the manager approached, a tall woman with grey streaked hair and an Italian silk scarf wound round her neck. 'Hello, Ruth, you've made it,' she said warmly. 'And in time. We've already had some admirers. I've started taking names. I think we'll get a good number of orders.

Ruth nodded mutely, grateful and overwhelmed. She had wanted to call Sally, to tell her she'd arrived, that it wasn't as terrifying as she'd feared. But Sally was at home, curled under blankets with flu, her voice thin and raspy that morning. 'Go,' she'd said. This is your night, darling. I'll be here when you get back.'

The sound of her name pulled her back to the room.

'Ruth, could you join us over here?'

The manager called her again from the other side of the room. A man in a tailored navy suit was standing beside her, pointing at a large, wide mouthed urn. Ruth crossed the space slowly. She was wearing a simple charcoal dress and a string of freshwater pearls Sally had given her on her last birthday. She felt exposed, like clay before the kiln. But when the man turned and smiled, something settled.

He was asking about the glaze: how she'd achieved the uneven, riverbed texture. She explained, carefully but softly, trying to keep her voice from shaking. One by one, others drifted over. They asked questions, made polite remarks, used words like 'tactile', 'ancient,' and 'delicate'. She smiled and thanked them and nodded, though she felt like a ghost floating between islands of conversation.

And then, she saw him.

Mark Van de Watering — the wealthy gallery patron who had first spoken to her at Simpsons, on her birthday. Such a handsome man and one that had featured in one or two daydreams of Ruth's since then. Sally, being the rude thing she was had told her to, 'go for it' of course but Ruth had told her that she was now too old for that sort of shenanigans! But now, looking at him in his dark suit he looked so handsome. He was across the room now, standing close to a dark haired man, their heads bent together…their fingers intertwined.

Ruth's breath caught. She hadn't expected that, although she supposed she should have. It wasn't jealousy, not exactly — she had never harboured illusions. But something in her soul dropped, the way a bird might when startled by a heavy breeze.

She disappointedly quickly turned away towards a nearby table, pretending to study a set of stoneware cups when a moment later, she felt a light touch on her elbow.

'Ruth,' Mark said warmly, 'I'm so glad you made it. And you've already got a crowd. Isabell tells me she's taking plenty of orders.' He smiled, then gestured beside him. 'I'd like you to meet someone. This is my brother — Nigel.'

Ruth looked up.

Nigel was obviously younger than Mark but like him he was tall and lean, with hair the colour of old oak. His eyes were gentle, unassuming, but curious — the way someone might look at a work of art and want to understand the story behind it. He offered his hand with a smile.

'It's an honour,' he said. 'Mark's been talking about your work for months. He was right', it's stunning. May I offer you my congratulations.'

Ruth managed a confused smile, and for a moment, all the noise in the room receded.

'I'll leave you two to chat for a moment excuse me.'

They talked. First about the pieces. Then about kilns, and glazes, and Cornwall, where Nigel had once lived for a year in a house with no central heating and taught himself to cook soup on a wood stove. Then about the weather, and books, and the light in late March, and why London always felt lonelier in spring than in winter.

She wasn't sure how long they stood there. At some point, a waiter passed by with a tray and she took a glass of wine. Her hand no longer shook. A bell chimed multiple times somewhere — the front door opening and closing. Mark and Isabell circled the room like conductors, collecting compliments and names for the order book.

And all the time Ruth stood beside Nigel, her cheeks warm from the wine, her heart a little unmoored. Eventually, the crowd began to thin. A few friends stayed behind to speak to Mark while others lingered by the door with coats and umbrellas. Eventually Mark reappeared at their side.

'We're heading off,' he said with a glance to his own lady companion. 'But I hope you two will continue your conversation.' He smiled, and then to Nigel, 'don't keep her out too late. Ruth? Where are you staying?'

'The Kingsley Hotel, Holborn.'

Ruth laughed and the sound surprised her.

Nigel laughed too. 'There's a fab wine bar down the road. It's quiet, has a good Rioja, and the chairs are ugly but comfortable. May I buy you a tipple to celebrate?'

She hesitated only a second remembering Sally's words, then nodded.

The wine bar was narrow and dimly lit, with tiny lamps shaped like tulips on each table. They sat by the window and ordered one bottle, then another. They talked of nothing and everything. She told him about the farm, about Sally, about the feel of wet clay between her fingers. He told her about his work as a barrister, and how he wanted to write a novel one day but didn't yet know what it would be about.

The hours slipped by like silk.

At one point, Ruth saw their reflection in the window her face softened by laughter. His hand, resting lightly near hers. A pause. A breath. She looked away quickly, her heart fluttering like it hadn't in years. Something was shifting, she could feel it, not like an earthquake, but like the slow turn of the tide. And she was still standing. Still here. But there was doubt. Why was she drawn to these upper class families? Was this going to be a repeat of what happened previously?

Mindful of the time Nigel escorted her by cab to the Kingsley Hotel and they stood outside rather nervously as he took her hand.

'Ruth? I am so glad to have met you and I would be honoured if we could meet again.'

'Nigel? Surely, your brother has told you who I am?'

'He has mentioned who you *once* were and of course I am cognizant of your name and that is not the person who I see before me this evening.'

'And who is that?'

'A woman who is talented, intelligent…and desirable.'

'I'm older than you.'

'I know it's a cliche but it's just a number.'

'I don't know, Nigel. You are a lovely man and I like you very much but…'

'I tell you what. Spend a few days with me and I will charm you! We will spend some time together in London, take in the sights and you can get to know me better and then you can decide whether I'm fit for purpose. What do you say?'

'You are charming!'

'I know!'

'When then?'

'Tomorrow?'

'I can't, my friend is ill and I must look after her and I have orders to fulfil. May I call you? And I mean that. I will call you.'

'You promise?'

'I promise.'

'Then with that promise I will say good night. Good night, madam!'

Nigel bent forward and kissed her gently on her cheek and she smiled before she entered the lobby giving him one last look. He stood smiling and raised his hat which she thought was charming.

When Ruth arrived at Haven the next morning, she found Sally considerably improved but had a surprising story to tell. So, over an extended breakfast after Sally's private nurse left, she told her an astonishing story.

'It's lucky the nurse was here because I wasn't able to get to the door and I heard her speaking to a man. I could tell it was a man. But then up she comes and tells me that there's a man called, Benedict downstairs wanting to speak to me. And I thought, Benedict? I don't know anybody called, Benedict. Then it hits me.'

'Your ex husband…'

'Dead right.'

'Christ! What did you do?'

'I said, show him up. And up he came and, God! What a wreak of a man. I reckon he must have lost half of his weight since the last time I saw him. He was like a bloody pole. He stood in the doorway of my bedroom, his eyes all sunken in some old suit and literally, I thought, what the F!'

'Why was he there?'

'Well, I got him to sit and it turns out that the woman he married after divorcing me died from some sort of bone cancer a few months previously and the thing was, he really had no idea why he was there.'

'That's weird.'

'Tell me about it. As he was telling it, he didn't look right and I got the feeling he was confused he was there… oh, I don't know why he was there.'

'But the nurse was there?'

'Thank God, yes. I told him to go and make himself a coffee while the nurse made me comfortable and while he was downstairs I told her everything and she understood. I told her that a full explanation would have to follow later. Anyway she phoned the local gendarme who sent along a constable who removed him peacefully I may add and so far I haven't heard or seen him since but whether he's going to return I don't know.'

'I'm so sorry I wasn't here for you.'

'Don't be silly. I'm sorry I missed your grand debut. Now, how did it go? I want full details!'

Sally enjoyed listening to everything Ruth had to say about the previous evening and was proud of her but she sat up and became more attentive when Ruth started to talk about the last part of the evening.

'You went to a *bar*? With him!'

'It was a wine bar. Not a scruffy old boozy pub. It was quiet and discreet.'

'Ruth, you old devil! His *brother*! Oh, look at you! You like him, don't you? If you were sixteen, you'd be blushing!'

'He's handsome and charming of course. Impeccable manners and that's what troubles me.'

'Why should that trouble you?'

'Because he and his brother come from an upper class family and if you remember, I don't exactly fit in with those sort of people? Remember, I shot one of them?'

'Darling, that was twenty-five years ago and the bloody world's moved on since then and you have to. The only thing you need to ask yourself is, is he a nice man? Is he a good man? Is he? What does your guts tell you?'

'My guts are confused.'

'Does he know about you?'

'Yes he knows all about me. He's a barrister!'

'Well, that will be useful if you get in trouble with the law again! Sorry, that's good, and he wants to see you again?'

'He's made it plain he would very much like to see me again.'

'That's wonderful, so what's stopping you?'

'My guts?'

'Ruth? You got to take a chance, my darling. You've overcome so many hurdles. This could be your last hurdle. Take a chance my darling.'

The first week of April brought with it a shy kind of spring: hesitant and pale at first, but full of quiet promise. In Hyde Park, daffodils tipped their yellow heads toward the last of the watery sunlight of the day, and the air, though still touched with a wintry crispness, held a gentleness that made breathing a pleasure.

Ruth stood at the park gate near Lancaster Gate tube station, her gloved hands wrapped tightly around each other as she waited. She hadn't been to Hyde Park in years, perhaps not since before prison, before David, before all of it and the space felt both enormous and yet comfortingly familiar. She had forgotten how vast London could feel when it opened up, shedding its noise in favour of green and birdsong.

Then she saw Nigel, striding lightly through the gate toward her, his collar turned up against the breeze, a boyish smile widening as he caught her eye. He looked like a man who belonged in the spring—carefree, fresh faced, unkempt in a way that suggested strength and confidence.

'I hope I haven't kept you waiting,' he said, falling into step beside her as they entered the park.

'Not at all,' Ruth smiled. 'I was early. It's my habit.'

They walked slowly, not touching, the distance between them filled with the soft crunch of gravel and the occasional chirp of a bold robin. Hyde Park was busy with other Londoners who had caught the scent of spring and decided to chase it, but it never felt crowded. The wide footpaths and endless green absorbed everyone.

'It's strange,' Ruth said after a pause. 'I used to come here as a teenager. But I haven't been in ages. It feels like another life.'

Nigel glanced at her. 'That's not necessarily a bad thing, is it? Other lives? Sometimes I think each of us need a few.'

She smiled, turning her head toward the Serpentine, where ducks bobbed on the pale water. 'Yes. I suppose I've had at least two. Maybe more.'

They talked easily, their conversation light but never shallow. She told Nigel about her studio, her ceramics and how something as soft and wet as clay could, under the right conditions, become hard enough to last for centuries. And Nigel told her about the gallery, and how his brother

Mark could spot talent in places no one else bothered to look. He also spoke briefly about his work as a commercial barrister working in Middle Temple Gardens.

As they crossed a small footbridge near the Dell, the sun caught the water, and for a moment everything around them shimmered in gold. Ruth stopped without thinking, and Nigel paused too, watching her face more than the view.

'You really see things, don't you?' he said softly.

Ruth turned towards him, a little caught off guard. 'Do I?'

'Yes,' he said. 'That's what I noticed at your exhibition. You don't just make beautiful things. You observe. You translate.'

She felt a warmth rise to her face, not exactly embarrassment, but something close. Praise always unsettled her. Praise from men especially. But what he had said was true because since she had been a child she had always observed things about nature and had drawn things and had secretly wanted to be an artist. But that hidden passion was drowned with the coming of puberty particularly given the family and the society into which she had been born.

'Thank you,' she said, letting her gaze drift back to the water. 'That means a lot.'

By the time they left the park and caught a cab toward Knightsbridge, the last of the light was slipping behind the rooftops. London glowed in its usual amber and grey twilight. The bistro Nigel had chosen was tucked discreetly off a side street, a place Ruth had never noticed before, though she'd passed the area countless times.

Inside, it was warm, dimly lit by pendant bulbs and flickering candles. The maître d' greeted Nigel like a regular, and they were seated at a small table by the window. The menus were slim, handwritten and seasonal. Ruth ordered grilled sea bass with lemon and rosemary while Nigel chose venison.

For the first few minutes, they spoke about the food, the lighting and the way the music wasn't too loud. But then, as the wine flowed and the edge of formality wore away, the conversation deepened.

Ruth found herself talking about Sally and how the farm had become both a refuge and a cage: how watching someone grow older, in pain and in limitation, had changed her perspective on what it meant to live freely.

Nigel listened without interruption, only nodding now and then. When she finished, he didn't offer platitudes. He simply reached for his glass and said, 'you're brave, Ruth. Not in a noisy way. But quietly. And I think that's rarer.'

They lingered over dessert—shared, though she'd protested at first. Chocolate tart with blood orange. He insisted she have the last bite. She let him.

When the bill came, he paid without fuss. Outside, the street was quieter now, the evening cooled. The cab they hailed drove slowly, as if unwilling to break the day.

As they parted at the entrance to her usual hotel, Ruth touched his arm.

'Thank you, Nigel. I didn't think I'd enjoy myself today as much as I did.'

He smiled, eyes crinkling. 'Then we'll have to do it again. Soon.'

And she nodded, still unsure what exactly she'd started, but knowing that something new had begun.

Several telephone calls later.

It had rained earlier in the day, but by evening the streets of Soho were drying under a soft amber light, reflected in scattered puddles and the glazed shopfronts along Old Compton Street. Ruth stood beneath the Prince Edward Theatre's gilt awning, glancing up at the Evita poster lit with theatrical confidence. She smoothed the front of her jacket, aware of the flutter in her chest. Nigel appeared moments later, uncharacteristically breathless and apologetic, brushing a stray lock of hair from his forehead as he greeted her with a grin.

'Only five minutes late,' he said. 'Which, considering the state of the Northern line, might qualify as early.'

Ruth smiled. 'You're lucky I didn't give up and go back to the hotel.'

'You'd never miss, Evita!'

He was right, of course. She'd mentioned in passing that she'd always been curious about the show, how an actress, a woman, could rise to power and be worshipped and reviled in equal measure. The notion had struck a chord. And now here they were, tickets in hand, weaving into the plush interior of the theatre where the red velvet seats and golden ornamentation offered a kind of old world sanctuary from the chaos outside.

As the lights dimmed and the overture swelled, Ruth felt herself swept along. The spectacle was dazzling, but it was the intimacy of the performances that caught her off guard. Eva's hunger, her rise, the adoration and the bitter loneliness that followed—it was as though the spotlight cracked her open. She felt her throat tighten at unexpected moments, especially during, 'You Must Love Me,' when the mask slipped and grief rose to the surface.

She didn't look at Nigel during the performance, but she felt his presence keenly, like a warmth at her side. At the final applause, he leaned in and whispered, 'That was extraordinary. Thank you for making me see it.'

'Me?' she laughed. 'You're the one who bought the tickets.'

He shrugged. 'Still. I think you led me here.'

They found a small Italian restaurant on a quiet street beyond the theatre crowds, candle lit and low ceilinged, with old wine bottles repurposed as candlesticks. Nigel ordered a bottle of red without asking, he seemed to know instinctively what she liked, and they fell into conversation easily. The wine loosened them both, but it wasn't only that. It was the comfort of time already shared. There was no need for flirtation, no affectation, just talk.

They spoke about the performance, yes, but also about other things, Ruth's past jobs, Nigel's struggles with his own difficult work on occasions and the sometimes strained relationship with his brother, Mark. He was candid in a way that surprised her, speaking about their mother, and the shadow of expectations that had shaped both brothers differently. Mark had always been the businessman, the curator while Nigel had been the dreamer who had been expected to become something more practical, something he'd quietly refused which is why he chose the legal world.

She asked him in what case he was involved at the moment.

'Nothing spectacular, just insurance fraud,' he said, 'down to earth nuts and bolts.'

'You make that sound like hard work,' she said gently.

He smiled. 'Maybe it is. The work is constant.'

By the time Nigel hailed a cab on Shaftesbury Avenue, the night had settled into a cool hush. They rode back to her hotel with the music of the theatre not only echoing in Ruth's mind, but with a warmth that lingered from their shared laughter and the steady way Nigel had looked at her, as though time were a thing to be held gently, not rushed. Once again he had kissed her on her cheek.

Two weeks latter they met again, this time in daylight. The Tate Gallery stood noble and white against a pale sky, its classical columns softened by climbing shadows as the sun shifted westward. Inside, the gallery offered space to breathe. Ruth had always loved its quietude, the way it held both chaos and clarity on its walls.

They wandered side by side, letting their conversation ebb and flow between silences, pausing often. At a Francis Bacon piece, Nigel tilted his head.

'It's violent, but somehow not cruel,' he said.

Ruth nodded slowly. 'Like waking from a nightmare and realising it was only your own mind punishing you.'

They turned corners and came upon unfamiliar works, raw, provocative, bright with new voices. Ruth found herself drawn to a ceramic installation, jagged and asymmetric, unlike anything she would make. Yet it made her fingers twitch with inspiration.

'You're thinking about the clay,' Nigel said, quietly amused.

'I can't help it. It's a sickness. But actually I'm also thinking about what some of the wardresses in Holloway would have thought of me now doing this.'

'Whatever do you mean?'

'All this is so highbrow and they thought of me as a common bitch. It's so laughable.'

'It goes deep with you doesn't it. Your past I mean.'

'Yes it's the sort of thing that never really goes away.'

'I accept you for what you are, you know. You must believe that.'

'For what I am. That's an interesting sentence.'

'No,' he said. 'It's love.'

They sat on a bench opposite a vast abstract canvas that seemed to move as the light changed. Ruth let the moment stretch, not needing to fill it. Nigel's hand was near hers on the bench, and for the first time in years, she felt a desire to close that small space between them…not out of need, but out of recognition. She didn't act on it, not yet. But the thought stayed with her.

They had tea in the café downstairs. He talked about a novel he was planning and she listened intelligently but her mind could not forget what he said that he accepted her for what she was.

When she returned to the farm that evening, the spring light casting long shadows across the fields, Sally naturally asked how her day had been.

This time Ruth smiled. 'It was…illuminating. He said he accepts me for what I am.'

London was warming by degrees. Late spring stretched across rooftops and riverbanks, coaxing crocuses to bloom and casting longer shadows in the afternoons. Ruth had begun to dress differently, an entirely new wardrobe, and she enjoyed choosing and buying it.

On a clear Thursday evening, she met Nigel outside Ronnie Scott's in Soho. He had secured the tickets days in advance. 'I know it's not ceramics,' he'd said, 'but I thought we might try something a little less… fired.' He grinned at his own wordplay, and Ruth had chuckled. She wore a dark wrap and a strand of antique glass beads. She preferred to wear things that did not cost the earth.

Inside, the room was intimate, low lit, the scent of old wood and whisky hanging in the air. A small quartet played with lush elegance, notes slipping like silk through the room. Nigel ordered them cocktails, an old fashioned for himself, and a French 73 for Ruth, who only agreed when he told her it was what Ava Gardner used to drink.

They spoke little while the band played. Ruth let herself lean back in the curve of the banquette, her gaze moving from the saxophonist's fingers to Nigel's profile, lit intermittently by candlelight. He didn't know she was watching him: he was absorbed entirely in the music. She felt an ache that wasn't pain, more like recognition. How long had it been since she had let herself sit beside someone like this, with no need to guard her thoughts?

Afterwards, they walked back through Soho, the streets alive with laughter and spilled light. 'Did you enjoy it?' he asked.

She nodded. 'I liked the way they weren't afraid to leave space between the notes. So much music tries to fill every second.'

For one second she was going to add that her father used to be a musician but she did not want to take the conversation in that direction so she held her tongue.

'And people,' he added, glancing at her. 'We fill the silence because we're frightened of what it might say.'

They stopped at a late night patisserie and shared a slice of pear tart, standing under a neon sign. Her coat was buttoned up to her throat, but her cheeks were warm.

That weekend, Ruth invited Nigel to her studio, a converted outbuilding at the far edge of the farm. Sally had arranged for a ramp to be built some months earlier, and Nigel wheeled her out into the sunlight before joining Ruth among her shelves of clay and glazes.

'I'm no artist,' he said, staring at a coil of earthenware. 'I once glued two fingers together in school with PVA.'

'You'll be fine,' Ruth replied, handing him an apron and pulling her hair into a knot. 'Just don't try to make anything serious. Make a shape that feels like laughter, or calm.'

The studio smelled of earth and lemon oil. Morning light slanted in through dusty panes. As she worked at her wheel, shaping a shallow bowl, Ruth watched Nigel beside her at the hand building table. He had rolled a piece of clay into a ridiculous spiral—something between a snail and a storm cloud.

She laughed. 'That's either genius or nonsense.'

'Possibly both,' he said proudly.

They grew messy with clay, smearing lines across their forearms, teasing each other. At one point, he accidentally splashed slip onto her apron and tried to wipe it away, only making it worse.

'You're a menace,' she told him, but she didn't step back.

There was a pause then, not unlike the ones in the music from earlier that week—intentional, open and waiting.

Nigel looked at her hands. 'You create things from mud and heat and time. It's alchemy, Ruth.'

She felt a sting behind her eyes. 'It's survival,' she said quietly. 'For a long time, I made things because it was the only way I could keep going.'

He touched her wrist, lightly. 'And now?'

She met his gaze. 'Now, I think I do it because it's the only way I can tell the truth.'

The trees were beginning to blossom. The orchard beyond the field was laced with white, and a pair of swallows dipped in the air like brushstrokes. Ruth glanced through the window, the clay cooling on her fingertips. She didn't know what tomorrow would bring—whether this thing between them would hold or falter—but here, in the quiet warmth of her studio, she felt the ground beneath her was finally beginning to settle.

Their eyes met and Nigel pulled her gently towards her. She folded easily into his arms and their lips touched as Ruth's eyes closed. She knew instantly the past was gone. There was no more, David. No more, Desmond. No more anybody else. There was just this gorgeous gentle handsome man who cared for her.

Nigel hadn't told Ruth where they were going. He simply had telephoned and said, 'Pack for the weekend. Nothing fancy. Something warm.' When the taxi pulled up outside Marylebone Station, she raised an eyebrow, half smiling. 'You're abducting me, then?'

'If I were, I'd at least bring wine and better shoes,' he grinned, shouldering her overnight bag.

The train trundled northwest through green stained glass, towns melting into pasture and hills. Ruth watched the countryside unfold—hedgerows and lambs, church spires blinking in the mist. With each mile, London slipped further away, as did the clatter of galleries and the weight of past decades.

They arrived in Moreton-in-Marsh before midday where a rental car waited for them. The air was fresh with a faint sweetness and a promise of wild flowers and damp earth. Nigel drove without haste, meandering along quiet lanes rimmed with low stone walls.

Their lodgings was a converted shepherd's cottage on the edge of Upper Slaughter—the sort of place where silence had texture. The walls were thick, the windows latticed, and the hearth still smelled faintly of smoke and lavender polish. In the garden, a blackbird sang from the bare branches of an apple tree. Ruth stood still in the doorway, breathing it in.

'Do you like it?' Nigel asked, setting down their bags.

She nodded. 'I haven't been anywhere this quiet since... I don't know when.'

'No 'phones. No clocks. No noise,' he said, and added softly, 'just us.'

That afternoon, they wandered slowly into the village. Ruth wore an old wool coat and Nigel borrowed a walking stick from the inn for no reason other than he liked the feel of it. They found a crumbling church with a moss covered sundial and lingered by a river no wider than a bath, its water crystal clear. In a tiny tea room, they ordered scones with too much cream and sat side by side on a bench worn smooth by time.

'Tell me something you've never told anyone,' she said, lightly—but not playfully.

He paused, then said, 'I used to dream of being a pianist. Before I did what I chose to do. But I gave it all up after taking half a dozen lessons.'

Ruth smiled. 'What happened?'

'I realised that I didn't have a head for music.'

'Oh, love!'

He shrugged, laughing a little. 'Don't get me wrong, I love music I just can't hold a tune.'

She thought about it a moment. 'That might be the most beautiful thing you've told me.'

That night, it rained—a soft, unbothered drizzle, tapping against the windows. They stayed in, lighting a fire and opening a bottle of red. Ruth had brought one of her smaller pieces—a fired porcelain bowl glazed in midnight blue—and placed it on the mantelpiece almost without thinking. It looked as though it belonged there.

Later, Nigel sat cross legged on the rug, turning the bowl in his hands. Do you name your work?

'Only the ones I keep. That one's called, After Silence.'

'It's full of space.'

She nodded. 'I wanted to create something quiet enough to hold grief.'

He didn't answer immediately, then said, 'I lost someone once too. A long time ago. My father.'

Their eyes met across the firelight. Ruth felt her breath catch. 'It was for David.' she said softly.

Nigel nodded. 'You don't have to explain. I guessed.'

But she wanted to. 'It was so long ago. And for a long time, I didn't think I'd feel anything like this again. Not joy. Not hunger. Certainly not…love.'

The word sat between them, bright and real.

He reached for her hand. 'You're not alone anymore, Ruth.'

There was no ceremony to the moment, no swelling music. Just the hush of flame and rain, the gentle tremor of two people no longer pretending they weren't falling in love. Ruth leaned against his shoulder, her head resting in the space between his neck and collar. His arm slipped around her, warm and sure.

They didn't speak for a long time after that. The fire hissed, the rain thickened, and the world outside their cottage fell away.

Chapter 21
December 1983

The farm was its normal clamorous self that morning when Ruth awoke. She heard the identifiable and distant sound of several thousand hens plus the farmworkers already hard at work and before she moved, she thought briefly about what she had planned to do that day.

Then it was out of bed and to the kitchen to brew coffee. She remembers waving to Amere, one of the workers from shed two, from the kitchen window. She had spoken to him often as he had expressed a desire himself to learn as much as he could about ceramics.

The coffee brewed, she took a tray to Sally's room and knocked gently.

'Hi, honey. You awake?'

There was no answer.

'Honey…I've got your coffee…'

A strange sensation settled in her chest. Something wasn't right. Ruth hesitated before opening Sally's bedroom door. The sight before her was eerily peaceful. Sally lay in her bed, her hands resting lightly over the duvet, her head turned gently to one side, her hair partly obscuring part of her face as if she had drifted away peacefully with no distress. Ruth simply saw the quiet surrender of a beautiful life that had slipped away.

For a long moment, Ruth didn't move. Then, she stepped forward and reached towards her as if she could undo the moment, as if touching Sally's arm might bring her back. As if trying to understand where she had gone. As if to wake her. But the coldness under her fingertips was final.

Ruth remembers little of what happened next. She remembers calling the emergency services but the next two days became a blur. A doctor arrived and gave her something to relax her and Harry took overall charge of the household. Nigel arrived on the third day and stayed over and that helped Ruth as he organised Sally's funeral. This was only accomplished after a telephone call by Mr Chantree, Sally's solicitor who informed her that the autopsy confirmed that she had passed away due to natural causes.

'What does that mean, Nigel? There was nothing wrong with her!'

They had had dinner and were now sitting around a crackling wood fire in the front room. Boxes of Christmas decorations were scattered around the room unopened. To all intense and purposes, Christmas was cancelled.

'I suspect he means, Ruth that her immune system was compromised from being disabled for so long. Something like that. Her heart gave out.'

'She had a beautiful heart.'

'I know, sweetheart. I'm so sorry.'

'What am I supposed to say at her funeral?'

'Tell the truth about her. With the same amount of love that you showed her in life. You don't have any other choice.'

'Thank you, my darling.

The funeral in St Jude's village church was held in the biting grip of early January, the sky a dull grey ceiling pressing down on the gathered mourners while snow gently fell. Ruth's son, André was there, standing a little apart, as if unsure where his presence belonged while Nigel stood next to Ruth in close support. The ceremony was modest, as Sally would have wanted: no excessive displays, just quiet Christian words with sleet settling over the coffin as it descended into the earth. Afterwards, there was a warm drink for everybody at the farm but Ruth felt disconnected from the entire day, as if she were watching from outside herself, detached from the reality that her closest friend was truly gone. Nigel found her in one of the barns and she was shivering.

'Darling, what are you doing out here without a coat?'

'I was remembering a woman called, Mary Dooley.'

'Who's she?'

'You wouldn't have known her. She was an insignificant little woman. Just turned eighteen which is why she'd been sent to Holloway. I'd been in there for about two years when she got given a six month stretch for shop lifting…'

'Why are you out here thinking of her, darling?'

'Because me and her kind of hit it off you see and I liked her. She had spirit and she told me about herself. How she was raped by one of her father's parishioners. How her father hadn't believed her. How he and her mother had thrown her out of their house onto the streets. How she had begged them for food. How she had dossed down wherever she could, getting help from the Sally Ann you know, that sort of thing. But then finally after giving birth to a child, resorting to stealing food for it and getting caught. They took away her baby of course.'

'Did the prison give her any help?'

Ruth shook her head. 'No, nobody reached her in time. She hung herself in her cell. I suppose she'd had enough punishment. Poor, Mary Dooley.'

'And her baby?'

'In those days there was a mother and baby unit in Holloway. If a prisoner had a long sentence and had no family, then the child was adopted. That's what happened to Mary's infant. That little baby would be about twenty-eight years old now and I was wondering what she had made of herself.'

'Darling? Come in out of the cold. Come on. You're catch your…come on.'

A week later, Ruth accompanied by Nigel sat in Mr Chantree's office in Brick Court off Middle Temple Lane, the smell of aged paper and furniture polish filling the room. The legal formalities seemed cold against the weight of what had happened. The reading of Sally's will was clinical: facts arranged in legal jargon, a life's worth of decisions condensed into a few pages, simple and to the point. Sally had left her entire estate to her.

The words landed heavily. In the quiet of the office, surrounded by books and legal pads, Ruth felt the full weight of it. The land, the house, the animals, the company…all of it was now hers. She hadn't asked for it. She hadn't planned for it. And yet, here she was, standing on the threshold of an entirely new responsibility. She wasn't sure if she was grateful or terrified.

'Mr Chantree? Is that it?'

'It is, Mrs Ellis. I have enjoyed a remarkable partnership with Mrs Wilson and I am of course deeply saddened that it has come to an end as I regarded her as a close friend.'

'But surely you will want to continue looking after the interests of the company?'

'If that is what you would like me to do then I certainly would have no objection whatsoever. Indeed I would be honoured.'

'Then please draw up any papers you need for me to sign, Mr Chantry. And let us continue our relationship for I am sure that is what Sally would have liked.'

After the meeting concluded and they found themselves standing in noisy Fleet Street, Nigel lingered. His presence had been steady since Sally had been discovered…

sometimes offering quiet support, and yet other times remaining respectfully distant.

'I hope I'm not being too pushy, Ruth but my mother is shopping today in town,' he said, his tone careful. 'And I wonder if this might be a good time for you to meet her.'

Ruth blinked, caught off guard. They had never spoken much about his mother. She knew he and his brother were wealthy and although they were not titled she imagined his family had a pile of old bricks somewhere.

Nigel was relieved to see her smile.

'So, she wants to see why her son is dating the old murderer?'

'Ruth! It's not that…but, of course, she's heard about you,' he said, watching her carefully.

'And what has she heard?'

A flicker of a smile touched Nigel's lips. 'It's more like what she's read. Enough to make her curious.'

Ruth exhaled slowly, feeling the weight of everything: the funeral, the farm, the situation into which she had stepped.

'Well, then. She might as well hear the truth from me. But I want to go back to my hotel first.'

They took a taxi to an expensive hotel close to Marble Arch, where its vast lounge exuded a quiet, cultivated luxury. Its dimly lit corners glowed with the amber hues of vintage lamps, their soft, forgiving light casting long shadows over polished mahogany tables and velvet drapery. The air was tinged with the faint scent of brandy and polished leather, a comforting but oppressive warmth that made Ruth think of ancestral portraits and stately rooms where one's voice never echoed. After being accompanied to the seating area, Nigel ordered drinks, his speech deliberate and controlled.

Ruth was more than aware she was not appropriately dressed for a first meeting with her boyfriend's mother but she was not unduly concerned. While she had changed into one of her better outfits–a dark wool skirt and a cashmere cardigan–she couldn't help but feel out of place amid the understated opulence of this world. It wasn't the clothes, though: it was the sense that she didn't fit into this tapestry of lineage and privilege. Yet, she told herself, that didn't matter. Not anymore.

She would have been put out even a few years previously but she had attended so many charity events where she had been the soul topic of attention she had long ago realised she now had weight to her life and that counteracted any previous doubts her former life had imposed upon her. Therefore meeting this upper class lady no longer held any fears for her. Even though she fully and easily remembered how she had been cut dead so easily by Blakely's family all those years ago because of what and who she was and what she did. She unconsciously pouted and muttered under her breath. 'What a bloody fool I was.'

'What was that, my darling?'

'Oh, sorry, Nigel. Nothing. Just a passing random thought.'

Nigel leaned closer. 'She'll be down shortly,' he said, placing his hand gently on hers. The drinks soon arrived and minutes later so did Nigel's mother: a slender woman with high cheekbones and silver streaked hair swept elegantly back. She wore a cream silk blouse beneath a tailored wool coat in a shade of soft charcoal. She entered the lounge with the calm assurance of someone for whom fine hotels and liveried staff were as familiar as her own living room. Nigel stood. Ruth deliberately did not.

'Nigel,' she said with a practiced smile, leaning in to offer her son a cool kiss on the cheek before straightening to take in Ruth with a brief but unmistakable assessment. 'And this must be, Ruth.'

Only then did Ruth stand, extending her hand. 'So pleased to meet you, Mrs Van de Watering.'

The older woman's handshake was firm, her eyes the clear, assessing grey of a morning sea.

'So good to meet you at last, my dear. May I offer you my deepest commiserations on the loss of your friend.' she replied, her voice warm but with that peculiar crispness Ruth associated with the well bred. They sat, and Mrs Van de Watering folded her white gloved hands in her lap.

'Thank you so very much, Mrs Van de Watering. That's very thoughtful of you.'

Nigel, ever the attentive son, leaned forward. 'What will you have to drink mother? Your usual?'

'Thank you, Nigel. A dry sherry, if you please.'

He signalled to the waiter, and they slipped into the kind of polite, surface conversation Ruth had always found mildly exhausting. They spoke of the weather first, then moved quickly to the recent renovations at the Royal Academy, where Mrs Van de Watering was a patron. Ruth found herself nodding at the right moments, her smile practiced, if a little tight.

'And you work with ceramics, I understand?' Mrs Van de Watering's question came smoothly, her tone a shade too bright and rather untruthful as it was highly unlikely that a woman in her position would never have heard of such an award winning women artist and Ruth saw Nigel's head turn disbelieving in his mother's direction. However, Ruth smiled and continued.

'I do, yes,' Ruth replied, relaxing a little at the chance to speak about her passion. 'Mostly hand thrown pieces. I've been working with porcelain lately. It's more challenging, but I find it...deeply satisfying.'

'Porcelain?' The older woman's brows lifted almost imperceptibly. 'Ah, that must require a delicate touch. Not easy to master, I should think.'

'It can be unforgiving,' Ruth agreed, catching the slight edge to the compliment. 'But that's part of the appeal.'

Mrs Van de Watering nodded, a thin, polite smile on her lips. 'Nigel has always had an eye for the arts,' she said, reaching for her sherry as the waiter returned. 'Though, of course, our family has always leaned more towards the, well, classical forms. Portraiture. Sculpture. You know how it is.'

Ruth returned the smile, choosing to take the comment in the spirit of polite conversation rather than mild condescension. 'I think all art forms have their place,' she replied. 'Some of the most powerful works I've seen are from self taught artists. There's a purity to it.'

Mrs Van de Watering inclined her head, an acknowledgment rather than agreement. She took a delicate sip of her drink. 'Of course. And you met through Mark, I believe? At his gallery?'

'Yes,' Ruth said, glancing at Nigel, whose expression was carefully neutral. 'He's been incredibly supportive.'

'Oh, Mark is a dear,' Mrs Van de Watering continued. 'He's good at finding talent, though of course, he can be a bit...impulsive at times. But then, I suppose that's what makes him so charming.'

Ruth felt the subtle currents of the conversation, the gentle steering of tone and topic, and for a moment, she was back at one of those awkward society gatherings with David, all those years ago. She felt the old urge to say something sharp, to test the boundaries of this carefully polite exchange, but she caught Nigel's eye and thought better of it.

Mrs Van de Watering placed her empty glass on the small side table and clasped her hands together, leaning towards Ruth. 'And are you planning to stay in London long, my dear?'

The question was perfectly reasonable, but Ruth heard the deeper question within it. How permanent are you in my son's life? How much should I invest in this conversation?

She smiled, tilting her head. 'I'm taking things as they come. I think that's best, don't you?'

A brief pause, the tiniest flicker of surprise in the older woman's eyes. 'Indeed,' she said, her tone warming. 'Indeed.'

They exchanged a few more polite remarks, the conversation drifting to safer, broader topics. And when the meeting finally drew to a close, Ruth felt the warm weight of Nigel's hand on her back as they made their way out, his mother's gaze following them like a question.

In the taxi back at Ruth's hotel, Nigel took her hand. 'You did well,' he whispered, kissing her cheek. 'Better than I expected.'

'I don't know how that went at all!'

'I do love you, you know.'

'And I you, Nigel. Come and stay next weekend?'

'Of course I will. You get home safely.'

In her room after undressing, Ruth felt her pulse and found it to be steady. She picked up a copy of Sally's printed funeral service, one she intended to frame and stared at her friend's photograph. It had been taken a few years after Ruth had arrived at Haven and she remembered that day as they had been having a picnic by the stream with Amelia, Ava, David and Daisy and she wonder where Daisy was and what she was doing. She would probably be in her forties now! And this caused her to remember people from Holloway such as the Indian woman, Laila and the kindness of Wardress Floyd and Grainger. What were they all doing now in this brave new world? Well, she was still here. Still standing.

Chapter 22

It took a visitor from the past to break Ruth's long spell of grieving and this occurred during the height of the summer two years later during a mild thunderstorm. Ruth certainly had not stopped working during that time as her accountant would testify. For during those two years, her personal manager, Mr Box organised twenty galleries and numerous other charity events around the country raising money for various concerns.

At Haven, well on its periphery, a long temporary wooden shed had been erected and that is where a number of students arrived each day to work and learn under the tutelage of Miss Taylor who was directly responsible for the work put out by Ruth. Once this arrangement had its kinks ironed out, the apprenticeship plan worked perfectly and it offered Ruth an excellent opportunity to choose those young people whom she thought might benefit from extra tuition.

Her grieving did not interfere with her deepening relationship with Nigel though and she experienced many things for the first time one of which was when they flew to Tunisia for a week's holiday. It had been spring and she had been fifty-nine and with the help of Miss Taylor, had brought an entirely new wardrobe consisting of a travel outfit, a daywear one and a swimwear one which was comprised of a classic one piece swimsuit in deep burgundy with a matching pareo for modesty when parading around the hotel pool and evening wear: an elegant but simple maxi dress in black with leather sandals.

She was nervous about the flight of course but Nigel's reassuring smile helped her along with a few whiskeys. It was thankfully a direct flight from London Gatwick to Tunis Carthage Airport and only took three hours. To the compliment of the clinking of cocktail glasses and a smoky cabin, Ruth even managed to fall asleep! Nigel had to nudge her to wake up! They stepped off the plane and immediately felt the dry heat and the distinct scent of jasmine and warm dust, the North African sun sharp even in the early morning.

The Abou Nawas Le Palace was renowned for its elegance and panoramic sea views and as Nigel had booked in advance that is what they saw. After drinks were delivered, they sat on their spacious veranda in silence taking in the view until Ruth spoke.

'I think I have to be dreaming. I'm back in my cell in Holloway and this is but a dream.'

Nigel smiled. 'And I am part of your imagination?'

'What a journey this has been.'

'It's not over yet, my darling. I came here as a youth and there is so much to see. Explore Carthage, Medina of Tunis, Sidi Bou Saïd. Perhaps we could take a day trip to the Sahara, riding camels over the dunes. We are close to Matmata, where the Star Wars sets were filmed. And there's always the sandy beaches of Hammamet. I remember I used to love them.'

'No, silly! I meant my journey! From you know what to…here.'

'Oh, I'm sorry. Yes, of course. You were being reflective. No, you are not dreaming, darling. You are here, with me and we are very happy.'

'Yes, we are, aren't we.'

'Yes, my darling. We are.'

Ruth touched his arm and lifted up her sunglasses.

'I'm hungry! Lunch?'

'Perfect.'

The midday sun hung high over the Gulf of Tunis, its bright reflection shimmering like molten gold on the waves. Ruth shaded her eyes as they approached a seaside restaurant, the air alive with the scent of grilling fish and the sharp tang of salt. Nigel, walking a step ahead, glanced back to catch her gaze, his grin easy and relaxed as he took a quick photograph. She envied that about him, the way he could move so effortlessly through the world, his shoulders always loose, his head always held high. He looked so English in his Panama hat.

The waiter, dressed in a crisp white shirt and black apron, guided them to a shaded terrace table draped in pale linen. From here, they had a perfect view of the sea, the water a deep, sparkling blue, cut through occasionally by the ghostly shadows of passing yachts.

'I'm glad you're hungry,' Nigel said, pulling out her chair for her, a small, gentlemanly gesture that still caught her off guard at times. 'Because I've heard the food here is five stars.' She thanked him with a slight smile, settling herself and removing her wide brimmed sunhat, smoothing a few stray curls back into place.

'I think I could manage a little something,' she smiled, her tone light, though her eyes lingered for a moment on the gently rolling sea. She wondered if he caught the slight tremor in her voice, if he sensed the way her heart felt both too full and too hollow in this strange and beautiful place.

Nigel took the wine list, his brow furrowing as he scanned the options. 'Shall we start with a bottle of the local rosé? Something crisp to cut through this heat?'

'Perfect,' she replied, her gaze wandering to the brightly coloured fishing boats bobbing in the distance, their hulls a cheerful splash of blues and reds against the sun bleached shore. Briefly she imagined the lives of the fishermen who sailed them, their hands thick with calluses, their skin bronzed by the unrelenting sun.

The waiter returned with the wine, his movements practiced and smooth as he poured a measure into Nigel's glass for approval. Nigel took a sip, swirled it thoughtfully, then nodded. The waiter filled both their glasses before retreating silently back into the cool shadows of the restaurant.

Ruth lifted her glass, the pale pink liquid catching the sunlight. 'To new adventures,' she said, clinking her glass gently against his.

Nigel's eyes met hers over the rims of their glasses, his gaze warm and steady. 'And to second chances,' he added, his voice low, his smile tinged with a hint of something she couldn't place — gratitude, perhaps, or something deeper.

They sipped the cool wine in companionable silence, the only sounds the gentle lap of the waves against the rocks below and the soft clinking of cutlery from nearby tables. After a moment, Nigel leaned forward, resting his elbows on the table, his face shaded by the dappled sunlight filtering through the terrace's awning.

'Have you thought about where you want to take your ceramics?' he asked, his tone genuinely curious. 'I mean, beyond the galleries, of course.'

Ruth set her glass down, tracing the edge with one finger as she considered his question. 'I'm not sure,' she admitted. 'I've never been one for grand plans. Mr Box takes care of my day to day business affairs and everything ticks long rather nicely. My work... it's always felt small and personal.'

Nigel nodded, his expression thoughtful. 'I get that. But your pieces have a voice. They say something. And maybe it's time the larger world started listening.'

She felt a blush creep up her neck, a warmth that had nothing to do with the Mediterranean sun. 'You think so?'

'I know so,' he replied, his tone as certain as the steady rhythm of the waves behind them. 'You ought to know there have been organisations that are beginning to become interested in you such as, the Contemporary Applied Arts, the Crafts Council Gallery, the V&A of course, the Tate and even regional galleries. Has not Mr Box talked to you about any of these?'

The waiter returned, placing a platter of freshly grilled sea bream between them, the skin crackling and fragrant, accompanied by a simple salad of tomatoes, olives, and crisp lettuce, gleaming with a sheen of olive oil. The scent rose up, rich and inviting, and Ruth felt a sudden, sharp pang of hunger.

'Oh, this smells fantastic! No, he has not. Now you are making me wonder whether he is competent enough to do the job at that level. Perhaps that is why he has not said anything.'

'Ruth, I'm sorry to have mentioned it. We are on holiday. Let's forget all about it until we get home. Shall we do that?'

Ruth smiled and they ate and drank slowly, their conversation drifting between the past and the future, their laughter mingled with the soft chatter of the other diners around them causing Ruth to feel something unfamiliar to stir within her — a quiet, contented kind of happiness, fragile yet undeniable, like the first hesitant green shoots of spring.

Later that evening, as the sun dipped below the horizon, casting the Gulf in shades of burnt orange and deep indigo, they found themselves on the balcony of their hotel room, the sea breeze cool against their sun warmed skin. The distant hum of waves was their only companion as the lights of Tunis began to flicker to life along the distant shoreline.

Nigel had opened a second bottle of wine, and they leaned together against the balcony rail, their shoulders brushing, their glasses held loosely in their hands.

'I've never been one for grand gestures,' Nigel said, his voice quiet, almost lost beneath the gentle crash of the waves. 'But I've been thinking about this for a while now.'

Ruth turned to him, the soft lines of his face cast in shadow, his eyes reflecting the last golden light of the day.

'I don't know what the future holds, and I'm not naive enough to think that life won't throw us a few more curveballs.' He hesitated, his jaw tightening. 'But I do know that I want to face them with you.'

He set his glass down on the small iron table beside them, then reached into the pocket of his linen trousers. For a moment, he hesitated, his fingers brushing against the fabric, and then, with a nervous chuckle, he drew out a small, velvet lined box.

Ruth felt her breath catch, and her eyes widened.

'Ruth,' he said, opening the box to reveal an elegant gold ring, the diamond catching the last light of the day. 'Will you do me the honour of becoming my wife?'

For a heartbeat, she felt as if the world had stopped, the air around them holding its breath, the sea itself pausing in anticipation. And then, with a trembling smile and eyes that shone in the fading light, she whispered, 'Yes…thank you.'

Nigel's grin broke wide, his relief palpable, and he slipped the ring onto her finger before pulling her into his arms, their laughter mingling with the whisper of the waves far below. Their lips met, their eyes closed and they were in paradise. For the first time in what felt like a lifetime, Ruth allowed herself to believe in a future filled with love as well as possibilities.

That visitor from the past arrived at Haven on a Sunday in the autumn and so Ruth was virtually alone. Only the manager was venturing out every so often due to the weather to make sure the storm was not inflicting any damage on the enclosures. In her studio, under the somewhat comforting noise of the rain hammering on the roof, Ruth was working a piece according to her memory of a scene she had witnessed in Tunis of a boy holding a cup of water, a scene which had moved her, when she heard three taps on the window next to the door. Believing it was the manager, she glanced up distractedly but instantly saw it was not he. Curiously she walked across and peered at the face that looked decidedly familiar yet she did not recognise the woman at all.

Who was dripping wet so quickly she opened the door.

'Yes? this is private property you know.'

'Miss Ellis? Ruth Ellis? It's me. Daisy? I used to work for Sally, remember?'

Ruth immediately remembered the day she was introduced to Sally's original four workers, three girls and one lad and then how confused she had become over the girl. This one, thinking that because of her age, she could have been the child she had lost.

'Miss Ellis?'

'Oh, I'm sorry, come in, come in. You're soaking! But what are you doing here? Let me look at you. Let me take your mac. I'll make you a coffee.'

'Thank you, that's so kind of you.'

'I didn't recognise you. The last time I saw you, you left to get married. A tall chap with long hair if I remember.'

'Yes, that was Mike and it was a happy marriage until he died.'

'Oh, I am so sorry. May I ask what happened?'

'A motorbike accident on the A259, the Bognor Road seven years ago. I've been living with my mother ever since.'

'I'm so very sorry. Please take a seat and excuse the mess! But what brings you here today?'

'Well, firstly I wanted to say that I'm sorry to have missed Sally's funeral. The reason is I didn't even know. My mother lives in Edinburgh and I didn't know. I only knew when an old friend wrote to me a few weeks ago so that's why I felt I had to come down here. But there was something else because, Sally did mention, oh, years ago that she said that I seemed to have some sort of an effect on you when we first met and I wanted to ask you if that was true.'

Ruth smiled and she could see the young girl in her now. Fair haired, cheeky faced, a nice smile.

'Yes, Daisy, I remember now. There was something about you that struck me that day but it had nothing to do with you. Because years previously I lost a child at three months and seeing you at your age sort of made me think that had my own child lived, he or she would have been about your age, that's all. It struck me in that way that's all, that day.'

'And here I am today!'

'How old are you, Daisy?'

'Thirty-five.'

'You have children?'

'We tried. We tried so hard but it didn't happen. I don't know if the fault was me or him. We never got that far before…'

'I'm sorry.'

'It was a bad night for driving. Icy and foggy. It was ten days before Christmas and the police said it wasn't his fault.' He was the love of my life, Miss Ellis.'

'Call me, Ruth.'

Daisy offered her a smile. 'I'm so sorry about Sally. You have Haven now?'

'Yes, she left it to me. What do you do with yourself?'

'Nothing. Not a thing. Mum is ill. Dad died a year ago and mum's going senile and I look after her. It's a full time job. Each day I wonder if she recognises me.'

'Oh, that sort of senility. I know the type. There is a word for it but I can't remember what it is. Who is looking after her while you're here?'

'I have a friend who is a carer. She's got a week's holiday and she's giving me four days which is a blessing and that's all I have.'

'Daisy? This is a terrible thing to say because I'm implying things but in the future if ever you need a position I can always find work for you here. You can have one of the cottages.'

'That's so very kind of you, Ruth thank you so much. I have no other family and I will sell mum and dad's house so I don't know where I will stand but I'm almost certain that I won't be staying in Scotland but I will love to keep in touch.'

'And I will definitely be inviting you to my wedding.'

Daisy's mouth opened a little as did her eyes. 'Oh! How wonderful. I had no idea. Congratulations. Who is the lucky man?'

'He is the brother of the man who originally found me as an artist.'

'Oh, I am so pleased for you. Please send me a RSPV! I shall treasure that.'

Ruth and Nigel decided on a spring wedding to take place the following year, mainly because Ruth felt that now she was sixty, she felt that time was catching up with her. However, as mature as she was and as popular and as celebrated as she was, she found that getting married and becoming part of an old established English family was not going to be so easy because her mother in law to be began to demand situations which did not appeal to her at all.

Ruth desired a small wedding but her voice was drowned out almost immediately in this regard and although she protested, eventually the weight of Nigel's family went against her. Although Nigel fully understood, Ruth also understood that the resultant publicity would be extremely good for her career. And in that regard he was not wrong.

Because the fact was that once the newspapers got hold of the fact that the eminent and prize winning artist and one time murderer and now chicken farmer was going to marry into a wealthy upper middle class British family, they were not able to send enough reporters after her wanting an interview.

Therefore, Mr Box over the Christmas period and leading up to spring was kept extremely busy and the lane leading to Haven was chaotic with reporters, television crews and police trying to maintain order to allow legitimate lorries through so that the main business of the farm could continue. As Ruth complained bitterly to anybody who would listen, 'it's become a bloody nightmare.'

Yet interviews were given and by March the chaos and the interest in her had almost died away but not fully. Through a discreet amount of negotiation, Ruth paid for a professional carer to look after Daisy's mother because she wanted Daisy to be her bridesmaid. Daisy, being thrilled to have been asked, had given her answer immediately.

The Van de Watering estate in Surrey was a nineteenth-century collection of buildings mostly built in the Regency style and was enclosed by some two thousand acres of woodland and scrub. As Nigel told his wife to be, 'it's good for riding but nothing else because all the decent farming land had been sold off pre first world war.'

As family tradition dictated, Nigel was to be married in the local church, a tiny twelfth-century romanesque and that is where Ruth and he first met the vicar and where the banns were called. By mid April Mr Box discovered Ruth sitting by herself one Sunday afternoon.

She sat on the rough, weathered stone beside the stream, her boots sinking into the damp, moss covered earth. The stream babbled over smooth, time worn rocks, a soothing sound that usually calmed her nerves, but today it only seemed to mock her with its effortless freedom. She drew her cardigan tighter around her shoulders, the early April air still sharp with the tail end of winter, and let her gaze drift across the meadow, where the first brave wildflowers were beginning to bloom.

She heard the crunch of gravel behind her before the shadow fell across her shoulder. She didn't turn: there was no need. The footsteps were too sure, too deliberate to be anyone but Mr Box. She allowed herself a tight smile. He had a way of finding her, even when she made a point of slipping away.

'Ruth,' his voice was crisp. He hesitated, clearly unaccustomed to finding her outside the gallery or her studio, and cleared his throat. 'I've been looking for you.'

'I needed some air,' she replied without turning, her fingers tracing the rough surface of the stone beneath her. 'And space. You seem intent on taking both from me these days.'

He stepped into her line of sight, careful to avoid a patch of wet ground, his polished brogues incongruous against the wild, untamed grass. He wore his usual dark, three piece suit, despite the mud that clung to the fringes of his trouser cuffs. She glanced at him, catching the faintest flicker of discomfort as he took in his surroundings.

'I can't imagine you've come to admire the view,' she said, meeting his eyes with a raised brow.

Mr Box clasped his hands behind his back, rocking on his heels as if considering how to begin. 'It's about the interviews,' he said finally, his tone carefully neutral.

Ruth closed her eyes, drawing in a deep breath of cold, fresh air. 'Of course it is.'

'They're insisting on at least one major piece for the Sunday Times,' he pressed on, his voice tightening a fraction. 'And there's a request from the BBC for a radio interview. They're hoping you might discuss your... remarkable journey. From Holloway to high society.'

Ruth's eyes snapped open, her fingers curling into fists. 'Is that how they are still seeing it? As some sort of grim fairy tale?' She gave a short, bitter laugh. 'As if I've somehow been polished up, fit to be paraded for their amusement.'

Mr Box flinched, his composure slipping for a moment. 'It's not as simple as that, Ruth. You're about to marry into a very prominent family. You know there are expectations.'

'Expectations,' she repeated, her voice low, dangerously calm. 'Yes, I'm beginning to understand all about those.'

She looked back at the stream, watching the water twist and turn over the stones, unconstrained by anything but its own nature.

'It feels like my life isn't my own anymore. I'm to be married in some old church I don't even like, to a man I love, yes, but on terms that seem entirely his family's.'

Mr Box shifted, a hint of discomfort crossing his usually impassive face. 'You'll be gaining a great deal, too, Ruth. Stability, respectability…'

'Oh, spare me the lecture,' she cut in sharply, the sudden steel in her voice making him straighten.

'I know what I'm gaining, but I also know what I'm losing. My independence. My privacy. My freedom.' She turned to face him fully, her eyes fierce. 'Is that really a proper price to pay?'

He hesitated, the stream's soft gurgling filling the sudden silence.

'Nigel adores you, he said at last, his voice quieter, less the polished manager and more the man behind the mask. 'And you him. That has to count for something.'

'It does,' she whispered, her eyes dropping to the ground, her anger deflating as quickly as it had flared. 'It counts for everything.'

They stood in the damp meadow for a long moment, the wind rustling through the new leaves, the stream singing softly at their feet. Finally, Mr Box cleared his throat again, glancing back toward the distant shape of the estate house. 'I'll let them know you'll consider the interviews,' he said, a note of quiet relief in his voice.

'I suppose I must,' Ruth said, her tone weary but resigned. She turned back to the water, the muscles in her jaw tight as she forced the words out. 'But it doesn't mean I have to like it.'

He gave a small, respectful nod, the corner of his mouth twitching in the ghost of a smile. 'I'll leave you to your air and space then, Ruth.'

With that, he turned and made his way back across the meadow, his figure quickly swallowed by the long spiky grass and the shifting shadows of the early spring sun. Ruth listened to his footsteps fade, her eyes fixed on the rushing stream, wondering how long she could keep herself from being swept away.

Chapter 23

The church stood alone on a low rise in the centre of the village, its ancient stones mottled with lichen and the long shadow of time. The squat, square tower, unyielding against the sharp spring wind, had watched over centuries of whispered vows, of joy and grief, of whispered prayers and stifled sobs. As Ruth stepped through the thick wooden doors, their iron hinges cold under her touch, she felt the chill of those centuries settle around her shoulders, a weight as solid as the stone walls themselves.

Ruth's dress, chosen with a careful blend of restraint and elegance, whispered of a different era–soft ivory silk, the high neckline edged with delicate, hand stitched lace that crept over her collarbones like the tentative touch of a lover. The bodice was fitted, its gentle curves echoing the classical simplicity she had come to appreciate in her pottery. The sleeves, long and gently tapered, ending below her wrists, the lace cuffs brushing her skin like a ghost of some forgotten past. The skirt fell in soft, graceful folds, trailing enough to rustle against the cold stone floor as she walked. She had foregone a veil, choosing instead a single, delicate sprig of white heather pinned into her hair–a nod to her new life in the countryside.

Daisy with a cascade of dark curls and a mischievous glint in her eye, standing behind her at the altar, had insisted on a dress of deep, forest green–a dramatic contrast to Ruth's understated ivory, but one that suited her spirit. She had clasped Ruth's hands tightly before they stepped into the nave, whispering with a grin, 'Don't let them scare you, Ruth. You've faced worse than a church full of stiff upper lips.' That made her smile.

Nigel was already at the altar, his back straight, his face set with a quiet, steady resolve. He turned as the old organ creaked to life, its pipes groaning out the first notes of the bridal march, and for a moment, Ruth felt the years melt away–the decades of solitude, of bruised pride and lingering shame, dissolving in the warm, steadfast light of his eyes. She saw her son and his wife, then her grandson and granddaughter and her sister but thankfully not her father. Then she saw Mr Box in a new suit ready to give her away.

The ceremony was brief, the vicar's voice rising and falling in the measured, lilting tones of ancient English. Ruth barely heard the words, her thoughts drifting to the small crowd gathered in the hard, wooden pews behind her–a scattering of family, friends, and a few tentative friends from Nigel's world, their expressions ranging from polite curiosity to thinly veiled disapproval. Sally, always Ruth's anchor, was missing of course, her absence a silent ache in Ruth's chest.

When the service was over, when the rings had been exchanged and the vicar's hand had pressed hers with a firm, paternal warmth, Ruth turned to face the world as Mrs Van de Watering. The small congregation rose to their feet, the echo of clapping hands filling the cold stone nave, and Ruth felt a strange, unexpected rush of warmth–not of triumph, but of something close.

Thirty-six hours later, Ruth found New York was a riot of neon and noise, the city's pulse a stark, shocking contrast to the quiet corners of Surrey and the solemn whispers of the twelfth-century church. They stayed at The Plaza, their suite high above the chaotic thrum of Fifth Avenue, and every morning Ruth woke to the distant wail of sirens and the clatter of yellow cabs. She wandered the city's canyons, hand in hand with Nigel, her eyes wide at the endless cascade of lights, the steam rising from the subway grates, the kaleidoscope of faces rushing past them on the crowded sidewalks. Each morning the city showed her impossible fashions and impossible actions and she heard impossible snippets of languages she had never heard before and saw values that shocked her.

They spent lazy afternoons in Central Park, the sharp tang of spring air mingling with the earthy scent of thawing ground. They wandered through the Met, their footsteps echoing in vast, marbled halls, pausing to admire the cool, ancient lines of Greek statues and the sweeping, dramatic brushstrokes of European masters. One evening, they took the Staten Island Ferry, the wind tearing at their hair as they watched the Statue of Liberty drift past, her torch a distant, defiant flame against the steel grey water.

On another night, they found themselves pressed into the dark, smoky confines of the Village Vanguard, the slow, sultry wail of a saxophone curling through the shadows like a whispered promise. Ruth felt the music thrumming in her bones, its rhythm as steady and unhurried as Nigel's heartbeat beneath her cheek. One night, high above the city at the Rainbow Room, Ruth leaned into Nigel's shoulder, his arm warm around her waist, and whispered, 'I worry this will end. That I'll wake up and find it was all some impossible dream.'

He smiled, pressing a kiss to her hair. 'It's not a dream, my darling. Because you've already lived through the nightmare. This–this is the part you thought you'd never get to.'

They returned to England on a grey, windswept morning, the plane's wheels skimming the wet tarmac of Heathrow with a soft, bump. Ruth watched the rain streak across the small, oval window, the fog pressing in like a damp, clinging shroud. Nigel squeezed her hand, his own gaze fixed on the distant outlines of London's familiar, brooding skyline.

'I wonder how your chickens are doing?'

Their new house, a substantial property with a hundred acres, close to Seasalter, stood on a gentle rise, its windows turned toward the sea, the salt wind forever brushing its stones like the breath of some ancient, slumbering giant. It was a house of wide, low beams and crooked doorways, of creaking floorboards and cool, flagstone floors, its walls thick with the quiet, unspoken histories of those who had lived there before.

Ruth wandered around the immediate overgrown garden on their first morning, her shoes sinking into the soft, rain soaked earth, the sharp scent of wet grass rising around her. She paused by a low, crumbling wall where the sea stretched out in an endless, mist shrouded expanse, the white peaks of distant waves breaking against the horizon. She closed her eyes, the cold wind whipping her hair against her cheeks, and felt a slow, quiet peace settle over her–a feeling she had never felt before.

When she turned back to the house, she saw Nigel standing in the doorway, his figure a dark, solid outline against the warm, flickering glow of the fire he had lit in the great, stone hearth. He raised a hand, his smile small but genuine, and for the first time in years, Ruth felt as though she had truly arrived home.

Ruth would keep the farm, of course. Its low, familiar shapes would remain a constant on the horizon, a reminder of the life she had built–and the one she had finally chosen to leave behind. But this–this house by the sea–would be her future, a place where the past, for once, felt like nothing more than the echo of a distant, fading tide.

Nigel clicked the clunky mouse, watching as the slow, grey progress bar crept across the screen. The modem crackled and hissed in protest as it dialled into the distant server. Finally, the screen refreshed, and his inbox appeared–a jumble of plain text and crude, blocky fonts. Email still felt like a novelty, even in 1994, a strange, disembodied kind of conversation with the outside world.

'Blast!'

'What is it, my darling?' Ruth wandered into his office. 'Bad news?'

'It's the Birmingham office. They would like me up there for the Brancaster case on the twelfth for ten days and I did promise them.'

'Are you going?'

'I fear I must, my darling. I'm sorry.'

'I will miss you.'

'I've really had enough of this. It's retirement time I think.'

'But you love your work.'

'But not if it takes me away from you for any extended time.'

'There will be other times to spend with the family.'

'How's your hip today?'

'A little easier than yesterday but it's still early in the morning yet. When are you leaving?'

'Tomorrow morning I think. You'll give my love to everybody won't you?'

'Of course my darling.'

The sea breeze swept through the open French doors, carrying with it the crisp, salty air of Seasalter. Ruth moved slowly through the kitchen helped by her assistant, her hands busy with the final touches on the cake–a simple but towering creation, thickly iced and generously topped with late summer berries. She stepped back, eyeing it critically, then smiled.

'What do you think, Pam?'

'Let's hope he's not a diabetic, Ruth! Because of the amount of sugar you've put in it!'

'He had a sweet tooth when he was a kid.'

From the living room, she heard the low rumble of Graham's voice, chatting with his younger sister. The boy: no, not a boy anymore, a young man of twenty-one, was arguing the merits of a TV programme to his younger sister, Violet. Who, when Ruth peeked at her could see her eyes occasionally flitting towards the window, clearly more interested in the gulls circling the distant waves.

Violet, all teenage energy and too-cool-for-family gatherings attitude, had draped herself over the arm of the sofa, flicking through one of the glossy fashion magazines Ruth kept on the coffee table. Ruth noted with a small pang of recognition that the sixteen year old had that same restless, ferocious spark she'd once had at that age, the sense of being too big for the world around her, constantly looking for edges to push against.

Heather's voice drifted in from the patio, where she and André were inspecting the rose bushes. André, now fifty, still carried himself with the calm, understated confidence of a man who had long ago made peace with his place in the world. His hair had thinned, and his frame had filled out in that solid, comfortable way that middle age often brings, but his eyes still held the same sharp, thoughtful glint Ruth remembered from his childhood.

As she slid the cake onto a waiting stand, she caught her own reflection in the glass oven door and she wished once again that Nigel was there to celebrate her son's birthday. Her silver hair was pinned up in a loose chignon, a few rebellious strands escaping to frame her face. She smoothed her apron, took a breath, and felt a familiar warmth bloom in her chest–the quiet, steady pulse of contentment she had never expected to find.

With Pam pushing the cake on a trolly, she stepped into the living room, catching the tail end of Graham's enthusiastic explanation of something or other he'd been watching. Violet looked up as Ruth entered, and for a brief moment, Ruth saw the girl's expression soften, the flicker of a real smile passing over her sharp features.

'Alright, everyone,' she said, clapping her hands together with a bright, mischievous smile. 'Enough chatting. Let's see if the old man can still blow out fifty candles. Pam? The champagne please.'

Soon they were munching on Pam's sugary efforts and drinking to André's health, even Violet although she was only allowed one glass.

'So Violet, I haven't seen much of you this summer. How are you getting on with your education?'

'Alright, I suppose.'

'Tell granny the truth,' said Heather. 'She's doing very well. And we are very proud of her. She's completed her GCSEs and she'll be starting her A-Levels next year. Ten subjects you took wasn't it? English Language, English Literature, maths, and science history, geography, french, art, music, IT and others I can't remember.'

'MUM!'

'Well, I'm proud of you. You ought to be proud.'

'Goodness me, child, we have a genius in the family!'

'Nan, it's only remembering stuff, that's all.'

'But do you know where you are going with all this?'

'What do you mean?'

'Well, do you want to go to university and afterwards what are you going to do?'

'Yeah, I'd like to go to university and then I'd like to become a solicitor or a barrister, something in the legal world, like Nigel.'

'Oh, I'm sure he would be able to help you in that regard.'

'Maybe.'

The room fell silent until André spoke.

'I don't think you've put enough sugar in this cake, mum.'

Ruth grinned knowing that she did.

'Graham? You still seeing that young lady? What was her name? The tattooed one?'

'Nan! She had one small tattoo on her shoulder. It was a flower. Get over it! And yes, we are still seeing each other. I wanted to bring her today but as she's now got a nose ring mum thought that the shock of it might kill you so she thought it best she not come!'

'Heather? You allow your children to talk to their grandmother like that?'

Heather lifted her hands up in a gesture of helplessness and rolled her eyes.

'Kids! Can't live with 'em, can't kick 'em out.'

'Nan?' said Violet, 'You've told us stories of women in Holloway who had tats all over their bodies and that was back in the days of the dinosaurs.'

'Cheeky little mare! They were hardened criminals.'

'Mum?' smiled André, they're winding you up.'

'All right. I give in. The old crippled lady gives in.'

'But we all love you, mum. And it's a shame Nigel isn't here.'

'Yes. On your sixtieth as well.'

'So, mum. How's your own work going? Your collection of awards seems to be growing monthly!'

André looked at a handsome piece of Victorian craftsmanship, standing over six feet tall. Its dark, polished mahogany frame gleamed with a rich, reddish brown hue, the grain catching the light from the nearby window. The base featured a deep, panelled plinth, carved with intricate scrollwork and acanthus leaves, the sort of detail that spoke of patient, meticulous hands at work.

Its glass fronted cabinet, framed with fine, fluted columns, was topped with a gently curved pediment, carved with a crest of interwoven leaves and flowers–a nod to the natural world that inspired so much of Ruth's work. Inside, the shelves were thick and sturdy, their edges lined with a faint gold filigree, perfectly echoing the ornate Victorian taste for both elegance and excess.

The brass fittings, though tarnished with age, still caught the light in a pleasing way, their simple, understated design a quiet contrast to the flamboyant woodwork. At the base, two small, glass fronted drawers provided a place for more personal mementos her occasional sketches, handwritten notes, and fragments of her earliest pottery experiments.

Inside, Ruth's awards, a small army of polished plaques, shimmering medals, and engraved crystal, stood proudly, each a testament to her skill and the long, hard road from the rough clay of her early work to the refined artistry she had become known for.

'My personal work is slowing, darling if the truth be told. Not a word must be said outside this room but age is catching up with me and arthritis is finally taking its toll and I can no longer mould the clay without pain.'

'I'm sorry, mum I had no idea.'

'The tutelage, apprenticeship and guardianship part of my life is going well of course and I have no fears for that but, c'est la vie.'

Her family left before the sun set and their departure caused Ruth to become reflective. Particularly after Pam left. Pam was a Godsend, a local woman and had been working for her for over five years. Having nobody else to talk to, Ruth poured herself a glass of wine and stepped into her studio and turned on the heating.

After tying on her apron, Ruth sat at her wheel, her hands resting on the cool, smooth surface of the unshaped clay. She flexed her fingers, felt the familiar twinge in her knuckles, that slow, creeping ache that had been settling into her bones over the past year. Amongst the sound of the chickens she could still hear Sally's voice, long gone now but echoing in the corners of her mind, urging her to take care, to rest those hands, to slow down.

She closed her eyes, letting the memories swirl around her–the sharp, clean crack of a bone dry bowl coming off the shelf, the soothing, hypnotic spin of the wheel beneath her fingers, the quiet satisfaction of a perfectly glazed vase. She had built a second life from these hands, shaped a world of colour and form and purpose out of mud and fire. And now, it seemed, her own body was turning against her, slowly setting her hands in clay as if they too were destined to become part of the earth again.

The pain had a rhythm to it, a slow, insistent throb that mirrored the pulse of her own heartbeat. She flexed her fingers again, watched the pale, mottled skin stretch over swollen joints, and felt a fresh wave of anger rise up inside her. She had fought too hard to build this life, too many years clawing her way out of the darkness, to be brought down now by her own treacherous body.

With a grunt of frustration, she pushed herself away from the wheel and stood, her chair scraping loudly against the studio floor. She felt the warmth of the radiator, noticed the high, dust streaked windows, felt the cool concrete beneath her feet, and tried to focus on the world outside– the distant cry of a gull, the whisper of the sea against the shingle. But the low pain was still there, clinging to her like a second skin, and she knew that no amount of sunlight or sea air could wash it away.

That night, she lay in bed, the sheets cool and soft against her skin, the mattress gently sagging beneath her weight. She curled her fingers into the pillow, felt the ache spread from her knuckles to her wrists, up into her elbows, like a slow, creeping frost. She stared at the darkened ceiling, her mind drifting through the years, back to the early mornings and late nights in the studio, the long hours of shaping, carving, smoothing and glazing.

She had always been a woman of action, a doer, someone who fought against the tide rather than let it carry her away. But now, in the silence of the bedroom, she felt the cold fingers of fear creeping into her heart. What if this was the beginning of the end? What if the clay, which had once been her salvation, would now be her undoing?

She closed her eyes, felt the slow, steady thud of her pulse in her fingertips, and whispered into the darkness, 'c'est la vie.'

Recognising that her business and her livelihood was coming to an end, Nigel too decided to take early retirement so that they could not only spend more time together but take holidays together as well. Therefore they not only explored England but the furthest extent of Europe as well and it was during the first part of the 21st century that they had one of their finest and last romantic encounters.

The wind off the Mediterranean was sharp and cool with the bite of early spring, but the sun shone bright and clear, casting a warm, golden glow over the terracotta rooftops and the narrow, winding streets of Marseille. Ruth sat on the splendid balcony of their hotel room, her hands resting on the wrought iron railing, fingers curled around the cool, painted metal. Below, the harbour sparkled with a thousand points of light, the white sails of the yachts swaying gently against the deep, cobalt blue of the water.

Nigel stepped out behind her, slipping an arm around her waist, his chin resting lightly on her shoulder. 'Not a bad way to welcome the 21st century, eh?'

She smiled, leaning into him, feeling the solid warmth of his blue blazer against her back. 'Not bad at all,' she murmured, her eyes following the lazy swoop of a seagull as it dipped low over the water, catching the sunlight on its wings. She took a deep breath, tasting the salt and brine on the air, feeling it settle in her lungs, sharp and invigorating.

'I thought I might take you to that little bistro that the concierge recommended,' he said, his lips brushing against her hair. 'The one with the excellent wine?'

She laughed, a low, throaty sound that carried on the breeze. 'Yes, let's. And I want to walk down to the old port again. It's so charming–all that history, the weight of the centuries… I love that. Makes you feel small, but in a good way.'

Nigel's arm tightened around her, his fingers finding hers, their wedding bands finding each other.

'I'm glad you said that,' he whispered. 'Because I've booked us on a little boat trip this afternoon. Out to the islands. I thought you might like to see the Château d'If.'

She turned in his arms, her silver hair catching the sunlight, her eyes bright with a familiar, mischievous glint. 'The Château d'If? You old romantic.'

'Only for you, Ruth,' he said, leaning in to kiss her cheek.

Below them, the sounds of the city drifted up–the hum of mopeds, the chatter of the street vendors, the distant clatter of dishes from the cafes lining the waterfront. She closed her eyes, letting the warmth of the sun and the steady, reassuring strength of Nigel's embrace wash over her, and felt a quiet, fierce gratitude bloom in her chest.

Seventy-five, she thought, with a small, secret smile. Seventy five and still reaching for the horizon.

But it was to be their last trip. For in August 2003, Pam arrived at her usual time and took Ruth and Nigel their usual tea and coffee in bed and after began to prepare breakfast.

Ruth's hip was hurting her more than usual that morning so she was using an extra cane and as Pam recognise the signs she brought her an extra pain relieving tablet.

'Do you want me to phone, Doctor Edmund?'

'Not necessary, Pam. I probably slept wrong. it will ease up later on. I'll take a walk round the garden.'

'You know how stubborn she is,' winked Nigel.

'I am not,' she grumbled. 'Anyway, what time are you leaving?'

'Peter's collecting me at nine-thirty. Pam! What have you done to this coffee? It's lovely!'

'It's that new brand from Brazil that you ordered last month.'

'Oh, yes. Please order some more. Now, darling, please take it easy won't you? Don't run about the garden in your usual manner!'

'Husband! I'm seventy-seven! When was the last time you saw me rush around anywhere?'

'I'm just saying. Goodness me, is that the time? Okay, must shower.'

'Wear that gold tiepin, Her Majesty gave you and apologise for my absence.'

'As if I'd forget to do that!'

Pam found Ruth collapsed near her beloved herb garden at eleven o'clock that morning. She had been looking for her because she had not appeared for her morning cup of tea and she found her unresponsive but alive. When questioned by the police she told them that she had no idea how long she had been lying there.

Several hours later the overhead lights were too bright and stark white against the dull beige of the hospital walls, casting sharp shadows over the bed where Ruth lay, her face pale against the thick, institutional pillow. The steady, rhythmic beeping of the heart monitor pulsed through the small, sterile room, a quiet but relentless reminder that life still clung to her fragile form. The faint, antiseptic smell of disinfectant hung in the air, sharp and unforgiving.

Dr. Patel entered the room, his steps quick but measured, his white coat swishing around his legs. He paused at the foot of Ruth's bed, flipping through the thin stack of notes on his clipboard, his eyes flicking over the complex tangle of wires and tubes that connected her to the surrounding machines. He sighed softly, pressing his lips into a thin line before stepping closer to her side.

'Mrs Van de Watering,' he said, his voice low but clear, leaning in so his words wouldn't carry beyond the thin curtain that separated her bed from the bustling corridor beyond. 'Ruth. Can you hear me?'

For a moment, there was no response, just the faint, shallow rise and fall of her chest beneath the starched hospital sheets. Then, slowly, her eyelids fluttered, a faint crease forming between her brows as if she were struggling to remember where and who she was.

'Ruth,' Dr. Patel continued, his tone softening as he reached out to gently touch her wrist, his fingers pressing against the thin, papery skin to find her pulse.

'You're in the Queen Elizabeth. The Queen Mother Hospital. You collapsed, but you're safe now. You're in good hands.'

Her eyes slowly focused, the grey blue irises that had once sparked with mischief and defiance were now clouded with confusion and fear. She opened her mouth, her lips dry and cracked, and managed a faint, hoarse whisper. 'Nigel...'

'He's on his way,'

Dr. Patel assured her, gently releasing her wrist and straightening up. He reached for the small plastic cup of water on the bedside table, carefully guiding the straw to her lips. She took a small, tentative sip, her throat convulsing as the cool liquid slid down.

A few moments later, the door to the room swung open, and Nigel, proceeded by a nurse, stepped in, his face pale, eyes wide with worry, the faintest hint of a tremor in his hands as he crossed the small, clinical space to her bedside. He leaned over her, one hand reaching out to gently cradle her cheek, his thumb brushing over the soft, lined skin.

'Ruth,' he whispered, his voice thick with a mixture of fear and relief, his breath coming in short, shallow gasps. 'My love...'

She managed a faint, trembling smile, her eyes locking onto his, and in that brief, fragile moment, the years seemed to fall away, the decades of hardship and heartbreak dissolving into the soft, flickering light of the hospital room.

'I'm here,' she whispered, her voice stronger now, the faintest hint of defiance creeping back into her tone. 'I'm still here.'

Nigel leaned against the wall outside Ruth's room, his eyes fixed on the dull, scuffed floor tiles, his mind racing with unspoken fears. Dr. Patel approached, his expression serious but not grim, his steps quick and precise as he came to stand beside Nigel.

'Mr Van de Watering,' he said, his tone gentle but direct, 'I've finished reviewing the test results. Ruth has suffered a minor stroke.'

Nigel's head snapped up, his heart clenching painfully in his chest. 'A stroke?' he repeated, the word tasting bitter and foreign on his tongue.

Dr. Patel gave a small nod, his hands folded neatly over his clipboard. 'Yes. It was a transient ischemic attack, or TIA. Essentially, it's a temporary disruption in the blood supply to the brain. It can cause sudden weakness, confusion, or loss of coordination, but the good news is that it's often a warning sign.'

'A warning?' Nigel's voice cracked, his fingers curling into tight fists at his sides.

'What...what does that mean for her?'

'With the right medication and lifestyle changes, she can recover well.'

Dr. Patel assured him, his dark eyes steady and calm.

'Modern drugs can significantly reduce the risk of a more severe stroke in the future. Blood thinners, cholesterol lowering medication, and perhaps some physical therapy to help with any lingering weakness.'

Nigel let out a long, shuddering breath, his shoulders sagging with a mixture of relief and lingering fear.

'So she's not...it's not...'

'It's not the end,' Dr. Patel said firmly, offering a small, reassuring smile. 'But it is a wake up call. She'll need to take it easy for a while, but she's a strong woman. I have no doubt she'll pull through.'

Nigel closed his eyes for a moment, letting the words wash over him, feeling the tight, suffocating knot in his chest begin to loosen. He forced a small, shaky smile in return. 'Thank you, doctor.'

Dr. Patel placed a reassuring hand on his shoulder, giving it a small, firm squeeze before turning back down the corridor, his white coat swishing softly behind him, leaving Nigel alone in the cold, echoing hallway to gather his thoughts.

September 1994 seemed to arrive early that year. A September garden in the cold felt like a place caught between seasons. The air was sharp, each breath tinged with the earthy scent of damp soil and decaying leaves. The late blooms–dahlias, asters, and rudbeckia–clung stubbornly to their fading colour, their petals edged with the first touches of frost. The grass, once lush and green, had turned brittle and patchy, crunching underfoot. The wind whispered through the skeletal branches of the trees, scattering the first fallen leaves, their crisp, curling forms rustling like dry paper. Ruth and Nigel's garden felt quieter now, its vibrant summer pulse stilled, settling into the slow, reflective rhythm of autumn.

And it was this scene they looked at. She from her wheelchair and he standing behind her and both waiting by their computer.

'You ought to have been here on his 50th birthday, Nigel. That cake was so sweet!'

I know. But I did get to taste it, darling, remember?'

'Oh yes, of course. I forgot. I forget so much nowadays. Now, what are we doing here today?'

'We are wishing André a happy sixtieth birthday by video link because he's on holiday in Japan with Heather.'

'My, my, how the world changes. Young Violet is a barrister in London and Graham is in senior management. Everybody's growing up and we're growing old.'

'You speak for yourself, young lady!'

'I do so love you, Nigel.'

'Back at you, my darling. For ever and ever.'

'How did I ever managed to land you? Hello! Is this him?'

The screen turned blue and after some distortion there was André and Heather sitting side by side in what looked like a hotel bedroom.

'Konnichiwa, mum! Konnichiwa, Nigel!'

'What's he saying, Nigel? Connie what?'

'Get closer, darling. Can you see them?'

The call lasted for some ten minutes and after a little confusion Ruth was very happy to speak to her son. But after the call had ended Nigel noticed there was a sadness about her. He watched as Ruth closed the laptop, the faint glow of the screen reflecting in her eyes before it flickered into darkness. She sat there for a moment, her hands resting on the closed lid, her expression thoughtful and distant.

'Sixty years old,' she murmured, her voice almost lost in the hum of the kitchen refrigerator. She drew a slow, steady breath, then rose from the chair with a deliberate care that made Nigel's heart ache. He had long since become attuned to the subtle shifts in her energy, the moments when the years seemed to weigh more heavily on her slender frame.

'You alright, my darling?' he asked, his tone light but laced with concern.

She managed a small, thin smile, one that didn't reach her eyes. 'Just tired. I think I'll lie down for a while before dinner.'

He watched her as she left the room, the soft rustle of her long cardigan trailing behind her, the gentle creak of the stairs as she ascended to their bedroom. For a moment, the house felt too large, the rooms too quiet, and Nigel found himself lingering over the small details of the kitchen–the worn edges of the oak table they had picked out together, the faint marks on the tiled floor from years of bustling activity, the kettle she still preferred to use over the electric one.

He straightened the tablecloth, adjusted an askew chair, then moved to the sink, rinsing the few teacups and saucers they had used for the call. He glanced through the window above the sink, out to the garden where Ruth's pots and sculptures sat half hidden in the shadows of the gathering twilight. The creeping tendrils of a wild clematis had claimed one of her early pieces, a tall, angular vase with rough, finger pressed edges that he remembered her shaping on a cool spring morning, her sleeves rolled up, brow furrowed in concentration.

It struck him, as he placed the last cup on the drying rack, how much of their life together had been shaped by those small, shared moments–the early mornings in the studio, the quiet walks along the coastline, the countless dinners where silence held as much meaning as words.

Later, as they sat together over a modest dinner–grilled sea bass with new potatoes and a salad prepared by Pam–Nigel reached across the table, taking her hand in his.

'You seemed a little off after the call earlier,' he said gently, his thumb tracing the faint veins on the back of her hand, now cool to the touch. 'Was it something André said?'

She looked up, her eyes meeting his in the soft candlelight. The years had left their mark on her, lines etched deeply at the corners of her eyes, her once sunlit hair now a soft, silvery grey. But her gaze remained sharp, unflinching, as if the fire within her had only burned more fiercely with age.

'It's just…it struck me,' she said, her voice low and thoughtful, 'how much of his life I've missed. Sixty years. A whole lifetime. I should have been there, watching him grow, guiding him, holding his hand through all those small moments. and I'm also thinking of Georgina.'

She paused, looking at their joined hands, her thumb brushing against his in an unconscious gesture of gratitude.

'And now he's on the other side of the world, and I'm here, staring at him through a screen. I wonder if either of them ever thinks of me as their mother, or the woman who left when they were too young to understand why.'

Nigel felt a familiar pang of helplessness when dealing with this, the ache of wanting to soothe a wound that time itself had carved.

'You've made the best of what you had, Ruth. You gave André the freedom to choose his own path, to become his own man. And as for Georgina? She was so young and so far out of your reach.'

She met his eyes again, the candlelight catching the faint shimmer of tears she quickly blinked away. 'I know,' she whispered, her grip on his hand tightening for a moment. 'I know. But it still hurts. The not knowing. The missed years.'

He leaned across the table, brushing his lips against her knuckles. 'You've given him and your grandson a chance to live their lives. That's no small thing, Ruth.'

She closed her eyes, leaning into his touch for a moment, letting the warmth of his affection seep into her. When she looked at him again, the flicker of pain in her eyes had softened, replaced by the quiet resilience he had come to admire so deeply.

'Thank you,' she said, her voice steadying. 'For being here. For understanding.'

Nigel held her gaze for a moment longer, then released her to pour them each a small glass of wine, the deep red liquid catching the flicker of the candlelight as it swirled into the glass.

They ate in silence, the soft clink of cutlery on porcelain the only sound between them, each lost in thought. Nigel found himself recalling the early days of their relationship—the nervousness of their first meetings, the way she had gradually let her guard down, revealing the sharp, quick witted woman beneath the hardened shell of survival.

As he refilled their glasses, he glanced at her again, her eyes now focused on the window, where the last of the day's light was giving way to the deep blue of night. She had come so far, he thought, through so much—the trials of her youth, the years of solitude, the quiet triumphs of her later life—and yet this small, nagging ache for the son she had once held in her arms still lingered, a wound that time and distance had only deepened.

'Here's to making the most of the years we have left,' he said softly, raising his glass.

Ruth turned to him, a faint smile returning to her lips. She raised her glass in reply, the faint clink of their glasses echoing softly in the quiet room.

It was eleven days after Ruth's 79th birthday, a quiet affair in which she and Nigel spent the evening enjoying a Chinese takeaway and renting, The English Patient that Nigel awoke the following morning and knew immediately that something was not right for when he touched his wife's shoulder she was abnormally cold and he shivered in response. Fetching Pam who was making tea she dialled for the emergency services and afterwards, the morning became an unsettling blur to everybody. The crew that arrived confirmed that Ruth had died during the night and given the status of her, the police and the coroner's office soon followed and the house immediately settled into mourning.

Nigel's solicitor, agent and his brother, Mark arrived during the afternoon and a statement for the press was issued. And for the next ten days Mark never left Nigel's side. Despite repeated requests from the media the funeral was a private one conducted in St Jude's Church with the internment taking place next to Ruth's old friend Sally which came as a surprise to everybody except Nigel. Before the funeral, André had telephoned Nigel, somewhat surprised.

'Did you know about this?'

'Of course I did. It was your mother's wish always to be buried next to Sally. It's in her will.'

'But she didn't mention anything to me.'

'She didn't mention it to anybody, André, except me. Being placed alongside the person who made her life comfortable after Holloway was very important to her and she made the decision decades ago and I fully supported her. That's where I will be buried as well. Next to her. Yes we know it's a bit of a journey, but it's what she wanted and as her executor I take my responsibilities seriously so these are her last wishes. All the cars will be leaving here on the third.'

The November wind whipped through the ancient yew trees that stood like silent sentinels around St Jude's Church, their twisted branches clawing at the grey sky. The church itself, a weathered stone building that had stood through centuries of English history, now played host to one final act in the life of a woman who had, against all odds, found peace in her later years.

Mourners gathered in the small churchyard, their breath steaming in the chill air as they pulled their coats tighter against the bitter wind. A few of the women, faces veiled in black, clutched at their hats as the wind threatened to steal them away. The scent of wet leaves and cold stone filled the air.

Inside, the church was a place of shadows and candlelight, the stone walls absorbing the whispered conversations of those who had come to pay their final respects. The mourners filled the old wooden pews, their faces a mix of grief and quiet reflection. Some had known Ruth in her wild, rebellious youth, others in the calmer, creative decades that had followed. Her impact, both as an artist and as a survivor of a life that had once seemed destined for tragedy, had drawn a disparate crowd.

At the front of the congregation sat Ruth's family. Her husband Nigel, his white hair carefully combed, sat with his head bowed, his hands clasped tightly in his lap. To his left, Ruth's son André, leaned forward holding his wife's hand, his shoulders hunched against the weight of loss. Next to him sat Graham, Ruth's grandson, tall and solemn in a dark suit, his young face reflecting a quiet, private grief alongside, Violet his sister, who was close to tears. Ruth's sister, frail now and leaning heavily on her cane, also dabbed at her eyes with a lace handkerchief, her thin fingers trembling.

A few rows behind them, dignitaries from the world of art filled the pews. Faces familiar from gallery openings, critics who had once dissected Ruth's work, and fellow artists who had admired her fierce independence sat in sombre reflection. They, too, felt the loss of a woman who had brought such fire and passion to the world of ceramics, her pieces a testament to the life she had rebuilt from the ashes of her youth.

The vicar, an elderly man with a shock of white hair and a deep, resonant voice, stepped up to the pulpit and looked over the congregation. He adjusted his glasses, his fingers lingering for a moment on the worn edge of the lectern. The organ stopped.

'We gather here today to honour the life of, Ruth Van de Watering,' he began, his voice steady but tinged with sadness. 'A woman of great strength, creativity, and resilience. She leaves behind a legacy not only in the world of art, but in the hearts of all who knew her.'

As he spoke, the church seemed to draw a collective breath, the flickering candle flames reflecting in the polished brass of the altar cross. The vicar's words, echoing off the stone walls, carried a weight that spoke to the long, often difficult path Ruth had walked.

'Ruth faced many trials in her life,' he continued, his gaze moving slowly over the gathered mourners, 'but in the end, she found peace. She found love, and she found purpose. Her work stands as a testament to that journey, each piece a fragment of a life fully lived.'

He paused, his eyes moving to the closed casket at the front of the church, a simple oak box adorned with white lilies and a single spray of late flowing forget me nots, their delicate blue petals a quiet echo of Ruth's long ago youth.

After the eulogy, the congregation rose to sing a final hymn, their voices swelling to fill the cold stone space. The sound, rich and powerful, seemed to cling to the rafters, hanging in the air long after the final notes had faded. And then finally they were treated to one of Ruth's favourite pieces of music, Litolff's Concerto Symphonique No. 4

(because according to Ruth, nobody can feel sad listening to it) during which the pallbearers stepped forward to carry the casket from the church.

The mourners followed in a slow, sombre procession. Outside, the wind caught their coats once more as they moved towards the small plot beneath a gnarled yew tree where Ruth would be laid to rest beside her dear friend Sally. The mostly oblique gravestones around them, their inscriptions softened by the passage of time, seemed to lean in as if to offer silent comfort.

Nigel, standing beside the open grave, reached for André's arm, his grip firm despite the years. André in return, placed a comforting hand over his, the unspoken bond between them stronger in that moment.

As the coffin was lowered into the cold, damp earth, Nigel stepped forward, his shoulders straight despite the weight of his grief. He reached into his coat pocket and withdrew a small, pale piece of Ruth's ceramic work: a delicate white bird, its wings spread as if in flight. With a steady hand, he placed it on the edge of the casket before stepping back, his eyes never leaving the dark, gaping hole in the earth.

Finally, as the first fistful of earth struck the casket's lid with a hollow, muffled thud, the wind swept through the churchyard once more, lifting a handful of dry leaves into the air. They swirled briefly before settling again, their journey complete. And so, with quiet dignity, Ruth was laid to rest, her life a story written in clay, fire, and an unbroken spirit.

…however, here she lays in St Mary's Church in Old Amersham, still. Year after year. Not pardoned. Our reality, not that contented one. No experiences, but a wintry, untimely, frightened death. We are the poorer for it, for her son never saw his mother mature, we never saw her art, our sons and daughters died without her, and the light of the world vanished when we let her go.

HMP HOLLOWAY

By January 1843 the Court of Common Council and the Court of Aldermen of the City of London agreed that the existing Giltspur Street prison was inadequate and that a new house of correction was needed. An area outside the City was chosen at Holloway where the City had purchased some land as a cemetery during a cholera epidemic in 1832.

Plans by James Buntstone Bunning were approved by the Secretary of State on 29th January 1848. A tender of £92,290 from William Trego was accepted in 1849. The foundation stone was laid by the Lord Mayor, Sir James Duke, on 26th September 1849. Trego went bankrupt in October 1850 and between November 1850 and January 1851 worked stopped. John Jay took up the contract in January 1851 and the house of correction opened on 6th October 1852.

Debtors were admitted to the prison in 1870. The prison was entered through two gatehouses. The plan was radial with four cell blocks for adult males, an administration block, a juvenile block and a female block. The majority of the buildings were constructed of brick. A number of alterations to cell blocks were made between 1881 and 1890, a new male hospital was erected in 1883-4, new reception blocks and a laundry were built in 1886 and a new female infirmary in 1891-2. The prison became all female in 1902. In 1905 a new wing was opened. By the 1930s the prison was found to be inadequate and by 1968 it was concluded that the prison should be demolished and a new one built on the site.

If you have enjoyed this novel then his other works, consisting of, drama, fantasy and true life (as of July 2025) are as follows:

Ruth Ellis-A Life Lived

Ruth Ellis. The last woman hanged in Britain.

But what if she hadn't been?

In this deeply moving reimagining of Ruth's life, here is not her final chapter. From prison gates to quiet fields, gallery walls to private heartbreaks, Ruth must navigate the long shadow of the past while trying to shape a future history never allowed her. Based on meticulous research and emotional truth, this novel offers not an alternative verdict, but an alternative life — one of survival, sorrow, and the possibility of redemption.

A powerful act of literary resurrection. A story not of what was, but what might have been.

From the author of the popular reimagining of Edith Thompson's life comes another unforgettable journey into the fragile line between justice and fate.

A Life Lived

A Life Lived is best described as counterfactual, and originated from real events. The Thompson and Bywaters' affair, which, during 1922-23, scandalised England. Stepping into Edith's life, we are shown events which could have been. An authentic life, emotionally moving and even humorous.

A Life, Lived is a family saga concentrating on the life of Edith Thompson had she been allowed to live. It focuses on her one child, her new husband, her family and profession. We journey with her as the twentieth-century unfolds, as she experiences the Second World War, and after into her old age. She begins new relationships, watches her grandchild and her other adopted children grow. Finally, she remarries, moves out of the country, and finds refuge from the publicity she has generated all her life. The publicity of the woman who was nearly hung.

ISBN 978-1-4709-8733-6

The Following Years

The Following Years is based on the true and tragic events, which occurred during 1922-1923 and ended in the deaths of two men and a woman; the Thompson and Bywaters' case. So outrageous and horrendous was the woman's execution that her case was discussed in parliament decades later. The ordeal she endured evokes disgust even today. The Following Years is a semi-fictional story about Edith Thompson's family and how they dealt with the horror, guilt and shame of having a family member executed. It follows the life of Edith's family concentrating on her sister, Avis.

ISBN 978-1-4709-8733-6

A Romp In Time: The Beginning

Lord Timus is a vicious and unforgiving aristocratic who has the means of travelling across the centuries. After betraying him once too many times, his sulky and vindictive lady assistant, Vah, assisted by the plucky and occasionally funny, Anne Boleyn and her apoplectic mother, Elizabeth the First become friends with two gay men from modern day London. It's a recipe for the most ludicrous of wacky adventures as they attempt to stay one step ahead of the psychopathic Lord.

A Romp In Time is a fantastic time travel comedy (but one with a heart) that takes 'The Grandfather Paradox', and mocks it relentlessly before wringing its neck and throwing its dead body on a heap!

ASIN: B0DYV593W4

A Romp In Time: Confusion Overload

A Romp In Time: Confusion Overload is a fast paced exploit consisting of dashing between the centuries with the final aim of eliminating Lord Timus after he has seemingly come back to life.

It is a farcical, profoundly irreverent, madcap comedy (but one with a heart) primarily intended for the older teenager and those in their twenties. Recommencing in 2020, it is a gentle, tongue-in-cheek, fantasy comedy that never takes itself seriously.

This unique yarn pushes further into the realms of absurdity by introducing luminaries such as John Fowles, Oscar Wilde, Douglas Adams, Agatha Christie (which is why she disappeared for eleven days in 1926 of course), Brooklyn Beckham who is Prime Minister in 2030, Shakespeare and Molly Thompson, (not a luminary) a humble beggar with aspirations who once worked the streets of London in the early nineteenth-century. Joining this merry eclectic mix is The Spice Girls and HG Wells.

ASIN: B0DYV7L42Z

A Romp In Time: The Blackmailer

Four years on from crazily jumping about the centuries after putting right half a dozen wrongs is a long time. Long enough for the seasoned time travelling duo, Stewart and Frankie to marry and become respectable...

Until a sharp lady journalist threatens them with exposure because of a tiny, tiny error that the jocular Frankie once made near the Tower of London.

Intimidated and coerced into submission if they do not comply to her one abnormal request, with the help of their friend Anne Boleyn and their other friend, the beautiful alien, Vah, Stewart and Frankie begin another wild and surreal adventure (but one with a heart) moving through time and other realities.

But is Anne now ready for love after meeting the cunning and duplicitous, Smithers? Why is Stewart's deceased mother alive? How does the very dead Timus fit into it all? And heavens…Frankie with a full head of hair?

Naturally, Molly Thompson, their narrator is on hand to tell you of their travels, and also to explain how her penmanship has improved and why Frankie and Stewart are not the same gay ridiculing couple as they used to be.

ASIN: B0DYTJJTW9

A Romp In Time: Qartin: The Vampire World

A Romp In Time: Qartin: The Vampire World poses yet another problem for Stewart, Frankie, Anne B and Vah's narrator, Miss (now Mrs) Molly Thompson. For the escapade in which they find themselves, perplexes even the mature understanding of their original nineteenth-century lady of the night turned archivist.

As if the notion of time travel wasn't difficult enough for Molly to comprehend, her knotty problem is how to document what happened when Vah decides she wants to rescue her long lost sister, Vibeta from a thousand years ago. Alternate universes, doppelgängers, multiple timelines and worst of all, Qartin; an earth like parallel world where royal cannibalistic humans pray to the half-blind goddess, Vampas are only a few instances that poor Molly has to chronicle in the correct order.

This story (one with a heart!) contains distasteful confusion, abhorrent blood sacrifices, Stewart and Frankie's diminishing love for each other and an insane deranged princess...it's all here proving that their fourth adventure will be their toughest and most revolting yet.

ASIN: B0DG63K78P

A Romp In Time: Doppelgängers

This fifth story (but one with a heart) about the time travelling, mind-boggling adventures of Stewart, Frankie, Vah and Anne Boleyn ought to have you reaching for your pity stick as Molly T, their narrator, many times felt obliged to apologise for her lack of skill in replicating their adventure. But how could she when she was forced to deal with Frankie, an older Frankie, Stewart and an older Stewart, a younger Vah and an old insane Vah? As Molly once shouted at Stuart, 'throw away your logic hat, 'Doppelgängers is insane!'

Nevertheless, along with being blackmailed by Stewart and Frankie's new millennial neighbours, the essential recovery of a Traveller at the place where the android of Anne Boleyn was once executed and trying to understand how a close friend of Anne could be remembered and yet not exist, all becomes reasonably probable under the pen of Molly T.

ASIN: B0DYQ1KSWT

A Romp In Time: Treachery, Betrayal and Vindictiveness

In Molly's sixth description of her friend's unusual lives, there is treachery, betrayal, vindictiveness and all round bad feelings. The combined strain of time travelling over such a long period has finally burst causing unexpected and tragic consequences. Stewart undergoes an unthinkable life changing transformation and Frankie and others do something unimaginable causing relationships to be shattered.

In attempting to recover Vah's gold machine which has been stolen, and attempting to rescue Molly's assumed sister from the year 1800, a vicious psychopathic killer is let loose in modern London essentially changing it. Imagine no World War One and Two and horror of horrors, no Tesco! In attempting to correct their errors, even the notion of Christianity is threatened.

Molly T, Lord Timus' former wife, the group's wordsmith, wrote with her heart on her sleeve, but life will never be the same again for the friends of, those who, Romp In Time.

ASIN: B0DYPH9FRM

A Romp In Time: The Ending

Molly T, your essential chronicler originally from the nineteenth-century is not happy. By her own admittance she is what is known in literary circles as an unreliable narrator. But given the unorthodox, dangerous and interminable circumstances that had the possibility to turn a person upside down, inside out and virtually insane, how could she be otherwise?

Nevertheless, this question must be asked. Is what has happened up to the present day, really her responsibility? Because, what is written here is the truth as told to her by her friends.

Since 2019, when she had agreed to Vah's request that she lovingly documented their exploits, Molly, to all intents, virtually illiterate at the time, agreed as she had the assistance of the great JF.

She imagined, given her early nineteen-century intellect at the time that it would be interesting and even a pleasure documenting Vah and Anne's relationship grow and Stewart and Frankie's misjudged cynicism for each other as well as officially cataloguing all that happened in their crazy misadventures travelling through the centuries.

Except here we are in 2035, the last of her heptalogy, finding herself dealing with emotionally tragic events about which she or her friends had hardly any experience at all.

ASIN: B0DYZCM4HQ

THE MORROW SAGA.

The Morrow Family of Newgate Street, 1939

The final year of a lower class London family and friends living and working in Newgate Street before war engulfs them. There are funerals, affairs, deception, violence, and even a murder. And to those familiar with the Miriam series, there is a surprising visitor.

A novel with domineering mothers, obsessions with famous trials and hangings and frustration that the little corporal from Germany was going to take over their lives. Yet amongst the anger and heartache of their everyday existence, many of their frustrations arrive from realising they are subject to an unknown future…

ISBN: 978-1-326-81782-4

The Morrow Family of Newgate Street, 1940

As the second full year of the European war dawns for the Morrow family of Newgate Street, the pressure falls upon Maud to keep her growing family safe. Particularly as she has become a grandmother and has another new young person to care for. Changes in society are swift and not at all easy to accommodate as everything on the home front affects the family to a personal and greater degree.

Yet close friends who make life worth living surround her. Richard, once the love of her life, young people who test her patience, Bert, their family friend and supplier of black market goods and even his niece…

By the year's end, when the destruction of London begins, it will never be the same…and neither will the Morrow family of Newgate Street.

ISBN: 978-1-326-96239-5

The Morrow Family of Newgate Street, 1941

When the third year of war begins, Maud and her family are homeless and misplaced. Only Bert, an old friend of her dead husband has the ability to help them. Gradually Maud and her daughter begin to rebuild their lives taking on responsibility after responsibility as the deprivations of war continue to affect them. Although Maud continues to find great comfort in the love Richard has for her, the effects of the war changes the personalities of those she knows. And with that comes bitterness and frustration as everyone realises that this is a war than is not going to end any time soon.

There are more deaths of loved ones, an unknown brother arrives, two jail sentences, Maud's love for orphan Freddy is tested, in her circle of friends more babies are born and eventually, her love for William, her only son, is tested as the army turns him into a fighting man. A man he was not destined to be.

ISBN: 978-0-244-90531-6

The Morrow Family of Newgate Street, 1942

War is changing the Morrow family and their friends in unexpected ways. They have come to expect the deprivations, loss of loved ones and hard work. But bitterness, betrayal, rejection and hopelessness were new enemies. A surprising and tragic death from Miriam's family affects them greatly, and while Arabella continues her social descent, a surprising interloper takes her place as

London and its people become exhausted with no end yet in sight.

ISBN: 978-0-244-91814-9

The Morrow Family of Newgate Street, 1943

In this year Maud and her family learn that the physical horrors and disappointment of living through a world war extend beyond mere death. For despondency and demoralising events happen closer to home as her children change in ways she previously could not have imagined.

Would these occurrences have happened had the Germans not begun their quest for world domination? Just how long would it take to win the war as she and everybody else ask how many more needless deaths of soldiers, Jews, intellectuals, gypsies, ordinary civilians and the Nazis, so-called, undesirables would have to die?

As the Morrow family's tired and weary souls prevail under the gravest of situations, Maud and her husband, Richard both find the question impossible to answer. Yet, as they endure, bright speckles of happiness and even love occasionally whirl around them making their lives just bearable.

ISBN: 978-0-244-63540-4

The Morrow Family of Newgate Street, 1944

While everyday life becomes increasingly tedious for the Morrow family and their friends as they cope with the frustration at how long it is taking to defeat Nazism, hope appears in many forms. Yet new friendships, unexpected wealth, lost souls, conflicts with the law and accidents muddle the waters. As do illegitimate babies and news of deeds long ago committed. A second Blitz partly returns them to the condition they found themselves in back in 1940, but by the end of the year, as Europe is set ablaze with the Second Front, back on English soil, expectations that the war will end soon and that they will have a future is their greatest hope.

ISBN: 978-0-244-34932-5

The Morrow Family of Newgate Street, 1945

By the beginning of 1945, Maud and Richard knew it was only a matter of time before Hitler and his Nazi party was destroyed. The British, Americans, and the Russians along with twenty other countries were now converging with destructive force on Berlin. But such positive news meant little to the civilians of London who were dealing day by day with shortages of food, clothing and fuel as well as coping with business, reappearing scoundrels and life-changing accidents.

Old enemies are subject to retributive justice; corrupt men are arrested for indecency. There are deaths, births and before the last and final day, addressing and accepting the final powerful weapons of the Third Reich, the dreaded vengeance rockets that decimated cities.

However, just because the war concluded, and amid the triumphant joy of victory, family life was never going to be the same again for, The Morrow family of Newgate Street.

ISBN: 978-0-244-06132-6

The Morrow Family of Newgate Street, 1966

In the eighth and final novel describing the Morrow family of Newgate Street, we find them twenty-one years later during 1966. The business is now being managed by Maggie and Anthony who do not have a great deal of hope for its long-term future due to the changing requirements of Londoners, many of whom are daily commuters and not members of local families who had lived in the area for generations.

Maud and Richard are now in their seventies and retired. They live above the hardware store but still show a keen interest in it, as well as their family and friends.

However, many of those and their adult children have dissipated of course to various parts of the suburbs leaving them somewhat isolated and alone.

Therefore, the elderly couple find living in the modern world difficult because not only are they surrounded by powerful memories but find it increasingly difficult to accept the contemporary concepts that the youth enjoy such as free love, flower power, banning the bomb and drinking coffee on the pavement! With every passing year they know the world that offered them the best years of their life is fast disappearing.

Yet, they do their best to enjoy what time is left to them by visiting Forest Reach, roaming to Paris and Cornwall and catching up with old and valued friends as their deep affection for each other increases.

ISBN: 978-0-244-99572-0

NOVELS IN MOLLY'S BEST SELLING MIRIAM SERIES ARE:

Percy and Bert — A Miriam Story:

Miriam was born into a warm East London Edwardian family in 1907. The first of four daughters to Percy and Faith Burrow, her youthful years were as eventful as her father and his twin brother, the unmanageable and troublesome, Bert.

The boys, born in 1874, the sons of Emma and Samuel, residents of Smithfield were to see great changes in their lifetime. Join Percy and Bert as their lives are traced from birth to when Percy marries Faith and she tells him that they are expecting their first child. Meanwhile, Bert's vexatious young life prepares him for the kind of obliging and indispensably isolated man he is to become.

ISBN: 978-1-326-49843-6

Miriam's Early Years:

Miriam's Early Years tells the beginnings of her Edwardian, East London family. From her welcome birth to her newly married parents in the summer of 1907, we follow her through her early childhood, her schooling, the Great War, and the births of her three sisters, Emily, Sarah and Penelope. Upon reaching the gay twenties, she meets, Ray, her first husband, and gives birth to her children. Then, with World War Two approaching, darkness settles over her once happy life. When the electrical accident occurs, her life disintegrates until the fateful Saturday when two policemen knock at her door… ISBN: 978-1-291-59974-9

A Year In Holloway:

1938. Mrs Miriam Baxter, an ordinary housewife and mother of two small children, committed a misdemeanour in the form of theft. Her punishment was to be imprisoned in the infamous women's gaol, Holloway, House of Correction, North London.

Placed with the type of women, with whom she had never been in contact, Miriam has to learn to survive in a harsh environment that took away her freedom, her family and every-thing she had ever known.

Written with the help of authentic documents of the period, A Year In Holloway, details exactly what it would have been like to suffer imprisonment in a women's prison just before the beginning of the Second World War.

ISBN: 978-1-4475-0452-8

Miriam's War:

After spending eight months in Holloway prison, Miriam Baxter is released three days before war is declared in 1939. Overjoyed to see her children, her parents and her sisters, she spends the next five and a half years protecting, arguing and feeding them. She would call herself unremarkable. However, it is her determination and courage that takes her and her family through the Second World War.

ISBN: 978-1-291-04154-5

Miriam's Family Life:

It is the summer of 1945, and Miriam and her extended family are weary but disciplined by war, and accustomed to austerity. Throughout this period, she deals with more deaths, ill health, moving house, rationing and accidents; all the while guiding her loved ones through the deprivation and destitution that is the East-End of London. Yet, there are births, a new relationship for her and marriages. Conscription and the introduction of the National Health arrive at the end in 1948. As with, Miriam's War, and, A Year in Holloway, she copes daily, struggling with a situation that is unique and difficult. Her pathos, determination, humour and love are all she has.

ISBN: 978-1-291-06288-5

Miriam's Silver Years

This edition deals with the years 1948 to the stimulating one of 1963, a period when rationing and coupons still applied, and the long shadow of the Second World War still hung over Britain.

Through the threads of Miriam and her three sisters, we see how they cope with their increasingly complicated lives; the introduction of self-employment, marriages, births, deaths, moving house and television, as they embraced the second half of the twentieth-century, and the radical changes which followed World War Two. During this crucial time, a previously unknown family member shockingly makes himself known, she enjoys the holiday of a lifetime, the hub of her close family falls apart and she makes a final decision whether to stay in the East End or live out her years by the coast.

The Second World War and her time in Holloway Prison is now a distant memory. However, apart from the changes in her family, particularly as the decade of the, 'swinging sixties' arrive, she retains the love of her loyal husband, Roy, and still enjoys her enduring friendship with Rafa.

Miriam is now a dutiful grandmother, an extraordinarily fabulous aunt of an ever-increasingly large family, a servant of the community, and as a woman proudly moving from middle age into the remaining years of her life, a matriarchal force to be reckoned with.

ASIN : B0D4288KXB

Miriam's Golden Years:

Miriam's Golden Years takes us from 1963 until the nineteen nineties. A period when she bore the many deaths of her family and friends with dignity, but is more than pleased to welcome the beginning of her grandchildren, great grandchildren and great nephews and nieces, despite all their singular problems.

Equally remarkable, as the rest of her life had been, Miriam finds herself wrestling with the problems of social and political violence, the rise of female emancipation, decimalisation and the acceptance of becoming elderly while still caring deeply for her extended family and her beloved husband, Roy.

She has now gone beyond a matriarchal figure. She is host to memories long forgotten, a contributor to a decent way of life fast disappearing and part of a proud East End dynasty that her descendants will never forget.

ISBN: 978-1-291-48384-0

Miriam's Last Years:

Miriam is now eighty-seven and after Roy's death, still lives in the old rectory with Rafa alongside Florence and her twin girls. It is now a time of reflection, the promise of a great, great grandchild, and long conversations about the events and conditions that shaped her life. Yet even as her body moves inexorably into extreme old age, events continue around her that proves that even wheelchair bound, her clear and sound mind, alongside her remarkable memory, can still dispense sound advice and be more than useful to those who are charged with caring for her.

Miriam's Last Years also sees Rafa Barker in her twilight years when she too has become alone once more, abandoned by her only and only daughter over a shameful event from which she cannot face. A time when, surrounded by her close family and friend, she too takes a reflective sad look back on a lifetime of service and love as she cares for Miriam during her final days.

ISBN: 978-1-326-66152-6

Miriam's Presence at Christmas:

It is now Christmas and Miriam's now middle-aged youngest daughter, Florence and her two adult daughters, Faith and Betty are preparing for Christmas amid one of the most dreadful snowstorms to befall London in recent years. There are incidences aplenty; Rafa to be visited in a care home, a disaster or two, headstrong children, a husband who needs to be divorced and old and long memories are stirred. But as Faith, heavily pregnant with her third child comes to realize, the spirit of Miriam (real or imaginary?) is not so far away.

ISBN: 978-1-291-97868-1

Peter and April:

When Peter met April in the summer of 1946, his family speculated it was a match made in heaven. Therefore when the couple married in 1953, Miriam Barker hoped that her son would keep their large family together in Stratford. But the circumstances and excitement of the mid Nineteen Fifties overran the significance of his pedigree and, to his mother's dismay, Peter, a newly qualified policeman, bought a flat in Barkingside, historically part of Essex.

Here they would meet a variety of characters quite different from the ones they had known during their time in East London. Close friends, private confrontations, a death or two, secrets and pregnancy; these became subjects that were part of any newly married couple setting up in a new home. But seventeen years later, April's very existence is threatened…

ISBN: 978-1-326-06596-6

Miriam's Family Blitz:

On the 7 September 1940, the London Blitz began in earnest. This was when the Nazi Luftwaffe machine switched from daylight raids on military targets to heavy bomber raids at night focusing on large cities.

Miriam's Family Blitz, already broadly conceived in, Miriam's War by the same author, places her family's first fifteen days of the London Blitz under a magnifying glass. A period in which the mundane lives of her close family and friends in the East End found themselves experiencing front-line warfare for the first time, undergoing the inconvenient blackout, general restrictions and rationing. From the family's once relatively quiet life, and with Miriam, released from Holloway prison only one year previously, the intense and very real fear of invasion, gassing, destruction and death occupies almost their every thought.

ISBN: 978-1-326-29810-4

Daffodils in Autumn:

An autumn break for a young London mother... An isolated stretch of Dorset coastline... An unexplained phenomenon...

Daffodils in Autumn tells the unusual story of Sheryl Walters and her harrowing descent into paranoia and derangement as she and her daughter's past, present and future become meaningless, as nothing appears to be what it is.

Daffodils In Autumn has been described as a psychological time-travel fantasy. To offer a synopsis of the plot would be impossible without spoiling it as it does not contain a predictable ending but is, in its entirety, a kink.

However, it appears to be about a modern young, poorly educated mother and what happens to her and her daughter when they find themselves under impossible and inescapable circumstances.

ISBN: 978-1-4457-4259-5

Escape:

Harry Whittle is a sixteen-year-old son of an emotionally frustrated butler working in London. He fails in his attempt to join the army in 1916 because of his age.

As a punishment for his recklessness, Harry is sent to work on a wealthy estate in Devon where he befriends the owner's sixteen-year-old daughter, Blanche who is slightly deranged due to her younger brothers abruptly disappearing five years previously.

While walking in the woods, miserable and homesick, Harry and Blanche are unaccountably and instantaneously catapulted into the unsolved misadventure of what happened to Blanche's brothers.

Henceforth, they are forced to endure a fantastic and inexplicable agenda of unimaginable circumstances, so scarcely credible that madness threatens to engulf them as they hope to return to normality.

ISBN: 978-1-326-02127-6

The Herb Girl:

A novel about the great divide, the complication that may be the after-life, our relation-ship with it, and what we believe it could be.

By way of a damning gypsy's curse, a Scots-born female rogue, savage inexplicable accidents, murder and two of the oldest sexual dysfunctions known to civilization, The Herb

Girl chronicles a few months in the life and close family of a bewitching, heavily pregnant, Cornish-bred herbalist, whose life is not entirely guiltless. The Herb Girl is a self-contained maze, a story involving poisoning, manslaughter, spiritualism, explosives, and rage. But who is the narrator? What is his wholly abhorrent secret and why is he so personally judgmental?

ISBN 978-1-291-90618-9

Carry on Corsets:

A comedy set in 1972 about a battle between an ancient and respectable company of corset makers and, Aphrodisiac, a place of swinging, knicker-clad females.

As I see the cast:

Sir Cyril Strumpet The Third--Kenneth Williams.

Lord Strumpet--Peter Butterworth.

Frederick Hofen-Stoffen-Hoffen-Stoffen--Jim Dale.

Miss Demi More--Hattie Jacques.

Mr. Muff--Charles Hawtrey.

Sidney Rabbit--Sidney James.

Bunny Rabbit--Joan Sims.

Munchie--Bernard Bresslaw.

Ever Perky--Barbara Windsor.

Libby Rabbit--Patsy Rowlands.

Mr. Tesy--Frankie Howerd.

The Reverend Thrush--Kenneth Connor.

Anton Cashmere--Leslie Phillips.

Harmony Didit--Esma Cannon.
Miss Tumbledown--Valerie Leon
ISBN: 978-1-84753-137-7

Seven Sisters:

A drama about a deformed child. It tells the story of a girl born into a wealthy Devon-shire family in the 1960s with the condition of Polydactyly, and who is given up for adoption, finds herself...and love. It tells of her fostering, her cruel upbringing, the friendships she makes, and of her eventual success as she finds that rarest flower; love. Set amongst a world of poetry and astronomy it ends at the climax of one of nature's most memorable events.

ISBN: 978-1-4092-1176-1

Executrix:

A story of retribution and redemption set in an intelligent, dystopian capitalist society obsessively consumed with consumer voting and finance.

Livina is an orphan, who has been trained from birth in, Brook, a state-run, military-style training camp, to become an executioner working at High Tower Transmissions, a privately owned UK prison which is owned by the multinational company, Mergam whose profitable influence extends to the upper echelons of parliament.

Mergam makes its money by allowing visual transmissions of its authorized punishments by terrestrial transmission and the Internet. Through a twenty-four hour, pay-as-you-watch scheme, the worldwide audience can attempt to amend the decisions of the courts. Often, the fate of reviled prisoners can be altered by how many votes have been cast. The amount of votes can dictate the punishment, which are varied.

Livina however, has an inherent kindness about her, almost a spirituality, even though she consistently remains true to her military-style upbringing, wholeheartedly convinced that her actions are helping society to become a better place. Therefore, occasionally she brings about a swift ending on those upon whom she is charged to carry out the ultimate punishment. However, she is friendless, suffers from a type of borderline Aspergers condition, has an obsessive-compulsive character, and is to a greater extent, unemotional and distant be-cause of her high position. Nevertheless, she befriends a childhood friend by the name of Winter, who has fallen on hard times, and entered the system himself on minor charges. Against the rules, Livina falls deeply in love, and becomes pregnant.

ISBN: 978-1-4457-0689-4

The Angel from the Sea:

The Angel From The Sea is a supernatural story and describes the events that occur after an Edwardian young lady called Clara pleads for assistance against a member of her family who is brutal towards her. Whereupon, one of the oldest feminine forces in the world appears as the uncontrollable Moganna. However, having demanded the presence of this ungovernable intelligence, Clara and her heinous family find themselves at the mercy of Moganna's ruthlessness and inhumanity. Moganna refers to herself as an angel, but as the innocent Clare soon discovers, a better name for the power she has unleashed is, a Cacodaemon.

ISBN: 978-1-291-52345-4

Saturn's Return:

Saturn's Return is a romantic comedy. Alan Brown is a wealthy and young, wisecracking, stuttering, clumsy black businessman living the high life in London and engaged to Maria, his cheating, loudmouth but stunningly beautiful girlfriend. Upon the death of his mother, honouring a deathbed agreement, he travels to Africa to find his father, but while there, meets the mysterious and alluring Kali. Whereupon he discovers far more about himself than he ever thought possible.

ISBN: 978-1-4457-6621-8

Stronger Than War:

In the late summer of 1972, Lawrence De Havilland, a successful and analytical surgeon discovers Miss Jennifer Compton-Hepburn, an attractive thirty-year-old, Leading Officer with the WRNS outside his house in Cheyne Walk, Chelsea.

Her mannerisms and appearance pose an exotic problem for Lawrence for which there is no logical explanation. Distressed from shock and injuries arising from an apparent explosion, Jennifer tells Lawrence an unreasonable story, which forces him to accept the impossible, and to acknowledge that love is stronger than war.

ISBN: 978-1-4461-6592-8

The Christmas Eve Ghost:

A phantasmagorical ghost story. In Victorian London, two elderly spinster sisters who have not spoken to each other for fifty years because of a youthful tragedy, share a house that once belonged to their parents. The reason for their bitter feud remains unknown even to their closest friends. But on Christmas Eve, 1881, the past returns to offer them one last chance to redeem themselves, and show that Christmas really is a magical time of year.

ISBN: 978-1-4467-3994-5

Bad Girl:

London, 2013. Bad Girl is a modern story about Angela Tenneb, an attractive psychopathic London woman. She is a drug dealer, addict, bully, thief and extortionist.

She was once a happy and innocent child of a contented family. That was before she and her twin sister; Ann arrived home from school one hot summer afternoon in the 1990s to find their mother laughing insanely in a room awash with blood and in the process of sawing her husband and his lover into pieces.

Now, in 2013, Angela pits herself against society, pushing boundaries. She has become a bad girl. But events near Christmas, when her mother is released from prison, becomes a weekend when the bad girl becomes truly evil, adding kidnapping and murder to her villainy.

ISBN: 978-1-4710-9423-1

Bad Girl 2:

Angela Tenneb is now 42 and has spent 18 years in prison, one third of her time in solitary confinement. Now, in the year 2030, she is released on licence.

Living with her widowed twin sister, Ann in Camden Town and having become religious, she is now meek, compliant and thoroughly rehabilitated.

However, her murderous past can never be forgotten. Her enemies will not let her forget and neither will they forgive.

ASIN: B087FYF6TQ

The Cornish Wheel:

1965. At eighteen years of age, Jack Webber is friendless and not the most popular of men, despite belonging to a wealthy London family. Shy and slightly dysfunctional from a lifetime of abuse, and recovering from pneumonia, he is sent to convalesce at Kelynek House in Western Cornwall, which is owned by his estranged uncle and his young wife, a passionless, yet mysterious native of the area. There, Jack quickly falls in love with Jacque-line, a twenty-seven year old reclusive woman artist and writer of children's novels who lives, apparently in 1946, in an isolated cottage.

However, this is not just a regular time-travel fantasy love story. For what Jack ultimately uncovers is immeasurably far more bizarre, abnormal and disturbing.

ASIN: B006IWWYVC

The Tragic and Transgendered World of Margaret Allen

The reason the transgendered man, Margaret 'Bill' Allen became a murderer has con-founded criminologists. Since his execution at Strangeways Prison in January 1949 for the brutal murder of the eccentric Nancy Ellen Chadwick, sociologists (particularly those working in the sociology of deviance) and those in the behavioural sciences, such as psychologists and psychiatrists as well as lay authors have attempted to understand why.

In this short book, a transgendered woman herself, Molly Cutpurse attempts to cast some new and personal light on what has become known as a tragic and misunderstood case. Of Bill's guilt, there is no doubt. But upon examining the details of his life, there re-mains a degree of shame over the way he was treated at his trial and after in prison, and of the lack of mercy afforded to him.

ISBN: 978-1-4717-4214-9

The Detective:

Hoping to emulate his hero, the great fictional detective, Sherlock Holmes, and coming from a wealthy family in Ghana, Mr Gabriel Chukwumereije, posing as a simpleton, is in reality, an intelligent, good looking, arrogant and wealthy sociopath who arrives in London willing to do and say anything to advance his cause. His only problem is…it is 1960.

Becoming involved with what seems at first a trivial matter of inexplicably received profoundly immoral and wicked Christmas cards, as the case unravels, the narrative widens and extends back to the dark days of the Blitz and thenceforth to murder as his investigation takes its toil of the local's lives.

Taking a position as a cleaner in a local police station, in an era when racism was on the increase, Chukwumereije's socially inept manner and his lying and deceptive sociopathic nature destroys everything he touches.

ISBN: 978-1-4717-1516-7

Dark Man:

When purity is not enough. North London, 1936. Father Forrest is an inherently decent priest consumed by impure corporal thoughts. He has little possibility of ethical growth. When his secretary's young daughter dies, the tragedy stimulates a series of events, which contribute to obsession, misfortune and blackmail.

It will take a chance meeting with an unscrupulous young woman, the sudden reason-less death of his demented mother, a fortuitous brush with an elderly ex woman prisoner and combating an evil and vicious thug before he is able to come to terms with his moral struggle.

This is a character-driven novel. You won't get any cute Hollywood endings here!

ISBN: 978-1-291-53303-3

Waterleigh Nursing Home:

Waterleigh Nursing Home is primarily about a young carer, Ms Erin Flynn and, Sarah Graham, a new type of patient who is forced to take up permanent residence due to early onset dementia.

Although Erin is regarded as one of the best carers in the home, she is not without personal family problems. However, the elderly and confused Sarah brings out more than the caring side of her, proving that even during our last days, all of us can be useful as we connect with each other. Because of where it is set, there can be no happy ending. What happens is logical and unavoidable. Yet life continues.

ISBN: 978-1-291-25156-2

OBSESSIONS:

Obsessions is an irregular glimpse into the pennilessness life of Miss Hester Martin-Compter, the only child of a once wealthy banking family, destined by a deranged mind to live amongst the poverty of the Whitechapel area of London during the interwar years, World War Two and the nineteen fifties.

A bewildering, self-obsessed passion, infatuations by others and a tenuous, bizarre connection with Whitechapel's most infamous murderer, Jack the Ripper shapes her life and destiny as she and her mother, Cecelia learns to live amongst the impoverished residents about which the child previously had no knowledge.

At first, living a hand-to-mouth existence, and becoming friends with a variety of idiosyncratic local characters, as decades pass, Hester's introverted self disappears as, through marriage and friendships gained, she learns to trust herself as she embraces the opportunities of the middle of the twentieth-century.

ISBN: 978-1-291-71151-6

The Mystery of Bleak House:

In 1975, Mary Park, the only daughter of a wealthy and respected dynasty whose family accommodation is in Bloomsbury Square, London, is being driven beyond endurance by domestic and marital responsibilities, financial pressures and intellectual frustration. A separation from her philandering husband and the concern of her teenage daughter taking drugs occupy a large amount of her time. However, rumours, arriving from an unprincipled and grievous mathematician, a man desperate to redeem his own family heritage, informs her that her grandfather once built an extraordinary machine that offered the possibility of changing the entire world. Mary will need to confront her family's shadowy past and endure obscure and repugnant painful memories before she can unravel the mystery of what her mother used to call, 'Bleak House'.

ISBN: 978-1-291-87356-6

Lies, Secrets and Infidelity:

When a London private investigator arrives in Torquay in 1955, he allows people to believe that he is a tourist. Brought in privately to investigate the death of an elderly woman who was almost buried alive, one by one he exposes the sordid and complex family secrets of its most respectable town members.

ISBN: 978-1-291-93811-1

The Angel, the Coward and the Parasite-A Faerie Tale?

A Faerie Tale for adults. Roistered Pheoden is a young man of limited wisdom who lives in the port city of King's Scallion on the coastline of the Vihq Ocean, which lays within the Trallaedel Kingdom.

His life is uneventful until he meets, Dane Haddix, a transvestite and sexual predator who shows him that, 'there is no cure for pleasure'.

Through Dane though, Risteard meets and marries the spirited and vivacious sorceress and psychic, Miss Siùsaidh Molde who is truly to change the rest of his life.

Yet Risteard cannot rise above his past, and when Lort, an older, passive and sadomasochistic man insinuates himself into their everyday lives, nothing will ever be the same again.

ISBN: 978-1-326-13452-5

The House In Carter Lane:

A four-part novel set in Clifton Buildings, Carter Lane near St Paul's cathedral. The landlord is a miserly and deliberately cruel moneylender called, Mr Scrooge.

Mr and Mrs Percy Radcliffe are an impoverished, newly married couple struggling to run a funeral business in 1843. Their descendants run the same business in 1892, and during the December blitz of 1940 as well. And finally there are eight people living their solitary lives in 2009 in converted flats.

On their Christmas days, over the centuries, what have these people in common? Is their good fortune because they happen to live in the same house, or is there a more spiritual and indefinable reason? Have their Christmas experiences anything to do with what happened to the old money lender One Christmas morning all those years ago?

Yes, Miriam Baxter visits! And Bert too! Thematically, the novel deals with elements of fate, luck and serendipity. There's no neat resolution and no definitive full stop.

Of course that's what most readers want or need these days, but I'm not going to let you off so lightly! In this novel, algorithm has not taken the place of soul.

ISBN: 978-1-326-20014-5

The Chemist's Son:

London 1963

A physiologically disturbing account of an imaginary or real event. Mr William Mills is a widower and pharmacist whose shop is near St Paul's Cathedral. When his twin children, John and Jane discover an abandoned Roman ruin under the shop's cellar, it leads them to series of disturbing events. Nonetheless, many years later, when John writes about their experience, is he writing the truth or hiding something malevolent?

ISBN: 978-1-326-82195-1

The Soul In The Machine:

The future: The ability to map the human cortex neurone by neurone has been perfected by way of scanning. While people live, it is now possible to place a copy of a person's personality into data storage. A Similarity. The main reason is so the bereaved can communicate with them after death. Geolog is a world leader in this technology. For two middle-aged sisters, Mia and Emma, living on an isolated farm on the periphery of Hastings, this technology divides them. When Mia's husband is murdered in Hong Kong and she uses his Similarity online, a family secret is revealed forcing them to ask some profound questions about life and the continuance of the human soul. And all the time, Geolog, the technology giant, is monitoring them.

ISBN: 978-1-326-26057-6

Holloway, House of Correction:

Holloway, House of Correction is an alternative fantasy and documents the unlikely friendship between two women; Victoria, wealthy, beautiful and recently married, and the impoverished Margaret, the only surviving daughter of Victorian England's most prolific serial murderer, Mary Ann Cotton. Both live close to the old Holloway Gaol when it became a women's only prison in the spring of 1902.

ISBN: 978-1-326-38773-0

Misplaced:

On a warm and late summer evening in 2015, after her boyfriend dumps her, Essex girl, Donna Rigg drunkenly smashes her car into a pillar-box. She is taken to hospital where she is diagnosed with concussion.

Over the next few weeks, her perception changes, for she begins to see the world as it was fifty-five years previously in 1960. On a follow-up visit for an MRI, she becomes frightened and argues with staff. Becoming aggressive and overhearing she could be sectioned, she runs from the hospital and vanishes in the grounds as 1960 actually becomes her reality...

Misplaced was written (optimistically) as literary fiction and as a first person narration. It is focused more on theme than on plot. As Donna describes her adventure, it certainly risks losing its way with no simplistic logical ending.

ISBN: 978-1-326-44663-5

The Appearance of the Woman:

A fantasy grounded in reality.

In 1963 when Miss Donna Lawson discovers an unconscious woman on a deserted stairwell at London's Fenchurch Street Station, she calls for help immediately, little realising that the bizarrely dressed lady wearing late Victorian clothes is about to offer her an experience that will change her perception on life and love. That is if she can shake off the suspicion that she has become the central figure in what could be an elaborate hoax. Her reservations are not made any easier by the sordid and hidden activities of her boyfriend, but at least are eased by the appearance of one good man.

ISBN: 978-1-326-63463-6

The Atwall Twins.

It is during the last and late days of December 1941 when the lonely but wealthy Miss Ada Atwall begins to receive telephone calls from a young and disabled woman called Sarah Atwall who claims to be speaking from the future. Fascinated by occultism and astrology since a tragedy devastated her family thirty years previously, Ada uses Sarah's knowledge to advance her own popularity. Enter Mr Emerson Farthingale, a profoundly immoral son of a bishop who is determined to uncover the truth.

ISBN: 978-1-326-75006-0

Slavery

Love is vulnerability. Love screams. Unrequited love destroys. Love is pain. Love is eternal. We hang on to love. We hang on for love. We exist with the absence of love. Occasionally, love is so very close that we can touch it. We feed love. Love feeds us. Sometimes love rules us. Never the opposite. Love is nuits blanches. Sometimes love pulls us apart until death. Sometimes it loves us back. In all its forms, to love is painful. We serve the one we love. We become its slave. Paul was one such slave.

ISBN 978-1-4457-5076-7

The Chronologically Challenged Funeral Director

Take a lone and eccentric woman scientist called, Miftley from ninety-four years in the future, a devastating curse from a thousand old family who practise Wicca, a present day hypochondriac young funeral director called Dennis (the spitting image of Eric Morecambe) whose business is in Southend-on-Sea, and Fenella, the love of his life who doesn't want him. Mix in the erotic dance of the tango, a comic journey that can only lead to an uncertain doom, and you have, The Chronologically Challenged Funeral Director.

ISBN 978-1-4457-6926-4

Supertranny

The comic adventures of a modern mythological individual who lives side by side with us in our world. Supertranny lives in the heart of a great nation. Born with unimaginable gifts, she lives in the hearts and souls of those she helps. She is imaginative, humorous and spectacularly beautiful! Moreover, she has a wardrobe to die for as well! An ordinary soul, mostly doing any job she can, but a Supertranny when she hears that cry for help with her super hearing. Only three people know her masculine identity and they have vowed never to reveal it. Day and night, people go about their business soundly, knowing that there is someone here on earth who is unbreakable and who has unimpeachable moral fibre and character. She protects the innocent and saves the stupid and unworthy. Her name has become legion. Her acts, supernatural, for she is… Supertranny! But from out of the earth rises a savagely fierce and ancient monster, intent on subduing the population. His presence takes Supertranny to the edge of her capabilities.

ISBN 978-1-4452-0969-2

The Bitter Rose and the Thorn

Lara Everett is a sensitive, childless widow of twenty years. She is settled, has buried her childhood dreams, is financially solvent and addicted to being alone. She would not call herself depressed, just unhappy. However, fate allows William (Bill) Lee, a shrewd and resourceful man, a man entirely unsuitable for any woman, to cross her threshold and take hold of her heart.

Hypnotised by his personality, Lara finally has no choice but to take the hardest path and realise that it is not his physical presence that is important but something far more formidable and ultimately satisfying.

Set in 1969 and with memories going back to World War Two, The Bitter Rose and the Thorn is a narrative account of a woman choosing to abandon her catastrophic past and move towards a more self-fulfilling life.

ISBN: 978-0-244-69575-0

I was left in 1871 Book 1

Luna is a 23 year old music student in her third year at university. She is a product of her age. A formidable and intelligent millennium woman.

An outspoken, foul-mouthed, fitness freak. A non-smoking, vegetarian, and a passionate supporter of equality for women, LGBT and animal rights as well.

While training for the London Marathon, 2018, she is knocked to the ground in a collision with a woman outside Temple Gardens on Victoria Embankment. But that was only the beginning of the day her life entirely changed… It's not a comedy. Actual time travel never is.

ASIN: B07GYWR3BP

I went back to 1872 Book 2

In the following months after returning from her experience in the nineteenth-century, Luna finds she has fallen prey to anxiety and depression. She realises the catastrophic mistake she made and unhappily appreciates that she has to return to the past to rectify it. However, her closest friend, Sophia insists she accompany her.

But this collaboration hardly ends well because while dealing with a terminal illness, mental incapacity and a violent assault, Luna, for the sake of her baby and a vulnerable Victorian waif, is eventually forced to make decisions she would not normally undertake.

ASIN: B07K12ZFBW.

I returned to 1873 Book 3

Half a year after returning from 1872, Luna and Rose are living together in Sophia's flat. Relations with her parents have soured and Luna's conscience is troubling her over Sophia's death to the extent that she is making herself ill. The only decent thing in her life is Rose who struggles to live in 2019.

Making friends with another young woman called Eleanor who works at their Pizza restaurant, Lulu conceives the idea of threatening Mr Quick into letting her travel back just one more time to stop Sophia from dying of sepsis. However, she greatly underestimated Mr Quick's reaction and he punishes her by sending her to 1873 to spend a year there. Left to cope on her own, she has no choice but to seek help from the wealthy family who looked after her previously…

ASIN: B07MK77M55

I arrived back in 1870 Book 4

Luna is not in the best place mentally. Nobody except her friend Sophia fully realises what has happened to her. Only Luna knows the power and influence Mr Quick has over her life and the way he has altered her thoughts. As much as she is unable to erase the child, Rose from her thoughts, she feels a great need to rescue her but finds herself lacking in courage. But then Mr Quick, running to his own unknown and mysterious agenda, makes the decision for her and therefore Luna is once again plunged back in time with the intention of rescuing Rose. Who is not the child she remembers. However, the vagaries of time-travel mess with her once again, this time equally severely as she is forced to face two nineteenth-century sinners and criminals. The rescue succeeds...but can Luna be sure that her adventure is now over?

ISBN: 978-0-244-15972-6

I was sent to 1968 Book 5

During the summer of 2021. Luna settled into complacency. She enjoys her job at the MusicRoom and shares Sophia's flat. However, her relationship with her parents has not thawed as they still refuse to believe her story.

But, in November, Mr Quick visits her again and tells her that once she does one last trip for him, then he will never visit her again. She immediately and strongly refuses but then when Mr Quick offers her an impossible arrangement and it's one she simply cannot refuse. Therefore, with great reluctance, she agrees and as Sophia wants to go with her, they travel to 1968 to the same house in Royal Crescent where their instructions are to steal a rare bible from its library.

The assignment itself was simple enough but Luna had not reckoned for Sophia to fall hopelessly in love with a disreputable man. Therefore, Luna returns by herself bringing with her a young Egyptian servant, Asim and that seems to be the end of that. Except when she visits Camille in Park Street, a shocking event takes place which must be resolved.

ISBN: 9798354171057

I was coerced to go to 1913 Book 6

The sixth adventure in the Time Girl series sees Luna's mind beginning to unravel as she attempts to more fully understand Mr Quick's reasons why he choose her and why he continues to send her to the past.

She is beginning to feel that the secretive man and herself are somehow connected as he judges her capable of delivering a letter to her son, James in 1913, who is now forty-three years of age.

Although at first the plan appears to succeed, an encounter with a murderer derails it setting in motion a series of events that does nothing to ease Luna's fragile mind.

When combined with the constant and tiresome efforts of the reporter, Tris Green who is determined to get her story, Luna's frustration and mental health suffers. Particularly when she and her friend, Sophia continue to look after Iris, Rose and Asim whom she had brought from the past and who continue to have problems adjusting to 2021.

Yet one more trip, this time to a place previously unimaginable, causes Luna to doubt her sanity.

ASIN: B0BP847ZRB

I was sent to 1840 Book 7

After five arduous years, Luna's seventh and final adventure under the administration of the mysterious Mr Quick, finds her tired and emotional. Yet, just as she is fatalistic to experience another exploit, answers and enlightenment arrive from an unexpected quarter. Which concurrently makes her angry and yet gives her the courage to continue.

Sent to spend a year in 1840, proves to be a dark period for Luna and Tris as they are exposed to the extremely unpleasant dying legacy of the French Revolution and a psychopathic man who exists where he should not be.

However, by now, at almost twenty-eight years old, Luna forces herself to make one of the most profound and hardest decisions of her life and she optimistically hopes she will be able to end what ought to have ended years previously and do what is right for not only all concerned but for her future and the rest of her life.

ASIN: B0BTX9M26W

The Angel of Death

The Angel of Death is a bleak and fictional account of the United Kingdom's prison system.

When terrorists commit an act of genocide resulting in the deaths of over eleven thousand Londoners, the Prime Minister, under pressure of intense social media, announces a new government initiative as the death penalty is no longer practicable.

The new legislation called, the Safe Limitation Act is rushed through Parliament and a woman neurosurgeon is employed to run the scheme.

But however successful the program, she is eventually betrayed by the government, rejected by her family and spurned by her friends, undergoing the most consequential counteraction by the population in living memory.

ISBN: 978-0-244-18617-3

The Woman who won Euromillions

South London widow, Edith Aveling loves her two daughters and her son. She undoubtably lives for them. She'd do anything for them. She even works all hours as a minimum wage domestic to give her mature children all they need after her husband died in tragic circumstances eleven years previously.

Then, on one average day, never having bought any before, in an act of imprudence, she purchases a single EuroMillions lottery ticket and finds herself the recipient of over £137,000,000. She consequently thanks her good sense that she asked to remain anonymous as she finds her situation overwhelming.

Yet overnight, try as she might to keep her family the way they were, her life becomes a struggle to keep the honesty of her children and to prevent herself from losing everything of value as she invariably becomes a different type of woman with whom she is not familiar at all.

ISBN: 978-0-244-50176-1

THEM

Enter the unconventional middle class world of the Bailey family as they experience their lives against the backdrop of the queerest event ever to have occurred to the world.

Gilbert is an enthusiastic rebuilder of antique motor cycles and a collector of Nazi memorabilia, while his wife, Drusilla, earns her living as a dominatrix and part-time reseller of occult literature.

Together with Peter, Drusilla's ill-treated ten year old son from her first marriage and Danial, Gilbert's multimillionaire friend from school, they become party to a challenging worldwide event that eventually takes human destiny to another level.

ISBN: 978-0-244-86564-1

The Children of Farthing Green

Imagine the knock of leather on willow on a summer's afternoon; the call of an umpire, 'owzat!' Tea on the greenish of lawns; a white haze over the long spiky grass beneath the trees of a summer meadow; polished brass and a whiff of steam as an express comes to a standstill at a country halt; church bells drifting in snatches on a lazy breeze; the taste of blackberries in the sun and ladies in their white dresses and hats cycling to church.

Set in 1924 close to an idyllic Cornish village by the sea, this sounds peaceful and lovely, doesn't it? How wrong can you be?

When sixteen year old Bethany loses her parents, she is sent to spend the summer on the estate of Farthing Green. There, along with her cousins, Lamorna and Simon, she will solve a four hundred year old mystery that contains a suggestion of the supernatural.

ASIN: B08NF235Z1

The Luckiest Man in the World

Unidentified flying objects are unusual things, aren't they? They come, they go, rarely leaving a physical imprint on humanity.

Enter John Crabtree. A bespectacled Doctor of Mathematics, possibly a genius, knowledgeable, obsessive, marginally autistic and originally, innocent. A young London man who enjoys a quiet life and who once was revered as being the luckiest man in the world. Here is his story. In his own words.Thematically, the novel deals with greed, obsession, and desire.

ISBN: 9798706522513

Miss Wetherby's return to London, 1939

Miss Clementine Wetherby moved to Bombay with her parents in 1899. In the summer of 1939, when her mother and father are violently murdered by separatists connected to the Salt Rebellion, she returns to her childhood home in London accompanied by her closest friend, Miss Aadhirai Varma. However, the congenial, courteous and respectful Victorian world she remembers so thoroughly has vanished and the prolonged malefic shadow of the Second World War is about to arrive.

ISBN: 9798743202317

Miss Wetherby's Life in 1940.

Miss Clementine Wetherby, accompanied by her closest friend, Miss Aadhirai Varma, have now settled in a fashionable house in the London borough of Snaresbrook and due to Clementine's parent's estate they have enough money to live out the war in comfort. However, the hostility between the free world and Nazi Germany means that their lives don't go as planned. With the help of a number of local, free spirited retainers and domestic help, Clementine and Aadhirai navigate their way through an increasingly complex year with humour and determination while Clementine begins to enjoying the personal attention of her solicitor.

ASIN: B0999K2R98

Miss Wetherby's Time in 1941

Along with her closest friend, Aadhirai, and Jeremy her new sweetheart, Miss Wetherby begins to fully experience the harshness of a London devastated by war, with its limitations of food, clothes and travel, at the same time as realising that death could put an end to everything at any moment.

Many issues concerning their friends remain unresolved causing great anguish but comfort can always be found in the smallest of ways. However, while there are new and hopeful relationships for some, other issues can only be resolved by estrangement, imprisonment or even death.

Nevertheless, as Miss Wetherby's personal triumphs and tragedies are played out against the larger canvas of the Second World War, on the days when she reminisces about her former life in India that she remembers so dearly, she realises that even now, in her new life, by the war's end, she feels she will have lost many new friends.

All the same, Miss Wetherby, as was her father, is competitive and she accepts that, as a woman who was once raised in such a tender Victorian manner, she has earned the right to fight for the things in which she believes. Therefore, her indomitable spirit soars, even when it seems her own death is near.

ASIN: B09HFWZF8F

Miss Wetherby's Challenges in 1942

By the close of 1942, Miss Wetherby could certainly count on ten fingers the amount of challenges she had had to endue during that year .

By the middle of the summer, news concerning the European war at least was promising as the Wehrmacht had seemingly and finally met their match against the Russians along the Eurasian steppes.

Taking each day one at a time, Clementine and Aadhirai continued to engage and participate on the home front overcoming every obstacle that arrives with cups of tea and home grown fortitude.

From being close to death at the beginning of the year to having an increased amount of hope and trust that the end of the military action could be in sight by December, through Jeremy's increasing love for her and Aadhirai's loyal friendship, through prayer, moments of joy and high spirits, she endures the hardness of rationing, personal pain, dramatic loss of close friends, and even the deaths of those whom she would called friends.

ASIN: B09NRGB4BL

Miss Wetherby's Path to Victory, 1943, 1944, 1945.

There was no doubt that four years of war were finally taking its toil on Clementine and her family and friends. To the point that she, Jeremy and Aadhirai found themselves fatigued as many more demands were made on them.

Although the once promised Nazi invasion never materialised, that did not mean that working towards a successful end of the war could stop. Women who were working as maids and cooks found themselves ordered to work in factories while those men who came of age were ordered to report for military service. Ordinary men and women made distressing sacrifices and more than a few of Clementine and Aadhirai's friends were taken one by one leaving ruptures in their lives that would not easily heal.

At night, a disordered London was still a dangerous city populated by thieves and looters who took advantage of the continuing blackout. And while the arrival of American troops injected new and unexpected life into those who were so tired but who welcomed them, friends and foes were buried or never heard of again while at the same time blessings came from unexpected new life.

Yet new acquaintances continued to arrive, Christmases, birthdays and other war-related celebrations were still acknowledged. And while those who lived in Clementine's three houses waited for the war to play out and end, they each knew that life would never be the same again. Moreover, when the end of the war finally presented itself, it brought both tragedy and surprises.

ASIN: B09V38BGSX

Magic?

Dartmoor, twenty-three days before Christmas 1962 and England is about to suffer the coldest winter in living memory where temperatures plummeted and lakes, rivers and sections of sea froze as blizzards and gusts reaching force eight swept across South West England.

Mary and Alice Acker are twin sisters who, along with their younger brother, Robert, run a non-profit charity for their horse and donkey sanctuary.

One evening, when they hear their border collie barking continuously, Mary enters their largest barn where she sees a dark figure of a man lying unconscious on the straw-covered concrete floor and mysteriously noticed there was no sign of how he got there.

It was the beginning of a set of circumstances that would profoundly affect the Acker family.

ASIN: B0B36DPT4Q

The Man On The Bench

August 1939. World War Two is about to control the lives of every Londoner. Viscount Douglas Harris-Churchill, an aristocratic young man with a unique but questionable ability spends his days on a bench within the shadow of St Paul's Cathedral. He is approached by Susan Spencer, a young, working class widow and mother. Both lives will be changed irrevocably…eventually.

ISBN: 9798862157802

Downfall

At the height of her success Ruth Wright was the wealthiest woman in the world with an estimated personal fortune of £1 trillion having developed, with the assistance of her savant autistic daughter, Lillith Wright, the most powerful and intelligent AI search engine in history. She entertained royalty, politicians and the most famous celebrities from around the world. But after completing a jail term for vehicular manslaughter and underestimating her husband's greed, she was reduced to signing on for Universal Credit having become the most hated woman in the world. This is her own unblemished story about how she grew her empire and then lost it along with her daughter, her sister, her mother and her entire life.

ASIN: B0CQWG6X9L

The Heartache Of Marjory X by Stick Woman

A downtrodden and naive mother, Marjorie X becomes controversial and eventually discovers her strength that helps prevent the destruction of her family.

Too controversial for an author's regular work, Stick Woman steps in as a replacement. A Roman à clef.

ISBN: 9798301004346

Short stories and reflections

A collection of short stories, essays, musings and reflections from 1990 to 2020.

Printed in Dunstable, United Kingdom